FEVER

Charles Martel is a brilliant cancer researcher who discovers that his own daughter is the victim of leukemia. The cause: a chemical plant conspiracy that not only promises to kill her, but will destroy him as a doctor and a man if he tries to fight it . . . With chilling accuracy and riveting suspense, Robin Cook portrays the struggle of one family searching for the truth from a corporation and a medical establishment all too willing to ignore the fate of one little girl . . .

DR. ROBIN COOK, a graduate of Columbia Medical School, finished his postgraduate medical training at Harvard. He is the author of *Seizure, Shock, Abduction, Vector, Toxin, Chromosome 6, Contagion,* and numerous other bestselling novels.

CONTAGION

A shattering scenario based on medical fact—a battle for survival waged in the hot zone of a deadly new virus . . .

"FAST . . . EXCITING . . . SPINE-TINGLING."

—*Denver Post*

ACCEPTABLE RISK

His most shocking thriller—a timely and terrifying glimpse into the dangers of antidepressant drugs . . .

"STERN AND BRACING . . . A SUSPENSEFUL THRILLER."

—*San Francisco Chronicle*

FATAL CURE

One of the most controversial books Robin Cook has ever written—a terrifying look at the darker implications of managed health care in America . . .

"A RIVETING PLOT, FILLED WITH ACTION."

—*San Diego Union-Tribune*

"A HAIR-RAISING, CAUTIONARY TALE ABOUT THE POSSIBLE PITFALLS OF IMPENDING HEALTH CARE REFORM IN AMERICA."

—*Detroit News*

TERMINAL

Brain cancer patients are miraculously cured—when the rising cost of research sparks a medical conspiracy that lowers the price on human life . . .

"A SPELLBINDER . . . UNBEARABLE TENSION."

—*Houston Chronicle*

"STRAIGHT OUT OF TODAY'S HEADLINES." —*UPI*

continued . . .

BLINDSIGHT

How far will people go to obtain donors for eye operations? Murder is beyond comprehension. But seeing is believing . . .

"GRABS THE READER . . . MAINTAINS SUSPENSE WITH SURPRISING STORY TWISTS."
—*Pittsburgh Press*

"RIVETING."
—*Nashville Banner*

VITAL SIGNS

Dr. Cook explores the frightening possibilities of experimental fertilization—the passion to create life, and the power to destroy it . . .

"CONSTANT SUSPENSE . . . BELIEVABLE AND CHILLING."
—*Houston Chronicle*

"VINTAGE COOK . . . NONSTOP ACTION."
—*Kirkus Reviews*

HARMFUL INTENT

The explosive story of a doctor accused of malpractice—a fugitive on the run who pierces the heart of a shocking medical conspiracy . . .

"A REAL GRABBER!"
—*Los Angeles Times*

"TRULY EXCITING."
—**Associated Press**

MUTATION

On the forefront of genetic research, a brilliant doctor tries to create the son of his dreams—and invents a living nightmare . . .

"HOLDS YOU PAGE AFTER PAGE."
—Larry King, *USA Today*

"*REALLY* FRIGHTENING."
—*Booklist*

MORTAL FEAR

A major scientific breakthrough becomes the ultimate experiment in terror when middle-aged patients begin to die—of old age . . .

"A CHILLING ODYSSEY INTO THE ORIGINS OF LIFE—AND DEATH."
—*New York Times*

"COOK'S BEST BOOK SINCE *COMA*."
—*People*

OUTBREAK

Murder and mystery reach epidemic proportions when a devastating plague sweeps the country . . .

"HIS MOST HARROWING MEDICAL HORROR STORY."
—*New York Times*

"THE ULTIMATE NIGHTMARE . . . SPINE-TINGLING INTRIGUE AND FEVER-PITCHED ACTION."
—Associated Press

Titles by Robin Cook

SEIZURE
SHOCK
ABDUCTION
VECTOR
TOXIN
INVASION
CHROMOSOME 6
CONTAGION
ACCEPTABLE RISK
FATAL CURE
TERMINAL
BLINDSIGHT
VITAL SIGNS
HARMFUL INTENT
MUTATION
MORTAL FEAR
OUTBREAK
MINDBEND
GODPLAYER
BRAIN
SPHINX
COMA
THE YEAR OF THE INTERN

FEVER

ROBIN COOK

BERKLEY BOOKS, NEW YORK

THE BERKLEY PUBLISHING GROUP
Published by the Penguin Group
Penguin Group (USA) Inc.
375 Hudson Street, New York, New York 10014, USA
Penguin Group (Canada), 90 Eglinton Avenue East, Suite 700, Toronto, Ontario M4P 2Y3, Canada
(a division of Pearson Penguin Canada Inc.)
Penguin Books Ltd., 80 Strand, London WC2R 0RL, England
Penguin Group Ireland, 25 St. Stephen's Green, Dublin 2, Ireland (a division of Penguin Books Ltd.)
Penguin Group (Australia), 250 Camberwell Road, Camberwell, Victoria 3124, Australia
(a division of Pearson Australia Group Pty. Ltd.)
Penguin Books India Pvt. Ltd., 11 Community Centre, Panchsheel Park, New Delhi—110 017, India
Penguin Group (NZ), Cnr. Airborne and Rosedale Roads, Albany, Auckland 1310, New Zealand
(a division of Pearson New Zealand Ltd.)
Penguin Books (South Africa) (Pty.) Ltd., 24 Sturdee Avenue, Rosebank, Johannesburg 2196,
South Africa

Penguin Books Ltd., Registered Offices: 80 Strand, London WC2R 0RL, England

This is a work of fiction. Names, characters, places, and incidents either are the product of the author's imagination or are used fictitiously, and any resemblance to actual persons, living or dead, business establishments, events, or locales is entirely coincidental.

FEVER

A Berkley Book / published by arrangement with the author

PRINTING HISTORY
G. P. Putnam's Sons edition published in 1982
Signet edition / January 1983
Berkley edition / January 2000

Copyright © 1982 by Robert Cook.

ISBN: 0-425-17420-4

BERKLEY®
Berkley Books are published by The Berkley Publishing Group,
a division of Penguin Group (USA) Inc.,
375 Hudson Street, New York, New York 10014.
BERKLEY is a registered trademark of Penguin Group (USA) Inc.
The "B" design is a trademark belonging to Penguin Group (USA) Inc.

PRINTED IN THE UNITED STATES OF AMERICA

20   19   18   17   16   15   14   13   12   11   10

To the joy of my family—
it began with my parents,
now shared with my wife.

FEVER

PROLOGUE

The poisonous molecules of benzene arrived in the bone marrow in a crescendo. The foreign chemical surged with the blood and was carried between the narrow spicules of supporting bone into the farthest reaches of the delicate tissue. It was like a frenzied horde of barbarians descending into Rome. And the result was equally as disastrous. The complicated nature of the marrow, designed to make most of the cellular content of the blood, succumbed to the invaders.

Every cell exposed to the benzene was assaulted. The nature of the chemical was such that it knifed through the cell membranes like steel through butter. Red cells or white, young or mature, it made no difference. Within some lucky cells where only a few molecules of benzene entered, enzymes were able to inactivate the chemical. In most others the destruction of the interior membranes was immediate.

Within minutes the concentration of the benzene had soared to the point that thousands of the poisonous molecules had reached the very heart of the marrow, the primitive, finely structured stem cells. These were the actively dividing units, serving as the source of the circulating blood cells, and their activity bore witness to hundreds of millions of years of evolution. Here, being played out moment by moment, was the incredible mystery of life, an organization more fantastic than the wildest scientific dream. The benzene molecules indiscriminately penetrated these busily reproducing cells, interrupting the orderly replication of the DNA molecules. Most of these cells either halted the life processes in a sudden agonal heave or, having been released from the mysterious central control, tumbled off in frenzied undirected activity like rabid animals until death intervened.

After the benzene molecules had been washed away by repeated surges of clean blood, the marrow could have recovered except for one stem cell. This cell had been busy for years turning out an impressive progeny of white blood cells whose function, ironically enough, was to help the body fight against foreign invaders. When the benzene penetrated this cell's nucleus, it damaged a very specific part of the DNA but did not kill the cell. It would have been better if the cell had died because the benzene destroyed the fine balance between reproduction and maturation. The cell instantly divided and the resulting daughter cells had the same defect. No longer did they listen to the mysterious central control and mature into normal white blood cells. Instead they responded to an unfettered urge to reproduce their altered selves. Although they appeared to be relatively normal within the marrow, they were different from other young white blood cells. The usual surface stickiness was absent, and they absorbed nutrients at an alarmingly selfish rate. They had become parasites within their own house.

After only twenty divisions there were over one million of these lawless cells. By twenty-seven divisions there were over one billion; they then began to break free from the mass. First a trickle of sick cells entered the circulation, then a steady stream, finally a flood. These cells charged out into the body eager to establish fertile colonies. By forty divisions they numbered over a trillion.

It was the beginning of an aggressive, acute myeloblastic

leukemia in the body of a pubescent girl, starting December 28, two days after her twelfth birthday. Her name was Michelle Martel and she had no idea except for a single symptom: she had a fever!

ONE

A cold January morning tentatively fingered its way over the frigid landscape of Shaftesbury, New Hampshire. Reluctantly the shadows began to pale as the winter sky slowly lightened, revealing a featureless gray cloud cover. It was going to snow and despite the cold, there was a damp sting to the air; a sharp reminder that off to the east lay the Atlantic.

The red brick buildings of old Shaftesbury huddled along the Pawtomack River like a ghost town. The river had been the support, the lifeblood of the town; it sprang from the snow-laden White Mountains in the north and ran to the sea in the southeast. As the river coursed past the town, its smooth flow was interrupted by a crumbling dam and a large waterwheel that no longer turned. Lining the riverbanks were block after block of empty factories, reminders of a more prosperous age when New England mills were the center of the textile industry. At the extreme southern end of town, at the foot of Main Street, the last brick mill building was occupied by a chemical operation called Recycle, Ltd., a rubber, plastic, and vinyl recycling plant. A wisp of acrid, gray smoke rose from a large phallic smokestack and merged with the clouds. Over the whole area hung a foul, choking odor of burnt rubber and plastic. Surrounding the building were enormous piles of discarded rubber tires, like the droppings of a gigantic monster.

South of the town the river ran through rolling, wooded hills, interspersed by snow-covered meadows and bordered by fieldstone fences erected by settlers three hundred years before. Six miles south of the town the river took a lazy curve to the east and formed an idyllic six-acre peninsula of land. In the center was a shallow pond connected to the river by an inlet. Behind the pond rose a hill capped by a white-framed Victorian farmhouse with gabled roofs and gingerbread trim. A long winding driveway bordered with oaks and sugar maples led down to the Interstate 301 heading south toward Massachusetts. Twenty-five yards north of the house was a weather-beaten barn nestled in a copse of evergreens. Built on piles at the edge of the pond was a miniature copy of the main house; it was a shed turned playhouse.

It was a beautiful New England landscape, like a January calendar scene, except for a slight macabre detail: there were no fish in the pond and no encircling vegetation within six feet.

Inside the picturesque white house, the pale morning light diffused through lace curtains. By degrees the gathering dawn gently nudged Charles Martel from the depths of a satisfying sleep. He rolled over onto his left side, enjoying a contentment he'd been afraid to acknowledge for the past two years. There was a sense of order and security in his life now; Charles had never expected to experience this again after his first wife had been diagnosed with lymphoma. She had died nine years ago, leaving Charles with three children to raise. Life had become something to endure.

But that was now in the past, and the awful wound had slowly healed. And then to Charles's surprise, even the void had been filled. Two years ago he had remarried, but he still was afraid to admit how much his life had changed for the better. It was safer and easier to concentrate on his work and the day-to-day necessities of family life than to acknowledge his newly regained contentment and thereby admit to the ultimate vulnerability, happiness. But Cathryn, his new wife, made this denial difficult because she was a joyous and giving person. Charles had fallen in love with her the day he met her and had married her five months later. The last two years had only increased his affection for her.

As the darkness receded, Charles could see the placid profile of his sleeping wife. She was on her back with her right arm casually draped on the pillow above her head. She looked much younger than her thirty-two years, a fact that initially had emphasized the thirteen years' difference in their ages. Charles was forty-five and he acknowledged that he looked it. But Cathryn looked like twenty-five. Resting on his elbow, Charles stared at her delicate features. He traced the frame of her provocative widow's peak, down the length of the soft brown hair to her shoulder. Her face, lit by the early morning light, seemed radiant to Charles and his eyes followed the slightly curved line of her nose, noticing the flare of her nostrils as she breathed. Watching her he felt a reflex stirring deep within him.

He looked over at the clock; another twenty minutes before the alarm. Thankfully he lowered himself back into the warm nest made by the down coverlet and spooned against his wife, marveling at his sense of well-being. He even looked forward to his days at the institute. Work was progressing at an ever-increasing pace. He felt a twinge of excitement. What if he, Charles Martel, the boy from Teaneck, New Jersey, made the first real step in unraveling the mystery of cancer? Charles knew that it was becoming increasingly possible, and the irony was that he was not a formally trained research scientist. He'd been an internist specializing in allergy when Elizabeth, his first wife, had become ill. After she died he gave up his lucrative practice to become a full-time researcher at the Weinburger Research Institute. It had been a reaction against her death, and although some of his colleagues had told him that a career change was an unhealthy way to work out such a problem, he had flourished in the new environment.

Cathryn, sensing her husband was awake, turned over and found herself in an enveloping hug. Wiping the sleep from her eyes, she looked at Charles and laughed. He looked so uncharacteristically impish.

"What's going on in that little mind of yours?" she asked, smiling.

"I've just been watching you."

"Wonderful! I'm sure I look my best," said Cathryn.

"You look devastating," teased Charles, pushing her thick hair back from her forehead.

Cathryn, now more awake, realized the urgency of his arousal. Running her hand down her husband's body, she encountered an erect penis. "And what is this?" she asked.

"I accept no responsibility," said Charles. "That part of my anatomy has a mind of its own."

"Our Polish Pope says a man should not lust after his wife."

"I haven't been. I've been thinking about work," Charles teased.

As the first snowflakes settled on the gabled roofs, they came together with a depth of passion and tenderness that never failed to overwhelm Charles. Then the alarm went off. The day began.

Michelle could hear Cathryn calling from far away, interrupting her dream; she and her father were crossing a field. Michelle tried to ignore the call but it came again. She felt a hand on her shoulder, and when she turned over, she looked up into Cathryn's smiling face.

"Time to get up," her stepmother said brightly.

Michelle took a deep breath and nodded her head, acknowledging that she was awake. She'd had a bad night, full of disturbing dreams which left her soaked with perspiration. She'd felt hot beneath the covers and cold out of them. Several times during the night she thought about going in to Charles. She would have if her father had been alone.

"My goodness, you look flushed," said Cathryn, as she

opened the drapes. She reached down and touched Michelle's forehead. It felt hot.

"I think you have a fever again," said Cathryn sympathetically. "Do you feel sick?"

"No," said Michelle quickly. She didn't want to be sick again. She did not want to stay home from school. She wanted to get up and make the orange juice, which had always been her job.

"We'd better take your temperature anyway," said Cathryn, going into the connecting bath. She reappeared, alternately flicking and examining the thermometer. "It will only take a minute, then we'll know for sure." She stuck the thermometer into Michelle's mouth. "Under the tongue. I'll be back after I get the boys up."

The door closed and Michelle pulled the thermometer from her mouth. Even in that short a time, the mercury had risen to ninety-nine. She had a fever and she knew it. Her legs ached and there was a tenderness in the pit of her stomach. She put the thermometer back into her mouth. From where she lay she could look out the window and see her playhouse that Charles had made out of an ice shed. The roof was covered with new-fallen snow and she shivered at the cold scene. She longed for spring and those lazy days that she spent in that fantasy house. Just she and her father.

When the door opened, Jean Paul, age fifteen, was already awake, propped up in bed with his physics book. Behind his head the small clock radio played a soft rock and roll. He was wearing dark red flannel pajamas with blue piping, a Christmas gift from Cathryn.

"You've got twenty minutes," Cathryn said cheerfully.

"Thanks, Mom," said Jean Paul with a smile.

Cathryn paused, looking down at the boy, and her heart melted. She felt like rushing in and swooping him into her arms. But she resisted the temptation. She'd learned that all the Martels were somewhat chary about direct physical contact, a fact that initially had been a little hard for her to deal with. Cathryn came from Boston's Italian North End where touching and hugging was a constant. Although her father had been Latvian, he'd left when Cathryn was twelve, and Cathryn had grown up without his influence. She felt 100 percent Italian. "See you at breakfast," she said.

Jean Paul knew that Cathryn loved to hear him call her Mom and gladly obliged. It was such a low price to pay for the warmth and attention that she showered on him. Jean Paul had been conditioned by a very busy father and seen himself eclipsed by his older brother, Chuck, and his irresistible baby sister, Michelle. Then came Cathryn, and the excitement of the marriage, followed by Cathryn's legal adoption of Chuck, Jean Paul, and Michelle. Jean Paul would have called her "grandmother" if she wanted. He thought he loved Cathryn as much as his real mother; at least what he could remember of her. He'd been six when she died.

Chuck's eyes blinked open at the first touch of Cathryn's hand but he pretended sleep, keeping his head under his pillow. He knew that if he waited she'd touch him again, only a little more forcibly. And he was right, only this time he felt two hands shake his shoulder before the pillow was lifted. Chuck was eighteen years old and in the middle of his first year at Northeastern University. He wasn't doing that well and he dreaded his upcoming semester finals. It was going to be a disaster. At least for everything but psychology.

"Fifteen minutes," said Cathryn. She tousled his long hair. "Your father wants to get to the lab early."

"Shit," said Chuck under his breath.

"Charles, Jr.!" said Cathryn, pretending to be shocked.

"I'm not getting up." Chuck grabbed the pillow from Cathryn's hands and buried himself.

"Oh, yes you are," said Cathryn, as she yanked the covers back.

Chuck's body, clad only in his undershorts, was exposed to the morning chill. He leaped up, pulling the blankets around him. "I told you never to do that," he snapped.

"And I told you to leave your locker-room language in the

locker room," said Cathryn, ignoring the nastiness in Chuck's voice. "Fifteen minutes!"

Cathryn spun on her heel and walked out. Chuck's face flushed in frustration. He watched her go down the hall to Michelle's room. She was wearing an antique silk nightgown that she'd bought at a flea market. It was a deep peach color, not too different from her skin. With very little difficulty, Chuck could imagine Cathryn naked. She wasn't old enough to be his mother.

He reached out, hooked his hand around the edge of his door, and slammed it. Just because his father liked to get to his lab before eight, Chuck had to get up at the crack of dawn like some goddamn farmer. The big deal scientist! Chuck rubbed his face and noticed the open book at his beside. *Crime and Punishment.* He'd spent most of the previous evening reading it. It wasn't for any of his courses, which was probably why he was enjoying it. He should have studied chemistry because he was in danger of flunking. God, what would Charles say if he did! There had already been a huge blowup when Chuck had not been able to get into Charles's alma mater, Harvard. Now if he flunked chemistry . . . Chemistry had been Charles's major.

"I don't want to be a goddamn doctor anyway," Chuck snapped, as he stood up and pulled on dirty Levi's. He was proud of the fact that they'd never been washed. In the bathroom he decided not to shave. He thought maybe he'd grow a beard.

Clad in a terrycloth lava-lava, which, unfortunately, emphasized the fifteen pounds he'd gained in the last ten years, Charles lathered his chin. He was trying to sort through the myriad facts associated with his current research project. The immunology of living forms involved a complexity which never failed to amaze and exhilarate him, especially now that he thought he was coming very close to some real answers about cancer. Charles had been excited before and wrong before. He knew that. But now his ideas were based on years of

painstaking experimentation and supported by easily repro-
ducible facts.

Charles began to chart the schedule for the day. He wanted
to start work with the new HR7 strain of mice that carried
hereditary mammary cancer. He hoped to make the animals
"allergic" to their own tumors, a goal which Charles felt was
coming closer and closer.

Cathryn opened the door and pushed past him. Pulling her
gown over her head, she slipped into the shower. The water
and steam billowed the shower curtain. After a moment she
pulled back the curtain and called to Charles.

"I think I've got to take Michelle to see a real doctor," she
said before disappearing back behind the curtain.

Charles paused in his shaving, trying not to be annoyed by
her sarcastic reference to a "real" doctor. It was a sensitive
issue between them.

"I really thought that marrying a doctor would at least guarantee good medical attention for my family," shouted Cathryn
over the din of the shower. "Was I wrong!"

Charles busied himself, examining his half-shaved face, noticing in the process that his eyelids were a little puffy. He
was trying to avoid a fight. The fact that the family's "medical
problems" spontaneously solved themselves within twenty-
four hours was lost on Cathryn. Her newly awakened mother
instincts demanded specialists for every sniffle, ache, or bout
of diarrhea.

"Michelle still feeling lousy?" asked Charles. It was better
to talk about specifics.

"I shouldn't have to tell you. The child's been feeling sick
for some time."

With exasperation, Charles reached out and pulled back the
edge of the shower curtain. "Cathryn, I'm a cancer researcher,
not a pediatrician."

"Oh, excuse me," said Cathryn, lifting her face to the water.
"I thought you were a doctor."

"I'm not going to let you bait me into an argument," said
Charles testily. "The flu has been going around. Michelle has

a touch of it. People feel lousy for a week and then it's over."

Pulling her head from beneath the shower, Cathryn looked directly at Charles. "The point is, she's been feeling lousy for four weeks."

"Four weeks?" he asked. Time had a way of dissolving in the face of his work.

"Four weeks," repeated Cathryn. "I don't think I'm panicking at the first sign of a cold. I think I'd better take Michelle into Pediatric Hospital and see Dr. Wiley. Besides, I can visit the Schonhauser boy."

"All right, I'll take a look at Michelle," agreed Charles, turning back to the sink. Four weeks was a long time to have the flu. Perhaps Cathryn was exaggerating, but he knew better than to question. In fact, it was better to change the subject. "What's wrong with the Schonhauser boy?" The Schonhausers were neighbors who lived about a mile up the river. Henry Schonhauser was a chemist at M.I.T. and one of the few people with whom Charles enjoyed socializing. The Schonhauser boy, Tad, was a year older than Michelle, but because of the way their birthdays fell, they were in the same class.

Cathryn stepped out of the shower, pleased that her tactic to get Charles to look at Michelle had worked so perfectly. "Tad's been in the hospital for three weeks. I hear he's very sick but I haven't spoken with Marge since he went in."

"What's the diagnosis?" Charles poised the razor below his left sideburn.

"Something I've never heard of before. Elastic anemia or something," said Cathryn, toweling herself off.

"Aplastic anemia?" asked Charles with disbelief.

"Something like that."

"My God," said Charles, leaning on the sink. "That's awful."

"What is it?" Cathryn experienced a reflex jolt of panic.

"It's a disease where the bone marrow stops producing blood cells."

"Is it serious?"

"It's always serious and often fatal."

Cathryn's arms hung limply at her sides, her wet hair like an unwrung mop. She could feel a mixture of sympathy and fear. "Is it catching?"

"No," said Charles absently. He was trying to remember what he knew of the affliction. It was not a common illness.

"Michelle and Tad have spent quite a bit of time together," said Cathryn. Her voice was hesitant.

Charles looked at her, realizing that she was pleading for reassurance. "Wait a minute. You're not thinking that Michelle might have aplastic anemia, are you?"

"Could she?"

"No. My God, you're like a med student. You hear of a new disease and five minutes later either you or the kids have it. Aplastic anemia is as rare as hell. It's usually associated with some drug or chemical. It's either a poisoning or an allergic reaction. Although most of the time the actual cause is never found. Anyway, it's not catching; but that poor kid."

"And to think I haven't even called Marge," said Cathryn. She leaned forward and looked at her face in the mirror. She tried to imagine the emotional strain Marge was under and decided she'd better go back to making lists like she did before getting married. There was no excuse for such thoughtlessness.

Charles shaved the left side of his face wondering if aplastic anemia was the kind of disease he should look into. Could it possibly shed some clue on the organization of life? Where was the control that shut the marrow down? That was a cogent question because, after all, it was the control issue which Charles felt was key to understanding cancer.

With the knuckle of his first finger, Charles knocked softly on Michelle's door. Listening, he heard only the sound of the shower coming from the connecting bathroom. Quietly he opened the door. Michelle was lying in bed, facing away from him. Abruptly she turned over and their eyes met. A line of tears which sparkled in the morning light ran down her flushed cheeks. Charles's heart melted.

Sitting on the edge of her eyelet-covered bed, he bent down

and kissed her forehead. With his lips he could tell she had a fever. Straightening up, Charles looked at his little girl. He could so easily see Elizabeth, his first wife, in Michelle's face. There was the same thick, black hair, the same high cheekbones and full lips, the same flawless olive skin. From Charles, Michelle had inherited intensely blue eyes, straight white teeth, and unfortunately a somewhat wide nose. Charles believed she was the most beautiful twelve-year-old in the world.

With the back of his hand he wiped the wetness from her cheeks.

"I'm sorry, Daddy," said Michelle through her tears.

"What do you mean, sorry?" asked Charles softly.

"I'm sorry I'm sick again. I don't like to be a bother."

Charles hugged her. She felt fragile in his arms. "You're not a bother. I don't want to even hear you say such a thing. Let me look at you."

Embarrassed by her tears, Michelle kept her face averted as Charles pulled away to examine her. He cradled her chin in the palm of his hand and lifted her face to his. "Tell me how you feel. What is bothering you?"

"I just feel a little weak, that's all. I can go to school. Really I can."

"Sore throat?"

"A little. Not much. Cathryn said I couldn't go to school."

"Anything else? Headache?"

"A little but it's better."

"Ears?"

"Fine."

"Stomach?"

"Maybe a little sore."

Charles depressed Michelle's lower lids. The conjunctiva was pale. In fact, her whole face was pale. "Let me see your tongue." Charles realized how long it had been since he'd done clinical medicine. Michelle stuck out her tongue and watched her father's eyes for the slightest sign of concern. Charles felt under the angle of her jaw and she pulled her tongue back in.

"Tender?" asked Charles as his fingers felt some small lymph nodes.

"No," said Michelle.

Charles had her sit on the edge of the bed, facing away from him, and he began to draw up her nightgown. Jean Paul's head came into the room from the connecting bathroom to tell her the shower was free.

"Get out of here," yelled Michelle. "Dad, tell Jean Paul to get out."

"Out!" said Charles. Jean Paul disappeared. He could be heard laughing with Chuck.

Charles percussed Michelle's back somewhat clumsily but well enough to be convinced that her lungs were clear. Then he had her lie back on her bed, and he drew her nightgown up to just below her nascent breasts. Her thin abdomen rose and fell rhythmically. She was thin enough for him to see the recoil of her heart after each beat. With his right hand, Charles began to palpate her abdomen. "Try to relax. If I hurt you, just say so."

Michelle attempted to remain still but she squirmed beneath Charles's cold hand. Then it hurt.

"Where?" asked Charles. Michelle pointed and Charles felt very carefully, determining that Michelle's abdomen was tender at the midline. Putting his fingers just beneath the right ribs he asked her to breathe in. When she did, he could feel the blunt edge of her liver pass under his fingers. She said that hurt a little. Then with his left hand under her for support, he felt for her spleen. To his surprise he had no trouble palpating it. He'd always had trouble with that maneuver when he was in practice and he wondered if Michelle's spleen wasn't enlarged.

Standing up, he looked at Michelle. She seemed thin, but she'd always been slender. Charles started to run his hand down her legs to feel the muscle tone, then stopped, noticing a series of bruises. "Where'd you get all these black-and-blue marks?"

Michelle shrugged.

"Do your legs bother you?"

"A little. Mostly my knees and ankles after gym. But I don't have to go to gym if I have a note."

Straightening up again, Charles surveyed his daughter. She was pale, had minor aches and pains, a few lymph nodes, and a fever. That could be just about any minor viral illness. But four weeks! Maybe Cathryn was right. Maybe she should be seen by a "real" doctor.

"Please, Dad," said Michelle. "I can't miss any more school if I'm going to be a research doctor like you."

Charles smiled. Michelle had always been a precocious child and this indirect flattery was a good example. "Missing a few days of school in the sixth grade is not going to hurt your career," said Charles. "Cathryn is going to take you to Pediatric Hospital today to see Dr. Wiley."

"He's a baby doctor!" said Michelle defiantly.

"He's a pediatrician and he sees patients up to eighteen, smarty pants."

"I want you to take me."

"I can't, dear. I've got to go to the lab. Why don't you get dressed and come down for some breakfast?"

"I'm not hungry."

"Michelle, don't be difficult."

"I'm not being difficult. I'm just not hungry."

"Then come down for some juice." Charles lightly pinched Michelle's cheek.

Michelle watched her father leave her room. Her tears welled up anew. She felt horrid and did not want to go to the hospital but worst of all, she felt lonely. She wanted her father to love her more than anything in the world and she knew that Charles was impatient when any of the kids got sick. She struggled up to a sitting position and braced herself against a wave of dizziness.

"My God, Chuck," said Charles with disgust. "You look like a pig."

Chuck ignored his father. He got some cold cereal, poured

milk over it, then sat down to eat. The rule for breakfast was that everyone fended for themselves, except for the orange juice which Michelle usually made. Cathryn had made it this morning.

Chuck was wearing a stained sweater and dirty jeans, which he wore so long that he walked on the frayed bottoms. His hair was uncombed and the fact that he hadn't shaved was painfully apparent.

"Do you really have to be so sloppy?" continued Charles. "I thought that the hippie look was passé now and that college kids were becoming respectable again."

"You're right. Hippie is out," said Jean Paul, coming into the kitchen and pouring orange juice. "Punk is in now."

"Punk?" questioned Charles. "Is Chuck punk?"

"No," laughed Jean Paul. "Chuck is just Chuck."

Chuck looked up from his cereal box to mouth some obscenities at his younger brother. Jean Paul ignored him and opened his physics book. It occurred to him that his father never noticed what he wore. It was always Chuck.

"Really, Chuck," Charles was saying. "Do you honestly feel you have to look that bad?" Chuck ignored the question. Charles watched the boy eat with growing exasperation. "Chuck, I'm speaking to you."

Cathryn reached over and put her hand on Charles's arm. "Let's not get into this discussion at breakfast. You know how college kids are. Leave him be."

"I think I at least deserve an answer," persisted Charles.

Taking in a deep breath and blowing it out noisily through his nose to punctuate his annoyance, Chuck looked into his father's face. "I'm not a doctor," he said. "I don't have to adhere to a dress code."

The eyes of the father and the older son met. Chuck said to himself: "Take that, you smart-ass son-of-a-bitch, just because you got good grades in chemistry you think you know everything, but you don't." Charles examined the face of this son of his, marveling how much arrogance the boy could manufacture with so little basis. He was intelligent enough but hopelessly lazy. His performance in high school had been such that Harvard had rejected him, and Charles had a feeling that he wasn't doing well at Northeastern. Charles wondered where he, as a father, might have gone wrong. But such musing was made difficult by the personality of Jean Paul. Charles glanced at his other son: neat, easygoing, studious. It was hard to believe that both boys had sprung from the same genetic pool and grown up together. Charles's attention returned to Chuck. The boy's defiance had not altered, but Charles felt his interest in the issue wane. He had more important things to think about.

"I hope," said Charles evenly, "your appearance and your grades have nothing in common. I trust you are doing all right at college. We haven't heard much about that."

"I'm doing all right," said Chuck, finally dropping his eyes back to his cereal. Standing up to his father was something new for Chuck. Before he'd gone to college, he had avoided any confrontation. Now he looked forward to it. Chuck was sure that Cathryn noticed and approved. After all, Charles was a tyrant with Cathryn as well.

"If I'm going to drive the station wagon into Boston, I'm going to need some extra cash," said Cathryn, hoping to change the subject. "And speaking of money, the oil people called and said they won't deliver until the account is settled."

"Remind me tonight," said Charles quickly. He didn't want to discuss money.

"Also my semester tuition has never been paid," said Chuck.

Cathryn looked up from her food and glanced at Charles, hoping he would refute Chuck's allegation. Semester tuition amounted to a lot of money.

"I got a note yesterday," said Chuck, "saying that the tuition was way overdue and that I wouldn't get credits for my courses if it weren't paid."

"But the money was taken out of the account," said Cathryn.

"I used the money in the lab," explained Charles.

"What?" Cathryn was aghast.

"We'll get it back. I needed a new strain of mice and there was no more grant money until March."

"You bought rats with Chuck's tuition money?" asked Cathryn.

"Mice," corrected Charles.

With a delicious sense of voyeurism Chuck watched the discussion unfold. He'd been getting notes from the bursar for months, but he'd not brought them home, hoping for a time when he could bring it up without his performance being at issue. It couldn't have worked out better.

"That's just wonderful," said Cathryn. "And how do you expect we are to eat from now until March after Chuck's bill is paid?"

"I'll take care of it," Charles snapped. His defensiveness was coming out as anger.

"I think maybe I should get a job," said Cathryn. "Do they need extra typing at the institute?"

"For Christ's sake. It's not a crisis!" said Charles. "Everything's under control. What you should do is finish that Ph.D. thesis of yours so that you can get a job that uses your training." Cathryn had been trying to finish her thesis in literature for almost three years.

"So now it's because I haven't gotten my Ph.D. that Chuck's tuition isn't paid," said Cathryn sarcastically.

Michelle stepped into the kitchen. Both Cathryn and Charles looked up, their conversation momentarily forgotten. She'd dressed herself in a pink monogrammed sweater over a white cotton turtleneck, making her look older than her twelve years. Her face, framed by her jet-black hair, seemed extraordinarily pale. She went over to the counter and poured herself some orange juice. "Ugh," said Michelle, taking a taste. "I hate it when the juice is filled with bubbles."

"Well, well," said Jean Paul. "If it isn't the little princess playing sick to stay home from school."

"Don't tease your sister," commanded Charles.

Suddenly, Michelle's head snapped forward with a violent sneeze, sloshing juice from her glass to the floor. She felt a surge of liquid come from her nose and she automatically leaned forward, catching the stream in an open palm. To her horror, it was blood. "Dad!" she cried, as the blood filled her cupped hand and splattered to the floor.

In unison, Charles and Cathryn jumped up. Cathryn snatched a dish towel while Charles picked Michelle up and carried her into the living room.

The two boys looked at the small pool of blood, then at their food, trying to decide what effect the episode had on their appetites. Cathryn came running back, pulled a tray of ice cubes from the freezer, then rushed back to the living room.

"Ugh," said Chuck. "You couldn't get me to be a doctor if you paid me a million dollars. I can't stand blood."

"Michelle always manages to be the center of attention," said Jean Paul.

"You can say that again."

"Michelle always manages to . . . " repeated Jean Paul. It was easy and fun to ride Chuck.

"Shut up, stupid." Chuck got up and threw the remains of his Grape-Nuts down the disposal. Then, skirting the blood on the floor, he headed up to his room.

After four mouthfuls, Jean Paul finished his cereal and put his dish in the sink. With a paper towel, he wiped up Michelle's blood.

"Good gravy," said Charles as he went outside through the kitchen door. The storm had brought a northeast wind, and with it the stench of burnt rubber from the recycling plant. "What a stink."

"What a shit hole of a place to live," said Chuck.

Charles's frayed emotions bristled at the impudence, but he refrained from saying anything. It had already been a bad enough morning. Setting his jaw, he tucked his chin into his sheepskin jacket to keep out the blowing snow and trudged toward the barn.

"As soon as I can, I'm going to head for California," said

Chuck, following in Charles's footsteps. There was about an inch of new snow.

"Dressed the way you are, you'll fit in perfectly," said Charles.

Jean Paul, bringing up the rear, laughed, his breath coming in concentrated puffs of vapor. Chuck spun and shoved Jean Paul off the shoveled pathway, into the deeper snow. There were some angry words but Charles ignored them. It was too cold to pause. The little gusts of wind felt abrasive and the smell was awful. It hadn't always been that way. The rubber plant had opened in '71, a year after he and Elizabeth had bought the house. The move had really been Elizabeth's idea. She wanted her children to grow up in clear, crisp air of the country. What an irony, thought Charles, as he unlocked the barn. But it wasn't too bad. They could only smell the plant when the wind came from the northeast and, thankfully, that wasn't very often.

"Damn," said Jean Paul, staring down at the pond. "With this new snow, I'm going to have to shovel my hockey rink all over again. Hey, Dad, how come the water never freezes around Michelle's playhouse?"

Leaving the piece of pipe against the door to keep it open, Charles looked out over the pond. "I don't know. I never thought about it. Must be something to do with the current because the area of open water connects with the inlet from the river, and the inlet isn't frozen either."

"Ugh," said Chuck, pointing beyond the playhouse. There on the apron of frozen mud surrounding the pond was a dead mallard. "Another dead duck. I guess they can't stand the smell, either."

"That's strange," said Charles. "We haven't seen ducks for several years. When we first moved here I used to hunt them from Michelle's playhouse. Then they disappeared."

"There's another one," cried Jean Paul. "But he's not dead. It's flopping around."

"Looks drunk," said Chuck.

"Come on, let's go help it."

"We haven't much time," cautioned Charles.

"Oh, come on." Jean Paul took off over the crusted snow.

Neither Charles nor Chuck shared Jean Paul's enthusiasm, but they followed just the same. When they reached him, he was bending over the poor creature who was in the throes of a seizure.

"God, it's got epilepsy!" said Chuck.

"What's wrong with him, Dad?" asked Jean Paul.

"I haven't the faintest idea. Avian medicine is not one of my strongest subjects."

Jean Paul bent down to try to restrain the bird's pitiful spasms and jerks.

"I'm not sure you should touch it," said Charles. "I don't know if psittacosis is carried by ducks."

"I think we should just kill it and put it out of its misery," said Chuck.

Charles glanced at his older son, whose eyes were glued to the sick bird. For some reason Chuck's suggestion struck Charles as cruel even though it was probably correct.

"Can I put it in the barn for the day?" pleaded Jean Paul.

"I'll get my air rifle and put it out of its misery," said Chuck. It was his turn to get back at Jean Paul.

"No!" commanded Jean Paul. "Can I put it in the barn, Dad? Please?"

"All right," said Charles, "but don't touch it. Run up and get a box or something."

Jean Paul took off like a rabbit. Charles and Chuck faced each other over the sick bird. "Don't you feel any compassion?" asked Charles.

"Compassion? You're asking me about compassion after what you do to all those animals in the lab? What a joke!"

Charles studied his son. He thought he saw more than disrespect. He thought he saw hatred. Chuck had been a mystery to Charles from the day he reached puberty. With some difficulty he suppressed the urge to slap the boy.

With his usual resourcefulness, Jean Paul had found a large cardboard box as well as an old pillow. He'd cut open the pillow and filled the box with the feathers. Using the collapsed pillow as a protective rag, he picked up the duck and put it into the box. As he explained it to Charles, the feathers would both protect the duck from injuring himself if he had another seizure and keep it warm. Charles nodded his approval and they all climbed into the car.

The five-year-old red, rusted Pinto complained as Charles turned the key. Because of a series of holes in the muffler the Pinto sounded like an AMX tank when it finally started. Charles backed out of the garage, slid down the drive, and turned north on Interstate 301, heading toward Shaftesbury. As the old car picked up speed, Charles felt relief. Family life could never be made to run smoothly. At least in the lab the variables had a comforting predictability and problems lent themselves to the scientific method. Charles was growing less and less appreciative of human capriciousness.

"All right!" he shouted. "No music!" He switched off the radio. The two boys had been fighting over which station to hear. "A little quiet contemplation is a good way to begin the day."

The brothers looked at each other and rolled their eyes.

Their route took them along the Pawtomack River and they got glimpses of the water as it snaked its way through the countryside. The closer they got to Shaftesbury, the more intense the stench became from Recycle, Ltd. The first view of the town was the factory's smokestack spewing its black plume into the air. A harsh whistle shattered the silence as they came abreast of the plant, signaling a changing of shift.

Once past the chemical plant the odor disappeared as if by magic. The abandoned mills loomed on their left as they proceeded up Main Street. Not a person was in sight. It was like a ghost town at six forty-five in the morning. Three rusting steel bridges spanned the river, additional relics of the progressive era before the great war. There was even a covered bridge but no one used that. It was totally unsafe and kept up just for the tourists. The fact that no tourists ever came to Shaftesbury hadn't dawned on the town fathers.

Jean Paul got out at the regional high school at the northern end of town. His eagerness to start his day was apparent in the rapid way he said good-bye. Even at that hour a group of his friends were waiting, and they entered the school together. Jean Paul was on the J.V. basketball team and they had to practice before classes. Charles watched his younger son disappear, then pulled the car out into the street heading toward I-93 and the trip into Boston. They didn't hit traffic until they were in Massachusetts.

For Charles, driving had a hypnotic effect. Usually his mind trailed off into the complexities of antigens and antibodies, protein structure and formation while he operated the car by some lower, more primitive parts of his brain. But today he began to find himself sensitive to Chuck's habitual silence, then irritated by it. Charles tried to imagine what was on his older son's mind. But try as he could, he realized he had absolutely no idea. Snatching quick looks at the bored, expressionless face, he wondered if Chuck thought about girls. Charles realized that he didn't even know if Chuck dated.

"How is school going?" asked Charles as casually as possible.

"Fine!" said Chuck, immediately on guard.

Another silence.

"You know what you're going to major in?"

"Nah. Not yet."

"You must have some idea. Don't you have to start planning next year's schedule?"

"Not for a while."

"Well, what course do you enjoy the most this year?"

"Psychology, I guess." Chuck looked out the passenger window. He didn't want to talk about school. Sooner or later they'd get around to chemistry.

"Not psychology," said Charles, shaking his head.

Chuck looked at his father's cleanly shaven face, his broad but well-defined nose, his condescending way of speaking with his head tilted slightly back. He was always so sure of himself, quick to make judgments, and Chuck could hear the derision in his father's voice as he pronounced the word "psychology." Chuck worked up his courage and asked: "What's wrong with psychology?" This was one area in which Chuck was convinced his father was not an expert.

"Psychology is a waste of time," said Charles. "It's based on a fundamentally false principle, stimulus-response. That's just *not* how the brain works. The brain is not a blank *tabula rasa*, it's a dynamic system, generating ideas and even emotions often irrespective of the environment. You know what I mean?"

"Yeah!" Chuck looked away. He had no idea what his father was talking about, but as usual it sounded good. And it was easier to agree, which is what he did for the next fifteen minutes while Charles maintained an impassioned monologue about the defects of the behavioral approach to psychology.

"How about coming over to the lab this afternoon?" said Charles after an interval of silence. "My work has been going fabulously, and I think I'm close to a breakthrough of sorts. I'd like to share it with you."

"I can't today," said Chuck quickly. The last thing he wanted was to be shepherded around the institute where everyone kowtowed to Charles, the famous scientist. It always made him feel uncomfortable, especially since he didn't understand a thing that Charles was doing. His father's explanations always started so far above Chuck's head that he was in constant terror of a question which could reveal the depths of his ignorance.

"You can come at any time at all, at your convenience, Chuck." Charles had always wished he could share his enthusiasm for his research with Chuck, but Chuck had never shown any interest. Charles had thought that if the boy could see science in action, he'd be irresistibly drawn to it.

"No. I got a lab and then some meetings."

"Too bad," said Charles. "Maybe tomorrow."

"Yeah, maybe tomorrow," said Chuck.

Chuck got out of the car on Huntington Avenue and, after a perfunctory good-bye, walked away in the wet Boston snow.

Charles watched him go. He looked like some late-sixties car-
icature, out of place even among his peers. The other students
seemed brighter, more attentive to their appearance, and almost invariably in groups. Chuck walked by himself. Charles
wondered if Chuck had been the most severely hurt by Elizabeth's illness and death. He'd hoped that Cathryn's presence
would have helped, but ever since the wedding, Chuck had
become more withdrawn and distant. Putting the car in gear,
Charles headed across the Fenway toward Cambridge.

TWO

Crossing the Charles River via the Boston University Bridge, he began to plan his day. It was infinitely easier to deal with the complications of intracellular life than the uncertainties of child rearing. At Memorial Drive Charles turned right, then after a short distance, left into the parking area of the Weinburger Research Institute. His spirits began to rise.

As he got out of his car, he noticed a significant number of cars already there, which was unusual at that time of the morning; even the director's blue Mercedes was in its spot. Mindless of the weather, Charles stood for a moment puzzling over all the cars, then started toward the institute. It was a modern four-storied, brick-and-glass structure, somewhat akin to the nearby Hyatt Hotel but without the pyramid profile. The site was directly on the Charles River and nestled between Harvard and M.I.T., and directly across from the campus of Boston University. No wonder the institute had no trouble locating recruits.

The receptionist saw Charles approach through the mirrored glass and pressed a button, sliding open the thick glass door. Security was tight because of the value of the scientific instrumentation as well as the nature of some of the research, particularly the genetic research. Charles started across the carpeted reception area, saying good morning to the newly acquired and coy Miss Andrews, who tilted her head down and watched Charles from beneath her carefully plucked eyebrows. Charles wondered how long she would last. The life of receptionists at the institute was very short.

With an exaggerated double take, Charles stopped at the main hall and stepped back so he could see into the waiting room. In a haze of cigarette smoke a small crowd of people were milling about excitedly.

"Dr. Martel . . . Dr. Martel," called one of the men.

Surprised to hear his name, Charles stepped into the room and was instantly engulfed by people, all talking at the same time. The man who had first called to Charles stuck a microphone just inches from his nose.

"I'm from the *Globe*," shouted the man. "Can I ask you a few questions?"

Pushing the microphone to the side, Charles began a retreat to the hall.

"Dr. Martel, is it true you're going to take over the study?" shouted a woman grabbing onto Charles's coat pocket.

"I don't give interviews," shouted Charles as he broke from the small crowd. Inexplicably the reporters stopped at the threshold of the waiting room.

"What the hell is going on?" muttered Charles as he slowed to a fast walk. He hated the media. Elizabeth's illness had for some reason attracted the attention of the press and Charles had felt repeatedly raped as their private tragedy had been "trivialized" for people to read while having their morning coffee. He entered his lab and slammed the door.

Ellen Sheldon, Charles's laboratory assistant for the last six years, jumped. She'd been concentrating in the stillness of the lab while setting up the equipment to separate serum proteins. As usual she had arrived at seven fifteen to prepare for Charles's invariable arrival at seven forty-five. By eight

Charles liked to be into the day's work, especially now that things were going so well.

"If I slammed the door like that, I'd never hear the end of it," said Ellen, irritated. She was a darkly attractive woman of thirty who wore her hair piled on her head except for vagrant wisps which trailed down alongside her neck. When he'd hired her, Charles got some jealous kidding from his colleagues, but in truth, Charles had not appreciated her exotic beauty until he'd worked with her for several years. Her individual features were not exceptional; it was the whole package that was intriguing. But as far as Charles was concerned, the most important aspects were her intellect, her eagerness, and her superb training at M.I.T.

"I'm sorry if I scared you," said Charles, hanging up his coat. "There's a bunch of reporters out there, and you know how I feel about reporters."

"We all know how you feel about reporters," agreed Ellen, going back to work.

Charles sat down at his desk and began going through his papers. His laboratory was a large rectangular room with a private office connected by a door in the back. Charles had eschewed the office and put a functional metal desk in the lab, converting the office into an animal room. The main animal area was a separate wing off the back of the institute, but Charles wanted some of his experimental animals nearby in order to closely supervise their care. Good experimental results depended heavily on good care of the animals and Charles was particularly attentive to details.

"What are all the reporters doing here anyway?" asked Charles. "Did our fearless leader make some scientific breakthrough in his bathtub last night?"

"Be a little more generous," scolded Ellen. "Someone has to do the administrative work."

"Excuse me," said Charles with sarcastic exaggeration.

"Actually, it is something serious," said Ellen. "The episode with Brighton was leaked to the *New York Times*."

"These new generation doctors certainly like publicity," said

Charles, shaking his head in disgust. "I thought that after that rave review in *Time* magazine a month ago he would have been satisfied. What the hell did he do?"

"Don't tell me you haven't heard?" said Ellen incredulously.

"Ellen, I come here to work. You of all people should know that."

"True. But this Brighton situation . . . Everybody knows about it. It's been the in-house gossip for at least a week."

"If I didn't know you better, I'd think you were trying to hurt my feelings. If you don't want to tell me, don't. In fact, from your tone of voice, I'm beginning to think I'd rather not know."

"Well, it's bad," agreed Ellen. "The head of the animal department reported to the director that Dr. Thomas Brighton had been sneaking into the animal lab and substituting healthy mice for his own cancer-carrying animals."

"Wonderful," said Charles with sarcasm. "Obviously the idea was to make his drug appear miraculously effective."

"Exactly. Which is all the more interesting because it's been his drug, Canceran, that has gotten him all the recent publicity."

"And his position here at the institute," added Charles, as he felt his face redden with contempt. He'd disapproved of all the publicity Dr. Thomas Brighton had garnered, but when he'd voiced his opinion he'd realized people had thought he was jealous.

"I feel sorry for him," said Ellen. "This will probably have a big effect on his career."

"Am I hearing right?" asked Charles. "You feel sorry for that little conniving bastard? I hope they throw his cheating ass right out of medicine. That guy is supposed to be a medical doctor. Cheating on research is as bad as cheating on patient care. No! It's worse. In research you can end up hurting many more people."

"I wouldn't be so quick to judge. Maybe he was under a lot of pressure because of all the publicity. There could have been extenuating circumstances."

"When it comes to integrity, there are no extenuating circumstances."

"Well, I disagree. People have problems. We're not all supermen like you."

"Don't give me any of that psychology bullshit," said Charles. He was surprised at the malice implied in Ellen's comment.

"Okay, I won't. But a little human generosity would do you good, Charles Martel. You don't give a damn about other people's feelings. All you do is take." Ellen's voice trembled with emotion.

A strained silence fell over the lab. Ellen ostensibly went back to her work. Charles opened his lab book, but he could not concentrate. He hadn't meant to sound so angry and obviously he had offended Ellen. Was it true he was insensitive to others' feelings? It was the first time Ellen had ever said anything negative about him. Charles wondered if it had anything to do with the brief affair they'd had just before he'd met Cathryn. After working together so many years it had been more the result of propinquity than romance, coming at a time when Charles had finally come out of the immobilizing depression following Elizabeth's death. It had only lasted a month. Then Cathryn had arrived at the institute as temporary summer help. Afterwards he and Ellen had never discussed the affair. At the time Charles had felt it was easier to let the episode slip into the past.

"I'm sorry if I sounded angry," said Charles. "I didn't mean to. I got carried away."

"And I'm sorry I said what I did," said Ellen, her voice still reflecting deeply felt emotion.

Charles wasn't convinced. He wanted to ask Ellen if she really thought he was insensitive, but he didn't have the nerve.

"By the way," added Ellen. "Dr. Morrison wants to see you as soon as possible. He called before you arrived."

"Morrison can wait," said Charles. "Let's get things going here."

• • •

Cathryn was irritated at Charles. She wasn't the kind of person who tried to suppress such feelings; besides, she felt justified. In light of Michelle's nosebleed, he could have altered his sacred schedule and taken Michelle to Pediatric Hospital himself. After all, he was the doctor. Cathryn had horrible visions of Michelle's nose bleeding all over the car. Could she bleed to death? Cathryn wasn't sure, but the possibility seemed real enough to terrify her. Cathryn hated anything associated with disease, blood, and hospitals. Why such things bothered her she wasn't sure, although a bad experience at age ten with a complicated case of appendicitis probably contributed. They'd had trouble making the diagnosis, first at the doctor's office, then at the hospital. Even to that day she vividly remembered the white tiles and the antiseptic smell. But the worst had been the ordeal of the vaginal exam. No one tried to explain anything. They just held her down. Charles knew all this, but he had still insisted on getting to the lab on schedule and letting Cathryn accompany Michelle.

Deciding there was a certain safety in numbers, Cathryn sat down at the kitchen phone to call Marge Schonhauser to see if she wanted a ride into Boston. If Tad was still in the hospital there was a good chance she would. The phone was picked up on the second ring. It was Nancy, the Schonhausers' sixteen-year-old daughter.

"My mother's already at the hospital."

"Well, I just thought I'd try," said Cathryn. "I'll see if I can tell her while I'm there. But if I don't get her, tell her I called."

"Sure," said Nancy. "I know she'd be glad to hear from you."

"How's Tad doing?" asked Cathryn. "Is he coming home soon?"

"He's awfully sick, Mrs. Martel. He had to have a marrow transplant. They tested all us kids and little Lisa was the only one who matched. He's living in a tent to protect him from germs."

"I'm terribly sorry to hear that," said Cathryn. She could feel a little of her strength drain away. She had no idea what a marrow transplant was, but it sounded serious and scary. She said good-bye to Nancy and hung up the phone. For a moment she sat thinking, dreading the emotional aspect of the confrontation with Merge, feeling the guilt of not having called sooner. Tad's illness made her own fears about Michelle's nosebleed seem petty by comparison. Taking a deep breath, Cathryn went into the living room.

Michelle was watching the *Today* show, propped up on the couch. After some orange juice and rest, she felt considerably better, but she was still upset. Although Charles had not said it, she was certain he was disappointed in her. The nosebleed had been the final aggravation.

"I called Dr. Wiley's office," said Cathryn as brightly as she could, "and the nurse said we should come as soon as possible. Otherwise we might have a long wait. So let's get the show on the road."

"I feel much better," said Michelle. She forced a smile but her lips trembled.

"Good," said Cathryn. "But you stay still. I'll get your coat and stuff." Cathryn started for the stairs.

"Cathryn, I think I'm all right now. I think I can go to school." As if to substantiate her opinion, Michelle swung her legs to the floor and stood up. Her smile wavered through a flurry of weakness.

Cathryn turned and looked at her adopted daughter, feeling a rush of affection for his little girl whom Charles loved so dearly. Cathryn had no idea why Michelle would want to deny her illness unless she was afraid of the hospital like Cathryn was. She walked over and put her arms around the child, hugging her close. "You don't have to be afraid, Michelle."

"I'm not afraid," said Michelle, resisting Cathryn's embrace.

"You're not?" asked Cathryn, more to have something to say. She was always taken by surprise to have her affection refused. Cathryn smiled self-consciously, her hands still resting on Michelle's shoulders.

"I think I should go to school. I don't have to take gym if you give me a note."

"Michelle. You haven't been feeling right for a month. You had a fever this morning. I think it's time we did something."

"But I feel fine now, and want to go to school."

Taking her hands off Michelle's shoulders, Cathryn examined the defiant face in front of her. In so many ways Michelle remained a mystery. She was such a precise, serious little girl who seemed mature for her age, but for some reason always kept Cathryn at arm's length. Cathryn wondered how much of it was due to Michelle's losing her mother at age three. Cathryn felt she knew something about growing up with only one parent because of her own father's abandonment.

"I tell you what we'll do," said Cathryn, debating with herself the best way to handle the problem. "We'll take your temperature again. If you still have a fever, we go. If you don't, then we won't."

Michelle's temperature was 100.8.

An hour and a half later, Cathryn pulled the old Dodge station wagon into the garage at Pediatric Hospital and took a ticket from the machine. Thankfully it had been an uneventful ride. Michelle had spoken very little during the trip, only answering direct questions. To Cathryn she seemed exhausted and her hands lay immobile in her lap like a puppet's, waiting to be moved from above.

"What are you thinking?" asked Cathryn, breaking the silence. There were no parking spaces available and they kept driving from one level to the next.

"Nothing," said Michelle without moving.

Cathryn watched Michelle out of the corner of her eye. She wanted so much to get Michelle to let down her guard, to let Cathryn's love in.

"Don't you like to share your thoughts?" persisted Cathryn.

"I don't feel good, Cathryn. I feel really bad. I think you are going to have to help me out of the car." Cathryn took one look at Michelle's face, and abruptly stopped the car. She reached out and put her arms around the child. The little girl didn't resist. She moved over and put her head on Cathryn's breast. Cathryn felt warm tears touch her arm.

"I'll be glad to help you, Michelle. I'll help you whenever you need me. I promise."

Cathryn had the feeling that she'd finally crossed some undefined threshold. It had taken two and a half years of patience, but it had paid off.

Blaring auto horns brought Cathryn back to the present. She put her car in gear and started forward, pleased that Michelle continued to hold on to her.

Cathryn felt more like a real mother than she ever had before. As they pushed through the revolving door, Michelle acted very weak and allowed Cathryn to help her. In the lobby a request for a wheelchair was promptly filled, and although Michelle initially resisted, she let Cathryn push her.

For Cathryn, the happiness in the new closeness to Michelle helped dull the specter of the hospital. The decor helped, too; the lobby was paved with a warm Mexican tile and the seating was done in bright oranges and yellows. There were even lots of plants. It was more like a luxury hotel than a big city hospital.

The pediatric offices were equally nonthreatening. There were five patients already in Dr. Wiley's waiting room. To Michelle's disgust, none was over two years of age. She would have complained except she glimpsed the examining rooms through an open door and remembered why she was there. Leaning toward Cathryn she whispered, "You don't think I'll get a shot, do you?"

"I have no idea," said Cathryn. "But afterwards if you feel up to it, we can do something fun. Whatever you like."

"Could we go visit my father?" Michelle's eyes brightened.

"Sure," said Cathryn. She parked Michelle next to an empty seat, then sat down herself.

A mother and a whimpering five-year-old boy emerged from the examining room. One of the mothers with a tiny baby got up and went in.

"I'm going to ask the nurse if I can use the phone," said Cathryn. "I want to find out where Tad Schonhauser is. You're okay, aren't you?"

"I'm okay," said Michelle. "In fact, I feel better again."

"Good," said Cathryn as she got up. Michelle watched Cathryn's long brown hair bounce on her shoulders as she walked over to the nurse, then dialed the phone. Remembering her father say how much he liked it, Michelle wished hers were the same color. Suddenly she wished she were really old, like twenty, so she could be a doctor and talk to Charles and work in his lab. Charles had said that doctors didn't have to give shots; the nurses do. Michelle hoped she didn't have to get a shot. She hated them.

"Dr. Martel," called Dr. Peter Morrison, standing at the doorway to Charles's lab. "Didn't you get my message?"

Straightening up from loading serum samples into an automatic radioactivity counter, Charles looked at Morrison, administrative head of the department of physiology. The man was leaning on the doorjamb, the fluorescent ceiling light reflecting off the lenses in his narrow tortoiseshell glasses. His face was taut, angry.

"I'll be by in ten or fifteen minutes," said Charles. "I just have a few more important things to do."

Morrison considered Charles's statement for a moment. "I'll be waiting in my office." The door closed slowly behind him.

"You shouldn't bait him," said Ellen, after Morrison had left. "All it can do is cause trouble."

"It's good for him," said Charles. "It gives him something to think about. For the life of me, I don't know what else he does in that office of his."

"Someone has to attend to the administration," said Ellen.

"The irony is that he once was a decent researcher," said Charles. "Now his entire life is dominated by his ambition to become director, and all he does is push papers, have meetings, go to lunch, and attend benefits."

"Those benefits raise money."

"I suppose," said Charles. "But you don't need a Ph.D. in physiology to do that. I just think it is a waste. If the people donating money at those fund-raisers ever found out how little of it actually gets applied to research, they'd be appalled."

"I agree with you there," Ellen replied. "But why don't you let me finish loading these samples. You go see Morrison and get it over with because I am going to need you to help draw blood from the rats."

Ten minutes later Charles found himself climbing the metal fire stairs to the second floor. He had no idea why Morrison wanted to see him, although he guessed it was going to be another pep talk, trying to get him to publish a paper for some upcoming meeting. Charles had very different ideas from his colleagues about publication. It had never been his inclination to rush into print. Although research careers often were measured by the number of articles a doctor published, Charles's dogged dedication and brilliance had won him a greater respect from his colleagues, many of whom often said that it was men like Charles who made the great scientific discoveries. It was only the administration who complained.

Dr. Morrison's office was in the administrative area on the second floor where the halls were painted a pleasant beige and hung with somber oil paintings of past directors clothed in academic robes. The atmosphere was a world apart from the utilitarian labs on the ground and first floors and gave the impression of a successful law office rather than a nonprofit medical organization. Its opulence never failed to irritate Charles; he knew that the money had come from people believing they were contributing to research.

In this frame of mind, Charles made his way to Morrison's office. Charles was about to enter when he noticed that all the secretaries in the administration area were watching him. There was that same feeling of suppressed excitement that Charles had sensed when he arrived that morning. It was as if everyone were waiting for something to happen.

As Charles went inside, Morrison stood up from his broad mahogany desk and stepped around into the room with his hand outstretched. His earlier irritated demeanor had vanished. By habit Charles shook the hand but was baffled by the gesture. He had nothing in common with this man. Morrison was dressed in a freshly pressed pin-striped suit, starched white shirt, and silk tie; his hand-sewn loafers were professionally shined. Charles was wearing his usual blue oxford shirt, open at the collar, with his tie loosened and tucked between the second and third buttons; his sleeves were rolled up above his elbows. His trousers were baggy khakis and his shoes, scuffed cordovans.

"Welcome," said Morrison as if he hadn't already seen Charles that morning. With a sweep of his hand he motioned for Charles to sit on the leather couch in the rear of the office, which afforded a view out over the Charles River. "Coffee?" Morrison smiled, showing very small, very white, even teeth.

Charles declined, sat back on the couch, and folded his arms. Something strange was going on and his curiosity was piqued.

"Have you seen the *New York Times* today?" asked Morrison.

Charles shook his head negatively.

Morrison walked over to his desk, picked up the paper, and directed Charles's attention to an article on the front page. His gold identification bracelet slid out from beneath his shirt sleeve as he pointed. SCANDAL AT THE WEINBURGER CANCER INSTITUTE.

Charles read the first paragraph, which paraphrased what Ellen had already told him. That was enough.

"Terrible, eh?" intoned Morrison.

Charles nodded half-felt agreement. Although he knew that such an incident would have a negative effect on fund-raising for a time, he also felt that it would take some of the unearned emphasis away from this new drug, Canceran, and hopefully return it to more promising areas. He felt that the answer to cancer lay in immunology, not chemotherapy, although he recognized the increasing numbers of cures achieved in recent years.

"Dr. Brighton should have known better," said Morrison. "He's just too young, too impatient."

Charles waited for Morrison to get to the point.

"We're going to have to let Dr. Brighton go," said Morrison.

Charles nodded as Morrison launched into his explanation of Brighton's behavior. Charles looked at Morrison's shining bald head. The little hair he had was located above his ears, connected in the back by a carefully combed swath.

"Just a minute," interrupted Charles. "This is all very interesting, but I do have an important experiment in progress downstairs. Is there something specific you wanted to tell me?"

"Of course," said Morrison, adjusting his cuff. His voice took on a more serious note and he brought the tips of his fingers together, forming a steeple. "The board of directors of the institute anticipated the *New York Times* article and had an emergency meeting last night. We decided that if we didn't act quickly the real victim of the Brighton affair would be the new and promising drug, Canceran. I assume you can understand this concern?"

"Of course," said Charles, but on the horizon of Charles's mind, a black cloud began to form.

"It was also decided that the only way to salvage the project was for the institute to publicly support the drug by appointing its most prestigious scientist to complete the tests. And I'm happy to say, Charles Martel, that you were chosen."

Charles closed his eyes and slapped a hand over his forehead. He wanted to storm out of the office, but he contained himself. Slowly he reopened his eyes. Morrison's thin lips were pulled into a smile. Charles could not tell if the man knew what his reaction was and was, therefore, teasing him, or if Morrison genuinely thought that he was conveying good news.

"I can't tell you how pleased I am," continued Morrison, "that the board of directors picked someone from my department. Not that I'm surprised, mind you. We all have been working tirelessly for the Weinburger. It's just nice to get this kind of recognition once in a while. And, of course, you were my choice."

"Well," began Charles in as steady a voice as he could manage. "I hope you convey to the board of directors my thanks for this vote of confidence, but unfortunately I'm not in a position to take over the Canceran project. You see, my own work is progressing extremely well. They will have to find someone else."

"I hope you're joking," said Morrison. His smile waned, then vanished.

"Not at all. With the progress I'm making, there is no way I can leave my current work. My assistant and I have been extremely successful and the pace is increasing."

"But you have not published a single paper for several years. That's hardly a rapid pace. Besides, funding for your work has come almost totally from the general operating funds of the institute; you have not been responsible for any major outside grants to the institute for a long, long time. I know that's because you have insisted on remaining in the immunological field of cancer research and until now I have backed you all the way. But now your services are needed. As soon as you finish the Canceran project, you can go back to your own work. It's as simple as that." Morrison stood up and walked back behind his desk to signify that as far as he was concerned the meeting was over, the matter decided.

"But I can't leave my work," said Charles, feeling a sense of desperation. "Not now. Things are going too well. What about my development of the process of the hybridoma? That should count for something."

"Ah, the hybridoma," said Morrison. "A wonderful piece of work. Who would have thought that a sensitized lymphocyte could be fused with a cancer cell to make a kind of cellular antibody factory. Brilliant! There are only two problems. One: it was many years ago; and two: you failed to publish the discovery! We should have been able to capitalize on it. Instead, another institution got the credit. I wouldn't count on the hybridoma development to ensure your position with the board of directors."

"I didn't stop to publish the hybridoma process because it was just a single step in my experiment protocol. I've never been eager to rush into print."

"We all know that. In fact, it's probably the major reason you're where you are and not a department head."

"I don't want to be a department head," yelled Charles, beginning to lose his patience. "I want to do research, not push around papers and go to benefits."

"I suppose that's meant as a personal insult," said Morrison.

"You can take it as you will," said Charles, who had abandoned his efforts at controlling his anger. He stood up, approached Morrison's desk, and pointed an accusing finger at the man. "I'll tell you the biggest reason I can't take over the Canceran project. I don't believe in it!"

"What the hell does that mean?" Morrison's patience had also worn thin.

"It means that cellular poisons like Canceran are not the ultimate answer to cancer. The presumption is that they kill cancer cells faster than normal cells so that after the malignancy is stopped the patient will still have enough normal cells to live. But that's only an interim approach. A real cure for cancer can only come from a better understanding of the cellular processes of life, particularly the chemical communication between cells."

Charles began to pace the room, nervously running his fingers through his hair. Morrison, by contrast, didn't move. He just followed Charles's gyrations with his eyes.

"I tell you," shouted Charles, "the whole attack on cancer is coming from the wrong perspective. Cancer cannot be considered a disease like an infection because it encourages the misconception that there will be a magic bullet cure like an antibiotic." Charles stopped pacing and leaned over the desk toward Morrison. His voice was quieter, but more impassioned. "I've been giving this a lot of thought, Dr. Morrison. Cancer is not a disease in the traditional sense, but an unmasking of a more primitive life-form, like those that existed at the beginning of time when multicellular organisms were evolving. Think of it. At one time, eons ago, there were only single-celled creatures who selfishly ignored each other. But then, after a few million years, some of them teamed up because it was more efficient. They communicated chemically and this communication made multicellular organisms like us possible. Why does a liver cell only do what a liver cell does, or a heart cell, or a brain cell? The answer is chemical communication. But cancer cells are not responsive to this chemical communication. They have broken free, gone back to a more primitive stage, like those single-cell organisms that existed millions of years ago. Cancer is not a disease but rather a clue to the basic organization of life. And immunology is the study of this communication."

Charles ended his monologue leaning forward on his hands over Morrison's desk. There was an awkward silence. Morrison cleared his throat, pulled out his leather desk chair, and sat down.

"Very interesting," he said. "Unfortunately, we are not in a metaphysical business. And I must remind you that the immunological aspect of cancer has been worked on for more than a decade and contributed very little to the prolongation of the cancer victim's life."

"That's the point," interrupted Charles. "Immunology will give a cure, not just palliation."

"Please," said Morrison softly. "I listened to you, now listen to me. There is very little money available for immunology at the present time. That's a fact. The Canceran project carries a huge grant from both the National Cancer Institute as well as the American Cancer Society. The Weinburger needs that money."

Charles tried to interrupt, but Morrison cut him off. Charles slumped back into a chair. He could feel the weight of the institute's bureaucracy surround him like a giant octopus.

Morrison ritually removed his glasses and placed them on his blotter. "You are a superb scientist, Charles. We all know that, and that's why we need you at this moment. But you're also a maverick and in that sense more tolerated than appreciated. You have enemies here, perhaps motivated by jealousy, perhaps by your self-righteousness. I have defended you in the past. But there are those who would just as soon see you go. I'm telling you this for your own good. At the meeting last night I mentioned that you might refuse taking over the Canceran project. It was decided that if you did, your position here would be terminated. It will be easy enough to get someone to take your place on a project like this."

Terminated! The word echoed painfully in Charles's mind. He tried to collect his thoughts.

"Can I say something now?" asked Charles.

"Of course," said Morrison, "tell me that you're going to take over the Canceran project. That's what I want to hear."

"I've been very busy downstairs," said Charles, ignoring Morrison's last comment, "and I'm moving very rapidly. I have been purposefully secretive but I believe that I am truly close to understanding cancer and possibly a cure."

Morrison studied Charles's face, trying to garner a hint as to his sincerity. Was this a trick? A delusion of grandeur? Morrison looked at Charles's bright blue eyes, his high lined forehead. He knew all about Charles's past, his wife's death, his sudden move from clinical medicine into research. He knew that Charles was a brilliant worker, but a loner. He suspected that Charles's idea of "truly close" might well constitute ten years.

"A cure for cancer," said Morrison, not bothering to smooth the sarcastic edge to his voice. He kept his eyes on Charles's face. "Wouldn't that be nice. We'd all be very proud. But . . . it will have to wait until the Canceran study is done. Lesley Pharmaceuticals, who holds the patent, is eager to get production rolling. Now, Dr. Martel, if you'll excuse me, I have work to do. The matter is closed. The Canceran lab books are available, so get cracking. Good luck. If you have any problems let me know."

Charles stumbled out of Morrison's office in a daze, crushed at the prospect of being forced away from his own research at such a critical time. Aware of the quizzical stare from Morrison's prim secretary, Charles half ran to the fire stairs, banging open the door. He descended slowly, his mind reeling. Never in his life had anyone ever threatened to fire him. Although he felt confident he could get a job, the idea of being cast adrift even for a short time was devastating, especially with all his ongoing financial obligations. When he had given up his private practice, Charles had given up his status as moderately well-to-do. On his research salary, they barely made it, especially with Chuck in college.

Reaching the first floor, Charles turned down the hall, toward his lab. He needed some time to think.

THREE

It was their turn. A nurse who looked like she stepped out of a 1950s Doris Day movie called out Michelle's name and held the door open. Michelle gripped her stepmother's hand as they entered the inner office. Cathryn wasn't sure which one of them was more tense.

Dr. Wiley looked up from a chart, peering over half glasses. Cathryn had never met Dr. Jordan Wiley, but all the children knew him. Michelle had told Cathryn that she remembered coming to him for the chicken pox four years ago when she was eight. Cathryn was immediately taken by the attractiveness of the man. He was in his late fifties and exuded that comfortably paternal air that people traditionally associate with doctors. He was a tall individual with closely cropped graying hair and a bushy gray mustache. He wore a small, hand-tied red bow tie which gave him a unique, energetic look. His hands were large but gentle as he placed the chart on his desk and leaned forward.

"My, my," said Dr. Wiley. "Miss Martel, you have become a lady. You look very beautiful, a little pale, but beautiful. Now introduce me to your new mother."

"She's not my new mother," said Michelle indignantly. "She's been my mother for over two years."

Both Cathryn and Dr. Wiley laughed and after a moment's indecision, Michelle joined them, although she was not sure she got the joke.

"Please, sit down," said Dr. Wiley, motioning to the chairs facing his desk. As a consummate clinician, Dr. Wiley had started the examination the moment Michelle had entered his office. Besides her pallor, he'd noticed the girl's tentative gait, her slumped posture, the glazed look to her blue eyes. Spreading open her chart, which he'd reviewed earlier, he picked up a pen. "Now then, what seems to be the trouble?"

Cathryn described Michelle's illness with Michelle adding comments here and there. Cathryn said that it had started gradually with fever and general malaise. They'd thought she'd had the flu, but it would not go away. Some mornings she'd be fine; others she'd feel terrible. Cathryn concluded by saying that she'd decided it would be best to have Michelle checked in case she needed some antibiotics or something.

"Very well," said Dr. Wiley. "Now I'd like some time alone with Michelle. If you don't mind, Mrs. Martel." He came around from behind his desk and opened the door to the waiting room.

Momentarily nonplussed, Cathryn got to her feet. She had expected to stay with Michelle.

Dr. Wiley smiled warmly and, as if reading her mind, said, "Michelle will be fine with me; we're old friends."

Giving Michelle's shoulder a little squeeze, Cathryn started for the waiting room. At the door she paused. "How long will you be? Do I have time to visit a patient?"

"I think so," said Dr. Wiley. "We'll be about thirty minutes or so."

"I'll be back before that, Michelle," called Cathryn. Michelle waved and the door closed.

Armed with some directions from the nurse, Cathryn retraced her steps back to the main lobby. It wasn't until she entered the elevator that her old fear of hospitals returned.

Staring at a sad little girl in a wheelchair, Cathryn realized that pediatric hospitals were particularly unnerving. The concept of a sick child made her feel weak. She tried to concentrate on the floor indicator above the doors, but a powerful, incomprehensible urge drew her eyes back to the sick child. When the doors opened on the fifth floor and she stepped off, her legs felt rubbery and her palms were sweaty.

Cathryn was heading for the Marshall Memorial isolation unit, but the fifth floor also contained the general intensive care unit and the surgical recovery room. In her emotionally sensitive state, Cathryn was subjected to all the sights and sounds associated with acute medical crisis. The beep of the cardiac monitors mixed with the cries of terrified children. Everywhere there was a profusion of tubes, bottles, and hissing machines. It was an alien world populated with a bustling staff who seemed, to Cathryn, to be unreasonably detached from the horror around them. The fact that these children were being helped in the long run was lost on Cathryn.

Pausing to catch her breath in a narrow hallway lined with windows, Cathryn realized that she was crossing from one building to another within the medical center. The hall was a peaceful bridge. She was alone for a moment until a man in a wheelchair with DISPATCHER written across the back motored past her. Glass test tubes and jars filled with all sorts of body fluid samples jangled in a metal rack. He smiled, and Cathryn smiled back. She felt better. Fortified, she continued on.

The Marshall Memorial isolation unit was easier for Cathryn to deal with. All the doors to the rooms were closed and there were no patients to be seen. Cathryn approached the nurses' station which seemed more like a ticket counter at a modern airport than the nerve center for a hospital ward. It was a large square area with a bank of TV monitors. A clerk looked up and cheerfully asked if he could help her.

"I'm looking for the Schonhauser boy," said Cathryn.

"Five twenty-one," said the clerk pointing.

Cathryn thanked him and walked over to the closed door.

She knocked softly. "Just go right in," called the clerk. "But don't forget your gown."

Cathryn tried the door. It opened and she found herself in a small anteroom with shelving for linen and other supplies, a medicine locker, a sink, and a large soiled-laundry hamper. Beyond the hamper was another closed door containing a small glass window. Before Cathryn could move, the inner door opened and a gowned, masked figure stepped into the room. With rapid movements the individual discarded the paper mask and hood in the trash. It was a young nurse with red hair and freckles.

"Hi," she said. The gloves went into the trash, the gown into the hamper. "You going in to see Tad?"

"I was hoping to," said Cathryn. "Is Mrs. Schonhauser in there, too?"

"Yup, she's here every day, poor woman. Don't forget your gown. Very strict reverse precautions."

"I . . ." started Cathryn, but the harried nurse was already through the door.

Cathryn searched through the shelves until she found the hoods and the masks. She put them on, feeling ridiculous. The gown was next but she put it on like a coat. The rubber gloves were more difficult and she never got the left one all the way on. With the half-empty fingers dangling from her hand, she opened the inner door.

The first thing she saw was a large plastic enclosure like a cage surrounding the bed. Although the plastic fragmented the image, Cathryn was able to make out Tad Schonhauser's form. In the raw fluorescent light the boy was a pale, slightly greenish color. There was a low hiss of oxygen. Marge Schonhauser was seated to the left of the bed, reading by the window.

"Marge," whispered Cathryn.

The masked and gowned woman looked up. "Yes?" she said.

"It's Cathryn."

"Cathryn?"

"Cathryn Martel."

"For goodness sake," said Marge when she was able to associate the name. She got up and put her book down. Taking Cathryn's hand, she led her back into the anteroom. Before the door closed behind them Cathryn looked back at Tad. The boy had not moved although his eyes were open.

"Thank you for coming," said Marge. "I really appreciate it."

"How is he?" asked Cathryn. The strange room, the gowning . . . it wasn't encouraging.

"Very bad," said Marge. She pulled off her mask. Her face was drawn and tense; her eyes red and swollen. "He had a marrow transplant twice from Lisa but it hasn't worked. Not at all."

"I spoke to Nancy this morning," said Cathryn. "I had no idea he was this sick." Cathryn could sense the emotion within Marge. It was just beneath the surface like a volcano, ready to erupt.

"I'd never even heard of aplastic anemia," said Marge, trying to laugh. But the tears came instead. Cathryn found herself crying in sympathy, and the two women stood there for several minutes weeping on each other's shoulder. Finally Marge sighed, pulled back slightly, and looked at Cathryn's face. "Oh, it is good of you to come. You don't know how much I appreciate it. One of the difficult things about serious illness is that people ignore you."

"But I had no idea," repeated Cathryn remorsefully.

"I'm not blaming you," said Marge. "I just mean people in general. I suppose they just don't know what to say or maybe they are afraid of the unknown, but it happens when you need people the most."

"I'm terribly sorry," said Cathryn, at a loss for something to say. She wished she'd called weeks ago. Marge was older than she, closer to Charles's age. But they got along well, and Marge had been gracious and helpful when Cathryn had first come to Shaftesbury. The other New Englanders had been very cold.

"I don't mean to take it out on you," said Marge, "but I feel so upset. The doctors told me this morning that Tad might be terminal. They're trying to prepare me. I don't want him to suffer, but I don't want him to die."

Cathryn was stunned. Terminal? Die? These were words that referred to old people, not to a young boy who just a few weeks ago was in their kitchen bursting with life and energy. With difficulty she resisted an urge to run back downstairs. Instead she hugged Marge.

"I just can't help but ask why," sobbed Marge, struggling to control herself and allowing Cathryn to hold her. "They say the good Lord has His reasons, but I'd like to know why. He was such a good boy. It seems so unfair."

Marshaling her strength, Cathryn began to talk. She hadn't planned what she was going to say. It just came out. She talked about God and death in a way that surprised her because she wasn't religious in the traditional sense. She'd been brought up a Catholic and had even talked briefly of becoming a nun when she was ten. But during college she had rebelled against the ritual of the Church and had become an agnostic of sorts, not bothering to examine her beliefs. Yet she must have made sense because Marge responded; whether it was to the content or just the human companionship, Cathryn didn't know. But Marge calmed down and even managed a weak smile.

"I've got to go," said Cathryn finally. "I've got to meet Michelle. But I'll be back and I'll call tonight, I promise." Marge nodded and kissed Cathryn before going back in with her son. Cathryn stepped out into the hall. She stood by the door breathing rapidly. The hospital had lived up to her fears after all.

"It doesn't seem to me that we have a whole lot of choice," said Ellen as she put her coffee mug on the counter. She was sitting on a laboratory stool, looking down at Charles who was slumped in his chair before his desk. "It's a shame to have to slow down on our work at this point, but what can we do? Maybe we should have kept Morrison informed of our progress."

"No," said Charles. His elbows were on the desk, his face in his hands, his coffee untouched. "If we'd done that he would have stopped us a dozen times to write some goddamned paper. We'd be years behind."

"That's the only way this could have been avoided," said Ellen. She reached out and put her hand on Charles's arm. Perhaps more than anyone, she realized how difficult this was for him. He detested any interference with his work, particularly an administrative interference. "But you're right. If they had known what we were doing, they would have been in here every day." She kept her hand on his arm. "It will be all right. We'll just slow down a little."

Charles looked up into Ellen's eyes, which were so dark that the pupils merged with the irises. He was acutely aware of her hand. Since their affair she'd scrupulously avoided touching him. Now in the same morning she'd accused him of insensitivity and held his arm: such confusing signals. "This Canceran nonsense is going to take some time," he said. "Six months to a year, and that's only if everything goes very smoothly."

"Why not do Canceran and our own work?" said Ellen. "We can extend our hours, work nights. I'll be willing to do it for you."

Charles stood up. Work nights? He looked at this woman whom he vaguely remembered sleeping with; it seemed so long ago. Her skin had been that same olive color as Elizabeth's and Michelle's. Although he had been physically attracted to Ellen, it had never seemed right with her; they were partners, coworkers, colleagues, not lovers. It had been an awkward affair; their lovemaking clumsy, like adolescents. Cathryn wasn't as beautiful as Ellen but from the beginning it was more comfortable, more fulfilling.

"I've got a better idea," said Charles. "Why don't I go over Morrison's head to the director and just lay the cards on the table, explain that it's infinitely more important for us to stay with our own work."

"I can't imagine it will help," cautioned Ellen. "Morrison

told you the decision came from the board of directors. Dr. Ibanez is not going to reverse that. I think you're just asking for trouble."

"And I think it's worth the risk. Help me get the lab books together. I'll show him what we've been doing."

Ellen slid off her stool and walked toward the door to the hall.

"Ellen?" called Charles, surprised by her actions.

She didn't stop. "Just do what you want, Charles. You always do anyway." The door closed behind her.

Charles's first impulse was to go after her. But the impulse cooled quickly. He'd expected her support. Besides, he had more important things to do than worry about Ellen's moods and behavior. Angrily, he put her out of his mind and concentrated on getting the main protocol book from his desk and the most recent data books from the workbench. Rehearsing what he would say, Charles headed back up the fire stairs.

The row of administrative secretaries warily monitored his progress down the hall. The entire group knew that he had been ordered to take over the Canceran study and that he wasn't happy with the idea.

Charles ignored the stares although he felt like a wolf in a chicken coop as he approached Dr. Carlos Ibanez's secretary, Miss Veronica Evans. Befitting her status, her area was separated from the rest of the room with paneled dividers. She'd been at the Weinburger even longer than Ibanez. She was a well-groomed woman of hefty proportions and indeterminate late middle age.

"I'd like to see the director," said Charles in a no-nonsense voice.

"Do you have an appointment?" No one intimidated Miss Evans.

"Just tell him I'm here," said Charles.

"I'm afraid . . ." began Miss Evans.

"If you don't tell him I'm here, I'm going to barge right in." Charles's voice was stiffly controlled.

Marshaling one of her famous, disdainful expressions, Miss

Evans reluctantly got up and disappeared within the inner office. When she reappeared, she merely held the door ajar and motioned Charles inside.

Ibanez's office was a large, corner room that faced south and east. Besides the Boston University campus, part of the Boston skyline could be seen across the partially frozen Charles River. Ibanez was seated at a monstrous, antique Spanish desk. The view was at his back. Seated in front of the desk was Dr. Thomas Brighton.

Laughing at some conversational point made before Charles arrived, Dr. Carlos Ibanez gestured with the long, thin cigar he was smoking for Charles to take a chair. A halo of gray smoke hung above the director's head like a rain cloud over a tropic island. He was a small man in his early sixties, given to sudden rapid movements, particularly of his hands. His perpetually tanned face was framed by silver hair and a silver goatee. His voice was surprisingly robust.

Charles sat, disturbed by Dr. Brighton's presence. On one hand, he was furious with the man, both on professional and personal grounds. On the other, he felt sorry for the doctor, having to face up to a scandal and the sudden dissolution of his life.

Dr. Brighton gave Charles a rapid but unmistakably disdainful glance before turning back to Dr. Ibanez. That single look was enough to undermine Charles's empathy. Charles studied Brighton's profile. As far as Charles was concerned, he was young: thirty-one years old. And he appeared younger than that: blond and handsome in an effete Ivy League sort of way.

"Ah, Charles," said Ibanez with some embarrassment. "I was just saying good-bye to Thomas. It's a shame that in his zeal to finish the Canceran project he acted foolishly."

"Foolishly," Charles burst out. "Criminally would be more accurate." Thomas flushed.

"Now, Charles, his motives were of the best. We know he did not mean to embarrass the institute. The real criminal is the person who leaked this information to the press, and we have every intention of finding him and punishing him severely."

"And Dr. Brighton?" asked Charles as if the man were not in the room. "Are you condoning what he did?"

"Of course not," said Ibanez. "But the disgrace he has suffered at the hands of the press seems punishment enough. It will be hard for him to get a job worthy of his talents for the next few years. The Weinburger certainly can't finance his career any longer. In fact, I was just telling him about an internal medical group in Florida in which I'm quite sure we can get him a position."

There was an uncomfortable pause.

"Well," said Dr. Ibanez, getting to his feet and coming around his desk. Brighton stood up as Dr. Ibanez approached him. Dr. Ibanez put his arm on Brighton's shoulder and walked him to the door, ignoring Charles.

"I'd appreciate any help you can give me," said Brighton.

"I hope you understand the reasons behind making you leave the institute so quickly," said Ibanez.

"Of course," returned Brighton. "Once the press gets onto something like this, they want to suck it dry. Don't worry about me, I'm glad to get out of the spotlight for a while."

Closing the door behind Brighton, Ibanez came back to his desk and sat down. His mood had abruptly switched to tired irritation. "Actually there are two people I'd like to strangle. The person from here who leaked the story and the reporter that wrote it. The press has a habit of blowing things out of proportion and this is a good example. Front page *New York Times*! Absurd!"

"It seems to me," said Charles, "that you're blaming the wrong people. After all, this is a 'moral issue,' not just an inconvenience."

Dr. Ibanez eyed Charles across the expanse of his desk. "Dr. Brighton should not have done what he did, but the moral issue does not bother me as much as the potential damage to the institute and to the drug, Canceran. That would change this from a minor affair to a major catastrophe."

"I just don't think that professional integrity is a minor affair," said Charles.

"I hope you're not lecturing me, Dr. Martel. Let me tell you something. Dr. Brighton was not motivated by any evil intent. He believed in Canceran and wanted to speed up its availability to the public. His fraud was the result of youthful impatience, which we've all been guilty of in one degree or another. Unfortunately in this case his enthusiasm got out of hand with the result being we've lost a very talented man, a phenomenal money raiser."

Charles moved to the edge of his seat. For him the issue was crystal clear and he was astounded that he and Ibanez could view the event from such fundamentally different perspectives. On the verge of unleashing a diatribe on the difference between right and wrong, Charles was interrupted by Miss Evans.

"Dr. Ibanez," called Miss Evans from the doorway. "You told me to tell you the moment Mr. Bellman arrived. He's here."

"Send him in!" shouted Ibanez, leaping to his feet like a boxer at the sound of the bell.

Jules Bellman, the institute's public relations man, came through the door like a puppy with his tail between his legs. "I didn't know about the *Times* until this morning," he squeaked. "I don't know how it happened, but it didn't come from anyone in my office. Unfortunately a great number of people knew."

"My assistant said it was the gossip of the institute," said Charles, coming to Bellman's rescue. "I think I was the only one who didn't know anything about it."

Ibanez glowered for another moment. "Well, I want the leak found." He didn't ask the P.R. man to sit down.

"Absolutely," said Bellman, his voice stronger. "I already think I know who was responsible."

"Oh?" said Ibanez, his eyebrows raising.

"The animal keeper who reported to you about Brighton

originally. I heard that he was pissed that he didn't get a bonus."

"Christ! Everybody wants a medal for doing their job," said
Ibanez. "Keep at it until you're sure. Now we have to talk
about the press. Here's how I want you to handle it. Schedule
a conference. Acknowledge that errors were found in the Canceran experimental protocol due to a severe time constraint,
but don't admit to any fraud. Just say that mistakes were un-
covered by the usual supervisory process that the administration routinely follows, and that Dr. Brighton has been granted
an unspecified leave of absence. Say that he has been under
great pressure to speed the delivery of the drug to the public.
Above all, emphasize that Canceran is the most promising an-
ticancer drug to come along in a long time. Then emphasize
that the error here was Brighton's and that the Weinburger
Institute still has full confidence in Canceran. And the way
you're going to do this is by announcing that we are putting
our most renowned scientist on the project, Dr. Charles Martel."

"Dr. Ibanez," began Charles, "I . . ."

"Just a minute, Charles," interrupted Ibanez. "Let me get
rid of Jules here. Now you think you've got all that, Jules?"

"Dr. Ibanez," Charles broke in. "I really want to say something."

"In a minute, Charles. Listen, Jules, I want you to make
Charles here sound like Louis Pasteur reincarnated, understand?"

"You got it," said Bellman excitedly. "Now, Dr. Martel.
Can you tell me your latest publications."

"Goddammit," shouted Charles, slamming his lab books
down on Ibanez's desk. "This is a ridiculous conversation.
You know I haven't published anything recently, mostly because I didn't want to take the time. But papers or no papers,
I've been making extraordinary progress. And it's all here in
these books. Let me show you something."

Charles reached over to open one of the lab books but Dr.
Ibanez restrained his arm. "Charles, calm down. You're not

on trial here, for God's sake. Actually it's probably better you haven't published. Right now interest as well as funding for immunological cancer research has slackened. It probably wouldn't be good for Jules to have to admit you've been working exclusively in this area because the press might suggest you were unqualified to take over Canceran."

"Give me strength," groaned Charles to himself through clenched teeth. He stared at Ibanez, breathing heavily. "Let me tell you something! The whole medical community is approaching cancer from the wrong perspective. All this work on chemotherapeutic agents like Canceran is only for palliative purposes. A real cure can only come from better understanding of the chemical communication among cells of which the immune system is a direct descendant. Immunology is the answer!" Charles's voice had built to a crescendo, and the last sentence held the fervor of a religious fanatic.

Bellman looked down and shuffled his feet. Ibanez took a long drag on his cigar, blowing the smoke in a long, thin stream.

"Well," said Dr. Ibanez, breaking the embarrassing silence. "That's an interesting point, Charles, but I'm afraid not everybody would agree with you. The fact of the matter is that while there is plenty of funding for chemotherapy research, there is very little for immunological studies . . ."

"That's because chemotherapy agents like Canceran can be patented whereas immunological processes, for the most part, cannot be," said Charles, impulsively interrupting Dr. Ibanez.

"It seems to me," said Ibanez, "that the old phrase, 'don't bite the hand that feeds you,' applies here. The cancer community has supported you, Dr. Martel."

"And I'm thankful," said Charles. "I'm not a rebel or a revolutionary. Far from it. All I want is to be left alone to do my work. In fact, that's why I came up here in the first place: to tell you that I don't feel capable of taking on the Canceran project."

"Nonsense!" said Ibanez. "You're more than capable. Obviously the board of directors thinks so."

"I'm not talking about my intellectual capabilities," snapped Charles. "I'm talking about my lack of interest. I don't believe in Canceran and the approach to cancer it represents."

"Dr. Martel," said Dr. Ibanez slowly, his eyes boring into Charles's face. "Are you aware that we are in the midst of a crisis? Are you going to sit there and tell me you cannot help because of a lack of interest? What do you think I'm running here, a federally endowed college? If we lose the grant for Canceran the whole institute is in financial jeopardy. You're the only person who is not already working under a National Cancer Institute grant and whose stature in the research community is such that this whole unfortunate brouhaha will be defused when you take over."

"But I'm at a critical point in my own research," pleaded Charles. "I know I haven't published and I know that I've been somewhat secretive. Maybe that was wrong. But I've been getting results and I think I have made an astounding breakthrough. It's right here." Charles tapped the cover of one of his lab books. "Listen, I can take a cancer cell, any cancer cell, and isolate the chemical difference between that cell and a normal cell from the same individual."

"In what animals?" asked Dr. Ibanez.

"Mice, rats, and monkeys," said Charles.

"What about humans?" asked Dr. Ibanez.

"I haven't tried it yet, but I'm sure it will work. It's worked flawlessly in all the species I've tried."

"Is this chemical difference antigenic in the host animal?"

"It should be. In all cases the protein seems to be sufficiently different to be antigenic but unfortunately I have not yet been able to sensitize a cancerous animal. There seems to be some kind of blocking mechanism or what I call a blocking factor. And that's where I am in my work, trying to isolate this blocking factor. Once I do, I intend to use the hybridoma technique to make an antibody to the blocking factor. If I can eliminate the blocking factor, I'm hoping the animal will then respond immunologically to its tumor."

"Whew!" whistled Bellman, not sure what to write in his pad.

"The most exciting thing," said Charles with enthusiasm, "is that it all makes scientific sense. Cancer today is a vestigial aspect of an ancient system whereby organisms could accept new cellular components."

"I give up," said Bellman. He closed his pad with a snap.

"What you are also saying, Dr. Martel," said Dr. Ibanez, "is that you have a long way to go in this work of yours."

"Absolutely," said Charles. "But the pace has been quickening."

"But there's no reason, except your preference, that you couldn't put this work aside for a period of time."

"Only that it appears so promising. If it turns out to be as fruitful as I expect, then it would be tragic, if not criminal, not to have it available as soon as possible."

"But it is only in your opinion that it appears so promising. I must admit it sounds interesting and I can assure you the Weinburger will support you as it has in the past. But first you are going to have to help the Weinburger. Your own interests must be postponed; you must take over the Canceran project immediately. If you refuse, Dr. Martel, you will have to take your research elsewhere. I want no more discussion. The issue is closed."

For a moment Charles sat there with a blank face reflecting his inner uncertainty. The enthusiasm he'd built up in presenting his work had elevated his expectations so that Ibanez's dismissal had a paralyzing effect, especially combined with the threat of being turned out of his lab. The suggestion of being fired was far more terrifying coming from Ibanez than from Morrison. Work and Charles's sense of self had been so closely connected that he could not imagine them severed. He gathered up his lab books with an effort.

"You're not the most popular man on the staff," added Ibanez gently, "but you can change that now by pitching in. I want you to tell me, Dr. Martel: Are you with us?"

Charles nodded his head without looking up, suffering the

final indignity of unconditional surrender. He turned and left without uttering another word.

After the door closed, Bellman looked back at Ibanez. "What a strange reaction. I hope he's not going to be trouble. That evangelistic attitude scares me to death."

"I feel the same way," said Ibanez pensively. "Unfortunately he's become a scientific fanatic, and like all fanatics, he can be difficult. It's too bad because he's such a first-rate researcher, maybe our best. But people like that can put us right out of business, especially in this era of reduced funding. I wonder where Charles thinks the money to run this place comes from. If the people down at the National Cancer Institute heard that monologue of his about chemotherapy, they'd throw a fit."

"I'm going to have to keep the press away from him," said Bellman.

Dr. Ibanez laughed. "At least that part will be easy. Charles has never cared for publicity."

"You sure he's the best man to take over Canceran?" said Bellman.

"He's the only man. No one else is available who has his professional reputation. All he has to do is finish the study."

"But if he screws up somehow . . ." worried Bellman.

"Don't even suggest it," said Ibanez. "If he mishandles Canceran at this point, we'd have to do something drastic. Otherwise we'll all be looking for a job."

Disgusted with himself, Charles dragged his way back down to his lab. For the first time in almost ten years, Charles nostalgically recalled private practice. It wasn't the one-on-one of clinical medicine that he longed for, but rather the autonomy. Charles was accustomed to being in control and until that moment he had not realized how little control he had at the Weinburger.

For the second time in the day, Charles slammed the door to his lab, rattling the glassware on the shelves and terrifying the rats and mice in the animal room. Also for the second time he startled Ellen, who deftly caught a pipette she'd knocked off the counter when she spun around. She was about to complain but when she saw Charles's face, she remained silent.

In a fit of misdirected rage, Charles slung the heavy lab books at the counter. One hit the floor while the others crashed into a distillation apparatus sending shards of glass all over the room. Ellen's hand flew up to protect her face as she stepped back. Still not satisfied, Charles picked up an Erlenmeyer flask and hurled it into the sink. Ellen had never seen Charles like this in all the six years they'd worked together.

"If you tell me I told you so, I'll scream," said Charles, flinging himself onto his metal swivel chair.

"Dr. Ibanez wouldn't listen?" asked Ellen, guardedly.

"He listened. He just wouldn't buy, and I caved in like a paper tiger. It was awful."

"I don't think you had any choice," said Ellen. "So don't be so hard on yourself. Anyway, what's the schedule?"

"The schedule is that we finish the Canceran efficacy study."

"Do we start right away?" asked Ellen.

"Right away," returned Charles with a tired voice. "In fact, why don't you go get the Canceran lab books. I don't want to talk to anyone for a while."

"All right," said Ellen softly. She was relieved to have an errand to take her out of the lab for a few minutes. She sensed that Charles needed a little time by himself.

After Ellen left, Charles didn't move and he tried not to think. But his solitude did not last long. The door was thrown open and Morrison stormed into the lab.

Charles swung around and looked up at Morrison, whose veins were standing out on the sides of his forehead like strands of spaghetti. The man was furious.

"I've had just about all I can tolerate," he shouted through blanched lips. "I'm tired of your lack of respect. What makes you think you're so important that you don't have to follow normal protocol? I shouldn't have to remind you that I am your department head. You're supposed to go through me when you have questions about administration, not to the director."

"Morrison, do me a favor," said Charles, "get the hell out of my lab."

Morrison's small eyes became suffused with a pale crimson. Minute beads of perspiration sprung up on his forehead as he spoke: "All I can say is that if it weren't for our current emergency, Charles, I'd see that you were thrown out of the Weinburger today. Lucky for you we can't afford another scandal. But you'd better shine on this Canceran project if you have any intentions of staying on staff here."

Without waiting for a response, Morrison stalked out of the lab. Charles was left with the low hum of the refrigerator compressors and the ticks of the automatic radioactivity counter. These were familiar sounds and they had a soothing effect on Charles. Maybe, he thought, the Canceran affair wouldn't be too bad; maybe he could do the study quickly, provided the experimental protocol was decent; maybe Ellen was right and they could do both projects by working some nights.

Suddenly the phone began to ring. He debated answering, hearing it ring three times, then four. On the fifth ring he picked it up.

"Hello," said the caller. "This is Mrs. Crane from the bursar's office at Northeastern University."

"Yes," said Charles. It took him a moment to associate the school with Chuck.

"Sorry to bother you," said Mrs. Crane. "But your son gave us the number. It seems that the $1650 semester tuition is way overdue."

Charles toyed with a small tin of paper clips, wondering what to say. Not being able to pay bills was a new experience.

"Mr. Martel, are you there?"

"Dr. Martel," said Charles, although as soon as he made the correction he felt foolish.

"Excuse me, Dr. Martel," said Mrs. Crane, genuinely compunctious. "Can we expect the money in the near future?"

"Of course," said Charles. "I'll have a check on its way. I'm sorry for the oversight."

Charles hung up. He knew that he'd have to get a loan immediately. He hoped to hell that Chuck was doing reasonably well and that he wouldn't major in psychology. He picked up the phone again, but didn't dial. He decided it would save time if he went directly to the bank; besides, he felt like he could use some fresh air and a little time away from the Morrisons and Ibanezes of the world.

FOUR

Flipping the pages of an old issue of *Time* magazine, Cathryn wrestled with a resurgence of anxiety. At first Dr. Wiley's waiting room had been a sanctuary from the horrors of the rest of the hospital, but as time passed uncertainty and foreboding began to reassert themselves. Glancing at her watch she saw that Michelle had been back in the examining area for over an hour. Something must be wrong!

She began to fidget, crossing and uncrossing her legs, checking her watch repeatedly. To her discomfort there was no conversation in the room and almost no movement except for the hands of a woman who was knitting and the erratic gestures of two toddlers playing with blocks. All at once Cathryn realized what was bothering her. Everything was too flat, without emotion. It was like a two-dimensional picture of a three-dimensional scene.

She stood up, unable to sit still for another moment. "Excuse me," she said walking over to the nurse. "My little girl, Michelle Martel. Do you have any idea how much longer she'll be?"

"The doctor hasn't told us," said the nurse politely. She sat with her back painfully straight so that her substantial buttocks protruded out the back of her chair.

"She's been in there for a long time," said Cathryn, searching for some reassurance.

"Dr. Wiley is very complete. I'm sure she'll be out shortly."

"Does he frequently take over an hour?" asked Cathryn. She felt superstitiously ambivalent about asking any questions at all, as if the asking would influence the ultimate outcome.

"Certainly," said the nurse receptionist. "He takes whatever time he needs. He never rushes. He's that kind of a doctor."

But why does he need all that time, wondered Cathryn as she returned to her seat. The image of Tad with his plastic cell kept returning to Cathryn's troubled mind. It was a horrifying shock to realize that children do get serious illnesses. She had believed that it was a rare occurrence that happened to someone else's child, a child one didn't know. But Tad was a neighbor, her daughter's friend. Cathryn shuddered.

Picking up yet another magazine, Cathryn glanced at the advertisements; there were smiling, happy people, shining floors, buying new cars. She tried to decide what to fix for dinner but never completed the thought. Why was Michelle taking so long? Two more mothers arrived with pink swathed parcels that were obviously babies. Then came another mother and child: a small boy about two with a huge violaceous rash that covered half his face.

The waiting room was now packed and Cathryn began to have trouble breathing. Getting up to make room for the second mother carrying her infant, Cathryn tried to avoid seeing the two-year-old with the horribly disfiguring rash. Her fears mounted. It had been over an hour and twenty minutes since she'd left Michelle. She realized she was trembling.

Once again she approached the nurse and self-consciously stood before her desk until the woman acknowledged her presence.

"Can I help you?" she said in a painfully courteous manner. Cathryn wanted to reach over and shake this woman whose starched whiteness inflamed Cathryn's precarious emotions.

She didn't need politeness, she needed warmth and understanding, an ounce of sensitivity.

"Do you think it could be possible," asked Cathryn, "to find out what's taking so long?"

Before the receptionist could respond, the door to her left opened and Dr. Wiley leaned into the room. He searched the waiting area until his eyes found Cathryn. "Mrs. Martel, can I speak to you for a moment?" His voice was noncommittal and he turned back inside, leaving the door ajar.

Cathryn hurried after him, nervously touching the flowered combs in her hair to be sure they were in place, and closed the door behind her carefully. Wiley had retreated to his desk but had not sat down in the chair. Instead he was half-sitting on the front edge, his arms folded across his chest.

Exquisitely sensitive to every nuance, Cathryn scrutinized Dr. Wiley's broad face. His forehead was deeply lined, something Cathryn hadn't noticed on her first encounter. The man didn't smile.

"We need your permission for a test," said Dr. Wiley.

"Is everything all right?" asked Cathryn. She tried to sound normal but her voice was too high.

"Everything is under control," said Dr. Wiley. Unfolding his arms, he reached out for a paper on his desk. "But we need to do a specific diagnostic test. I'm going to need your signature on this form." He handed the paper to Cathryn. She took it, her hand quivering.

"Where is Michelle?" Cathryn's eyes scanned the form. It was written in standard medicalese.

"She's in one of the examining rooms. You can see her if you'd like although I'd rather go ahead with this test before you do. It's called a bone marrow aspiration."

"Bone marrow?" Cathryn's head shot up. The words evoked the awesome image of Tad Schonhauser in his plastic tent.

"It's nothing to be alarmed about," said Dr. Wiley, noticing Cathryn's shocked response. "It's a simple test, very similar to taking a sample of blood."

"Does Michelle have aplastic anemia?" blurted Cathryn.

"Absolutely not." Dr. Wiley was perplexed at her response. "We want to do the test in order to try to make a diagnosis, but I can assure you Michelle does not have aplastic anemia. If you don't mind my asking, what made you ask that?"

"Just a few minutes ago I visited our neighbor's child who has aplastic anemia. When you said bone marrow, it . . ." Cathryn struggled to complete her own sentence.

"I understand," said Dr. Wiley. "Don't worry. I can assure you that aplastic anemia is not a possibility here. But we still want to do the test . . . just to be complete."

"Do you think I should call Charles?" asked Cathryn. She was relieved that Michelle couldn't have aplastic anemia and grateful to Dr. Wiley for eliminating it as a possibility. Although Charles had said aplastic anemia wasn't infectious, its proximity was frightening.

"If you'd like to call Charles, by all means. But let me explain a little. Bone marrow aspiration is done with a needle similar to the one we use for drawing blood. We use a little local anesthesia so it's practically painless, and it only takes a few moments. And once we have the results we'll be done. It's truly a simple procedure, and we do it often."

Cathryn managed a smile and said they could go ahead with the test. She liked Dr. Wiley, and she felt a visceral confidence in the man, especially since Charles had undoubtedly picked him from a group of pediatricians he knew well, back when Chuck had been born. She signed the forms where Dr. Wiley pointed, then allowed herself to be escorted out of the office and back into the crowded waiting room.

Michelle lay very still on the examining table. Even with her head propped up on the pillow her view was mostly ceiling with frosted glass over fluorescent lighting. But she could see a little wallpaper, enough to make out images of laughing clowns, rocking horses, and children with balloons. There was a sink in the room, and although she couldn't see it from where she was, she could hear the water dripping.

For Michelle the hospital had lived up to her fears. She'd

been stuck with needles three times. Once in each arm and once in a finger. Each time she'd asked if it was the last but no one would say, so she was afraid it might happen again, especially if she moved too much, so she stayed very still.

She felt embarrassed to be dressed so scantily. She had on a nightie of sorts, but it was open in the back, and she could feel her skin on the paper which covered the table. By looking down, she could see the mounds made by her toes beneath the white sheet that covered her. Even her hands were under the cover, clasped together over her stomach. She'd been shivering a little but didn't tell anyone. All she wanted was her clothes and to go home. Yet she knew the fever was back and she was afraid someone might notice and then want to stick her again. They had told her that the reason they needed her blood was to find out why she kept getting the fever.

There was a scraping sound, and the door to the examining room opened. It was the fat nurse, and she was backing into the room so that her form filled the doorway. She was pulling something, and Michelle heard the telltale sound of metal jangling against metal. Once clear of the door, the nurse swung around, pushing a small table on wheels. The table was covered with a blue towel. As far as Michelle was concerned, it didn't look good.

"What's that?" she asked anxiously.

"Some things for the doctor, sweetheart," said Miss Hammersmith, as if she were talking about treats. Her name tag was pinned high on her shoulder like a battle ribbon, above the band of her bosom which went around her chest like an innertube. There seemed to be as much flesh in the back as the front.

"Is it going to hurt?" asked Michelle.

"Sweetheart, why do you ask that kind of question? We're trying to help you." Miss Hammersmith sounded offended.

"Everything the doctor does hurts," said Michelle.

"Now that's hardly true," scoffed Miss Hammersmith.

"Ah, my favorite patient," said Dr. Wiley, opening the door with his shoulder. Coming into the room he kept his hands away from his body because they were wet and dripping onto the floor. Miss Hammersmith broke open a paper package, and Dr. Wiley carefully pulled out a sterile towel with his thumb and forefinger. Most alarming to Michelle, he was wearing a surgical mask.

"What are you going to do?" she asked, her eyes opened to their physical limits. She forgot her resolve about staying still and pushed herself up on one elbow.

"Well, I'm afraid I've got good and bad news," said Dr. Wiley. "I'm afraid you have to have one more little needle stick but the good news is that it will be the last for a while. What do you say?"

Dr. Wiley tossed the towel onto the counter by the sink and plucked out a pair of rubber gloves from a package Miss Hammersmith held open for him.

With growing dismay, Michelle watched him pull the gloves onto each hand, snapping the wrist portion into place and tugging on each finger in turn.

"I don't want any more needles," said Michelle, her eyes filling with tears. "I just want to go home." She tried not to cry but the harder she tried, the less successful she was.

"Now, now," soothed Miss Hammersmith as she began stroking Michelle's hair.

Michelle parried Miss Hammersmith's hand and tried to sit up, but she was restrained by a cinch about her waist. "Please," she managed.

"Michelle!" called Dr. Wiley sharply, then his voice softened. "I know you don't feel well, and I know this is hard for you, but we have to do it. It will be over in a moment if you help us."

"No!" said Michelle defiantly. "I want my father."

Dr. Wiley gestured to Miss Hammersmith: "Maybe Mrs. Levy could come in here for a moment and give us a hand."

Miss Hammersmith lumbered out of the room.

"Okay, Michelle, just lie back and relax for a moment," said Dr. Wiley. "I'm sure your dad will be real proud of you when

I tell him how courageous you were. This is only going to take a moment. I promise."

Michelle lay back and closed her eyes, feeling the tears run down the side of her face. Intuitively she knew that Charles would be disappointed if he heard that she'd acted like a baby. After all, it was going to be the last stick. But both her arms had been punctured and she wondered where they would do it.

The door opened again and Michelle propped herself up to see who it was. Miss Hammersmith came in followed by two other nurses, one of whom carried some leather straps.

"We won't need restraints, I don't think," said Dr. Wiley. "Okay, Michelle, now just lie back quietly for a moment."

"Come on, sweetheart," cajoled Miss Hammersmith, coming up alongside Michelle. One of the other nurses went around to the opposite side while the nurse who had been carrying leather straps went down to the foot of the table. "Dr. Wiley is the best doctor in the world and you should be so thankful he's taking care of you," said Miss Hammersmith as she pulled Michelle's sheet down over the child's legs. Keeping her arms stiffly against her side, Michelle half-heartedly tried to resist when Miss Hammersmith pulled up the nightie to expose the child's body from her nipples to her bony knees.

She watched while the nurse whisked the towel from the table with the wheels. Dr. Wiley busied himself with the instruments on it, his back to her. She could hear the tinkle of glass and the sound of fluid. When the doctor turned, he had a wet piece of cotton in each hand. "I'm just going to clean your skin a little," he explained as he began scrubbing Michelle's hipbone.

The water felt alarmingly cold to Michelle as it ran down her hip and pooled beneath her buttocks. This was a new experience, not like the previous needles. She strained to see what was happening, but the doctor gently urged her to lie back.

"It will be over in just a moment," said Miss Hammersmith. Michelle looked at the faces of the nurses. They were all smiling but they were fake smiles. Michelle began to feel panic. "Where are you going to stick me?" she shouted, trying again to sit up.

As soon as she moved, she felt strong arms grip her and force her back. Even her ankles were locked in an iron grasp. She was pressed firmly back onto the table, and the restriction inflamed her panic. She tried to struggle but felt the hold on her limbs tighten. "No!" cried Michelle.

"Easy now," said Dr. Wiley as he floated a gun-metal colored drape with a hole in the center over Michelle's pelvis and positioned it on her hipbone. Turning back to the small table, Dr. Wiley busied himself. When he reappeared in Michelle's view he was holding a huge syringe with three stainless steel finger rings.

"No!" cried Michelle and with all her might she tried to break from the grasp of the nurses. Instantly she felt the crushing weight of Miss Hammersmith settle on her chest, making breathing difficult. Then she felt the sharp pain of a needle pierce her skin over her hipbone followed by a burning sensation.

Charles bit off the corner of his pastrami on white, catching a stray piece of meat with his fingers before it fell to the desktop. It was a mammoth sandwich, the only good thing put out by the institute cafeteria. Ellen had brought it back to the lab since Charles did not want to see anyone and, except for his brief foray to the First National Bank, he'd stayed at his desk poring over the Canceran experimental protocol. He'd been through all the lab books, and to his surprise, he found them well-organized. He began to feel optimistic that completing the study would not be as difficult as he had initially imagined; maybe they could get it done in six months. He swallowed what he had in his mouth and chased it down with a slug of lukewarm coffee.

"The one good thing about this project," said Charles, wiping his mouth with the back of his hand, "is the size of the grants. For the first time we've got money to burn. I'll bet we can get that new automatic counter we've wanted as well as a new ultra centrifuge."

"I think we should get a new chromatography unit," said Ellen.

"Why not?" said Charles. "Having been railroaded into this project, we owe it to ourselves." He put the sandwich back down on the paper plate and picked up his pencil. "Here's the way we'll handle this thing. We'll start out with a dose of 1/16 of the LD50."

"Wait," said Ellen. "Being in immunology, it's been a while since I've done this kind of thing. Refresh me. The LD50 is the dose of a drug that causes 50 percent death in a large population of test animals. Right?"

"Right," said Charles. "We have the LD50 for mice, rats, rabbits, and monkeys from the toxicity studies done on Canceran before they started the efficacy studies. Let's start out with the mice. We'll use the RX7 strain bred for mammary tumors because Brighton ordered them and they're here."

With his pencil, Charles began to make a flow diagram of the project. While he wrote, he spoke, explaining to Ellen each step, particularly how they would increase the dosage of the drug and how they would expand the study to include rats and rabbits as soon as they got some preliminary data from the mice. Because the monkeys were so expensive they would not be used until the very end when the information from the other animals could be extrapolated and applied to a statistically significant group. Then, assuming positive results, a method of randomization would be worked out with each species to ensure suitable controls. These fresh animals would then be treated with the optimum dosage level of Canceran determined from the first part of the study. This portion of the project would be carried out so that neither Charles nor Ellen would know which animals had been treated until after each had been sacrificed and studied and recorded.

"Whew," sighed Ellen as she stretched her arms back. "I guess I didn't know what was involved."

"Unfortunately there's more," said Charles. "Each animal,

after they're autopsied, has to be studied not only microscopically, but also with the electron microscope. And . . ."

"All right already!" said Ellen. "I get the picture. But what about our own work? What are we going to do?"

"I'm not sure," said Charles. He put down his pencil. "I guess that's up to both of us."

"I think it's more up to you," said Ellen. She was sitting on a high stool with her back against the slate-topped workbench. She was wearing a white laboratory coat which was unbuttoned, revealing a beige sweater and a single strand of small, natural pearls. Her soft hands were folded together and lay still in her lap.

"Did you mean what you said about working nights?" asked Charles. In his mind he tried to estimate the feasibility of continuing the work on the mysterious blocking factor while they labored with Canceran. It would be possible, although they'd have to put in long hours and slow down considerably. But even if they were able to isolate a single protein in a single animal which functioned as a blocking agent, they'd have something. Even if only one mouse became immunized to its tumor, it would be spectacular. Charles was well aware that success with a single case was hardly a reason to generalize, but he felt that a single cure would provide the basis for convincing the institute to back his work.

"Look," said Ellen. "I know how much this work of yours means to you, and I know you think you're close to some sort of a conclusion. I don't know whether it's going to be positive or negative in the final analysis but that doesn't matter. You need to know. And you will. You're the most stubborn person I ever met."

Charles examined Ellen's face. What did she mean, stubborn? He didn't know whether it was a compliment or an insult, and he had no idea how the conversation had switched to his personality. But Ellen's expression was neutral, her unfathomable eyes unwavering.

Noticing Charles's stare, Ellen smiled, then said: "Don't look so surprised. If you're willing to work nights, so am I.

In fact, I can bring in some things to eat on the days we work evenings so we can have supper right here."

"I'm not sure you realize how tough it will be," said Charles. "We'd be practically living here."

"The lab is bigger than my apartment," said Ellen with a laugh, "and my cats take care of themselves."

Charles turned his gaze back to his recently concocted flow diagram. But he wasn't thinking about Canceran. He was wrestling with the advisability of working evenings with Ellen. "You understand that I have no idea whether I can get Morrison to pay you overtime?" he said.

"I don't . . ." began Ellen, but she didn't finish. The phone interrupted them.

"You answer it," said Charles. "I don't want to talk with anyone."

Ellen slid off her stool and, leaning on Charles's shoulder, reached across his desk for the receiver. Her hand rested on Charles as she said hello, but it was quickly removed. Abruptly she dumped the receiver in his lap and walked away. "It's your wife."

Charles fumbled for the phone as it slid between his legs, retrieving it by pulling on the coiled cord. Of all the times for Cathryn to be calling, he thought.

"What is it?" he asked impatiently.

"I want you to come over here to Dr. Wiley's office," said Cathryn in a stiffly controlled voice.

"What's going on?"

"I don't want to discuss it over the phone."

"Cathryn, this hasn't been a good morning for me. Give me an idea of what's happening."

"Charles, just come over here!"

"Cathryn, the roof has fallen in on top of me this morning. I can't leave now."

"I'll be waiting for you," said Cathryn. Then she hung up.

"Fuck!" shouted Charles as he slammed down the receiver. He swung around in his chair and saw that Ellen had retreated behind her desk. "On top of everything, Cathryn wants me over at the pediatrician's office but won't tell me what it's about. God! What else can happen today?"

"That's what you get for marrying a typist."

"What?" asked Charles. He'd heard but the comment seemed out of context.

"Cathryn doesn't understand what we are doing. I don't think she can comprehend the pressures you feel."

Charles peered quizzically at Ellen, then shrugged. "You're probably right. Obviously she thinks I can just drop everything and run over there. Maybe I should call Wiley and find out what's going on." Charles snapped the phone off the hook and started dialing, but midway he stopped. Slowly he replaced the receiver. The thought of Michelle planted a seed of concern under his irritation. Vividly he remembered the morning's nosebleed. "I'd better run over there. It won't take very long."

"But what about our schedule?" asked Ellen.

"We'll talk more when I get back. Meanwhile why don't you prepare the dilution of Canceran for the mice. We'll inject the first batch as soon as I return." Charles went over to the metal locker near the door and pulled out his coat. "Have the mice brought up here to our own animal room. It will make it a lot easier."

Ellen watched the door close behind Charles. No matter what she resolved outside of the lab, whenever she was face to face with him, it seemed that her feelings were hurt. Ellen knew it was absurd but she couldn't protect herself. And now she felt such a mixture of disappointment and anger that she could have cried. She had allowed the idea of working together at night to excite her. But it was stupid, adolescent. She knew deep down that it would not lead to anything and ultimately cause her more heartache.

Thankful for something specific to do, Ellen forced herself over to the counter where the sterile bottles of Canceran had been left. It was a white powder, like confectioner's sugar waiting for the introduction of sterile water. It wasn't as stable in solution as it was in solid form so it had to be reconstituted before it was used. She got out the sterile water, then used the desktop computer to work out the optimum dilution.

As she was getting out the syringes, Dr. Morrison came into the lab.

"Dr. Martel isn't here," said Ellen.

"I know," said Morrison. "I saw him leave the building. I wasn't looking for him. I wanted to talk to you for a moment."

Putting the syringe down, Ellen thrust her hands into her jacket pockets and came around the end of the counter to face the man. It was not usual for the head of the department of physiology to seek her out, especially behind Charles's back. Yet with everything else that had happened that morning, she wasn't all that surprised. Besides, Morrison's face had such a Machiavellian look that such intrigue seemed appropriate.

Coming over to her, Morrison produced a slim, gold cigarette case, snapped the case open, and extended it toward Ellen. When she shook her head, Morrison withdrew a cigarette. "May I smoke in here?" he asked.

Ellen shrugged. Charles didn't allow it but not because of danger. He just hated the smell. Ellen felt a stab of rebellious joy as she tacitly acquiesced.

Morrison produced a gold lighter that matched his cigarette case from his vest pocket and made an elaborate ritual out of lighting his cigarette. It was a staged gesture, designed to keep Ellen waiting.

"I suppose you know what has happened today concerning the Brighton case," said Morrison at length.

"A little bit," agreed Ellen.

"And you know that Charles has been selected to continue the Canceran study?"

Ellen nodded.

Morrison paused and blew smoke out in successive rings. "It's extremely important for the institute that this study be concluded . . . successfully."

"Dr. Martel has already started on it," said Ellen.

"Good. Good," said Morrison.

Another pause.

"I don't know exactly how to put this," said Morrison. "But

I'm concerned about Charles messing up this experiment."

"I don't think you have anything to worry about," said Ellen. "If there's one thing you can count on with Charles, it is scientific integrity."

"It's not his intellectual capabilities that concern me," said Morrison. "It's his emotional stability. To be perfectly candid, he seems a bit impulsive. He's hypercritical of everyone else's work and seems to feel he has a corner on the scientific method."

Impulsive? The word hit a familiar chord in Ellen's memory. As if it were yesterday she could remember the last evening she'd spent with Charles. They'd had dinner at the Harvest Restaurant, gone back to her apartment on Prescott Street, and made love. It had been a warm and tender night, but as usual Charles had not stayed over. He'd said he had to be home when the children woke up. The next day at work he had behaved as he always did, but they never went out again and Charles never offered a word of explanation. Then he'd married the temporary typist. It seemed like one day Ellen heard he'd been seeing this girl, and the next he was marrying her. Ellen agreed that impulsive was a good description of Charles; impulsive and stubborn.

"What do you want me to say?" said Ellen, struggling to bring her mind to the present.

"I guess I want you to reassure me," said Morrison.

"Well," said Ellen. "I agree that Charles is temperamental, but I don't think it will influence his work. I think you can count on him to do the Canceran study."

Morrison relaxed and smiled, his small teeth visible behind thin lips. "Thank you, Miss Sheldon. That's exactly what I wanted to hear." Reaching into the sink, he ran water on his half-smoked cigarette and dropped it into the wastebasket. "One other thing. I was wondering if you would do me and the institute a big favor. I'd like you to report any abnormal behavior on Charles's part in relation to the Canceran project. I know this is an awkward request, but the entire board of directors will be grateful for your cooperation."

"All right," said Ellen quickly, not sure how she really felt about it. At the same time she thought that Charles deserved it. She'd put forth a lot of effort for the man and he'd not appreciated it. "I'll do it with the proviso that anything I say remains anonymous."

"Absolutely," agreed Morrison. "That goes without saying. And, of course, you will report to me directly."

At the door, Morrison paused. "It's been nice talking with you, Miss Sheldon. I've been meaning to do it for some time. If you need anything, my office is always open."

"Thank you," said Ellen.

"Maybe we could even have dinner sometime."

"Maybe," said Ellen.

She watched the door close. He was a strange-looking man but he was decisive and powerful.

FIVE

Crossing the river by way of the Harvard Bridge, Charles struggled with a recalcitrant heater. He could not get the control arm to move to the heat position. As a consequence of his efforts, the Pinto swerved, to the dismay of neighboring motorists who responded by pressing their horns. In desperation, he hit the control with the heel of his hand only to be rewarded with the plastic arm snapping off and falling to the floor.

Resigning himself to the chill, Charles tried to concentrate on the road. As soon as he could, he turned right off Massachusetts Avenue and skirted the Back Bay Fens, a neglected and trash-littered park in the center of what once was an attractive residential neighborhood. He passed the Boston Museum of Fine Arts and then the Gardner Museum. As the traffic cleared, his mind wandered. To Charles it seemed emotionally cruel of Cathryn to leave him dangling, a victim of his own imagination. Could Michelle's nosebleed have started again? No, that seemed too simple. Maybe they needed to do some test like an IVP and Cathryn didn't want to give permission. No, there would be no reason why she wouldn't explain that over the phone. It had to be some medical problem.

Maybe appendicitis. Charles remembered the abdominal tenderness, the low-grade fever. Maybe it was a subacute appendicitis and they wanted to operate. And Charles knew how hospitals affected Cathryn. They made her crazy.

Entering Dr. Jordan Wiley's office, Charles was engulfed by a sea of anxious mothers and crying children. The crowded waiting room . . . that was a part of private practice that Charles did not miss. Like all doctors, his secretaries had an irritating propensity to book new, full workups in time slots reserved for simple return visits, resulting in a hopeless backup of patients. No matter what Charles had said, it had made no difference. He had always been behind in the office and had always been apologizing to the patients.

Charles searched for Cathryn in the press of women and children, but he didn't see her. He worked his way over to the nurse who was being besieged by a covey of mothers demanding to know exactly when they would be seen. Charles tried to interrupt but soon realized he had to wait his turn. Eventually he got the woman's attention and was impressed by her composure. If she was affected by the chaos around her, she did a superb job of not showing it.

"I'm looking for my wife," said Charles. He had to speak loudly to make himself heard.

"What's the name?" asked the nurse, her hands folded over a pile of charts.

"Martel. Cathryn Martel."

"Just a moment." As she rolled back in her chair and got to her feet, her face became serious. The women grouped around the desk eyed Charles with a mixture of respect and vexation. They were clearly jealous of the rapid response he'd elicited.

The nurse returned almost immediately, followed by a woman of impressive dimensions who Charles thought would make an appropriate mate for the Michelin tire man. He noticed her name tag: Miss A. Hammersmith. She motioned to Charles, and he obediently stepped around the desk.

"Please follow me," said the nurse. Her mouth, suspended

between two puckered cheeks, was the only part of her face that moved as she spoke.

Charles did as he was told, finding himself hurrying down a hall behind the bulk of Miss Hammersmith who effectively blocked his view. They passed a series of what Charles imagined were examining rooms. At the end of the hall she opened a paneled door and moved aside for Charles to enter.

"Excuse me," said Charles, squeezing past her.

"I guess we both could lose a few pounds," said Miss Hammersmith.

As Charles stepped into the room, Miss Hammersmith remained in the hall and softly closed the door behind him. Bookshelves lined one wall, filled with stacks of medical periodicals and some textbooks. In the center of the room was a round, blond oak table surrounded by a half dozen captain's chairs. One of them abruptly scraped back as Cathryn stood up. She was breathing audibly; Charles could hear the air enter and exit from her nose. It wasn't a smooth sound. It trembled.

"What . . ." began Charles.

Cathryn ran to him before he could speak and threw her arms around his neck. Charles put his hands on her waist and let her hold him for a few moments to regain her equilibrium. "Cathryn," he said at last, beginning to experience the bitter taste of fear. Cathryn's behavior was undermining his thought of appendicitis, of an operation, of something ordinary.

A horrid, unwelcome memory forced itself into Charles's mind: the day he'd learned of Elizabeth's lymphoma. "Cathryn," he said more sharply. "Cathryn! What is going on? What's the matter with you?"

"It's my fault," said Cathryn. As soon as she spoke she started to cry. Charles could feel her body shudder with the force of her tears. He waited, his eyes moving around the room, noticing the picture of Hippocrates on the wall opposite the bookshelves, the rich parquet floor, the Nelson's textbook of pediatrics on the table.

"Cathryn," said Charles at length. "Please tell me what's going on. What's your fault?"

"I should have brought Michelle in sooner. I know I should have." Cathryn's voice was broken by her sobs.

"What's wrong with Michelle?" asked Charles. He could feel panic tightening in his chest. There was a terrifying sense of déjà vu . . .

Cathryn strengthened her grip on Charles's neck as if he was her only salvation. All the control she'd marshaled before his arrival vanished.

Using most of his strength, Charles managed to break Cathryn's hold on his neck. Once he did so, she seemed to collapse. He helped her to a chair where she sank like a deflated balloon. Then he sat down beside her.

"Cathryn, you must tell me what is going on."

His wife looked up with great effort, her teal-blue eyes awash with tears. She opened her mouth, but before she could speak the door opened. Dr. Jordan Wiley stepped into the room.

Charles, his hands still resting on Cathryn's shoulders, turned at the sound of the closing door. When he saw Dr. Wiley he stood up, searching the man's face for a clue to what was happening. He had known Dr. Wiley for almost twenty years. It had been a professional rather than a social relationship, beginning while Charles was in medical school. Wiley had been his preceptor for third-year pediatrics and had impressed Charles with his knowledge, intelligence, and empathy. Later when Charles needed a pediatrician he'd called Jordan Wiley.

"It's good to see you again, Charles," said Dr. Wiley, grasping Charles's hand. "I'm sorry it's under such trying circumstances."

"Perhaps you could tell me what these trying circumstances are," said Charles, allowing annoyance to camouflage his fear.

"You haven't been told?" asked Dr. Wiley. Cathryn shook her head.

"Maybe I should step outside for a few moments," said Dr. Wiley.

He started to turn toward the door, but Charles restrained

him with a hand on his forearm. "I think you should tell me what this is all about," he said.

Dr. Wiley glanced at Cathryn, who nodded agreement. She was no longer sobbing but she knew she'd have difficulty speaking.

"All right," said Dr. Wiley, facing Charles once again. "It's about Michelle."

"I gathered that," said Charles.

"Why don't you sit down," said Dr. Wiley.

"Why don't you you just tell me," said Charles.

Dr. Wiley scrutinized Charles's anxious face. He saw that Charles had aged a lot since he was a student and was sorry that he had to be the messenger of more anguish and suffering; it was one of the few responsibilities of being a doctor that he detested.

"Michelle has leukemia, Charles," said Dr. Wiley.

Charles's mouth slowly dropped open. His blue eyes glazed as if he were in a trance. He didn't move a muscle; he didn't even breathe. It was as if Dr. Wiley's news had released a flood of banished memories. Over and over Charles heard, "I'm sorry to inform you, Dr. Martel, but your wife, Elizabeth, has an aggressive lymphoma . . . I'm awfully sorry to report that your wife is not responding to treatment . . . Dr. Martel, I'm sorry to say, but your wife has entered a terminal leukemic crisis . . . Dr. Martel, I'm terribly sorry to have to tell you that your wife died a few moments ago."

"No! It's not true. It's impossible!" shouted Charles with such vehemence that both Dr. Wiley and Cathryn were startled.

"Charles," began Dr. Wiley as he reached out and placed a sympathetic arm on Charles's shoulder.

With a lightning movement, Charles knocked Dr. Wiley's hand away. "Don't you dare patronize me!"

Despite her tears, Cathryn jumped up and caught Charles's arm as Dr. Wiley stepped back in surprise.

"Is this all some elaborate joke?" snapped Charles, shrugging off Cathryn's hand.

"It's not a joke," said Dr. Wiley. He spoke gently but firmly. "Charles, I know this is difficult for you, especially because of what happened to Elizabeth. But you have to get control of yourself. Michelle needs you."

Charles's mind was a jumble of incomplete thoughts and emotions. He wrestled with himself, trying to anchor his thoughts. "What makes you think Michelle has leukemia?" He spoke slowly, with great effort. Cathryn sat back down.

"The diagnosis in unequivocal," said Dr. Wiley softly.

"What kind of leukemia?" asked Charles, running his hand through his hair and looking out the window at the neighboring brick wall. "Lymphocytic?"

"No," said Dr. Wiley. "I'm sorry to say but it's acute myeloblastic."

I'm sorry to say . . . I'm sorry to say . . . a stock medical phrase that doctors resorted to when they didn't know what else to do and it echoed unpleasantly in Charles's head. I'm sorry to say your wife died . . . It was like a knife plunging into the heart.

"Circulating leukemic cells?" asked Charles, forcing intelligence to struggle against memory.

"I'm sorry to say, but there are," said Dr. Wiley. "Her white count is over fifty thousand."

A deathly silence descended over the room.

Abruptly Charles began to pace. He moved with quick steps, while his hands worked at each other as if they were enemies.

"A diagnosis of leukemia isn't certain until a bone marrow is done," he said abruptly.

"It's been done," said Dr. Wiley.

"It couldn't have," snapped Charles. "I didn't give permission."

"I did," said Cathryn, her voice hesitant, fearful she'd done something wrong.

Ignoring Cathryn, Charles continued to glower at Dr. Wiley.

"I want to see the smears myself."

"I've already had the slides reviewed by a hematologist," said Dr. Wiley.

"I don't care," said Charles angrily. "I want to see them."

"As you wish," said Dr. Wiley. He remembered Charles as a rash but thorough student. Apparently he hadn't changed. Although Dr. Wiley knew that it was important for Charles to substantiate the diagnosis, at that moment he would have preferred to talk about Michelle's extended care.

"Follow me," he said finally and led Charles out of the conference room and down the hall. Once the conference room door opened a cacophony of crying babies could be heard. Cathryn, initially unsure of what to do, hurried after the men.

At the opposite end of the corridor they entered a narrow room which served as a small clinical lab. There was just enough space for a counter and a row of high stools. Racks of urine samples gave the room a slightly fishy aroma. A pimply faced girl in a soiled white coat deferentially slid off the nearest stool. She'd been busy doing the routine urinalysis.

"Over here, Charles," said Dr. Wiley, motioning to a shrouded microscope. He plucked off the plastic cover. It was a binocular Zeiss. Charles sat down, adjusted the eyepieces, and snapped on the light. Dr. Wiley opened up a nearby drawer and pulled out a cardboard slide holder. Gently he lifted one of the slides out, being careful to touch only the edges. As he extended it toward Charles, their eyes met. To Dr. Wiley, Charles looked like a cornered animal.

Using his left hand, Charles took the slide between his thumb and first finger. In the center of the slide was a cover glass over what appeared to be an innocuous smudge. On the ground glass portion of the slide was written: MICHELLE MARTEL #882673 BONE MARROW. Charles's hand trembled as he placed the slide on the mechanical stage and put a drop of oil on the cover glass. Watching from the side he lowered the oil immersion lens until it just touched the slide and entered the oil.

Taking a deep breath, Charles put his eyes to the oculars and tensely began to raise the barrel of the scope. All at once a multitude of pale blue cells leaped out of the blur, choking off his breath, and forcing the blood to pound in his temples. A shiver of fear as real as if he were looking at his own death warrant blew through his soul. Instead of the usual population of cells in all stages of maturation, Michelle's marrow had been all but replaced by large, undifferentiated cells with correspondingly large irregular nuclei, containing multiple nucleoli. He was gripped by a sense of utter panic.

"I think you'll agree it's rather conclusive," said Dr. Wiley gently.

With a crash, Charles leaped to his feet, knocking his stool over backwards. An uncontrollable anger, anger pent up from the exasperating morning and now fired by Michelle's illness, blinded him. "Why?" he screamed at Dr. Wiley, as if the pediatrician were part of an encircling conspiracy. He grabbed a fistful of the man's shirt and shook him violently.

Cathryn leaped between the two men, throwing her arms around her husband. "Charles, stop!" she shouted, terrified of alienating the one person she knew they needed to help them. "It's not Dr. Wiley's fault. If anyone's to blame, it's us."

As if waking from a dream, Charles embarrassingly let go of Dr. Wiley's shirt, leaving the surprised pediatrician's bow tie at an acute angle. He bent down and righted the stool, then stood back up, covering his face with his hands.

"Blame is not the issue," said Dr. Wiley, fumbling nervously with his tie. "Caring for the child is the issue."

"Where is Michelle?" asked Charles. Cathryn did not let go of his arm.

"She's already been admitted to the hospital," said Dr. Wiley. "She's on Anderson 6, a floor with a wonderful group of nurses."

"I want to see her," said Charles, his voice weak.

"I'm sure you do," said Dr. Wiley. "But I think we have to discuss her care first. Listen, Charles." Dr. Wiley reached out a comforting hand, but thought better of it. Charles's fury had unnerved him. Instead he put his hands in his pockets. "We have here at Pediatric one of the world's authorities on childhood leukemia, Dr. Stephen Keitzman, and with Cathryn's permission I've already contacted him. Michelle is a very sick little girl, and the sooner a pediatric oncologist is on the case the better. He agreed to meet with us as soon as you arrived. I think we should talk to him, then see Michelle."

At first Cathryn wasn't sure about Dr. Stephen Keitzman. Outwardly he was the opposite of Dr. Wiley. He was a small, young-looking man with a large head and thick dark, curly hair. He wore rimless glasses on a skinny nose whose pores were boldly evident. His manner was abrupt, his gestures nervous, and he had a peculiar tic that he displayed during pauses in his speech. All at once he'd curl his upper lip in a sneer that momentarily bared his capped teeth and flared his nostrils. It lasted only an instant but it had a disquieting effect on people who were meeting him for the first time. But he was sure of himself and spoke with an authority that made Cathryn feel confidence in the man.

Certain that she would forget what was being told to them, she pulled out a small notebook and ballpoint pen. It confused her that Charles didn't seem to be listening. Instead he was staring out the window, seemingly watching the traffic inching along Longwood Avenue. The northeast wind had brought arctic air into Boston and the mixture of light rain and snow had turned to a heavy snow. Cathryn was relieved that Charles was there to take control because she felt incapable. Yet he was acting strangely: angry one minute, detached the next.

"In other words," summed up Dr. Keitzman, "the diagnosis of acute myeloblastic leukemia is established beyond any doubt."

Swinging his head around, Charles surveyed the room. He knew that he had a precarious hold on his emotions, and it made it difficult to concentrate on what Keitzman had to say. Angrily he felt he'd spent the whole morning watching people undermine his security, dislocate his life, destroy his family, rob him of his newly found happiness. Rationally he knew there was a big difference between Morrison and Ibanez on the one hand and Wiley and Keitzman on the other, but at the moment they all triggered the same unreasoning fury. Charles had great difficulty believing that Michelle had leukemia, particularly the worst possible type, the most deadly kind. He had already been through that kind of disaster; it was someone else's turn.

Listening half-heartedly, Charles examined Dr. Stephen Keitzman, who had assumed that typical condescending air of the physician in charge, doling out bits and pieces of information as if he were lecturing. Obviously Keitzman had experienced this scene many times before and his stock phrases like "I'm sorry to say" had an overused, insincere ring. Charles had the uncomfortable feeling that the man was enjoying himself, not in the same manner he'd enjoy a movie or a good meal, but in a more subtle, self-satisfied way: he was the center of attention in a crisis. This attitude abraded Charles's already frayed emotions, especially since he was more than familiar with the general material Dr. Keitzman was covering. Charles forced himself to remain silent while his mind's eye conjured up kaleidoscopic images of Michelle as she grew up.

"In order to allay the inevitable sense of guilt," continued Keitzman as he bared his upper teeth in one of his nervous grimaces, "I want to emphasize that the cause and date of onset of leukemia like Michelle's is unknown. Parents should not try to blame specific events for initiating the disease. The goal will be to treat the condition and bring about a remission. I'm pleased to be able to report that we have very favorable results with acute myeloblastic leukemia; something we didn't have ten years ago. Now we are able to engineer a remission in about eighty percent of cases."

"That's wonderful," said Charles, speaking for the first time. "But unlike the five-year cures you've been achieving with other forms of leukemia, can you tell us how long the remission lasts in Michelle's form of the disease." It was as if Charles had to goad Keitzman into revealing the worst news at once.

Keitzman pushed back his glasses and cleared his throat. "Dr. Martel, I am aware you know more about your daughter's disease than other parents I deal with. But since your field is not specifically childhood leukemia, I don't have any idea what you know and what you don't know. Therefore, I felt it best to have this discussion as if you knew nothing. And even if you are already familiar with these facts, perhaps they are helpful to Mrs. Martel."

"Why don't you answer my question?" said Charles.

"I think it is a more fruitful approach if we concentrate on obtaining a remission," said Dr. Keitzman. His nervous tic became more frequent. "My experience has shown that with the advances in chemotherapy, leukemia should be approached on a day-to-day basis. We have seen some spectacular remissions."

"Except in Michelle's type," snarled Charles. "Come on, tell us what the probability is of a five-year survival with acute myeloblastic leukemia."

Dr. Keitzman looked away from Charles's challenging eyes to Cathryn's frightened face. She had paused in her notetaking, gaping at Dr. Keitzman. He knew the meeting was going badly. He glanced at Dr. Wiley for support, but Dr. Wiley had his head down, watching his thumbnail play against his other fingers. Trying to avoid Charles's stare, Keitzman said in a low voice, "The five-year survival is not impressive in acute myeloblastic leukemia, but it's not impossible."

"Now you're getting closer to the truth," said Charles, jumping to his feet and leaning over Dr. Keitzman's desk. "But to be more exact, the median survival of acute myeloblastic leukemia if a remission is obtained is only one to two years. And, in Michelle's case, with circulating leukemic cells, her chances of a remission are a lot less than eighty percent. Wouldn't you agree, Dr. Keitzman?"

Taking his glasses off, Dr. Keitzman tried to think of how best to word his response. "There's some truth in what you say, but it is not a constructive way to view the disease. There are lots of variables."

Charles abruptly walked to the window, watching the dirty snow flutter past. "Why don't you tell Mrs. Martel what the

survival time of the nonresponder is . . . the patients who don't
have a remission."

"I'm not sure what good this . . ." began Dr. Keitzman.

Charles whirled around. "What good? You dare to ask? I'll
tell you what good it is. The worst thing about disease is the
uncertainty. Humans are capable of adapting to anything as
long as they know. It's the hopeless floundering that drives
people crazy."

Charles stormed back to Dr. Keitzman's desk as he spoke.
Eyeing Cathryn's pad, he grabbed it and threw it into the
wastebasket. "We don't need notes on this gathering! It's not
a goddamn lecture. Besides, I know all too well about leukemia." Turning back to Dr. Keitzman, Charles's face was
flushed. "Come on, Keitzman, tell us about the survival time
of nonresponders."

Keitzman moved back in his chair, his hands gripping the
edge of the desk as if he were prepared for flight. "It's not
good," he said finally.

"That's not good enough," snapped Charles. "Be more specific."

"All right!" said Dr. Keitzman. "Weeks, months at the
most."

Charles didn't answer. Having successfully backed Dr.
Keitzman into a corner, he was suddenly adrift. Slowly he
sank back down into his chair.

Keitzman's face recovered from a series of sustained
twitches as he exchanged sympathetic glances with Dr. Wiley.
Turning to Cathryn, he resumed his recommendations. "Now,
as I was saying. It is best to try to think of leukemia as a
nonfatal disease and to take each day as it comes."

"That's like telling a man on death row not to think about
death," mumbled Charles.

"Dr. Martel," said Dr. Keitzman sharply, "as a physician I
would expect your response to the crisis to be significantly
different."

"It's easy to respond differently," said Charles, "when it's not a member of your own family. Unfortunately I've been through this before."

"I think we should discuss therapy," offered Dr. Wiley, speaking for the first time.

"I agree," said Dr. Keitzman. "We must start treatment as soon as possible. In fact, I'd like to start today, immediately after all the baseline studies are done. But of course, we are going to need consent to treat because of the nature of the drugs."

"With the chance of a remission so slight, are you sure it's worth subjecting Michelle to the side effects?" Charles was speaking more calmly now, but he had a terrible vision of Elizabeth during those last months, the violent nausea, the loss of hair . . . He closed his eyes.

"Yes, I do," said Dr. Keitzman firmly. "I think it is well established that we have made significant advances in treating childhood leukemia."

"That's absolutely true," confirmed Dr. Wiley.

"There have been advances," agreed Charles, "but unfortunately in types of leukemia other than Michelle's."

Cathryn's eyes darted from Charles, to Keitzman, to Wiley. She expected and wanted unanimity on which she could build her hope. Instead she could feel nothing but dissension and animosity.

"Well," said Dr. Keitzman, "I believe in aggressively treating all cases, whatever the chances are for remission. Every patient deserves a chance at life, whatever the cost. Every day, every month, is precious."

"Even if the patient would rather end her suffering," said Charles, recalling Elizabeth's last days. "When the chances of a remission—let alone a cure—are less than twenty percent, I don't know if it's worth subjecting a child to the additional pain."

Dr. Keitzman stood up abruptly, pushing back his chair. "We obviously view the value of life very differently. I believe chemotherapy to be a truly remarkable weapon against cancer. But you are entitled to your opinion. However, it seems evi-

dent that you would prefer to find another oncologist or handle
your daughter's therapy yourself. Good luck!"

"No!" said Cathryn, leaping to her feet, terrified at the prospect of being abandoned by Dr. Keitzman, who Dr. Wiley had
said was the best. "Dr. Keitzman, we need you. Michelle needs
you."

"I don't think your husband shares your view, Mrs. Martel,"
said Dr. Keitzman.

"He does," said Cathryn. "He's just distraught. Please, Dr.
Keitzman." Turning to Charles, Cathryn put a hand on his
neck. "Charles, please! We can't fight this alone. You said this
morning you weren't a pediatrician. We need Dr. Keitzman
and Dr. Wiley."

"I think you should cooperate," urged Dr. Wiley.

Charles sagged under the weight of his brooding impotence.
He knew he could not care for Michelle even if he were convinced the current approach for her particular disease to be
wrong. He had nothing to offer and his mind was overloaded,
an emotional jumble.

"Charles, please?" Cathryn pleaded.

"Michelle is a sick little girl," said Dr. Wiley.

"All right," said Charles softly, once again forced to surrender.

Cathryn looked at Dr. Keitzman. "There! He said all right."

"Dr. Martel," asked Dr. Keitzman. "Do you want me to
serve as the oncologist on this case?"

With a sigh which suggested breathing to be a great effort,
Charles reluctantly nodded his head.

Dr. Keitzman sat down and rearranged some papers on his
desk. "All right," he said at length. "Our protocol for myeloblastic leukemia involves these drugs: Daunorubicin,
Thioguanine, and Cytarabine. After our workup we'll start immediately with 60 mg/m2 of Daunorubicin given IV by rapid
infusion."

As Dr. Keitzman outlined the treatment schedule, Charles's
mind tortured him by recalling the potential side effects of the
Daunorubicin. Michelle's fever was probably caused by an

infection due to her body's depressed ability to fight bacteria. The Daunorubicin would make that worse. And besides making her essentially defenseless for a host of bacteria and fungi, the drug would also devastate her digestive system and possibly her heart . . . besides that . . . her hair . . . God!

"I want to see Michelle," he said suddenly, leaping to his feet, trying to stifle his thoughts. Immediately he became aware that he had interrupted Dr. Keitzman in mid-sentence. Everyone was staring at him as if he had done something outrageous.

"Charles, I think you should listen," said Dr. Wiley, reaching up and grasping Charles's arm. It had been a reflexive gesture and only after he'd made contact did Dr. Wiley question its advisability. But Charles didn't react. In fact his arm felt limp and after the slightest tug, he sat back down.

"As I was saying," continued Dr. Keitzman, "I believe it is important to tailor the psychological approach to the patient. I tend to work by age: under five; school age; and adolescents. Under five it's simple; constant and loving supportive therapy. Problems start in the school-age group where the fear of separation from parents and the pain of hospital procedures are the major concerns of the child."

Charles squirmed in his seat. He didn't want to try to think of the problem from Michelle's point of view; it was too painful.

Dr. Keitzman's teeth flashed as his face momentarily contorted, then he continued, "With the school-age child, the patient is told no more than he specifically asks to know. The psychological support is focused on relieving the child's anxieties about separation."

"I think Michelle is going to feel the separation aspect a lot," said Cathryn, struggling to follow Dr. Keitzman's explanation, wanting to cooperate to please the man.

"With adolescents," said Dr. Keitzman without acknowledging Cathryn, "treatment approaches that of an adult. Psychological support is geared to eliminate confusion and uncertainty without destroying denial if that is part of the patient's defense mechanism. In Michelle's situation, unfortunately, the problem falls between the school age and the adolescent. I'm not sure what is the best way to handle it. Perhaps you people as parents might have an opinion."

"Are you talking about whether Michelle should be told she has leukemia?" asked Cathryn.

"That's part of it," agreed Dr. Keitzman.

Cathryn looked at Charles, but he had his eyes closed again. Dr. Wiley returned her gaze with a sympathetic expression that made Cathryn feel a modicum of reassurance.

"Well," said Dr. Keitzman, "it is an issue that demands thought. No decision has to be made now. For the time being, Michelle can be told that we are trying to figure out what's wrong with her. Before we go, does Michelle have any siblings?"

"Yes," said Cathryn. "Two brothers."

"Good," said Dr. Keitzman. "They should be typed to see if they match Michelle's HLA and ABO loci. We're probably going to need platelets, granulocytes, and maybe even marrow, so I hope one of them matches."

Cathryn looked at Charles for support but his eyes were still closed. She had no idea what Dr. Keitzman was talking about but she assumed Charles did. But Charles seemed to be having more trouble than she was with the news.

On the way up in the elevator, Charles fought to control himself. He'd never before experienced such painfully conflicting emotions. On the one hand he could not wait to see his daughter, to hold her and protect her; on the other he dreaded seeing her because he was going to have to come to terms with her diagnosis. And in that sense he knew too much. She would see it in his face.

The elevator stopped. The doors opened. Ahead stretched a pale blue hall with pictures of animals affixed like decals directly on the paint. It was busy with pajama-clad children of a variety of ages, nurses, parents, even hospital maintenance men grouped about a stepladder fixing the lights.

Dr. Wiley led them down the hall, skirting the ladder and passing the busy nurses' station. The charge nurse, seeing Dr.

Wiley from behind the chart racks, scurried out and caught up with them. Charles glanced down at the floor and watched his feet. It was as if he were looking at someone else. Cathryn was beside him with her arm thrust under his.

Michelle had a single room, painted the same shade of pastel blue as the hallway. On the left wall beside the door to the lavatory was a large, dancing hippopotamus. At the end of the room was a shaded window. To the right was a closet, a bureau, a night table, and a standard hospital bed. At the head of the bed was a stainless steel pole supporting a small plastic bag as well as an IV bottle. The plastic tubing snaked down and entered Michelle's arm. She turned from looking out the window when she heard the group enter.

"Hello, peanuts," said Dr. Wiley brightly. "Look who I brought to see you."

At the first glimpse of his daughter, Charles's dread of seeing her vanished in a wave of affection and concern. He rushed up to her and scooped her head in his arms, pressing her face against his. She responded by throwing her free arm around his neck and squeezing.

Cathryn stepped around the bed to the opposite side. She caught Charles's eye and saw that he was struggling to hold back tears. After a few minutes, he reluctantly released his hold, lowering Michelle's head to the pillow, and smoothing out her rich, dark hair to form a fan about her pale face. Michelle reached out for Cathryn's hand and grasped it tightly.

"How are you?" asked Charles. He was afraid that his precarious emotional state was apparent to Michelle.

"I feel fine now," said Michelle, obviously overjoyed to see her parents. But then her face clouded and turning to Charles, she asked: "Is it true, Daddy?"

Charles's heart leaped in his chest. She knows, he thought with alarm. He glanced at Dr. Keitzman and tried to remember what he had said about the proper psychological approach.

"Is what true?" asked Dr. Wiley casually, coming to the foot of the bed.

"Daddy?" pleaded Michelle. "Is it true I have to stay overnight?"

Charles blinked, at first unwilling to believe that Michelle wasn't asking him to confirm the diagnosis. Then when he was sure she didn't know she had leukemia, he smiled with relief. "Just for a few nights," he said.

"But I don't want to miss school," said Michelle.

"Don't you worry about school," said Charles with a nervous laugh. He eyed Cathryn for a moment who also laughed in the same hollow fashion. "It's important that you stay here for some tests so that we can find out what's causing your fever."

"I don't want any more tests," said Michelle, her eyes widening in fright. She'd had enough pain.

Charles was struck by how tiny her body was in the hospital bed. Her narrow arms looked incredibly frail as they poked out of the sleeves of the hospital gown. Her neck, which had always seemed substantial, now looked about the size of his forearm; she had the appearance of a delicate and vulnerable bird. Charles knew that somewhere in the heart of her bone marrow was a group of her own cells waging war against her body. And there was nothing he could do to help her—absolutely nothing.

"Dr. Wiley and Dr. Keitzman will only do the tests they absolutely need," said Cathryn, stroking Michelle's hair. "You're going to have to be a big girl."

Cathryn's comment awakened a sense of protectiveness in Charles. He recognized he couldn't do anything for Michelle, but at least he could protect her from unnecessary trauma. He knew too well that patients with rare diseases were often subjected to all sorts of physical harassment at the whim of the attending physician. With his right hand, Charles twisted the soft plastic bottle so he could see the label. Platelets. With his hand still holding the bottle, he turned to Dr. Wiley.

"We felt she needed platelets immediately," said Dr. Wiley. "Hers were only about twenty thousand."

Charles nodded.

"Well, I've got to be going," said Dr. Keitzman. Grasping one of Michelle's feet through the covers he said, "I'll be seeing you later, Miss Martel. Also there will be a few other doctors coming in to talk to you sometime today. We'll be giving you some medicine in that tube, so keep your arm nice and still."

Charles peered at the plastic tube: Daunorubicin! A fresh wave of fear washed over him, accompanied by a new urge to reach down and snatch his beloved daughter from the clutches of the hospital. An irrational thought passed through his mind: maybe the whole nightmare would disappear if he got Michelle away from all these people.

"I'm available anytime at all if you'd like to speak to me," said Dr. Keitzman as he moved to the door.

Cathryn acknowledged the offer with a smile and a nod. She noticed that Charles didn't look up from Michelle. Instead he sat on the edge of the bed and whispered something in her ear. Cathryn hoped his silence would not further antagonize the oncologist.

"I'll be right outside," said Dr. Wiley, following Dr. Keitzman. The charge nurse who hadn't spoken left, too.

In the hall Dr. Keitzman slowed his steps, giving Dr. Wiley a chance to catch up. Together they walked toward the nurses' station.

"I think Charles Martel is going to make this a very difficult case," said Dr. Keitzman.

"I'm afraid you're right," agreed Dr. Wiley.

"If it weren't for that poor sick child, I'd tell Martel to stuff it," said Dr. Keitzman. "Could you believe that bullshit about withholding chemotherapy? God! You'd think that someone in his position would know about the advances we've made with chemotherapy, especially in lymphocytic leukemia and Hodgkin's."

"He knows," said Dr. Wiley. "He's just angry. It's understandable, particularly when you know he's been through all this when his wife died."

"I still resent his behavior. He is a physician."

"But he's in pure research," said Dr. Wiley. "He's been away from clinical medicine for almost ten years. It's a good argument for researchers to keep one foot in clinical medicine to keep their sense of perspective alive. After all, taking care of people is what it's all about."

They reached the nurses' station, and both men leaned on the counter surveying the busy scene about them with unseeing eyes.

"Charles's anger did scare me for a moment," admitted Dr. Wiley. "I thought he'd totally lost control."

"He wasn't much better in my office," said Dr. Keitzman, shaking his head. "I've dealt with anger before, as I'm sure you have, but not like this. People get angry at fate, not the diagnosing physicians."

The two men watched an OR orderly skillfully navigate a gurney carrying a recent post-op down the corridor from the patient elevator. For a moment they didn't talk. The gurney carrying the child from recovery disappeared into one of the rooms, and several nurses hurried after it.

"Are you thinking about what I am?" asked Dr. Keitzman.

"Probably. I'm wondering just how stable Dr. Charles Martel is."

"Then we're thinking the same thing," said Dr. Keitzman. "Those sudden mood shifts in my office."

Dr. Wiley nodded. "Even given the circumstances, his reaction seemed inappropriate. But he's always been an odd duck. Lives someplace in the middle of nowhere in New Hampshire. He claimed it was his first wife's idea but after she died, he didn't move. And now he's got this wife living up there, too. I don't know. To each his own, I guess."

"His new wife seems fine."

"Oh, she's a peach. Adopted the kids, treats them like her own. I was afraid when they got married that she'd bit off more than she could chew, but she's adapted remarkably. She was devastated when I told her Michelle had leukemia, but I was pretty sure she'd deal with it better than Charles. In fact, that's why I told her first."

"Maybe we should talk just to her for a moment," suggested Dr. Keitzman. "What do you think?"

"Let's try." Dr. Wiley turned to face the nurses' station. "Miss Shannon! Could you come over here for a moment?"

The charge nurse came over to the two doctors. Dr. Wiley explained that they wanted to speak to Mrs. Martel without her husband and asked her if she wouldn't mind going down to Michelle's room and trying to engineer it.

As they watched Miss Shannon walk briskly down the hall, Dr. Keitzman's facial muscles jumped. "It goes without saying that the child is desperately ill."

"I thought as much when I saw her peripheral blood smear," said Dr. Wiley. "Then when I saw her bone marrow, I was sure."

"She could be a very rapidly terminating case, I'm afraid," said Dr. Keitzman. "I think she already has central nervous system involvement. Which means we have to commence treatment today. I want Dr. Nakano and Dr. Sheetman to see her right away. Martel is right about one thing. Her chance of a remission is very slim."

"But you still have to try," said Dr. Wiley. "At times like these I don't envy you your specialty."

"Of course I'll try," said Dr. Keitzman. "Ah, here comes Mrs. Martel."

Cathryn had followed Miss Shannon out into the hall, half-expecting to see Marge Schonhauser because the nurse had said someone was asking to see her. She hadn't been able to think of anyone else who knew that she was in the hospital. Once clear of the room, however, Miss Shannon confided that the doctors wanted to speak to her alone. It sounded ominous.

"Thank you for coming out," said Dr. Wiley.

"It's all right," said Cathryn, her eyes darting from one man to the next. "What's wrong?"

"It's about your husband," began Dr. Keitzman cautiously. He paused, trying to choose his words carefully.

"We're concerned that he may interfere in Michelle's treatment," Dr. Wiley finished the thought. "It's hard for him. First he knows too much about the disease himself. Then he already has watched someone he loved die despite chemotherapy."

"It's not that we don't understand his feelings. We just feel Michelle should have every chance at remission regardless of the side effects."

Cathryn examined the narrow, hawklike features of Dr. Keitzman and the broad, rounded face of Dr. Wiley. They were outwardly so different yet similar in their intensity. "I don't know what you want me to say."

"We'd just like you to give us some idea of his emotional state," said Dr. Keitzman. "We'd like to have some idea of what to expect."

"I think he will be fine," assured Cathryn. "He had a lot of trouble adjusting when his first wife died, but he never interfered with her treatment."

"Does he often lose his temper as he did today?" asked Keitzman.

"He's had an awful shock," said Cathryn. "I think it's understandable. Besides, ever since his first wife died, cancer research has been his passion."

"It's a terrible irony," agreed Dr. Wiley.

"But what about the kind of emotional outburst he demonstrated today?" asked Dr. Keitzman.

"He does have a temper," said Cathryn, "but he usually keeps it under control."

"Well, that's encouraging," said Dr. Keitzman. "Maybe it's not going to be so difficult after all. Thank you, Mrs. Martel. You've been most helpful, especially since I know you, too, have had a terrible shock. I'm sorry if we've said anything disturbing but we'll do our best for Michelle, I can assure you of that." Turning to Dr. Wiley, he said, "I've got to get things rolling. I'll speak to you later." He moved quickly, almost at a run, and was out of sight in seconds.

"He has some strange mannerisms," said Dr. Wiley, "but you couldn't get a better oncologist. He's one of the top people in the world in childhood leukemia."

"I was afraid he was going to abandon us when Charles acted up," said Cathryn.

"He's too good of a doctor for that," said Dr. Wiley. "He's only concerned about Charles because of your husband's attitude to chemotherapy, and aggressive treatment has to be started right away to get her into a remission."

"I'm sure Charles won't interrupt her treatment," said Cathryn.

"Let's hope not," said Dr. Wiley. "But we're going to count on your strength, Cathryn."

"My strength?" questioned Cathryn, aghast. "Hospitals and medical problems aren't my strong points."

"I'm afraid you'll have to overcome that," said Dr. Wiley. "Michelle's clinical course could be very difficult."

At that moment she caught sight of Charles emerging from Michelle's room. He spotted Cathryn and started toward the nurses' station. Cathryn ran down to meet him. They stood for a moment in a silent embrace, drawing strength from each other. When they started back toward Dr. Wiley, Charles seemed more in control.

"She's a good kid," he said. "Christ, all she's worried about is staying overnight. Said she wanted to be home in the morning to make the orange juice. Can you believe that?"

"She feels responsible," said Cathryn. "Until I arrived she was the woman of the house. She's afraid of losing you, Charles."

"It's amazing what you don't know about your own children," said Charles. "I asked her if she minded if I went back to the lab. She said no, as long as you stayed here, Cathryn."

Cathryn was touched. "On the way to the hospital we had a little talk, and for the first time I felt she really accepted me."

"She's lucky to have you," said Charles. "And so am I. I hope you don't mind my leaving you here. I hope you understand. I feel such a terrible powerlessness. I've got to do something."

"I understand," said Cathryn. "I think you're right. There

isn't anything you can do right now and it would be better if you can get your mind on something else. I'll be happy to stay. In fact, I'll call my mother. She'll come over and take care of things."

Dr. Wiley watched the couple come toward him, pleased to see their open affection and mutual support. The fact that they were acknowledging and sharing their grief was healthy; it was a good sign and it encouraged him. He smiled, somewhat at a loss for what to say as they arrived. He had to get back to his office which he knew was in chaos, but he wanted to be there if they still needed him.

"Do you have any extra of Michelle's blood?" asked Charles. His voice was businesslike, matter-of-fact.

"Probably," said Dr. Wiley. It wasn't a question he had expected. Charles had the uncanny ability to unnerve him.

"Where would it be?" asked Charles.

"In the clinical lab," said Dr. Wiley.

"Fine. Let's go." Charles started toward the elevator.

"I'll stay here with Michelle," said Cathryn. "I'll call if there is any news. Otherwise I'll see you home for dinner."

"Okay." He strode off purposefully.

Confused, Dr. Wiley hurried after Charles, nodding a quick good-bye to Cathryn. His encouragement regarding Charles's behavior was quickly undermined. Charles's mood had apparently tumbled off on a new and curious tangent. His daughter's blood? Well, he was a physician.

SIX

Clutching the flask of Michelle's blood, Charles hurried through the foyer of the Weinburger Institute. He ignored greetings by the coy receptionist and the security guard and ran down the corridor to his lab.

"Thanks for coming back," taunted Ellen. "I could have used some help injecting the mice with the Canceran."

Charles ignored her, carrying the vial of Michelle's blood over to the apparatus they used to separate the cellular components of blood. He began the complicated process of priming the unit.

Bending down to peer at Charles beneath the glassware shelving, Ellen watched for a moment. "Hey," she called. "I said I could have used some help . . ."

Charles switched on a circulatory pump.

Wiping her hands, Ellen came around the end of the workbench, curious to see the object of Charles's obvious intense concentration. "I finished injecting the first batch of mice," she repeated when she was close enough to be absolutely certain Charles could hear her.

"Wonderful," said Charles without interest. Carefully he in-

troduced an aliquot of Michelle's blood into the machine.
Then he switched on the compressor.

"What are you doing?" Ellen followed all his movements.

"Michelle has myeloblastic leukemia," said Charles. He
spoke evenly, like he was giving the weather report.

"Oh, no!" gasped Ellen. "Charles, I'm so sorry." She wanted
to reach out and comfort him but she restrained herself.

"Amazing, isn't it?" laughed Charles. "If the day's disasters
had remained localized to the problems here at the Weinburger, I'd probably just cry. But with Michelle's illness, everything is a bit overwhelming. Christ!"

Charles's laughter had a hollow ring to it but it struck Ellen
as somewhat inappropriate.

"Are you all right?" asked Ellen.

"Wonderful," said Charles as he opened their small refrigerator for clinical reagents.

"How does Michelle feel?"

"Pretty good right now but she has no idea of what she's
in for. I'm afraid it's going to be bad."

Ellen found herself at a loss for words. She blankly watched
Charles as he went about completing his test. Finally she found
her tongue. "Charles, what are you doing?"

"I have some of Michelle's blood. I'm going to see if our
method of isolating a cancer antigen works on her leukemic
cells. It gives me the mistaken impression I'm doing something to help her."

"Oh, Charles," said Ellen sympathetically. There was something pitiful about the way he acknowledged his vulnerability.
Ellen knew how much of an activist he was and Charles had
told her the feeling of powerlessness was what had been the
hardest for him when Elizabeth was ill. He had been forced
to just sit and watch her die. And now Michelle!

"I've decided we aren't going to stop our own work," said
Charles. "We'll continue while we work on Canceran. Work
nights if we have to."

"But Morrison is very insistent about exclusively concentrating on Canceran," said Ellen. "In fact, he came by while

you were out to emphasize that." For a moment Ellen debated about telling Charles the real reason Morrison stopped by, but with everything else that had happened, she was afraid to.

"I couldn't care less what Morrison says. With Michelle's illness, cancer has, once again, become more than a metaphysical concept for me. Our work has so much more promise than developing another chemotherapeutic agent. Besides, Morrison doesn't even have to know what we're doing. We'll do the Canceran work and he'll be happy."

"I'm not sure you realize how much the administration is counting on Canceran," said Ellen. "I really don't think it's advisable to go against them on this, particularly when the reason is personal."

For a moment Charles froze, then he exploded. He slammed his open palm against the slate countertop with such force that several beakers tumbled off the overhead shelves. "That's enough," he yelled to punctuate his blow. "I've had enough of people telling me what to do. If you don't want to work with me, then just get the fuck out of here!"

Abruptly Charles turned back to his work, running a nervous hand through his disheveled hair. For a few moments he worked in silence, then without turning he said, "Don't just stand there; get me the radioactive labeled nucleotides."

Ellen walked over to the radioactive storage area. As she opened the lock, she noticed that her hands were trembling. Obviously Charles was just barely in control of himself. She wondered what she was going to say to Dr. Morrison. She was certain she wanted to say something, because as her fear abated her anger grew. There was no excuse for Charles to treat her as he did. She wasn't a servant.

She brought the chemicals over and arrayed them on the counter.

"Thank you," he said simply, as if nothing had happened. "As soon as we have some B-lymphocytes I want to incubate them with the tagged nucleotides and some of the leukemic cells."

Ellen nodded. She couldn't keep pace with such rapid emotional changes.

"While I was driving over here, I had an inspiration," continued Charles. "The biggest hurdle in our work has been this blocking factor and our inability to elicit an antibody response to the cancer antigen in the cancerous animal. Well, I have an idea; I was trying to think of ways of saving time. Why not inject the cancer antigen into a related, noncancerous animal where we can be absolutely certain of an antibody response? What do you think about that?"

Ellen scrutinized Charles's face. Within seconds he'd metamorphosed from an infuriated child to the dedicated researcher. Ellen guessed that it was his way of dealing with the tragedy of Michelle.

Without waiting for an answer, Charles went on: "As soon as the noncancerous animal is immune to the cancer antigen, we'll isolate the responsible T-lymphocytes, purify the transfer factor protein, and transfer sensitivity to the cancerous animal. It's so fundamentally simple, I can't believe we didn't think of it before. Well . . . what's your impression?"

Ellen shrugged. In truth she was fearful of saying anything. Although the basic premise sounded promising, Ellen knew that the mysterious transfer factor did not work well in the animal systems they were using; in fact, it worked best with humans. But technical questions were not foremost in her mind. She wondered if it would be too obvious if she excused herself and went directly up to Dr. Morrison's office.

"How about getting the polyethylene glycol?" said Charles. "We're going to want to set up the equipment to produce a hybridoma with Michelle's T-lymphocytes. Also call the animal room and tell them we want a fresh batch of control mice, which we'll inject with the mammary tumor antigen. God, I wish there were more than twenty-four hours in a day."

"Pass the mashed potatoes," said Jean Paul after debating with himself for several minutes whether to break the silence that had descended over the dinner table. No one had spoken since he announced that the duck he'd put in the garage was "deader than a doorknob, stiff as a board." Ultimately his hunger had decided the issue.

"I'll trade you for the pork chops," said Chuck, tossing his head to remove some stringy hair from his eyes.

The boys exchanged platters. There was the clink of silver against china.

Gina Lorenzo, Cathryn's mother, eyed her daughter's family. Cathryn resembled her. They each had the same bony prominence on the bridge of the nose and the same large, expressive mouth. The major difference, other than the obvious twenty-plus years, was that Gina was so much heavier. She admitted she was twenty pounds overweight but in actuality it was more like sixty. Pasta was Gina's passion and she was not one to deny herself.

Lifting the bowl of fettucini, Gina gestured as if she were about to add to Cathryn's untouched plate. "You need some nourishment."

Forcing a smile, Cathryn shook her head no.

"What's the matter? You don't like it?" asked Gina.

"It's wonderful," said Cathryn. "I'm just not very hungry."

"You gotta eat," said Gina. "You, too, Charles."

Charles nodded.

"I brought fresh cannolis for dessert," said Gina.

"Oh, boy!" said Jean Paul.

Dutifully Charles took a bite of the fettucini but his stomach rebelled. He let the pasta sit in his mouth before trying to swallow it. The reality of the day's disasters had hit him with hurricane force once he'd left the frenzied environment he'd created in the lab. Work had been an emotional anesthetic and he had been sorry when it was time to pick up Chuck and drive home. And Chuck hadn't helped. Charles had waited until they were out of the Boston rush hour traffic before telling his son that his sister had a very serious kind of leukemia. Chuck's response had been a simple "Oh!" followed by silence. Then he had asked if there was any chance he might catch it.

At the time Charles did not say anything; he just gripped the steering wheel harder, marveling at the unabashed depths of his oldest son's selfishness. Not once did Chuck ask how Michelle was doing. And now as Charles watched Chuck gobble his pork chops, he felt like reaching over and throwing the selfish kid out of the house.

But Charles didn't move. Instead he began mechanically to chew his fettucini, embarrassed at his own thoughts. Chuck was immature. At least Jean Paul reacted appropriately. He'd cried and then asked when Michelle would be home and if he could go and see her. He was a good kid.

Charles looked at Cathryn, who kept her head down, pushing her food around her plate, pretending for her mother's sake to be eating. He was thankful that he had her. He didn't think he could handle Michelle's illness by himself. At the same time he realized how difficult it was for Cathryn. For that reason he had not said anything about the troubles at the institute, nor did he plan to. She had enough to worry about.

"Have some more pork chops, Charles," said Gina, reaching over and unceremoniously plopping a chop on his full plate.

He had tried to say no but the chop had already entered its ballistic arc. He looked away, trying to stay calm. Charles found Gina trying even under the best of circumstances, especially since the woman had never concealed her disapproval of her only daughter marrying a man thirteen years her senior with three kids. Charles heard another telltale *plop* and opened his eyes to see his mound of fettucini had grown.

"There," said Gina. "You need some more meat on your bones."

Charles restrained himself from grabbing a handful of fettucini and throwing it back into the bowl.

"How do they know Michelle has leukemia?" asked Jean Paul guilelessly.

Everyone turned to Charles, having been afraid to ask the question.

"They looked at her blood, then examined her bone marrow."

"Bone marrow?" questioned Chuck with disgust. "How do they get bone marrow to look at?"

Charles eyed his son, amazed at how easily Chuck could irritate him. To anyone else, Chuck's question might seem innocent, but Charles was sure the boy was motivated by morbid interest and not concern for his sister. "They get bone marrow by ramming a largebore needle into the breast bone or the hipbone, then sucking the marrow out," said Charles, hoping to shock Chuck into sympathy for Michelle.

"Ugh," said Chuck. "Does it hurt?"

"Terribly," said Charles.

Cathryn stiffened with a flash of imaginary pain, remembering that she'd been the one to consent to the test.

"God!" said Chuck. "Nobody is ever going to do a bone marrow on me!"

"I'm not so sure," said Charles without thinking. "Michelle's doctor wants both of you boys to go in to be tissue-typed. There's a chance one of you may match Michelle and can be a donor for platelets, granulocytes, or even a marrow transplant."

"Not me!" said Chuck, putting down his fork. "Nobody is going to stick no needle into my bones. No way!"

Slowly Charles placed his elbows on the table and leaned toward Chuck. "I'm not asking if you're interested, Charles Jr. I'm telling you that you're going into Pediatric Hospital to be tissue-typed. Do you understand me?"

"This is hardly a discussion for the dinner table," interrupted Cathryn.

"Will they really stick a needle into my bone?" asked Jean Paul.

"Charles, please!" shouted Cathryn. "This is no way to talk to Chuck about this kind of thing!"

"No? Well, I'm sick and tired of his selfishness," cried Charles. "He hasn't voiced one word of concern for Michelle."

"Why me?" yelled Chuck. "Why do I have to be a donor? You're the father. Why can't you be the donor, or are big-shit doctors not allowed to donate marrow?"

Charles leaped to his feet in blind fury, pointing a quivering finger at Chuck. "Your selfishness is only rivaled by your ignorance. You're supposed to have had biology. The father only donates half of the chromosomes to a child. There is no way I could match Michelle. If I could I'd change places with her."

"Sure! Sure!" taunted Chuck. "Talk's cheap."

Charles started around the table, but Cathryn leaped up and caught him. "Charles, please," she said bursting into tears. "Calm down!"

Chuck was frozen in his chair, gripping the sides with white knuckles. He knew that only Cathryn stood between him and disaster.

"In the name of the Father and the Son and the Holy Ghost," said Gina, crossing herself. "Charles! Beg the Lord for forgiveness. Don't abet the devil's work."

"Oh, Christ!" shouted Charles. "Now we get a sermon!"

"Don't tempt the Lord," said Gina with conviction.

"To hell with God," shouted Charles, breaking free of Cathryn's grip. "What kind of God gives a defenseless twelve-year-old leukemia?"

"You cannot question the Lord's way," said Gina solemnly.

"Mother!" cried Cathryn. "That's enough!"

Charles's face flushed crimson. His mouth voiced some inaudible words before he abruptly spun on his heels, wrenched open the back door, and stormed out into the night. The door slammed with a jolting finality that shook the bric-a-brac in the living room.

Cathryn quickly pulled herself together for the children's sake, busying herself with clearing the table and keeping her face averted.

"Such blasphemy!" said Gina with disbelief. Her hand was pressed against her bosom. "I'm afraid Charles has opened himself to the devil."

"How about a cannoli?" asked Jean Paul, carrying his plate to the sink.

With his father gone, Chuck felt a sense of exhilaration. He knew now that he could stand up against his father and win. Watching Cathryn clear the table, he tried to catch her eye. She had to have noticed how he stood his ground, and Chuck certainly noticed how Cathryn had backed him up. Pushing back his chair, he carried his plate to the sink and dutifully ran water over it.

Charles fled from the house with no goal other than to escape the infuriating atmosphere. Crunching through the crusted snow, he ran down toward the pond. The New England weather, true to form, had completely changed. The northeastern storm had blown out to sea and was replaced by an arctic front that froze everything in its tracks. Despite the fact he had been running, he could feel a raw chill, especially since he'd not taken the time to get his coat. Without a conscious decision, he veered left toward Michelle's playhouse, noting that the change in the wind had effectively eliminated the smell from the chemical factory. Thank God!

After stamping his feet on the porch to remove any snow, Charles bent over and entered the miniature house. The interior was only ten feet long and a central archway divided it roughly in two: one-half was the living room with a built-in banquette; the other the kitchen, with a small table and sink. The playhouse had running water (in the summer) and one electrical outlet. From about age six to nine Michelle had made tea here for Charles on Sunday summer afternoons. The small hotplate she used was still working and Charles switched it on for a little heat.

Sitting down on the banquette, he stretched his legs out and crossed them, conserving as much body heat as possible. Still he soon began to shiver. The doll's house was only a refuge from the icy wind, not from the cold.

As the solitude had the desired effect, Charles quickly calmed down, admitting that he had handled Chuck badly. Charles knew he had yet to come to terms with the disastrous day. He marveled how he had allowed himself to be lulled into a false sense of security over the last few years. He thought back to the morning . . . making love with Cathryn. In just twelve hours all the threads of his carefully organized world had unraveled.

Leaning forward so he could look up through the front window, Charles gazed at the canopy of sky. It had become a clear, star-studded night, and he could see forever, out into distant galaxies. The sight was beautiful but lifeless and all at once Charles felt an overwhelming sense of futility and loneliness. His eyes filled with tears, and he leaned back so that he couldn't see the terrible beauty of the winter sky. Instead he looked out over the snow-covered landscape of the frozen pond. Immediately in front of him was the area of open water Jean Paul had asked about that morning.

Charles marveled at the depths of his loneliness, as if Michelle had already been taken from him. He didn't understand these feelings although he guessed it might have something to do with guilt; if he had only been more attentive to Michelle's symptoms; if he had only paid more attention to his family; if he had only carried out his research faster.

He wished he could put everything aside and just work on his own project. Maybe he could find a cure in time for Michelle. But Charles knew that was an impossible goal. Besides, he could not oppose Dr. Ibanez so openly. He could not afford to lose his job or the use of his lab. Suddenly Charles understood the directors' cleverness in putting him on the Canceran project. Charles was disliked because of his unorthodoxy, but he was respected because of his scientific ability. Charles was a foil who lent the desired legitimacy that the project needed and a perfect scapegoat if the project failed. It was a decision of administrative genius.

In the distance Charles heard Cathryn's voice calling his name. In the frigid air the sound was almost metallic. Charles didn't move. One second he felt like crying, the next so weak that physical activity of any sort was impossible. What was he going to do about Michelle? If the chance of a remission faded, could he stand to watch her suffer with the treatment?

He moved over to the window and scraped off the frost his

breath had created. Through the clear areas he could see the
silver-blue snowscape and the patch of water directly in front
of him. Guessing that the temperature was close to zero,
Charles began to wonder about that open water. His original
explanation to Jean Paul that morning had been that the current
prevented it from icing over. But that was when the temperature hovered about the freezing mark. Now it was some thirty
degrees below that. Charles wondered whether there was much
current at that time of year. In the spring when the snows
melted in the mountain to the north, the river raged and the
pond rose by a foot-and-a-half. Then there would be current,
not now.

Suddenly Charles was aware of a sweet aromatic smell. It
had been there all the time but had not penetrated his consciousness until that moment. It was vaguely familiar, but out
of context. He'd smelled it before, but where?

Eager for a distraction, Charles began to sniff around. The
odor was about equal in intensity in the two rooms and strongest near the floor. Sniffing repeatedly, Charles tried to place
the smell in his past. Suddenly it came to him: organic chemistry lab in college! He was smelling an organic solvent like
benzene, toluene, or xylene. But what was it doing in the playhouse?

Braving the cold wind, Charles went out into the knife-sharp
night. With his right hand he clutched his sweater tightly
around his neck. Outside the aromatic odor was diminished
because of the wind, but by bending down at the side of the
playhouse, Charles determined the smell was coming from the
partially frozen mud around and under the structure. Making
his way down to the pond's edge, Charles scooped up some
of the icy water and brought it to his nose. There was no
mistaking it: the smell was coming from the pond.

He followed the gradual curve of the pond, walking along
the edge of the open water to the point where it merged with
the inlet from the river. Bending down again, he brought some
water to his nose. The odor was stronger. Breaking into a jog,
Charles followed the inlet to the juncture with the Pawtomack

River. It, too, was unfrozen. Again, Charles brought a sample to his nose. The odor was even more intense. The smell was coming from the river. Standing up, shaking from the cold, Charles stared upstream. Recycle, Ltd., the plastic/rubber recycling plant was up there. Charles knew from his chemistry background that benzene was used as a solvent for both plastics and rubber.

Benzene!

A powerful thought gripped his mind: Benzene causes leukemia; in fact it causes myeloblastic leukemia! Turning his head, Charles's eyes followed the trail of the unfrozen, open water. It led directly to the playhouse: the one spot Michelle had spent more time than any other.

Like a crazed man, Charles sprinted for the house. The uneven snow tripped him and he fell headlong, landing on his chest with his palms outstretched. He was unhurt save for a cut on his chin. Picking himself up, he ran more slowly.

When he reached the house, he thundered up the back steps and banged open the door.

Cathryn, already taut as a tightened bowstring, involuntarily shrieked as Charles hurled himself breathlessly into the kitchen. The dish she was holding slipped from her hands and shattered on the floor.

"I want a container," gasped Charles, ignoring Cathryn's reaction.

Gina appeared at the door to the dining room, her face reflecting terror. Chuck materialized behind her, then pushed past to gain access to the kitchen. He stepped between Charles and Cathryn. He didn't care if his father was bigger than he was.

Charles's breathing was labored. After a few seconds, he was able to repeat his request.

"A container?" asked Cathryn who'd regained some of her composure. "What kind of a container?"

"Glass," said Charles. "Glass with a tight top."

"What for?" asked Cathryn. It seemed like an absurd request.

"For pond water," said Charles.

Jean Paul appeared beside Gina who stuck out her arm to keep him from entering the kitchen.

"Why do you want pond water?" asked Cathryn.

"Christ!" managed Charles. "Is this an interrogation?" He started for the refrigerator.

Chuck tried to step in his way, but Charles merely swept the boy out of his path. Chuck stumbled, and Cathryn grabbed his arm, keeping him from falling.

Charles turned at the commotion and saw Cathryn restraining his son. "What the hell is going on here?" he demanded.

Chuck struggled for an instant, glaring at his father.

Charles looked from one face to another. Gina and Jean Paul looked shocked; Chuck, furious; and Cathryn, frightened. But no one spoke. It was as if the scene was a freeze frame in a motion picture. Charles shook his head in disbelief and turned his attention to the refrigerator.

He pulled out a jar of apple juice and closed the door. Without a moment's hesitation he dumped the remaining contents down the sink, rinsed the jar thoroughly, and yanked his sheepskin coat off its hook. At the door he turned to glance at his family. No one had moved. Charles had no idea what was happening but since he knew what he wanted to do, he left, closing the door on the strange scene.

Releasing her hold on Chuck, Cathryn stared blankly at the door, her mind going over the disturbing discussion she'd had with Dr. Keitzman and Dr. Wiley. She'd thought their questions about Charles's emotions had been ridiculous, but now she wasn't so sure. Certainly, flying out of the house in anger in the dead of winter without a coat, only to return a half hour later in great excitement, looking for a container for pond water, was curious at best.

"I'd never let him hurt you," said Chuck. He pushed back his hair with a nervous hand.

"Hurt me?" said Cathryn, taken by surprise. "Your father's not going to hurt me!"

"I'm afraid he's let in the devil," said Gina. "Once he's done that, you can't tell what he's going to do."

"Mother, please!" cried Cathryn.

"Is Charles going to have a nervous breakdown?" teased Jean Paul from the doorway.

"He's already had one," answered Chuck.

"That's enough of that," said Cathryn sternly. "I don't want to hear any disrespect for your father. Michelle's illness has upset him terribly."

Cathryn directed her attention to the broken dish. Was Charles having a nervous breakdown? Cathryn decided she'd discuss the possibility with Dr. Wiley in the morning. It was a terrifying thought.

Gingerly crossing the partially frozen mud, Charles approached the water's edge, then filled the jar. He screwed the cap on tightly before running back to the house.

Although the suddenness of his arrival surprised Cathryn, it had nowhere near the effect of his previous entrance. By the time Charles got to the refrigerator, Cathryn could react, and she reached out and grasped his arm.

"Charles, tell me what you are doing."

"There's benzene in the pond," hissed Charles, shaking off her grasp. He put the jar of pond water in the refrigerator. "And you can smell it in the playhouse."

Charles whirled back to the door. Cathryn ran after him, managing to get hold of his coat. "Charles, where are you going? What's the matter with you?"

With unnecessary force, Charles wrenched his coat free. "I'm going to Recycle, Ltd. That's where the goddamn benzene is coming from. I'm sure of it."

SEVEN

Charles pulled the red Pinto off Main Street and stopped in front of the gate in the hurricane fence surrounding Recycle, Ltd. The gate was unlocked and opened easily. He stepped back into his car and drove into the factory's parking area.

The evening shift couldn't have been too large because there were only a half dozen or so beat-up cars near the entrance to the old brick mill building. To the left of the factory, the huge piles of discarded tires rose up like miniature snowcapped mountains. Between the used tires and the building were smaller heaps of plastic and vinyl debris. To the right of the factory was a rubbish-strewn, empty lot bisected by the hurricane fence that ran down to the Pawtomack River. Beyond the fence the deserted mill buildings stretched for a quarter of a mile to the north.

As soon as Charles got out of his car, he was enveloped by the same stench that had assaulted his house that morning. It amazed him that people could live to the immediate west of town, the direction of the prevailing winds. Locking the car, he started toward the entrance, an unimposing aluminum storm door. Above it, RECYCLE, LTD. UNAUTHORIZED ENTRY FOR-

BIDDEN was written in block letters. Taped to the inside of the glass was a cardboard sign which said: INQUIRIES, followed by a local telephone number.

Charles tried the door, which was unlocked. If he had thought the odor bad outside, inside it was far worse. He found himself choking on the heavy, chemical-laden air in a small office of sorts. It was a plywood-veneer paneled room with a beat-up Formica counter that held a wire letter basket and a stainless steel bell, the kind you hit with the palm of your hand. Charles did just that, but the noise was swallowed up by the hisses and rumbles coming from within the factory proper.

Charles decided to try the inner door. At first it wouldn't open but when he pulled more forcibly it swung inward. As soon as it opened, Charles saw why it was insulated. It was as if it were a portal into hell itself. The combination of stench and noise was overpowering.

Charles entered a huge two-story-high room, poorly lit and dominated by a row of gigantic pressure-cooker-type apparatus. Metal ladders and catwalks ascended and crisscrossed in bewildering confusion. Large, clanking conveyor belts brought in piles of plastic and vinyl debris mixed with all sorts of disagreeable trash. The first people Charles saw were a pair of sweating men in sleeveless undershirts, with black-smudged faces like coal miners, sorting out the glass, wooden objects, and empty cans from the plastic.

"Is there a manager here?" yelled Charles, trying to be heard over the din.

One of the men looked up for an instant, indicated that he couldn't hear, then went back to his sorting. Apparently the conveyor belt didn't stop and they had to keep up with it. At the end of the belt was a large hopper which, when full, would rise up, position itself over an available pressure cooker, and dump its contents of plastic scrap. Charles saw a man with a large, scimitarlike knife up on the catwalk slit open two bags of chemicals, one white, the other black. With what appeared like great effort he dumped the two bags into the ovens in a great cloud of dust. For a moment the man disappeared from view. When he reappeared, he had closed the hatch and activated the steam, sending a fresh mixture of smoke, odor, and noise into the room.

Although Charles couldn't get anyone's attention, no one asked him to leave, either. Boldly he skirted the conveyor belts, keeping his eyes on the floor which was strewn with trash and puddles of oil and grease. He passed a cinder-block wall housing the automated machinery bringing in the tires to be melted down. It was from this area that the smell that Charles associated with the factory originated. Up close it was far more powerful.

Just beyond the wall, Charles found a large wire cage secured with a stout padlock. It was obviously a storeroom because Charles could see shelving with spare parts, tools, and containers of industrial chemicals. The walls were made of the same material that formed the hurricane fence outside. Charles put his fingers through the mesh to support himself while he scanned the labels on the containers. He found what he was looking for directly in front of him. There were two steel drums with benzene stenciled on the sides. There were also the familiar skull and crossbone decals warning that the contents were poisonous. As he looked at the drums, Charles was shaken by a new wave of rage.

A hand gripped Charles's shoulder and he spun about, flattening himself against the wire mesh.

"What can I do for you?" yelled a huge man trying to be heard over the thunderous din of the machinery. But the instant he spoke, a whistle blew above one of the plastic pressure cookers as it completed its cycle, making further conversation impossible. It burst open and belched forth an enormous amount of black, viscous, depolymerized plastic. The hot liquid was poured into cooling vats sending up billows of acrid vapors.

Charles looked at the man in front of him. He was a full head taller than Charles. His perspiring face was so pudgy that his eyes were mere slits. He was dressed like the other men

Charles had seen. His sleeveless undershirt was stretched over a beer belly of awesome dimensions. The man was supporting a dolly, and Charles noticed his massive forearms were professionally tattooed with hula dancers. On the back of his left hand was a swastika that he had apparently done himself.

As soon as the noise level sank to its usual deafening pitch, the worker tried again. "You checking our chemicals?" He had to shout.

Charles nodded.

"I think we need more carbon black," yelled the man.

Charles realized that the man thought he belonged there.

"What about the benzene?" yelled Charles.

"We got plenty of benzene. That comes in the hundred-gallon drums."

"What do you do with it after you use it?"

"You mean the 'spent' benzene? C'mere, I'll show you."

The man leaned his dolly against the wire cage and led Charles across the main room, between two of the rubber ovens where the radiant heat was intense. They ducked under an overhang and entered a hallway that led to a lunch room where the noise was somewhat less. There were two picnic tables, a soda dispenser, and a cigarette machine. Between the soda dispenser and the cigarette machine was a window. The man brought Charles over to it and pointed outside. "See those tanks out there?"

Charles cupped his hands around his eyes and peered out. About fifty feet away and quite close to the riverbank were two cylindrical tanks. Even with the bright moon, he couldn't see any details.

"Does any of the benzene go in the river?" asked Charles, turning back to the worker.

"Most of it is trucked away to God-knows-where. But you know those disposal companies. When the tanks get too full, we drain them into the river; it's no problem. We do it at night and it washes right away. Goes out to the ocean. To tell you the truth . . ." The man leaned over as if he were telling a secret: "I think that fucking disposal company dumps it into the river, too. And they charge a goddamn fortune."

Charles felt his jaw tighten. He could see Michelle in the hospital bed with the IV running into her arm.

"Where's the manager?" asked Charles, suddenly displaying his anger.

"Manager?" questioned the worker. He regarded Charles curiously.

"Foreman, supervisor. Whoever's in charge," snapped Charles.

"You mean the super," said the worker. "Nat Archer. He's in his office."

"Show me where it is," ordered Charles.

The worker regarded Charles quizzically, then turned and retraced their route to the main room where he indicated a windowed door at the end of a metal catwalk one flight up. "Up there," he said simply.

Ignoring the worker, Charles ran for the metal stairs. The worker watched him for a moment, then turned and picked up an in-house telephone.

Outside of the office, Charles hesitated for a moment, then tried the door. It opened easily and he entered. The office was like a soundproofed crow's nest with windows that looked out on the whole operation. As Charles came through the door, Nat Archer twisted in his chair, then stood up smiling in obvious puzzlement.

Charles was about to shout at the man when he realized he knew him. He was the father of Steve Archer, a close friend of Jean Paul's. The Archers were one of Shaftesbury's few black families.

"Charles Martel!" said Nat, extending his hand. "You're about the last person I expected to come through that door." Nat was a friendly, outgoing man who moved in a slow, controlled fashion, like a restrained athlete.

Taken off balance in finding someone he knew, Charles stammered that he wasn't making a social call.

"Okay," said Nat, eyeing Charles more closely. "Why don't you sit down?"

"I'll stand," said Charles. "I want to know who owns Recycle, Ltd."

Nat hesitated. When he finally spoke he sounded wary. "Breur Chemicals of New Jersey is the parent company. Why do you ask?"

"Who's the manager here?"

"Harold Dawson out on Covered Bridge Road. Charles, I think you should tell me what this is all about. Maybe I can save you some trouble."

Charles examined the foreman who'd folded his arms across his chest, assuming a stiff, defensive posture in contrast to his initial friendliness.

"My daughter was diagnosed to have leukemia today."

"I'm sorry to hear that," said Nat, confusion mixing with empathy.

"I'll bet you are," said Charles. "You people have been dumping benzene into the river. Benzene causes leukemia."

"What are you talking about? We haven't been dumping benzene. The stuff gets hauled away."

"Don't give me any of your bullshit," snapped Charles.

"I think you'd better get your ass out of here, man."

"I'll tell you what I'm going to do," fumed Charles. "I'm going to see that this shithole factory gets closed down!"

"What's the matter with you? You crazy or something? I told you we don't dump nothing."

"Hah! That big guy downstairs with the tattoos specifically told me you dumped benzene. So don't try to deny it."

Nat Archer picked up his phone. He told Wally Crab to get up to his office on the double. Dropping the receiver onto the cradle he turned back to Charles. "Man, you gotta have your head examined. Coming in here in the middle of the night, spoutin' off about benzene. What's the matter? Nothing good on the tube tonight? I mean I'm sorry about your kid. But really, you're trespassing here."

"This factory is a hazard to the whole community."

"Yeah? Well, I'm not so sure the community agrees with you."

Wally Crab came through the door as if he expected a fire. He skidded to a halt.

"Wally, this man says you told him we dumped benzene in the river."

"Hell no!" said Wally, out of breath. "I told him the benzene is taken away by the Draper Brothers Disposal."

"You fucking liar!" shouted Charles.

"Nobody calls me a fucking liar," growled Wally, starting for Charles.

"Ease off!" yelled Nat, putting a hand on Wally's chest.

"You told me," shouted Charles pointing an accusing finger in Wally's angered face, "when the tanks are too full, you drain them into the river at night. That's all I need. I'm going to shut this place down."

"Cool it!" yelled Nat, releasing Wally and grasping Charles's arm instead. He started walking Charles to the door.

"Get your hands off me," Charles shouted as he pulled free. Then he shoved Nat away from him.

Nat recovered his balance and thrust Charles back against the wall of the small office.

"Don't you ever touch me again," said Nat.

Charles had the intuitive sense to stay still.

"Let me give you some advice," said Nat. "Don't cause trouble around here. You're trespassing, and if you ever come back, you'll be very sorry. Now get the hell out of here before we throw you out."

For a minute Charles didn't know if he wanted to run or fight. Then, realizing he had no choice, he turned and went thundering down the metal stairs, and through the nightmarish mechanical maze on the main floor. He strode through the office and burst outside, thankful for the cold and relatively clean air of the parking lot. Once in the car, he gunned the engine mercilessly before shooting out through the gate.

The farther he got from Recycle, Ltd., the less fear he felt and the more anger and humiliation. Pounding the steering wheel, he vowed he'd destroy the factory for Michelle's sake no matter what it took. He tried to think of how he would go about doing it, but he was too irate to think clearly. The institute had a law firm on retainer; perhaps he'd start there.

Charles pulled off 301 into his driveway, pushing the accelerator to the floor, spinning the wheels and shooting gravel up inside the fenders. The car skidded first to one side and then the other. Out of the corner of his eye he could see the lace curtains of one of the living room windows part and Cathryn's face come into view for a second. He skidded to a stop just beyond the back porch and turned off the ignition.

He sat for a moment, gripping the steering wheel, hearing the engine cool off in the icy air. The reckless drive had calmed his emotions and gave him a chance to think. Perhaps it had been stupid to charge up to Recycle, Ltd. at that time of night, although he had to admit he'd accomplished one thing: he knew for certain where the benzene in the pond was coming from. Yet now that he thought about it, he recognized that the real issue was taking care of Michelle and making the hard decisions about treatment. As a scientist he knew that the mere presence of benzene in the pond did not constitute proof that it had caused Michelle's leukemia. No one had yet proved that benzene caused leukemia in humans, only in animals. Besides, Charles recognized that he was using Recycle, Ltd. to divert the hostility and anger caused by Michelle's sickness.

Slowly he got out of the car, wishing once again that he'd worked faster over the last four to five years on his own research so that now he might have something to offer his daughter. Immersed in thought, he was startled when Cathryn met him in the doorway. Her face was awash with fresh tears, her chest trembling as she fought to control her sobs.

"What's wrong?" asked Charles with horror. His first reaction was that something had happened to Michelle.

"Nancy Schonhauser called," Cathryn managed to say. "Little Tad died this evening. That poor dear child."

Charles reached out and drew his wife to him, comforting her. At first he felt a sense of relief as if Michelle had been spared. But then he remembered that the boy lived on the Pawtomack River just as they did, only closer to town.

"I thought I'd go over to see Marge," continued Cathryn. "But she's been hospitalized herself. She collapsed when they told her about Tad. Do you think I should go over to their house anyway and see if there is something I can do?"

Charles was no longer listening. Benzene caused aplastic anemia as well as leukemia! He'd forgotten about Tad. Now Michelle was no longer a single, isolated case of bone marrow disease. Charles wondered how many other families living along the course of the Pawtomack River had been struck. All the anger Charles had felt earlier returned in an overwhelming rush, and he broke free from Cathryn.

"Did you hear me?" asked Cathryn, abandoned in the center of the room. She watched Charles go over to the telephone directory, look up a number, and dial. He seemed to have forgotten she was there. "Charles," called Cathryn. "I asked you a question."

He looked at her uncomprehendingly until the connection went through. Then he directed his attention to the phone. "Is this Harold Dawson?" demanded Charles.

"It is," returned the manager.

"My name is Dr. Charles Martel," said Charles. "I was down at Recycle, Ltd. tonight."

"I know," said Harold. "Nat Archer called me a while ago. I'm sorry for any discourtesies you experienced. I wish you had made your visit during regular hours so I could have seen you."

"Discourtesies don't bother me," snapped Charles. "But dumping toxic waste, like benzene, into the river does."

"We are not dumping anything into the river," said Harold emphatically. "All our toxic chemical permits have been filed with the EPA and are up to date."

"Permits," scoffed Charles. "There is benzene in the river and one of your workers said Recycle's been dumping it. And benzene is damn toxic. My daughter has just come down with leukemia and a child just upriver from me died today of aplastic anemia. That's no coincidence. I'm going to shut you people down. I hope to God you have a lot of insurance."

"These are wild, irresponsible accusations," said Harold evenly. "I should tell you that Recycle, Ltd. is a marginal operation of Breur Chemical Corporation and they maintain this facility because they feel they are doing the community a service. I can assure you that if they thought otherwise, they would close the factory down themselves."

"Well, it goddamn well ought to be closed," shouted Charles.

"One hundred and eighty workers in this town might disagree," answered Harold, losing patience. "If you cause trouble, mister, I can guarantee you'll get trouble."

"I . . ." began Charles but he realized he was holding a dead phone. Harold Dawson had hung up.

"God!" Charles shouted as he furiously shook the receiver.

Cathryn took the phone away and replaced it in its cradle. She'd only heard Charles's side of the conversation, but it had upset her. She forced him to sit down at the kitchen table, and she shooed her mother away when she'd appeared at the door. Her face was streaked with tears, but she was no longer crying.

"I think you'd better tell me about the benzene," said Cathryn.

"It's a poison," fumed Charles. "It depresses the bone marrow somehow."

"And you don't have to eat it to be poisoned?"

"No. You don't have to ingest it. All you have to do is inhale it. It goes directly into the bloodstream. Why did I have to make that playhouse out of the old ice shed?"

"And you think it could have caused Michelle's leukemia?"

"I certainly do. Apparently she's been inhaling benzene all the time she's played there. Benzene causes the rare kind of leukemia that she has. It's too much of a coincidence. Especially with Tad's aplastic anemia."

"The benzene could have caused that?"

"Absolutely."

"And you think Recycle has been putting benzene into the river?"

"I know they have. That's what I found out tonight. And they're going to pay. I'll get the place shut down."

"And how are you going to do that?"

"I don't know yet. I'll talk to some people tomorrow. I'll get in touch with the EPA. Somebody is going to want to hear about it."

Cathryn studied Charles's face, thinking of Dr. Keitzman's and Dr. Wiley's questions. "Charles," began Cathryn, marshaling her courage. "This is all interesting and probably important but it seems to me that it's a little inappropriate at this time."

"Inappropriate?" echoed Charles with disbelief.

"Yes," said Cathryn. "We've just learned that Michelle has leukemia. I think that the primary focus should be taking care of her, not trying to get a factory shut down. There will always be time for that, but Michelle needs you now."

Charles stared at his young wife. She was a survivor, coping in a difficult situation with great effort. How could he hope to make her understand that the core of the problem was that he really didn't have anything to offer Michelle except love? As a cancer researcher he knew too much about Michelle's disease; as a physician he couldn't be lured into false hope by the panoply of modern medicine; as a father he was terrified of what Michelle was going to face because he'd gone through a similar situation with his first wife. Yet Charles was an activist. He had to do something, and Recycle, Ltd. was there to keep from facing the reality of Michelle's illness and his deteriorating situation at the Weinburger Institute.

Charles recognized that he couldn't communicate all this to Cathryn because she probably wouldn't understand it and if she did it would undermine her own hopes. Despite their intense love for each other, Charles accepted that he'd have to bear his burdens alone. The thought was crushing, and he collapsed in Cathryn's arms.

"It's been a terrible day," whispered Cathryn, holding

Charles as tightly as she could. "Let's go to bed and try to sleep."

Charles nodded, thinking, If I had only worked faster . . .

By a process so gradual as to be imperceptible, Michelle became aware that her room was lighter. The shade over the window now appeared dark with a light border rather than white with a dark border. Along with the gradual increase in illumination, the coming day was also heralded by the increased activity in the hallway. Michelle's door was open about six inches and the shaft of yellow incandescent light that came through had been a meager comfort for her during the interminable night.

Michelle wondered when Charles or Cathryn would come. She hoped it would be soon because she wanted, more than anything else, to go home to her own room, her own house. She couldn't understand why she had had to stay in the hospital because after her dinner, which she had barely eaten, no one had done anything to her other than look in and check that she was OK.

Swinging her legs over the side of the bed, Michelle pushed herself into a sitting position. She closed her eyes and steeled herself against a rush of dizziness. The movement exacerbated her nausea which had troubled her all night. Once she'd even gotten up when her saliva had pooled beneath her tongue, and she was afraid she was going to vomit. Holding on to the sides of the toilet, she'd retched but hadn't brought up anything. Afterwards, it had taken all her strength to get back into bed.

Michelle was certain she'd not slept at all. Besides the waves of nausea, she also had pains in her joints and abdomen, as well as chills. The fever, which had gone away the previous afternoon, was back.

Slowly Michelle slid off the bed onto her feet, gripping the IV pole. Pushing the pole in front of her, she began to shuffle to the bathroom. The plastic IV tubing still went into her left arm, which she kept as immobile as possible. She knew there was a needle on the end of the tubing and she was afraid that if she moved her arm, the needle would pierce her in some damaging way.

After going to the toilet, Michelle returned to her bed and climbed in. There was no way she could feel any more lonely or miserable.

"Well, well," beamed a redheaded nurse as she came bustling into the room. "Awake already. Aren't we industrious?" She snapped up the window shade unveiling the new day.

Michelle watched her but didn't speak.

The nurse went around the other side of the bed and plucked a thermometer out of a narrow stainless steel cup. "What's the matter, cat got your tongue?" She flicked the thermometer, examined it, bent down, and poked it into Michelle's mouth. "Be back in a jiffy."

Waiting until the nurse was out the door, Michelle pulled the thermometer out of her mouth. She did not want anyone to know she still had a fever in case that might keep her in the hospital. She held the thermometer in her right hand, near to her face so that when the nurse came back, she would be able to put it into her mouth quickly.

The next person through the door was a false alarm. Michelle got the thermometer back into her mouth, but it was a man in a dirty white coat with hundreds of pens stuffed in his pocket. He carried a wire basket filled with glass test tubes with different-colored tops. He had strips of rubber tubing looped through the edges of his basket. Michelle knew what he wanted: blood.

She watched, terrified, as he made his preparations. He put a rubber tube about her arm so tight that her fingers hurt and roughly wiped the inside of her elbow with an alcohol swab, even the tender spot where they'd taken blood the day before. Then using his teeth, he pulled the cap off a needle. Michelle wanted to scream. Instead, she turned her head to hide silent tears. The rubber was unsnapped, which caused about as much pain as when it was put on. She heard a glass tube drop into the wire basket. Then she felt another stab as he yanked the needle out. He applied a cotton ball to the puncture site, bent her arm so that it pressed against the cotton, and gathered up his things. He left without saying a single word.

With one arm holding the cotton ball and the other with the IV, Michelle felt totally immobilized. Slowly she unbent her arm. The cotton ball rolled aside revealing an innocent red puncture mark surrounded by a black-and-blue area.

"Okay," said the redheaded nurse, coming through the door. "Let's see what we've got."

Michelle remembered with panic that the thermometer was still in her mouth.

Deftly the nurse extracted it, noted the temperature, then dropped it into the metal container on Michelle's night table. "Breakfast will be up in a moment," she said cheerfully, but she didn't mention Michelle's fever. She left with the same abruptness with which she'd arrived.

"Oh, Daddy, please come and get me," said Michelle to herself. "Please hurry."

Charles felt his shoulder being shaken. He tried to ignore it because he wanted to continue sleeping, but the shaking continued. When he opened his eyes he saw Cathryn, already robed, standing by the bed holding out a steaming mug of coffee. Pushing himself up on one elbow, Charles took the coffee.

"It's seven o'clock," said Cathryn with a smile.

"Seven?" Charles glanced at the face of the alarm clock, thinking that oversleeping was not the way to increase the pace of his research efforts.

"You were sleeping so soundly," said Cathryn, kissing his forehead, "that I didn't have the heart to wake you earlier. We've got a big breakfast waiting downstairs."

Charles knew that she was making an effort to sound gay.

"Enjoy your coffee," said Cathryn. She started for the door. "Gina got up and made it before I was even awake."

Charles glanced down at the mug in his hands. The fact that Gina was still there was irritating enough. He did not want to have to feel beholden to her the first thing in the morning, but then he was holding the coffee and he knew she'd ask how it was and gloat over the fact that she'd arisen when everyone else was still asleep.

Charles shook his head. Such annoying thoughts were not the way to begin the day. He tasted the coffee. It was hot, aromatic, and stimulating. He admitted that he enjoyed it and decided to tell Gina before she'd have a chance to ask, and then thank her for getting up before the others, before she had a chance to tell them.

Carrying his coffee mug, Charles padded down the hall to Michelle's room. He paused outside of the door, then slowly pushed it open. He had half hoped to see his young daughter safely sleeping in her bed, but of course her bed was neatly made, her books and memorabilia compulsively arranged, her room as neat as a pin. "All right," said Charles to himself, as if he were bargaining with an all-powerful arbiter, "she has myeloblastic leukemia. Just let her case be sensitive to current treatment. That's all I ask."

Breakfast was a strained affair, overshadowed by Gina's forced ebullience and Charles's reserve. One fed the other in a self-fulfilling prophecy until Gina was chatting nonstop and Charles perfectly silent. Cathryn interrupted with complicated plans about who was going to do what, when. Charles stayed out of the domestic decision making and concentrated on planning his day's work at the institute. The first thing he wanted to do was check the well mice injected with the cancer antigen for signs of immunological activity. Most likely there would be no response with such a light dose and he would prepare to give them another challenge that afternoon. Then he would check the mice injected with the Canceran and reinject them. Then he would start work on a computer simulation of the way he envisioned the blocking factor worked.

"Charles, is that agreeable to you?" asked Cathryn.

"What?" questioned Charles. He'd tuned out all conversation.

"I will ride with you in the Pinto this morning, and you can drop me at the hospital. Chuck will take the station wagon, drop off Jean Paul, and drive himself to Northeastern. Gina has agreed to stay here and make dinner."

"I'll make your favorite," said Gina enthusiastically, "gnocchi."

Gnocchi! Charles didn't even know what gnocchi was.

"If I want to leave early," continued Cathryn to Charles, "I can go over to Northeastern and pick up the station wagon. Otherwise I'll come back with you. What do you say?"

Charles couldn't figure out how all these elaborate plans were making things any easier. The old method of his driving the boys and leaving the station wagon for Cathryn seemed far more simple, but he didn't care. In fact, if he decided to work that night, maybe it would be best if Chuck had the car because then Cathryn could come home with him in the afternoon.

"Fine with me," said Charles, finding himself watching Chuck who was in his usual breakfast posture, studying the cereal box as if it were Scripture. The boy was wearing the same clothes as yesterday and looked just as bad.

"I got a call from the business office yesterday," said Charles.

"Yeah, I gave them the number," said Chuck without looking up.

"I made arrangements at the bank for a loan," said Charles. "Should be available in a day or so, then the bill will be paid."

"Good," said Chuck, flipping the box so he could study the nutritional values on the side panel.

"Is that all you have to say? Good?" Charles turned his head toward Cathryn with a look that said: "Can you believe this kid?"

Chuck pretended he hadn't heard the question.

"I think we should be going," said Cathryn, getting to her feet and collecting the milk and butter to put into the refrigerator.

"Just leave everything," said Gina magnanimously. "I'll take care of it."

Charles and Cathryn were the first out of the house. A pale

winter sun hung low in the southeastern sky. As cold as it was inside the Pinto, Cathryn was relieved to get out of the biting wind.

"Damn," said Charles, blowing on his fingers. "I forgot the pond water."

For Cathryn's sake, Charles started the car, which was no easy task, before running back into the kitchen for the jar of pond water. He carefully wedged it behind his seat to keep it from spilling before he climbed into the car and fumbled with his seat belt.

Cathryn watched this procedure with the pond water with a certain misgiving. After her little talk to Charles the night before she'd hoped that he would concentrate on Michelle. But Charles had acted strangely from the moment she'd awakened him that morning. Cathryn had the scary feeling that her family was coming apart at the seams.

Watching Charles's silent profile as he drove, Cathryn began multiple conversations but abandoned each for various reasons, mostly because she feared any discussion would trigger her husband's temper.

When Route 301 merged with Interstate 93, Cathryn finally forced herself to speak: "How do you feel today, Charles?"

"Huh? Oh fine. Just fine."

"You seem so quiet. It's not like you."

"Just thinking."

"About Michelle?"

"Yes, and also my work."

"You're not still thinking of Recycle, Ltd., are you?"

Charles glanced at Cathryn for a moment, then turned his attention to the road ahead. "A little. I still think the place is a menace, if that's what you mean."

"Charles, there isn't something you're not telling me, is there?"

"No," said Charles too quickly. "What makes you ask that?"

"I don't know," admitted Cathryn. "You seem so far away since we heard about Michelle. Your mood seems to change so quickly." Cathryn's eyes darted over to watch Charles's reaction to her last comment. But Charles just drove on, and if there had been a reaction, Cathryn missed it.

"I guess I just have a lot on my mind," said Charles.

"You'll share it with me, won't you, Charles? I mean that's what I'm here for. That's why I wanted to adopt the children. I want you to share everything with me." Cathryn reached over and put her hand on Charles's thigh.

Charles concentrated on the road in front of him. Cathryn was voicing a conviction he'd held until yesterday, but now he realized that he couldn't share everything. His background as a physician had imparted experiences that Cathryn could not comprehend. If Charles told what he knew about the course of Michelle's illness, she'd be devastated.

Taking a hand from the steering wheel, Charles placed it over Cathryn's. "The children don't know how lucky they are," he said.

They rode in silence for a while. Cathryn wasn't satisfied, but she didn't know what else to say. In the far distance she could just make out the top of the Prudential building. The traffic began to increase, and they had to slow to forty miles per hour.

"I don't know anything about tissue-typing and all that," said Cathryn, breaking the silence. "But I don't think we should force Chuck to do something he doesn't want to do."

Charles glared at Cathryn for a moment.

"I'm sure he will come around," she continued when she realized that Charles wasn't going to speak. "But he has to agree on his own."

Charles took his hand off Cathryn's and gripped the steering wheel. The mere mention of Chuck was like stoking a smoldering fire. Yet what Cathryn was saying was undeniably true.

"You can't force someone to be altruistic," said Cathryn. "Especially Chuck, because it will only strengthen the worries he has about his sense of self."

"A sense of self is all he has," said Charles. "He didn't voice the slightest concern about Michelle. Not one word."

"But he feels it," said Cathryn. "It's just hard for him to express those feelings."

Charles laughed cynically. "I wish I believed it. He's just goddamned selfish. Did you notice his overwhelming appreciation when I told him I'd applied for a loan for his tuition?"

"What did you want him to do? Cartwheels?" returned Cathryn. "The tuition was supposed to be paid months ago."

Charles set his jaw. "Fine," he said to himself. "You want to side with the little bastard . . . just fine!"

Cathryn was instantly sorry she'd said what she had even though it was true. Reaching over, she put her hand on his shoulder. She wanted to draw Charles out, not shut him up. "I'm sorry I said that, but Charles, you have to understand that Chuck doesn't have your personality. He's not competitive and he's not the most handsome boy. But basically he's a good kid. It's just very hard growing up in your shadow."

Charles glanced sideways at his wife.

"Whether you know it or not," said Cathryn, "you're a hard act to follow. You've been successful in everything you've tried."

Charles did not share that opinion. He could have rattled off a dozen episodes in which he'd failed miserably. But that wasn't the issue: it was Chuck.

"I think the kid's selfish and lazy, and I'm tired of it. His response to Michelle's illness was all too predictable."

"He has a right to be selfish," said Cathryn. "College is the ultimate selfish experience."

"Well, he's certainly making the best of it."

They came to the stop-and-go traffic where 193 joined the southeast expressway and Storrow Drive. Neither spoke as they inched forward.

"This isn't what we should be worrying about," said Cathryn finally.

"You're right," sighed Charles. "And you're right about not forcing Chuck. But if he doesn't do it, he's going to wait a long time before I pay his next college bill."

Cathryn looked sharply at Charles. If that wasn't coercion, she had no idea what was.

Although at that time of morning there were few visitors, the hospital itself was in full swing, and Charles and Cathryn had to dodge swarms of gurneys moving tiny bedridden patients to and from their various tests. Cathryn felt infinitely more comfortable with Charles at her side. Still her palms were wet, which was her usual method of showing anxiety.

As they passed the bustling nurses' station on Anderson 6, the charge nurse caught sight of them and waved a greeting. Charles stepped over to the counter.

"Excuse me," said Charles. "I'm Dr. Martel. I was wondering if my daughter started her chemotherapy." He purposefully kept his voice natural, emotionless.

"I believe so," said the nurse, "but let me check."

The clerk who'd overheard the conversation handed over Michelle's chart.

"She got her Daunorubicin yesterday afternoon," said the nurse. "She got her first oral dose of Thioguanine this morning, and she'll start with the Cytarabine this afternoon."

The names jolted Charles but he forced himself to keep smiling. He knew too well the potential side effects and the information silently echoed in his head. "Please," said Charles to himself. "Please, let her go into remission." Charles knew that if it would happen, it would happen immediately. He thanked the nurse, turned, and walked toward Michelle's room. The closer he got, the more nervous he became. He loosened his tie and unbuttoned the top button of his shirt.

"It's nice the way they have decorated to brighten the atmosphere," remarked Cathryn, noticing the animal decals for the first time.

Charles stopped for a moment outside the door, trying to compose himself.

"This is it," said Cathryn, thinking that Charles was uncertain of the room number. She pushed open the door, entered, and pulled Charles in behind her.

Michelle was propped up in a sitting position with several

pillows behind her back. At the sight of Charles, her face twisted and she burst into tears. Charles was shocked at her appearance. Although he had not thought it possible, she looked even paler than she had the day before. Her eyes had visibly sunk into their sockets and were surrounded by circles so dark they looked like she had black eyes. In the air hung the rank smell of fresh vomit.

Charles wanted to run and hold her, but he couldn't move. The agony of his inadequateness held him back, although she lifted her arms to him.

Her disease was too powerful, and he had nothing to offer her, just like with Elizabeth eight years earlier. The nightmare had returned. In an avalanche of horror, Charles recognized that Michelle was not going to get better. Suddenly he knew without the slightest doubt that all the palliative treatment in the world would not touch the inevitable progression of her illness. Under the weight of this knowledge Charles staggered, taking a step back from the bed.

Although Cathryn did not understand, she saw what was happening and she ran to fill Michelle's outstretched arms. Looking over Cathryn's shoulder, Michelle met her father's eyes. Charles smiled weakly but Michelle decided that he was angry with her.

"It's so good to see you," said Cathryn, looking into Michelle's face. "How are you?"

"I'm fine," managed Michelle, checking her tears. "I just want to go home. Can I go home, Daddy?"

Charles's hands shook as he approached the foot of the bed. He steadied them on the metal frame.

"Maybe," said Charles evasively. Maybe he should just take her out of the hospital; take her home and keep her comfortable; maybe that was best.

"Michelle, you have to stay here until you're well," Cathryn said hurriedly. "Dr. Wiley and Dr. Keitzman are going to see that you get better just as soon as possible. I know it's hard for you, and we miss you terribly, but you have to be a big girl."

"Please, Daddy," said Michelle.

Charles felt helpless and indecisive, two unfamiliar and un-nerving emotions.

"Michelle," said Cathryn. "You have to stay in the hospital. I'm sorry."

"Why? Daddy," pleaded Michelle, "what's wrong with me?"

Charles vainly looked at Cathryn for help, but she was silent. He was the physician.

"I wish we knew," said Charles, hating himself for lying, yet incapable of telling the truth.

"Is it the same thing that my real mother had?" asked Michelle.

"No," said Charles quickly. "Absolutely not." Even that was a half lie; although Elizabeth had lymphoma, she died in a terminal leukemic crisis. Charles felt cornered. He had to get away to think.

"What is it then?" demanded Michelle.

"I don't know," said Charles as he guiltily checked his watch. "That's why you're here. To find out. Cathryn is going to stay with you to keep you company. I've got to get to the lab. I'll be back."

Without any warning, Michelle abruptly retched. Her slender body heaved, and she threw up a small amount of her recently consumed breakfast. Cathryn tried to get out of the way but some of the vomit got on her left sleeve.

Charles responded instantly by stepping into the corridor and yelling for a nurse. An aide only two doors down came flying in, expecting a crisis, and was pleased to discover it was a false alarm.

"Don't you worry, princess," said the woman casually, pulling off the soiled top sheet. "We'll have it cleaned up in a second."

Charles put the back of his hand against Michelle's forehead. It was moist and hot. Her fever was still there. Charles knew what caused the vomiting; it was the medicine. He felt a wave of anxiety wash over him. The small room was making him feel claustrophobic.

Michelle grabbed his hand and held it as if she'd slipped at the edge of an abyss and Charles was her only salvation. She looked into the blue eyes that were mirrors of her own. But she thought she saw firmness instead of acquiescence; irritation instead of understanding. She let go of the hand and fell back onto the pillow.

"I'll be over later, Michelle," said Charles, upset that the medicine was already causing potentially dangerous side effects. To the aide Charles said: "Does she have something ordered for nausea and vomiting?"

"Indeed she does," said the nurse. "There is a standing order for Compazine PRN. I'll get her some in a minute."

"Is it a needle?" cried Michelle.

"No, it's a pill," said the aide. "Provided your tummy keeps it down. If not, then it will have to go in your rump." She gave Michelle's foot a playful squeeze.

"I'll just walk Charles to the elevator, Michelle," said Cathryn, seeing Charles start for the door. She caught up with him in the hall, grabbing his arm. "Charles, what is the matter with you?"

Charles didn't stop.

"Charles!" cried Cathryn, yanking him around to face her. "What is it?"

"I've got to get out of here," said Charles, nervously stroking his hair. "I can't stand to see Michelle suffer. She looks terrible. I don't know what to do. I'm not sure she should get any of that medicine."

"No medicine?" cried Cathryn. Instantly she remembered that Dr. Keitzman and Dr. Wiley were worried that Charles might interrupt Michelle's treatment.

"Her vomiting," said Charles angrily. "That's only the beginning." Charles started to say that he was sure Michelle was not going to go into remission, but he held his tongue. There would be time for more bad news for Cathryn and for the present he did not want to destroy the hope.

"But the medicine is her only chance," pleaded Cathryn.

"I've got to go," said Charles. "Call me if there is any change. I'll be at the lab."

Cathryn watched Charles rush down the crowded corridor. He didn't even wait for the elevator. She saw him duck into the stairwell instead. When Dr. Wiley told her that they were going to rely on her strength, she had no idea what he'd meant. Now she was beginning to comprehend.

EIGHT

Charles turned into the institute parking lot, leaped out of the car, and pulled the jar of pond water from behind the seat. He ran across the tarmac and had to bang on the glass door before the receptionist opened it. Turning right instead of left in the main hallway, he ran down to the analysis lab. One of the technicians whom Charles respected was sitting on the countertop with his morning coffee.

"I want this water analyzed for contaminants," said Charles, out of breath.

"Rush job?" quipped the technician, noting Charles's excitement.

"Sorta," said Charles. "I'm particularly interested in organic solvents. But whatever else you can tell me about the water would be helpful."

The technician unscrewed the cap, took a whiff, and blinked. "Whew. I hope you don't use this stuff with your scotch."

Charles hurried back toward his own lab. His mind was pulsing with a confusion of thoughts which flashed in and out of his consciousness with bewildering rapidity.

He acknowledged that he had no way of rationally solving

the dilemma he felt about Michelle's treatment. Instead he decided to put his own research into high gear in the futile hope that he could accomplish something extraordinary in time for Michelle; and to try to have Recycle, Ltd. closed down. Revenge was a powerful emotion, and its presence dulled the anxiety about Michelle. By the time he reached the door to his lab, Charles found himself with clenched fists. But he hesitated, remembering his vow that morning to use his intelligence rather than his unreliable emotions. Composing himself, he calmly opened the door.

Ellen, who'd been busy reading the Canceran protocol at Charles's desk, slowly put the book down. There was a studied deliberateness to her movements, which bothered Charles even in his distracted state.

"Did the entire batch of mice get the mammary cancer antigen?" he demanded.

"They did," answered Ellen. "But . . ."

"Good," interrupted Charles, going up to their small blackboard. He picked up a piece of chalk and after erasing what was already on the board, he began diagramming the method they would use to assay the T-lymphocyte responses in the injected mice in order to chart their immunological response. When he finished, the small board was filled with an elaborate progression of steps. "Also," said Charles, putting down the chalk, "we're going to try something different. It's not meant to be scientific. Its purpose is to provide a kind of rapid survey. I want to make a large number of dilutions of the cancer antigen and begin a single mouse with each dilution. I know it will have no statistical significance. It's a shotgun survey, but it might be helpful. Now, while you check yesterday's mice and inject them with a second challenge of the cancer antigen, I'm going to make some calls." Charles wiped the chalk dust on his trousers, reaching for the phone.

"Can I say something now?" queried Ellen, cocking her head to the side with an I-told-you-so expression.

"Of course," said Charles, holding the receiver.

"I checked the mice who got the first dose of Canceran." She paused.

"Yeah?" said Charles, wondering what was coming.

"Almost all of them died last night."

Charles's face clouded with disbelief. "What happened?" He put down the receiver.

"I don't know," admitted Ellen. "There's no explanation except for the Canceran."

"Did you check the dilution?"

"I did," said Ellen. "It was very accurate."

"Any sign that they died from an infectious agent?"

"No," said Ellen. "I had the vet take a look. He hasn't autopsied any but he thinks they died of cardiac insult."

"Drug toxicity!" said Charles, shaking his head.

"I'm afraid so."

"Where's the original Canceran protocol?" asked Charles with mounting concern.

"Right there on your desk. I was glancing through it when you came in."

Charles picked up the volume and flipped through the toxicity section. Then he reached for the preliminary protocol they'd made up the day before. He scanned the figures. When he finished, he tossed the new protocol and the original onto his desk.

"That fucking bastard," snarled Charles.

"It has to be the explanation," agreed Ellen.

"Brighton must have falsified the toxicity data, too. Holy shit, that means the whole Canceran study that Brighton has spent two years on is no good. Canceran must be much more toxic than Brighton reported. What a joke! Do you know how much the National Cancer Institute has paid so far for testing this drug?"

"No, but I can guess."

"Millions and millions!" Charles slapped his forehead.

"What are we going to do?"

"We? What are *they* going to do! The whole project has to be started over, which means an additional three years!"

Charles could feel his vow to maintain an impassioned distance dissolve. To finish the efficacy study was one thing, but starting the whole Canceran project from scratch was something else. He would not do it, especially since now with Michelle ill he had to increase the pace of his own work.

"I have a feeling they'll still want us to do Canceran," said Ellen.

"Well I don't give a damn," snapped Charles. "We're finished with Canceran. If Morrison and Ibanez give us trouble, we'll slap them in the face with the proof that the toxicity study isn't worth the paper it's printed on. We'll threaten to tell the press. With that kind of scandal, I think even the National Cancer Institute might question where it's putting its money."

"I don't think it's going to be that easy," said Ellen. "I think we should . . ."

"That's enough, Ellen!" yelled Charles. "I want you to start testing for antibodies in our first batch of mice, then reinject them. I'll handle the administration in respect to Canceran."

Ellen angrily turned her back. As usual, Charles had gone too far. She began her work, making as much noise with the glassware and instruments as she could.

The phone rang under Charles's arm. He picked it up on the first ring. It was the technician down in analysis.

"You want a preliminary report?" asked the chemist.

"Please," snapped Charles.

"The major contaminant is benzene and it's loaded with it. But also there's lesser amounts of toluene, as well as some trichloroethylene and carbon tetrachloride. Vile stuff! You could practically clean your oil-base paintbrushes in it. I'll have a full report later this afternoon."

Charles thanked the man and hung up. The report was no surprise, but he was glad to have the documented proof. Involuntarily the image of Michelle appeared before him, and he forcibly blurred it by grabbing the Boston phone directory off the shelf over his desk. He hurried to the section for the Federal Government, finding a series of numbers for the Environmental Protection Agency. He dialed the general information number. A recording answered saying that the EPA was open from nine to five. It was not yet nine.

Charles then flipped to the section for the Commonwealth of Massachusetts. He wanted to find the incidence of leukemia and lymphoma along the course of the Pawtomack River. But there was no listing for a Tumor or Cancer Registry. Instead his eye caught the words "Vital Statistics." He called that number but got the identical recording he'd gotten calling the EPA. Checking the time, Charles realized that he had about twenty minutes before the bureaucratic offices would be open.

He went over to Ellen and began helping her set up to analyze whether any of the mice they'd injected with the mammary cancer antigen showed any signs of increased immunological activity. Ellen was obviously not speaking. Charles could tell she was angry and felt that she was taking advantage of their familiarity.

While he worked Charles allowed himself to fantasize about his latest research approach. What if the mice injected with the mammary cancer antigen responded to the antigen rapidly and the acquired sensitivity could be easily transferred to the cancerous mice via the transfer factor? Then the cancerous mice would cure themselves of that particular strain. It was beautifully simple . . . maybe too simple, thought Charles. If only it would work. If only he could speed up the whole process for Michelle . . .

The next time Charles looked up, it was well after nine. Leaving Ellen in her sullen mood, Charles went back to his desk and called the EPA General Information number. This time it was answered by a woman with a bored Boston accent.

Charles introduced himself and said he wanted to report serious dumping of poisonous material into a river.

The woman was not impressed. She put Charles on hold.

Another woman picked up, who sounded so similar to the first that Charles was surprised when she asked him to repeat his request.

"You've got the wrong extension," said the woman. "This

is the Water Programs Division and we don't handle dumping. You want the Toxic Chemicals Program. Just a minute."

Charles was again put on hold. There was a click followed by a dial tone. Charles dropped the receiver and grabbed the phone directory. Checking under the EPA he found the listing for Toxic Chemical Program and dialed it.

An identical voice answered. Charles wondered if they cloned people at the EPA. Charles repeated his request but was told that the Toxic Chemical Program had nothing to do with infractions and that he should call the number for Oil and Hazardous Material Spills. She gave it to him and hung up before he could reply.

He redialed, punching the numbers so hard that the tip of his middle finger tingled in protest.

Another woman! Charles repeated his request without trying to hide his annoyance.

"When did the spill take place?" asked the woman.

"This is continuous dumping, not a one-time accident."

"I'm sorry," said the woman. "We only handle spills."

"Can I speak to your supervisor?" growled Charles.

"Just a minute," sighed the woman.

Charles waited impatiently, rubbing his face with his hands. He was perspiring.

"Can I help you?" asked still another woman coming on the line.

"I certainly hope so," said Charles. "I'm calling to report that there is a factory regularly dumping benzene which is a poison."

"Well, we don't handle that," interrupted the woman. "You'll have to call the proper state agency."

"What?" yelled Charles. "What the hell does the EPA do then?"

"We are a regulatory agency," said the woman calmly, "tasked to regulate the environment."

"I would think that dumping a poison into a river would be something that would concern you."

"It very well could be," agreed the woman, "but only after

the state had looked into it. Do you want the number for the proper state agency?"

"Give it to me," said Charles wearily. As he hung up he caught Ellen staring at him. He glared and she went back to work.

Charles waited for the dial tone, then dialed again.

"Okay," said the woman after hearing his problem. "What river are you talking about?"

"The Pawtomack," said Charles. "My God, am I finally talking to the right people?"

"Yes, you are," reassured the woman. "And where is the factory you think is dumping?"

"The factory is in Shaftesbury," said Charles.

"Shaftesbury?" questioned the woman. "That's in New Hampshire, isn't it?"

"That's right but . . ."

"Well, we don't handle New Hampshire."

"But the river is mostly in Massachusetts."

"That might be," said the woman, "but the origin is in New Hampshire. You'll have to talk to them."

"Give me strength," muttered Charles.

"Excuse me?"

"Do you have their number?"

"No. You'll have to get it through Information."

The line went dead.

Charles called New Hampshire information and obtained the number to State Services. There was no listing for Water Pollution Control, but after calling the main number, Charles got the extension he wanted. Thinking that he was beginning to sound like a recording, he repeated his request once again.

"Do you want to report this anonymously?" asked the woman.

Surprised by the question, Charles took a moment to respond. "No. I'm Dr. Charles Martel, R.D. #1, Shaftesbury."

"All right," said the woman slowly, as if she were writing the material down. "Where does the alleged dumping occur?"

"In Shaftesbury. A company called Recycle, Ltd. They're discarding benzene in the Pawtomack."

"Okay," said the woman. "Thank you very much."

"Wait a minute," called Charles. "What are you going to do?"

"I'll turn this over to one of our engineers," said the woman. "And he'll look into it."

"When?"

"I can't say for certain."

"Can you give me an idea?"

"We're pretty busy with several oil spills down at Portsmouth, so it will probably be several weeks."

Several weeks wasn't what Charles wanted to hear.

"Are any of the engineers around now?"

"No. Both of them are out. Wait! Here comes one now. Would you like to speak to him?"

"Please."

There was a short delay before a man came on the line.

"Larry Spencer here!" said the engineer.

Charles quickly told the man why he was calling and that he'd like someone to check out the dumping immediately.

"We've got a real manpower problem in this department," explained the engineer.

"But this is really serious. Benzene is a poison, and a lot of people live along the river."

"It's all serious," said the engineer.

"Is there anything I can do to speed things up?" asked Charles.

"Not really," said the engineer. "Although you could go to the EPA and see if they're interested."

"That's who I called first. They referred me to you."

"There you go!" said the engineer. "It's hard to predict which cases they'll take on. After we do all the dirty work they usually help, but sometimes they're interested from the start. It's a crazy, inefficient system. But it's the only one we've got."

Charles thanked the engineer and rang off. He felt the man

was sincere and at least he'd said that the EPA might be interested after all. Charles had noticed the EPA was housed in the JFK Building at government center in Boston. He wasn't going to try another phone call; he decided he'd go in person. Restlessly Charles got to his feet and reached for his coat.

"I'll be right back," he called over to Ellen.

Ellen didn't respond. She waited several full minutes after the door closed behind Charles before checking the corridor. Charles was nowhere to be seen. Returning to the desk, Ellen dialed Dr. Morrison's number. She had convinced herself that Charles was acting irresponsibly, even taking into consideration his daughter's illness, and that it wasn't fair for him to jeopardize her job as well as his own. Dr. Morrison listened gravely to Ellen, then told her he'd be right down. Before he hung up he mentioned that her help in this difficult affair would not go unrecognized.

Charles felt a building frenzy when he left the Weinburger. Everything was going poorly, including his idea of revenge. After his time on the phone, he was no longer so positive he could do anything about Recycle, Ltd. short of going up there with his old shotgun. The image of Michelle in her hospital bed again rose to haunt him. Charles did not know why he was so certain she was not going to respond to the chemotherapy. Maybe it was his crazy way of forcing himself to deal with the worst possible case, because he recognized that chemotherapy was her only hope. "If she has to have leukemia," cried Charles shaking the Pinto's steering wheel, "why can't she have lymphocytic where chemotherapy is so successful."

Without realizing it, Charles had allowed his car to slow below forty miles an hour, infuriating the other drivers on the road. There was a cacophony of horns, and as people passed him, they shook their fists.

After stashing his car in the municipal parking garage, Charles made his way up the vast bricked walk between the JFK Federal Building and the geometric City Hall. The buildings acted as a wind tunnel and Charles had to lean into the gusts to walk. The sun was weakly shining at that moment, but a gray cloud bank was approaching from the west. The temperature was twenty-four degrees.

Charles pushed through the revolving door and searched for a directory. To his left was an exhibition of John F. Kennedy photographs and straight ahead, next to the elevator, a make-shift coffee and donut concession had been set up.

Dusting Charles with a fine layer of confectioner's sugar as she spoke, one of the waitresses pointed out the directory. It was hidden behind a series of smiling teenage photos of John F. Kennedy. The EPA was listed on the twenty-third floor. Charles scrambled onto an elevator just before the door closed. Looking around at his fellow occupants, Charles wondered about the strange predominance of green polyester.

Charles got out on the twenty-third floor and made his way to an office marked DIRECTOR. That seemed like a good place to start.

Immediately inside the office was a large metal desk and typing stand dominated by an enormous woman whose hair was permed into a profusion of tight curls. A rhinestone-encrusted cigarette holder, capped by a long, ultrathin ciga-rette, protruded jauntily from the corner of her mouth and competed for attention with her prodigious bosom that taxed the tensile strength of her dress. As Charles approached she adjusted the curls at her temples, viewing herself in a small hand mirror.

"Excuse me," said Charles, wondering if this was one of the women he'd spoken to on the phone. "I'm here to report a recycling plant that's dumping benzene into a local river. Whom do I speak with?"

Continuing to pat her hair, the woman suspiciously exam-ined Charles. "Is benzene a hazardous substance?" she de-manded.

"Damn right it's hazardous," said Charles.

"I suppose you should go down to the Hazardous Materials Division on the nineteenth floor," said the woman with a tone that suggested "you ignorant slob."

After eight flights of stairs, Charles emerged on nineteen,

which had a totally different atmosphere. All except weight-bearing walls were removed, so that one could look from one end of the building to the other. The floor was filled with a maze of chest-height metal dividers separating the area into tiny cubicles. Above the scene hung a haze of cigarette smoke and the unintelligible murmur of hundreds of voices.

Charles entered the maze, noticing there were poles resembling street signs, describing the various departments. The Hazardous Materials Division was helpfully adjacent to the stairwell Charles had used, so he began to look at the signs delineating the subdivisions. He passed the Noise Program, the Air Program, the Pesticide Program, and the Radiation Program. Just beyond the Solid Waste Program he saw the Toxic Waste Program. He headed in that direction.

Turning off the main corridor, Charles again confronted a desk serving as a kind of barrier to the interior. It was a much smaller desk and occupied by a slender black fellow who had apparently taken great effort to brush his naturally curly hair straight. To his credit, the man gave Charles his full attention. He was fastidiously dressed and when he spoke, he spoke with an accent almost English in its precision.

"I'm afraid you're not in the right section," said the young man after hearing Charles's request.

"Your division doesn't handle benzene?"

"We handle benzene all right," said the man, "but we just handle the permits and licensing of hazardous materials."

"Where do you suggest I go?" asked Charles, controlling himself.

"Hmmm," said the man, putting a carefully manicured finger to the tip of his nose. "You know, I haven't the slightest idea. This has never come up. Wait, let me ask somebody else."

With a light, springy step, the young man stepped around the desk, smiled at Charles, and disappeared into the interior of the maze. His shoes had metal taps and the sound carried back to Charles, distinct from the sounds of nearby typewriters. Charles fidgeted as he waited. He had the feeling his efforts were going to turn out to be totally in vain.

The young black came back.

"Nobody really knows where to go," he admitted. "But it was suggested that perhaps you could try the Water Programs Division on the twenty-second floor. Maybe they can help."

Charles thanked the man, appreciating at least his willingness to help, and returned to the stairwell. With dampened enthusiasm but augmented anger, Charles climbed the six flights of stairs to the twenty-second floor. When he'd passed the twenty-first floor he'd had to skirt a group of three young men passing a joint among them. They'd eyed Charles with brazen arrogance.

The twenty-second floor was a mix of offices with normal plasterboard walls alternating with open areas containing chest-high dividers. At a nearby watercooler, Charles got directions to the Water Programs Division.

Charles found the receptionist's desk but it was empty. A smoldering cigarette suggested the occupant was in the vicinity but even after a short wait, no one materialized. Emboldened by exasperation, Charles stepped around the desk and entered the interior office space. Some of the cubicles were occupied with people on the phone or busy at a typewriter. Charles wandered until he came upon a man carrying a load of federal publications.

"Pardon me," said Charles.

The man eased the stack of pamphlets onto his desk and acknowledged Charles. Charles went through his now-automatic routine. The man straightened the pile of pamphlets while he thought, then turned to Charles. "This isn't the right department for reporting that kind of thing."

"Jesus Christ!" Charles exploded. "This is the Water Department. I want to report a poisoning of water."

"Hey, don't get mad at me," defended the man. "We're only tasked with monitoring water treatment facilities and sewerage disposal facilities."

"I'm sorry," said Charles with little sympathy. "You have no idea how frustrating this is. I have a simple complaint. I know a factory that's dumping benzene into a river."

"Maybe you should try the Hazardous Substance department," said the man.

"I already did."

"Oh," said the man, still thinking. "Why don't you try the Enforcement Division up on twenty-three?"

Charles eyed the man for a moment, dumbfounded. "Enforcement Division?" echoed Charles. "Why hasn't someone suggested that before?"

"Beats me," said the man.

Charles muttered obscenities under his breath as he found another stairwell and climbed to the twenty-third floor. He passed the Financial Management Branch, the Personnel Branch, and the Program Planning and Development Branch. Just beyond the men's room was the Enforcement Division. Charles stepped inside.

A black girl with large, purple-shaded glasses looked up from the latest Sidney Sheldon novel. She must have been at a good part because she didn't hide her irritation at being bothered.

Charles told her what he wanted.

"I don't know anything about that," said the girl.

"Whom should I talk to?" said Charles slowly.

"I don't know," said the girl, going back to her book.

Charles leaned on the desk with his left hand, and with his right snatched away the paperback. He slammed it down on the desk so that the girl jumped back.

"Sorry I lost your place," said Charles. "But I'd like to speak to your supervisor."

"Miss Stevens?" asked the girl, unsure of what Charles might do next.

"Miss Stevens will be fine."

"She's not in today."

Charles drummed his fingers on the desk, resisting the temptation to reach over and give the girl a shake.

"All right," he said. "How about the next person in command who is here."

"Mrs. Amendola?" suggested the girl.

"I don't care what her name is."

Keeping a wary eye on Charles, the young woman got to her feet and disappeared.

When she reappeared, five minutes later, she had a concerned woman in tow who looked about thirty-five.

"I'm Mrs. Amendola, assistant supervisor here. Can I help you?"

"I certainly hope so," said Charles. "I'm Dr. Charles Martel and I'm trying to report a factory that is dumping poisonous chemicals into a river. I have been sent from one department to another until someone suggested there was an Enforcement Division. But when I arrived here the receptionist was somewhat less than cooperative, so I demanded to speak to a supervisor."

"I told him that I didn't know anything about dumping chemicals," explained the young black girl.

Mrs. Amendola considered the situation for a moment, then invited Charles to follow her.

After passing a dozen cubicles, they entered a tiny and windowless office enlivened with travel posters. Mrs. Amendola motioned toward a lounge chair and squeezed herself behind the desk.

"You must understand," said Mrs. Amendola, "we don't have people walking in off the street with your kind of complaint. But of course, that doesn't excuse rudeness."

"What the hell do you people enforce if it's not fouling the environment," said Charles with hostility. After leading him to her office to placate him, Charles had the feeling that she was just going to refer him to another department.

"Our main job," explained the woman, "is to make sure that factories handling hazardous waste have filed for all the proper permits and licenses. It's a law that they do this and we enforce the law. Sometimes we have to take businesses to court and fine them."

Charles lowered his face into his hands and massaged his

scalp. Apparently the absurdity that Mrs. Amendola was describing was not apparent to her.

"Are you all right?" Mrs. Amendola tilted forward in her chair.

"Let me be sure I understand what you're saying," said Charles. "The primary task of the Enforcement Division of the EPA is to make sure that paperwork gets done. It has nothing to do with enforcing the Clean Water Act or anything like that?"

"That's not entirely correct," said Mrs. Amendola. "You must remember that the whole concern for the environment is relatively new. Regulations are still being formulated. The first step is registering all users of hazardous materials and informing them of the rules. Then and only then will we be in a position to go after the violators."

"So, for now, unscrupulous factories can do what they want," said Charles.

"That's not entirely correct either," said Mrs. Amendola. "We do have a surveillance branch which is part of our analytical laboratory. Under the present administration our budget has been cut and unfortunately that branch is quite small, but that's the place your complaint should go. After they document a violation, they turn it over to us and we assign the case to one of the EPA lawyers. Tell me, Dr. Martel. What is the name of the factory you are concerned about?"

"Recycle, Ltd. in Shaftesbury," said Charles.

"Why don't we check their paperwork?" said Mrs. Amendola rising from her desk.

Charles followed the woman out of her tiny office and down a long corridor. She paused at a secured door and inserted a plastic card in a slot.

"We're going on-line with a pretty sophisticated data processor," said Mrs. Amendola, holding the door open for Charles, "so we're having to tighten security."

Inside the room the air was cooler and cleaner. There was no odor of cigarette smoke. Apparently the computer terminal's well-being was more important than employee health.

Mrs. Amendola sat down in front of a free terminal and typed in RECYCLE, LTD., SHAFTESBURY, N.H. There was a ten-second delay after which the cathode ray tube blinked to life. Recycle, Ltd. was described in computer shorthand, including the fact that it was wholly owned by Breur Chemicals of New Jersey. Then all the hazardous chemicals involved with the plant were listed, followed by the date applications for permit or license were filed and the date they were granted.

"What chemicals are you interested in?" said Mrs. Amendola.

"Benzene, mostly."

"Here it is, here. EPA hazardous chemical number U019. Everything seems to be in order. I guess they're not breaking any laws."

"But they're dumping the stuff directly in the river!" exclaimed Charles. "I know that's against the law."

The other occupants of the room looked up from their work, shocked at Charles's outburst. Churchlike speech was the unwritten law in the computer terminal room.

Charles lowered his voice. "Can we go back to your office?"

Mrs. Amendola nodded.

Back in the tiny office, Charles moved forward to the edge of the chair. "Mrs. Amendola, I'm going to tell you the whole story because I think you might be able to help me."

Charles went on to tell about Michelle's leukemia, Tad Schonhauser's death from aplastic anemia, his discovery and confirmation of the benzene in the pond, and his visit to Recycle, Ltd.

"My God!" she said when Charles paused.

"Do you have children?" asked Charles.

"Yes!" said Mrs. Amendola with true fear in her voice.

"Then maybe you can understand what this is doing to me," said Charles. "And maybe you can understand why I want to do something about Recycle, Ltd. I'm sure a lot of kids live along the Pawtomack. But obviously I need some help."

"You want me to try to get the EPA involved," said Mrs. Amendola. A statement, not a question.

"Exactly," said Charles, "or tell me how to do it."

"It would be best if you made your complaint in writing. Address it to me!"

"That's easy," said Charles.

"What about some documented proof? Could you get that?"

"I already have the analysis of the pond water," said Charles.

"No, no," said Mrs. Amendola. "Something from the factory itself: a statement by a former employee, doctored records, photos of the actual dumping. Something like that."

"It's possible, I suppose," said Charles, thinking about the last suggestion. He had a Polaroid camera . . .

"If you could supply me with some kind of proof, I think I could get the Surveillance Branch to confirm it, then authorize a full-scale probe. So it's up to you. Otherwise it will just have to wait its turn."

As Charles left the JFK Federal Building he was again fighting a feeling of depression. He was much less confident now about convincing any authority to do anything about Recycle, Ltd. Consequently, the idea of taking matters into his own hands was an increasingly enjoyable fantasy.

The more he thought about Breur Chemicals, the angrier he became that a handful of dull businessmen sitting around in oak-paneled conference rooms in New Jersey could destroy his happiness and rob him of that which he loved the most. Approaching the Weinburger, Charles decided he'd call the absentee parent company and let them know how he felt about them.

Since the Brighton scandal hit the media, security had been tightened at the Weinburger, and Charles had to knock on the massive glass door before it slid open. He was greeted by Roy, the guard, who demanded to see his identification.

"It's me, Roy," said Charles, waving his hand in front of Roy's face. "Dr. Martel."

"Orders," explained Roy, with his hand still outstretched.

"Administrative nonsense," mumbled Charles as he searched for his ID. "What next?"

Roy shrugged, waited to see the card, which Charles stuck two inches away from his face, then ceremoniously stepped aside. Even the usually coy Miss Andrews turned away without honoring him with her usual come-over-and-talk-to-me smile.

Charles ditched his coat, called information for New Jersey, and dialed Breur Chemicals. As he waited he looked around the lab wondering if Ellen was still offended. He didn't see her and decided she must be in the animal room. At that moment Breur Chemicals answered the phone.

Later Charles admitted to himself he should not have called. He'd already had enough bad experiences that morning to have guessed what it would have been like to try to call a giant corporation with what they would consider a bothersome complaint. Charles was switched over to a low-level man in the Public Relations department.

Rather than try to placate Charles, the man accused him of being one of those unpatriotic nuts whose stupid and unfounded environmental concerns were responsible for putting American industry in a poor competitive position with companies overseas. The conversation degenerated into a shouting match about dumping benzene with Charles saying they were and the man saying they were not.

He slammed the phone down and spun around in a fury, looking for a way to vent his anger.

The door to the corridor opened and Ellen entered.

"Have you noticed?" asked Ellen with irritating nonchalance.

"Noticed what?" snapped Charles.

"All the lab books," said Ellen. "They're gone."

Charles leaped to his feet, scanning his desk, then the countertops.

"There's no sense looking for them," said Ellen. "They're upstairs."

"What the hell for?"

"After you left this morning, Dr. Morrison stopped in to check on our progress with Canceran. Instead he caught me working with the mice we'd given the mammary cancer antigen. Needless to say, he was shocked that we were doing our own work. I'm supposed to tell you to go to Dr. Ibanez's office as soon as you appeared."

"But why did they take the books?" asked Charles. Fear blunted the edge of his anger. As much as he hated administrative authority, he also feared it. It had been that way ever since college where he'd learned that an arbitrary decision from the Dean's office could affect his whole life. And now the administration had invaded his world and arbitrarily taken his lab books which for Charles was like taking a hostage. The contents of the lab books were associated in his mind with helping Michelle, despite how far-fetched that was in reality.

"I think you'd better ask Dr. Morrison and Dr. Ibanez that question," said Ellen. "Frankly, I knew it was going to come to something like this."

Ellen sighed and tossed her head in an I-told-you-so fashion. Charles watched her, surprised at her attitude. It added to his feeling of isolation.

Leaving his lab, he wearily climbed up the fire stairs to the second floor and walked past the familiar row of secretaries and presented himself to Miss Veronica Evans for the second time in two days. Although she was obviously unoccupied, she took her sweet time looking up over her glasses at Charles.

"Yes?" she said as if Charles were a servant. Then she told him to wait on a small leather couch. Charles was certain that the delay was made to impress upon him that he was a pawn. Time dragged while Charles could not decide which was the stronger emotion: anger, fear, or panic. But the need to get back his lab books kept him in his place. He had no idea if they were technically his property or the institute's.

The longer he sat, the less certain he became that the books detailing his recent work would be a strong bargaining point. He began to wonder if Ibanez might actually fire him. He tried to think what he could do if he had trouble getting another research position. He felt so out of touch with clinical medicine that he didn't think he could do that. And if he got fired, he wondered with renewed panic if he'd still be covered by health insurance. That was a real concern because Michelle's hospital bills were going to be astronomical.

There was a discreet buzz on the intercom panel, and Miss Evans turned to Charles imperiously and said: "The director will see you now."

Dr. Carlos Ibanez stood up behind his antique desk as Charles entered. His figure was backlit from the windows, making his hair and goatee shine like polished silver.

Directly in front of the desk were Joshua Weinburger, Sr. and Joshua Weinburger, Jr., whom Charles had met at infrequent mandatory social functions. Although close to eighty, the senior seemed more animated than the junior, with lively blue eyes. He regarded Charles with great interest.

Joshua Weinburger, Jr. was the stereotypical businessman, impeccably attired, obviously extremely reserved. He glanced at Charles with a mixture of disdain and boredom, switching his attention back to Dr. Ibanez almost immediately.

Seated to the right of the desk was Dr. Morrison, whose dress mirrored Joshua Weinburger, Jr.'s in its attention to detail. A silk handkerchief, which had been carefully folded, then casually flared, protruded from his breast pocket.

"Come in, come in!" commanded Dr. Ibanez good-naturedly.

Charles approached Dr. Ibanez's huge desk, noticing the conspicuous lack of a fourth chair. He ended up standing between the Weinburgers and Morrison. Charles didn't know what to do with his hands, so he stuck them into his pockets. He looked out of place among these businessman with his frayed oxford-cloth shirt, his wide out-of-style tie, and poorly pressed slacks.

"I think we should get right to business," said Dr. Ibanez. "The Weinburgers, as co-chairmen of the board of directors, have graciously come to help us manage the current crisis."

"Indeed," said Weinburger, Jr., turning slightly in his chair so as to look up at Charles. He had a tremor of his head and it rotated rapidly in a short arc to and fro. "Dr. Martel, it's not the policy of the board of directors to interfere in the creative process of research. However, there are occasionally circumstances in which we must violate this rule and the current crisis is such a time. I think you should know that Canceran is a potentially important drug for Lesley Pharmaceuticals. To be very blunt, Lesley Pharmaceuticals is in precarious financial condition. Within the last few years, their patents have run out on their line of antibiotics and tranquilizers, and they are in desperate need of a new drug to market. They have committed their scarce resources into developing a chemotherapy line, and Canceran is the product of that research. They hold the exclusive patent on Canceran but must get the drug on the market. The sooner the better."

Charles studied the faces of the men. Obviously they weren't going to dismiss him summarily. The idea was to soften him up, make him understand the financial realities, then convince him to recommence work on Canceran. He had a glimmer of hope. The Weinburgers couldn't have risen to their positions of power without intelligence, and Charles began to formulate in his mind the way he would convince them that Canceran was a bad investment, that it was a toxic drug and would probably never be marketed.

"We already know what you discovered about the toxicity of Canceran," said Dr. Ibanez, taking a short puff on his cigar and unknowingly undermining Charles. "We realize that Dr. Brighton's estimates are not entirely accurate."

"That's a generous way of putting it," said Charles, realizing with dismay that his trump card had been snatched from him. "Apparently all the data in the Canceran studies done by Dr. Brighton has been falsified." He watched the reaction of the Weinburgers out of the corners of his eyes, hoping for a response but seeing none.

"Most unfortunate," agreed Dr. Ibanez. "The solution is salvaging what we can and going forward."

"But my estimates suggest the drug is extremely toxic," said Charles desperately, "so toxic, in fact, that it might have to be given in homeopathic doses."

"That's not our concern," said Joshua Weinburger, Jr. "That's a marketing problem, and that's the one department at Lesley Pharmaceuticals that is outstanding. They could sell ice to Eskimos."

Charles was dumbfounded. There wasn't even the pretense of ethicality. Whether the product would help people made no difference. It was business—big business.

"Charles!" said Dr. Morrison, speaking for the first time. "We want to ask if you could run the efficacy and toxicity studies concurrently."

Charles switched his gaze to Dr. Morrison and stared at him with contempt. "That kind of approach would be reducing inductive research to pure empiricism."

"We don't care what you call it," said Dr. Ibanez with a smile. "We just want to know if it could be done."

Joshua Weinburger, Sr. laughed. He liked aggressive people and aggressive ideas.

"And we don't care how many test animals you use," said Morrison generously.

"That's right," agreed Dr. Ibanez. "Although we'd recommend you use mice since they're considerably cheaper, you can use as many as you'd like. What we're suggesting is doing efficacy studies at a very wide range of dosages. At the conclusion of the experiment, new toxicity values could be extrapolated and then substituted for the falsified data in the original toxicity study done by Dr. Brighton. Simple as that, and we'd save lots of time! What do you say, Charles?"

"Before you answer," said Morrison, "I think I should warn you that if you refuse, it will be in the best interests of the institute to let you go and seek someone who will give Canceran the attention it deserves."

Charles looked from face to face. His fear and panic had disappeared. Anger and contempt remained. "Where are my lab books?" he asked with a tired voice.

"Safe and sound in the vault," said Dr. Ibanez. "They are the property of the institute but you will get them back as soon as you finish Canceran. You see, we want you to concentrate

on Canceran and we feel that having your own books might
be too much of a temptation."

"We can't emphasize enough the need for speed," added
Joshua Weinburger, Jr. "But as an added incentive, if you can
have a preliminary study done in five months, we'll give you
a bonus of ten thousand dollars."

"I'd say that is very generous," said Dr. Ibanez. "But you
don't have to decide right this moment. In fact, we have agreed
to give you twenty-four hours. We don't want you to feel
coerced. But just so you know, we will be making preliminary
inquiries into finding your replacement. Until then, Dr. Charles
Martel."

With disgust, Charles whirled and headed for the door. As
he reached it, Dr. Ibanez called out: "One other thing. The
board of directors and the administration want to convey their
condolences regarding your daughter. We hope she recovers
quickly. The Institute health plan, by the way, only holds
while you are actively employed. Good day, doctor."

Charles wanted to scream. Instead he ran the length of the
administrative department and thundered down the metal fire
stairs to his office, but once there, he didn't know whether he
wanted to stay. For the first time he felt that being part of the
Weinburger Institute was a disgrace. He hated the fact that
they even knew about Michelle. On top of that they were using
Michelle's illness as leverage against him. It was an outrage.
God!

He looked around his laboratory, his home for the last eight
years. He felt as if he knew every piece of glassware, each
instrument, every bottle of reagent. It didn't seem fair that he
could be rudely plucked from this environment at whim, especially now that he was making such progress.

His eye fell on the culture he'd set up with Michelle's leukemia cells. With great effort he went over to the incubator,
peering in at the rows of carefully arranged glass tubes. It
appeared to be progressing well, and Charles felt a much-
needed sense of satisfaction. As far as he could tell, his progress of isolating and augmenting a cancer antigen seemed to

work as well with human cells as it did with animal cells. Since it was already time for the next step, Charles rolled up his sleeves and tucked his tie inside his shirt. Work was Charles's anesthetic and he bent to the task. After all, he had twenty-four hours before he'd have to bow to the demands of the administration. He knew but did not want to admit to himself that he had to give in for Michelle's sake. He really had no choice.

NINE

Coming back from Beth Israel Hospital where she'd paid an unsuccessful visit to Marge Schonhauser, Cathryn felt she was being stretched to the limits of her endurance. She'd guessed that Marge must have been bad off or she wouldn't have been hospitalized, but she was still not prepared for what she found. Apparently some vital thread had snapped in Marge's brain when Tad had died, because she had sunk into an unresponsive torpor, refusing to eat or even sleep. Cathryn had sat with Marge in silence until a feeling of tension drove Cathryn away. It was as if Marge's depression were infectious. Cathryn fled back to Pediatric Hospital, going from the casualty of one tragedy to the beginning of another.

Rising in the crowded elevator to Anderson 6, she wondered if what happened to Marge could happen to her or even to Charles. He was a physician and she would have guessed he'd be more capable of dealing with this kind of reality, yet his behavior was far from reassuring. As difficult as she found hospitals and illness, Cathryn tried to gird herself against the future.

The elevator arrived at Anderson 6 and Cathryn struggled

to reach the front of the car before the doors closed. She was impatient to get back to Michelle, because the child had been very reluctant to let Cathryn leave. Cathryn had talked Michelle into letting her go after lunch by promising she'd be back in half an hour. Unfortunately it was now closer to an hour.

Michelle had clung to Cathryn earlier that morning after Charles had left, insisting that Charles was angry with her. No matter what Cathryn had said, she'd not been able to change Michelle's mind.

Now Cathryn pushed open Michelle's door, hoping the child might be napping. At first she thought perhaps she was, because Michelle didn't move. But then Cathryn noticed the child had kicked off the covers and slid down in the bed with one leg tucked under her. From the doorway Cathryn could see that Michelle's chest was heaving violently and worst of all, her face had an alarmingly bluish cast with deep maroon-colored lips.

Rushing to the bedside, Cathryn grasped Michelle by the shoulders.

"Michelle," she cried, shaking the child. "What's wrong?"

Michelle's lips moved and her lids fluttered open but only whites showed; her eyes were rolled up in their sockets.

"Help!" cried Cathryn, running for the corridor. "Help!"

The charge nurse came from behind the nurses' station followed by an LPN. From a room beyond Michelle's came another RN. They all rapidly converged on Michelle's room, pushing past the panic-stricken Cathryn. One went to either side of the bed, another to the foot.

"Call a code," barked the charge nurse.

The nurse at the foot of the bed sped over to the intercom and yelled for the clerk at the nurses' station to call a code.

Meanwhile the charge nurse could feel a rapid, thready pulse. "Feels like V-tack," she said. "Her heart's beating so fast it's hard to feel individual beats."

"I agree," said the other nurse, putting the blood pressure cuff around Michelle's arm.

"She's breathing but cyanotic," said the charge nurse. "Should I give her mouth-to-mouth?"

"I don't know," said the second nurse, pumping up the blood pressure cuff. "Maybe it would help the cyanosis."

The third nurse came back to the bed and straightened out Michelle's leg while the charge nurse bent over and, squeezing Michelle's nose shut, placed her mouth over Michelle's and blew.

"I can get a blood pressure," said the second nurse. "Sixty over forty, but it's variable."

The charge nurse continued to breathe for Michelle but Michelle's own rapid respiration made it difficult. The nurse straightened up. "I think I'm hindering her more than helping her. I'd better hold off."

Cathryn remained pressed against the wall, terrorized by the scene in front of her, afraid to move lest she be in the way. She had no idea what was happening although she knew it was bad. Where was Charles!

A woman resident was the first doctor to arrive. She came through from the hallway so quickly that she had to grab the edge of the door to keep from falling on the polished vinyl floor. She ran directly to the bedside, grasping Michelle's wrist for a pulse.

"I think she has V-tack," said the charge nurse. "She's a leukemic. Myeloblastic. Day two of attempted induction."

"Any cardiac history?" demanded the woman resident, as she leaned over and elevated Michelle's eyelids. "At least the pupils are down."

The three nurses looked at each other. "We don't think she has any cardiac history. Nothing was said at report," said the charge nurse.

"Blood pressure?" asked the resident.

"Last time it was sixty over forty but variable," said the second nurse.

"V-tack," confirmed the woman resident. "Stand back a second."

The woman resident made a fist and brought it down on

Michelle's narrow thorax with a resounding thump that made
Cathryn wince.

An extremely young-looking chief resident arrived followed
by two others pushing a cart filled with all sorts of medical
paraphernalia and crowned with electronic instrumentation.

The woman resident gave a terse explanation of Michelle's
condition while the nurses rapidly attached EKG leads to
Michelle's extremities.

The charge nurse leaned over to one of the other nurses and
told her to page Dr. Keitzman.

The electronic box on the top of the cart began to spew
forth an endless strip of narrow graph paper on which Cathryn
could see the red squiggles of an EKG. The doctors grouped
around the machine, momentarily forgetting Michelle.

"V-tack all right," said the chief resident. "With the dyspnea
and cyanosis she's obviously hemodynamically compromised.
What does that mean, George?"

One of the other residents looked up, startled. "Means we
should cardiovert her immediately . . . I think."

"You think right," concurred the chief resident. "But let's
draw up some Lidocaine. Let's see, the kid's about fifty kilo-
grams, no?"

"A little less," said the woman resident.

"All right, fifty milligrams of Lidocaine. Also draw up a
milligram of atropine in case she goes into bradycardia."

The team functioned efficiently as one resident drew up the
medications, another got out the electrode paddles, while the
third helped position Michelle. One paddle went under Michelle's back, the other anteriorly on her chest.

"All right, stand back," said the chief resident. "We'll use
a fifty-watt second shock to start, programmed to be delivered
at the R-wave. Here goes."

He pressed a button and after a momentary delay Michelle's
body contracted, her arms and legs jumping off the surface of
the bed.

Cathryn watched in horror as the doctors stayed bent over
the machine, ignoring Michelle's violent reaction. Cathryn

could see the child's eyes open in utter bewilderment and her head lift off the bed. Thankfully her color rapidly reverted to normal.

"Not bad!" yelled the chief resident, examining the EKG paper as it came out of the machine.

"John, you're getting good at this stuff," agreed the woman resident. "Maybe you should think about doing it for a living."

All the doctors laughed and turned to Michelle.

Dr. Keitzman arrived breathless, hands jammed into the pockets of his long white coat. He went directly to the bed, his bespectacled eyes quickly scanning Michelle's body. He snatched up her hand, feeling for a pulse.

"Are you okay, chicken?" he asked, getting out his stethoscope.

Michelle nodded but didn't speak. She appeared dazed.

Cathryn watched as John, the chief resident, launched into a capsule summary of the event in what was to Cathryn incomprehensible medicalese.

Dr. Keitzman's upper lip pulled back in a characteristic spasm as he bent over Michelle, listening to her chest. Satisfied, he checked a run of EKG paper offered by John. At that moment he caught sight of Cathryn pressed up against the wall. Keitzman glanced at the charge nurse with a questioning expression. The charge nurse, following his line of sight, shrugged.

"We didn't know she was in here," said the charge nurse defensively.

Dr. Keitzman walked over to Cathryn and put a hand on her shoulder.

"How about you, Mrs. Martel?" asked Dr. Keitzman. "Are you all right?"

Cathryn tried to talk but her voice wouldn't cooperate, so she nodded like Michelle.

"I'm sorry you had to see this," said Dr. Keitzman. "Michelle seems fine and she undoubtedly did not feel anything. But I know this kind of thing is shocking. Let's go out in the hall for a moment. I'd like to talk to you."

Cathryn strained upward to see Michelle over Dr. Keitzman's shoulder.

"She'll be okay for a moment," assured Dr. Keitzman. Then, turning to the charge nurse, he said, "I'll be just outside. I want a cardiac monitor in here, and I'd like a cardiac consult. See if Dr. Brubaker can see her right away." Dr. Keitzman gently urged Cathryn out into the corridor. "Come down to the nurses' station; we can talk there."

Dr. Keitzman led Cathryn down the busy corridor to the chart room. There were Formica Parsons tables, chairs, two dictating telephones, and the massive chart racks. Dr. Keitzman pulled out a chair for Cathryn and she gratefully sat down.

"Can I get you something to drink?" suggested Dr. Keitzman. "Water?"

"No, thank you," managed Cathryn nervously. Dr. Keitzman's extremely serious manner was a source of new anxiety and she searched the man's face for clues. It was hard to see his eyes through his thick glasses.

The charge nurse's head came through the door. "Dr. Brubaker wants to know if he can see the patient in his office."

Dr. Keitzman's face contorted for a second while he pondered. "Tell him that she just had an episode of V-tack and I'd prefer he see her before she's moved around."

"Okay," said the charge nurse.

Dr. Keitzman turned to Cathryn. He sighed. "Mrs. Martel, I feel I must talk frankly with you. Michelle is not doing well at all. And I'm not referring specifically to this latest episode."

"What was this episode?" asked Cathryn, not liking the initial tone of the conversation.

"Her heart speeded up," said Dr. Keitzman. "Usually it's the upper part of the heart that initiates the beat." Dr. Keitzman gestured awkwardly to try to illustrate what he was saying. "But for some reason, the lower part of Michelle's heart took over. Why? We don't know yet. In any case, her heart suddenly began to beat so fast that there wasn't time for the heart to fill properly, so it pumped inefficiently. But that seems to be under control. What is worrying me is that she does not seem to be responding to the chemotherapy."

"But she's just started!" exclaimed Cathryn. The last thing that Cathryn wanted was for her hope to be undermined.

"That's true," agreed Dr. Keitzman. "However, Michelle's type of leukemia usually responds in the first few days. On top of that Michelle has the most aggressive case that I've ever seen. Yesterday we gave her a very strong and very successful drug called Daunorubicin. This morning when we did her blood count, I was shocked to see that there was almost no effect on the leukemic cells. This is very unusual although it does happen occasionally. So I decided to try something a little different. Usually we give a second dose of this medicine on the fifth day. Instead I gave her another dose today along with the Thioguanine and Cytarabine."

"Why are you telling me this?" asked Cathryn, certain that Dr. Keitzman knew she would not understand much of what he was saying.

"Because of your husband's response yesterday," said Dr. Keitzman. "And because of what Dr. Wiley and I said to you. I'm afraid your husband's emotions will interfere and he'll want to stop the medicines."

"But if they're not working, maybe they should be stopped," said Cathryn.

"Mrs. Martel. Michelle is an extremely sick child. These medicines are her only chance for survival. Yes, it's disappointing that as yet they have been ineffective. Your husband is right in saying her chances are slim. But without chemotherapy, she has no chance at all."

Cathryn felt the stabbing pain of guilt; she should have brought Michelle to the hospital weeks ago.

Dr. Keitzman stood up. "I hope you understand what I'm saying. Michelle needs your strength. Now, I want you to call your husband and have him come over. He's got to be told what's happened."

•   •   •

Even before the automatic radioactivity counter began to record the electrons emanating from the series of vials, Charles knew that the radioactive nucleotides had been absorbed and incorporated into the tissue culture of Michelle's leukemic cells. He was now in the last stages of preparing a concentrated solution of a surface protein that differentiated Michelle's leukemic cells from her normal cells. This protein was foreign to Michelle's body but was not rejected because of the mysterious blocking factor that Charles knew was in Michelle's system. It was this blocking factor that Charles had wanted to investigate. If only he knew something about the method of action of the blocking factor, perhaps it could be inhibited or eliminated. He was frustrated to be so close to a solution and have to stop. At the same time he realized that it was probably a five-year project with no guarantee of success.

Closing the cover on the tissue culture incubator, he walked to his desk, vaguely wondering why Ellen had not appeared. He wanted to discuss the Canceran project with someone knowledgeable, and she was the only person he could trust.

He sat down, trying not to think about the recent humiliating meeting with Dr. Ibanez and the Weinburgers. Instead he recalled the frustrating visit to the EPA offices that didn't make him feel much better. Yet he could laugh at his own naiveté in thinking that he could walk into a government agency and expect to accomplish something. He wondered if there would be any way that he could get some sort of photographic proof of Recycle's dumping. It was doubtful, but he'd try.

Perhaps if he were responsible for getting the evidence, he should sue Recycle directly rather than waiting for the EPA to do so. Charles knew very little about law, but he remembered there was a source of information open to him. The Weinburger Institute law firm on retainer.

The left lower drawer was Charles's spot for miscellaneous pamphlets. Close to the bottom he found what he was looking for: a skinny red booklet entitled *Welcome Aboard: This Is Your Weinburger Cancer Institute*. In the back was a list of important phone numbers. Under services was Hubbert, Hubbert, Garachnik and Pearson, 1 State Street, followed by several phone numbers. He dialed the first.

Identifying himself, Charles was immediately switched to Mr. Garachnik's office. His secretary was particularly cordial and within minutes, Charles found himself talking with Mr. Garachnik himself. Apparently the Weinburger was a valued customer.

"I need some information," said Charles, "about suing a company dumping poisonous waste into a public river."

"It would be best," said Mr. Garachnik, "if we have one of our environmental law persons look into the matter. However, if your questions are general, perhaps I can help. Is the Weinburger Institute becoming interested in environmental pursuits?"

"No," said Charles. "Unfortunately not. I'm interested in this personally."

"I see," said Mr. Garachnik, his tone becoming cool. "Hubbert, Hubbert, Garachnik and Pearson does not handle personal Weinburger employee legal problems unless special arrangement is made with the individual."

"That could be arranged," said Charles. "But as long as I've got you on the phone, why don't you just give me an idea about the process."

There was a pause. Mr. Garachnik wanted Charles to realize that he felt Charles's inquiry beneath his stature as a senior partner. "It could be done as an individual or class action suit. If it were an individual suit, you'd need specific damages and if . . ."

"I've got damages!" interrupted Charles. "My daughter has come down with leukemia!"

"Dr. Martel," said Mr. Garachnik with irritation. "As a physician you should know that establishing causation between the dumping and the leukemia would be extremely difficult. However, with a class action suit for the purpose of securing an injunction against the factory, you don't need specific damages. What you do need is the participation of thirty to forty people. If you want to pursue this further, I suggest you contact Thomas Wilson, one of our new, younger lawyers. He has a particular interest in environmental matters."

"Does it matter that the company is in New Hampshire?" asked Charles quickly.

"No, other than that it must be sued in a New Hampshire court," said Mr. Garachnik, obviously eager to terminate the conversation.

"What if it's owned by a corporation in New Jersey?"

"That might and might not compound the difficulties," said Mr. Garachnik, suddenly more interested. "What factory in New Hampshire are you talking about?"

"A place called Recycle, Ltd. in Shaftesbury," said Charles.

"Which is owned by Breur Chemicals of New Jersey," added Mr. Garachnik quickly.

"That's right," said Charles, surprised. "How did you know?"

"Because on occasion we indirectly represent Breur Chemicals. In case you're not aware, Breur Chemicals owns the Weinburger Institute even though it's run as a nonprofit organization."

Charles was stunned.

Mr. Garachnik continued: "Breur Chemicals founded the Weinburger Institute when they expanded into the drug industry by purchasing Lesley Pharmaceuticals. I was against it back then, but Weinburger, Sr. was committed to the idea. I was afraid of an antitrust action, but it never materialized because of the nonprofit cover. In any case, Dr. Martel, you essentially work for Breur Chemicals and in that capacity, you'd better think twice about suing anyone."

Charles hung the phone up very slowly. He could not believe what he'd just heard. He'd never cared about the financial side of the institute except to the extent that the Weinburger could supply him with research space and equipment. But now he learned that he was working for a conglomerate which was ultimately responsible for dumping cancer-causing waste into a public river as well as running a research institute supposedly interested in curing cancer. As for Canceran, the parent company controlled both the drug firm holding the patents and the research firm chosen to ascertain its efficiency.

No wonder Weinburger was so interested in Canceran!

The phone jangled Charles's taut nerves as it rang under his outstretched hand. As the source of the recent dreadful revelation, Charles debated answering it. Undoubtedly it was the administration calling, bent on harassing him with more pressure and more deceit.

Abruptly Charles's mind switched to Michelle. The call could be about his daughter. He snatched the receiver from the cradle and pressed it to his ear.

He was right. It was Cathryn and her voice had the same stiff quality it had the day before. His heart jumped into his throat.

"Is everything okay?"

"Michelle is not doing so well. There's been a complication. You'd better come over."

Charles grabbed his coat and ran out of his lab. At the front entrance, he knocked on the massive glass door, impatient for it to open.

"All right, all right!" said Miss Andrews, pressing the door release under her desk.

Charles squeezed out before the door was fully opened and disappeared from sight.

"What's the matter with him?" asked Miss Andrews, pressing the close switch. "Is he crazy or something?"

Roy adjusted his worn holster and shrugged.

Charles concentrated on hurrying to keep from guessing what had happened to Michelle. But after crossing the Charles, he got bogged down in traffic on Massachusetts Avenue. As he inched forward, he couldn't help worrying about what he was going to find when he got to Pediatric Hospital. Cathryn's words kept echoing in his head: "Michelle is not doing so well. There's been a complication." Charles felt panic tighten his stomach into a painful knot.

When he reached the hospital, he rushed inside and forced his way onto a full elevator. Maddeningly the car stopped at every floor. Eventually it reached the sixth, and Charles pushed his way off and hurried down to Michelle's room. The door was almost closed. He entered without knocking.

An elegant blond-haired woman straightened up from leaning over Michelle. She'd been listening to the girl's heart before Charles's entry. On the opposite side of the bed was a young resident dressed in hospital whites.

Charles gave the woman a cursory glance and looked down at his daughter with empathy submerging all other emotions. He wanted to grab her and shield her, but he was afraid she had become too fragile. His trained eyes inspected her rapidly and could detect a worsening in her condition since that morning. There was a greenish cast to her face, a change Charles had associated during his medical training with ensuing death. Her cheeks had become hollow with the skin taut over her facial bones. Despite an intravenous line attached to both arms, she looked dehydrated from the vomiting and high fever.

Michelle, lying flat on her back, looked up at her father with tired eyes. Despite her discomfort she managed a weak smile and for a brief moment her eyes shone with the incredible luster that Charles remembered.

"Michelle," said Charles softly, bending down so his face was close to hers. "How do you feel?" He didn't know what else to say.

Michelle's eyes clouded and she began to cry. "I want to go home, Daddy." She was reluctant to admit how bad she felt.

Biting his lip Charles glanced up at the woman next to him, embarrassed by his overwhelming emotion. Looking back down at Michelle, he put his hand on her forehead and smoothed back her thick black hair. Her forehead was hot and damp. Her fever had risen. Michelle reached up and grasped his hand.

"We'll talk about it," said Charles, his lips quivering.

"Excuse me," said the woman. "You must be Dr. Martel.

I'm Dr. Brubaker. Dr. Keitzman asked me to see Michelle. I'm a cardiologist. This is Dr. John Hershing, our chief resident."

Charles made no effort to respond to the introductions. "What happened?"

"She had an acute episode of ventricular tachycardia," said Dr. Hershing. "We cardioverted her immediately, and she's been very stable."

Charles looked at Dr. Brubaker. She was a tall, handsome woman with sharp features. Her blond hair was piled on top of her head in a loose chignon.

"What caused the arrhythmia?" asked Charles, still holding Michelle's hand.

"We don't know yet," said Dr. Brubaker. "My first thoughts are either an idiosyncratic reaction to the double dose of Daunorubicin, or a manifestation of her basic problem: some kind of infiltrative myopathy. But I'd like to finish my exam, if I may. Dr. Keitzman and your wife are in the chart room at the nurses' station. I understand they are waiting for you."

Charles lowered his eyes to Michelle. "I'll be right back, sweetheart."

"Don't go, Daddy," pleaded Michelle. "Stay with me."

"I won't go far," said Charles, gently loosing Michelle's grip. He was preoccupied by Dr. Brubaker's statement that Michelle had received a double dose of Daunorubicin. That sounded irregular.

Cathryn saw Charles before he saw her and leaped to her feet, throwing her arms around his neck.

"Charles, I'm so glad you're here." She buried her face in his neck. "This is so difficult for me to handle."

Holding Cathryn, Charles glanced around the small chart room. Dr. Wiley was leaning against the table, his eyes on the floor. Dr. Keitzman was sitting opposite from him, his legs crossed, and his hands clasped together over his knee. He appeared to be examining the fabric of his slacks. No one spoke, but Charles felt nervous, his eyes darting from one doctor to the other. The scene seemed too artificial, too staged. Something was coming and Charles hated the theatrics.

"All right," said Charles challengingly. "What's happening?"

Dr. Wiley and Dr. Keitzman started to speak simultaneously, then stopped.

"It's about Michelle," said Dr. Keitzman finally.

"I assumed as much," said Charles. The vise on his stomach turned another notch tighter.

"She's not doing as we would have hoped," said Dr. Keitzman with a sigh, looking up into Charles's face for the first time. "Doctors' families are always the most difficult. I think I'll call it Keitzman's law."

Charles was in no mood for humor. He stared at the oncologist, watching the man's face twist into one of its characteristic spasms. "What's this about a double dose of Daunorubicin?"

Dr. Keitzman swallowed. "We gave her the first dose yesterday but she did not respond. We gave her another today. We've got to knock down her circulatory leukemic cells."

"That's not the usual protocol, is it?" snapped Charles.

"No," Dr. Keitzman replied hesitantly, "but Michelle is not a usual case. I wanted to try . . ."

"Try!" shouted Charles. "Listen, Dr. Keitzman," Charles snapped, pointing a finger in Dr. Keitzman's face. "My daughter isn't here for you to try things on. What you're really saying is that her chances of remission are so poor that you're ready to experiment."

"Charles!" said Cathryn. "That's not fair."

Charles ignored Cathryn. "The fact of the matter, Dr. Keitzman, is that you are so certain she's terminal you abandoned orthodox chemotherapy. Well, I'm not sure your experimentation isn't lessening her chances. What about this cardiac problem. She's never had any trouble with her heart. Doesn't Daunorubicin cause cardiac problems?"

"Yes," agreed Dr. Keitzman, "but not usually this fast. I don't know what to think about this complication and that's why I asked for a cardiac consult."

"Well, I think it's the medicine," said Charles. "I agreed to chemotherapy, but I assumed you would be using the standard doses. I'm not sure I agree with doubling the usual treatment."

"If that's the case, then perhaps you should retain another oncologist," said Dr. Keitzman wearily, standing up and gathering his things. "Or just handle the case yourself."

"No! Please!" said Cathryn, letting go of Charles and clutching Dr. Keitzman's arm. "Please. Charles is just upset. Please don't leave us." Cathryn turned frantically to Charles. "Charles, the medicine is Michelle's only chance." She turned back to Dr. Keitzman, "Isn't that right?"

"That is true," said Dr. Keitzman. "Increasing the chemotherapy, even if it is an unusual approach, is the only hope for a remission, and a remission has to be obtained quickly if Michelle is going to survive this acute episode."

"What are you proposing, Charles?" said Dr. Wiley. "To do nothing?"

"She's not going to go into remission," said Charles angrily.

"You can't say that," said Dr. Wiley.

Charles backed up, watching the others in the room as if they were going to force him into submission.

"How do you think she should be treated?" asked Dr. Wiley.

"We can't do nothing, Charles," pleaded Cathryn.

Charles's mind screamed for him to get away. Within the hospital, close to Michelle, he could not think rationally. The idea of causing Michelle additional suffering was a torture, yet the concept of just allowing her to die without a fight was equally abhorrent. There were no alternatives open to him. Dr. Keitzman was making sense if there was a chance they could get a remission. But if a remission was impossible, then they were merely torturing the dying child. God!

Abruptly Charles turned and strode from the room. Cathryn ran after him. "Charles. Where are you going? Charles, don't go! Please. Don't leave me."

At the stair he finally turned, gripping Cathryn's shoulders. "I can't think here. I don't know what's right. Each alternative is as bad as another. I've been through this before. Familiarity doesn't make it easier. I've got to pull myself together. I'm sorry."

With a feeling of helplessness Cathryn watched him go through the door and disappear. She was alone in the busy corridor. She knew that if she had to, she could handle the situation even if Charles couldn't. She had to, for Michelle's sake. She walked back to the chart room.

"The strange thing," said Cathryn with a tremulous voice, "is that you two anticipated all this."

"Unfortunately we've had some experience with families of physicians," said Dr. Keitzman. "It's always difficult."

"But it's usually not this difficult," added Dr. Wiley.

"We were talking while you were gone," said Dr. Keitzman. "We feel that something must be done to ensure continuity of Michelle's care."

"Some kind of guarantee," said Dr. Wiley.

"It's mostly because time is so important," said Dr. Keitzman. "Even if the treatment were stopped for a day or two, it could mean the difference between success and failure."

"We're not suggesting that Charles's concerns are unfounded," assured Dr. Wiley.

"Absolutely not," agreed Dr. Keitzman. "In Michelle's case, with circulating leukemic cells unresponsive to the Daunorubicin, the outlook is not the best. But I think she deserves a chance no matter what the odds. Don't you agree, Mrs. Martel?"

Cathryn looked at the two doctors. They were trying to suggest something but she had no idea what it was. "Of course," said Cathryn. How could she disagree? Of course Michelle deserved every chance.

"There are ways of making sure that Charles cannot arbitrarily stop Michelle's treatment," said Dr. Wiley.

"The powers need only be evoked if they are needed," said Dr. Keitzman. "But it's good to have them just in case."

There was a pause.

Cathryn had the distinct impression that the doctors expected her to respond, but she had no idea what they were talking about.

"Let me give you an example," said Dr. Wiley, leaning forward in his chair. "Suppose a child desperately needs a transfusion. If the transfusion is not given, then the child will die. And further, suppose that one of the parents is a Jehovah's Witness. Then there is a conflict between the parents as to the proper treatment of the child. The doctors, of course, recognize the need for the transfusion to save the child. What do they do? They have the court award guardianship to the consenting parent. The court is willing to do this to guarantee the rights of the child. It's not that they disrespect the beliefs of the nonconsenting parent. It's just that they feel it's unfair for one individual to deprive another of lifesaving treatment."

Cathryn stared at Dr. Wiley in consternation. "You want me to assume guardianship of Michelle behind Charles's back?"

"Only for the specific purpose of maintaining treatment," said Dr. Keitzman. "It might save the child's life. Please understand, Mrs. Martel, we could do it without your help. We would ask the court to appoint a guardian, which is what we do when both parents resist established medical treatment. But it would be much simpler if you participated."

"But you're not giving Michelle standard treatment anymore," said Cathryn, remembering Charles's words.

"Well, it's not that unusual," said Keitzman. "In fact I've been working on a paper about increased chemotherapeutic doses in cases as recalcitrant as your daughter's."

"And you must admit that Charles has been acting bizarrely," added Dr. Wiley. "The strain of this may be too great. He may be incapable of making sensible decisions. In fact, I'd feel much better if we could also get Charles to seek some professional help."

"You mean see a psychiatrist?" asked Cathryn.

"I think it would be a good idea," said Dr. Wiley.

"Please understand us, Mrs. Martel," said Dr. Keitzman,

"we're trying to do our best, and as Michelle's doctors our primary concern is her well-being. We feel we must do everything in our power."

"I appreciate your efforts," said Cathryn, "but . . ."

"We know it sounds drastic," said Dr. Keitzman, "but once the legal papers are obtained, guardianship doesn't have to be evoked unless the situation calls for it. But then if Charles tried to take Michelle off treatment or even out of the hospital, we'd be in a position to do something about it."

"An ounce of prevention is worth a pound of cure," said Dr. Wiley.

"The idea doesn't make me feel comfortable," said Cathryn. "But Charles has been very strange. I can't believe he left like he did just now."

"I can understand it," said Dr. Keitzman. "I can sense that Charles is a man of action, and the fact that he cannot do anything for Michelle must drive him mad. He's under a terrible emotional burden, and that's why I think he could benefit from professional help."

"You don't think he could have a nervous breakdown, do you?" asked Cathryn with increasing anxiety.

Dr. Keitzman looked at Dr. Wiley to see if he wanted to answer, then he spoke: "I don't feel qualified to say. Certainly the strain is there. It's a matter of how strong his defenses are."

"I think it's a possibility," said Dr. Wiley. "In fact, I think he's showing certain symptoms. He doesn't seem to be in command of his emotions and I think his anger has been inappropriate."

Cathryn was swept by a turmoil of emotion. The idea that she was capable of going between Charles, the man she loved, and his daughter, whom she'd learned to love, was unthinkable. And yet if the strain was too much for Charles, and he interrupted Michelle's treatment, she would have to share the blame for not having the courage to help the child's doctors.

"If I were to do as you ask," said Cathryn, "what would be the procedure?"

"Hold on," said Dr. Keitzman, reaching for the phone. "I think the hospital attorney could answer that better than I."

Almost before Cathryn knew what was happening, the meeting with the hospital attorney was over, and Cathryn was hurrying after the man in the Boston courthouse. His name was Patrick Murphy. He had freckled skin and indeterminate light brown hair that could have been red at one time. But by far his most distinguishing characteristic was his personality. He was one of those rare people whom everyone instantly liked, and Cathryn was no exception. Even in her distraught state, she had been charmed by his gentle and forthright manner and engaging smile.

Cathryn was not sure when the conversation with the attorney had changed from discussing a hypothetical situation to discussing an actual one. Making the decision to petition for legal guardianship for Michelle behind Charles's back was so difficult that Cathryn had welcomed its accomplishment by default. Patrick had assured Cathryn, as had Dr. Keitzman, that the legal powers would not be used except in the unlikely instance that Charles tried to stop Michelle's treatment.

Still Cathryn felt very uneasy about the whole affair, especially since she had not had time to see Michelle in the rush to get to the court before the 4 P.M. deadline.

"This way if you will," said Patrick, pointing to a narrow stairwell. Cathryn had never been in a courthouse before, and it was nothing like she'd imagined. She'd thought it would be grand in some symbolic way, standing as it did for the concept of justice. Yet the Boston courthouse, which was actually over one hundred years old, was dirty and depressing, especially since, for security reasons, the public was forced to enter through the basement.

After ascending the narrow steel stairs, which Cathryn could not believe served as the sole public entrance to the court, they reached the old main hall. Here there was at least a shadow of former grandness with an arched two-story ceiling; marble pilasters and marble floors. But the plaster was chipped and cracked, and the elaborate moldings gave the appearance they were about to break free and fall to the floor below.

. Cathryn had to run a few steps to catch up with Patrick as he turned into the Probate Court. It was a long, narrow room with a heavy, dusty appearance, especially with the hundreds of aged ledgers sitting sideways on their low shelves to the right. On the left was a long scuffed and pitted counter where a coterie of court employees seemed suddenly roused from their diurnal slumber at the prospect of quitting time.

As Cathryn surveyed the room she did not feel the confidence and reassurance she'd hoped. Instead its shabbiness evoked images of being snared in a quagmire of red tape. Yet Patrick did not allow Cathryn to stop. He pulled her over to a smaller counter at the end of the room.

"I'd like to speak to one of the Assistant Registers of Probate," said Patrick to one of the bored clerks. She had a cigarette in the corner of her mouth, making her cock her head to the side to keep the smoke from stinging her eyes. She pointed to a man facing away from them.

Hearing the request, the man turned; he was on the phone but put up a finger for them to wait. After finishing his conversation, he came over to Cathryn and Patrick. He was tremendously overweight, a middle-aged man with a thick, flaccid layer of fat that shook when he walked. His face was all jowls, wattles, and deep creases.

"We have an emergency," explained Patrick. "We'd like to see one of the judges."

"Hospital guardianship case, Mr. Murphy?" questioned the Assistant Register knowingly.

"That's correct," said Patrick. "All the forms are filled out."

"Must say, you fellows are getting efficient," said the man. He looked up at the face of the institutional clock. "My God, you're cutting it close. It's almost four. I'd better check to be sure Judge Pelligrino is still here."

He waddled through a nearby doorway, his arms swinging almost perpendicularly to his body.

"Glandular problem," whispered Patrick. He put his brief-case on the counter and snapped it open.

Cathryn looked at the attractive young lawyer. He was dressed in the typical attorney fashion with a boxy, Ivy League, pin-striped suit. The slacks were slightly rumpled, particularly behind the knees, and they were about two inches too short, exposing black-socked ankles. With great attentive-ness, he arranged the forms which Cathryn had signed.

"Do you really think I should do this?" asked Cathryn abruptly.

"Absolutely," said Patrick, giving her one of his warm, spontaneous smiles. "It's for the child."

Five minutes later they were in the judge's chamber, and it was too late to turn back.

As different as the Boston courthouse was from Cathryn's imagination, so was Judge Louis Pelligrino. Instead of an older, gowned, Socratic figure, Cathryn found herself sitting across from a disturbingly handsome man wearing a well-tailored designer's suit. After donning stylish reading glasses, he accepted the papers from Patrick saying, "Jesus Christ, Mr. Murphy. Why is it you always show up at four o'clock?"

"Medical emergencies, your honor, adhere to a biological rather than a probate clock."

Judge Pelligrino peered at Patrick sharply over his half-glasses, apparently trying to decide if Patrick's retort was clever or presumptuously brazen. A slow smile appeared as he decided on the former. "Very good, Mr. Murphy. I'll accept that. Now, why don't you fill me in on these petitions."

As Patrick skillfully outlined the circumstances surrounding Michelle's illness and treatment as well as Charles's behavior, Judge Pelligrino examined the forms, seemingly not paying attention to the young lawyer. But when Patrick made an insignificant grammatical error, the judge's head shot up, and he corrected him.

"Where are the affidavits by Doctors Wiley and Keitzman?" asked Judge Pelligrino as Patrick finished.

The lawyer leaned forward and anxiously thumbed through the papers in the judge's hands. He snapped open his briefcase, and with great relief found the two documents and handed them over with an apology.

The judge read them in detail.

"And this is the adopted mother, I presume," said Judge Pelligrino, capturing Cathryn's attention.

"Indeed it is," said Patrick, "and she is understandably concerned about maintaining the proper treatment for the young girl."

Judge Pelligrino scrutinized Cathryn's face, and she felt herself blush defensively.

"I think it's important to emphasize," added Patrick, "that there is no marital discord between Charles and Cathryn Martel. The only issue is the wish to maintain the established method of treatment advocated by the appropriate medical authorities."

"I understand that," said Judge Pelligrino. "What I don't understand or like is the fact that the biological father is not here to be cross-examined."

"But that's precisely why Mrs. Martel is asking for emergency temporary guardianship," said Patrick. "Just a few hours ago, Charles Martel rushed away from a meeting with Mrs. Martel and Michelle's doctors. Mr. Martel expressed the belief that Michelle's treatment, which is her only chance at survival, be stopped, then left the conference. And, off the record, the attending physicians are concerned about his mental stability."

"That sounds like something that should be part of the record," said the judge.

"I agree," said Patrick, "but unfortunately that would require Mr. Martel seeing a psychiatrist. Perhaps it could be arranged for the full hearing."

"Would you like to add anything, Mrs. Martel?" asked the judge, turning to Cathryn.

Cathryn declined in a barely audible voice.

The judge arranged the papers on his desk, obviously thinking. He cleared his throat before he spoke: "I will allow the emergency temporary guardianship for the sole purpose of maintaining the recognized and established medical treatment." With a flourish he signed the form. "I will also appoint a guardian *ad litim* on the petition for guardianship to serve until the full hearing on the merits, which I want scheduled in three weeks."

"That will be difficult," said the Assistant Register, speaking for the first time. "Your schedule is fully booked."

"The hell with the schedule," said Judge Pelligrino, signing the second document.

"It will be difficult to prepare for a hearing in just three weeks," protested Patrick. "We'll need to obtain expert medical testimony. And there is legal research to be done. We need more time."

"That's your problem," said the judge without sympathy. "You're going to be busy anyway with the preliminary hearing on the temporary guardianship. By statute that must be in three days. So you'd best get cracking. Also I want the father apprised of these proceedings as soon as possible. I want him served no later than tomorrow with a citation either at the hospital or at his place of work."

Cathryn sat bolt upright, stunned. "You're going to tell Charles about this meeting?"

"Absolutely," said the judge, rising. "I hardly think it fair to deprive a parent of his guardianship rights without telling him. Now if you'll excuse me."

"But . . ." blurted Cathryn. She didn't finish her statement. Patrick thanked the judge and hurried Cathryn out of the judge's lobby, back into the main room of the Probate Court.

Cathryn was distraught. "But you said we wouldn't use this unless Charles actually stopped treatment."

"That's correct," said Patrick, confused at Cathryn's reaction.

"But Charles is going to find out what I've done," cried Cathryn. "You didn't tell me that. My God!"

TEN

Although the sun had set on schedule at four-thirty, no one in New England had seen it go down, including Charles, who was parking at the base of Main Street in Shaftesbury at the time. A heavy bank of clouds had moved in from the Great Lakes. The New England meteorologists were trying to decide when the front was going to collide with a flow of warm air from the Gulf of Mexico. They all agreed it was going to snow, but no one could decide how much or when.

By five-thirty, Charles was still sitting behind the steering wheel of the Pinto parked in the lee of the row of deserted old mill buildings. Every so often he'd scrape off a bit of the frost on the inside of the windshield and peer out. He was waiting until it was completely dark. To keep warm he started the engine every quarter hour and let it idle for five minutes. Just after six he was satisfied that the sky was a uniformly dark blanket and he opened the door and got out.

Recycle, Ltd. was about two hundred yards ahead as evidenced mainly by the single light they had near the office door. It had started to snow with large flakes that settled like feathers in short swooping arcs.

Charles opened the trunk and collected his gear: a Polaroid camera, a flashlight, and a few sample jars. Then he crossed the snow to the shadow of the empty brick mill and started to trudge toward Recycle, Ltd. After leaving Cathryn at the hospital, he had tried to sort through his confusing emotions. He could not come to a decision about Michelle's treatment although intuition still told him that the child was not going to go into remission. He couldn't get himself to deny her treatment, but he couldn't bear to see her suffer more than she had to. He felt trapped. As a consequence, he welcomed the idea of heading up to Shaftesbury and trying to obtain some hard evidence of benzene dumping. At least that satisfied his emotional need for action.

As he came to the end of the building, he stopped and looked around the corner. He now had a full view of the factory that had taken over the last abandoned mill building in the long row.

With the Polaroid and flashlight in his coat pockets and the sample jars in his hands, Charles rounded the corner and headed toward the Pawtomack River, initially moving parallel to the hurricane fence. Once he could no longer see the light over the factory entrance, he cut diagonally across the empty lot, reaching the fence close to the riverbank. First the flashlight, then the sample jars were gently tossed over to land in the snow. With the camera slung over his shoulder, Charles grasped the mesh and began to climb. He teetered on the top, then leaped for the ground, landing on his feet but tumbling over onto his back. Fearful of being seen in the open lot, he gathered his things and hurried over to the shadow of the old factory.

He waited for a few moments, listening to the familiar sounds coming from inside the building. From where he was standing, he could look across the mostly frozen Pawtomack River and make out the trees on the opposite bank. The river was about fifty yards wide at that point. When he had regained his breath, he struggled along the building, heading for the corner facing the river. The going was difficult because the snow covered all sorts of trash and debris.

Charles reached the side of the building facing the river and, shielding his eyes from the lazy snowflakes, he looked down at his goal: the two metal holding tanks. Unfortunately, they were close to the opposite end of the building. After a short pause, Charles set out climbing through the rusted and twisted remains of discarded machinery, only to find himself barred from further advance by a granite-lined sluice about ten feet across and five feet deep. The sluice came from a low arch beneath the building and ran toward the river bank where it was dammed with wooden planks. About midway in the opposite masonry wall was a connecting channel to a large lagoon. The fluid in the sluice and in the lagoon was not frozen and it had the unmistakable acrid smell of discarded industrial chemicals.

Immediately adjacent to the factory, Charles saw that two stout planks had been laid across the sluice. Putting his sample jars down, Charles flipped the planks over to rid them of their veneer of snow and ice. Then, with great care, he struggled across the makeshift bridge holding the sample jars under his right arm and using his left to support himself against the building.

On the opposite side of the sluice the ground sloped down and Charles could approach the level of the lagoon. From the makeshift appearance of the setup, particularly the incompetently constructed dam, Charles knew that the discarded chemicals in the lagoon continuously made their way into the river. He wanted a sample of that syrupy fluid. He bent down at the edge and, holding on to the upper lip of one of the jars, collected a pint or so of the slowly bubbling sludge. Using a bit of snow, Charles wiped off the jar, capped it, and left it to be retrieved on the way back. Meanwhile he wanted a photo of the dam, which kept this chemical cesspool from totally emptying itself into the river below.

•   •   •

Wally Crabb had taken an early dinner break from the rubber ovens with the two guys he played poker with: Angelo De-Jesus and Giorgio Brezowski. Sitting at one of the picnic tables in the lunchroom, they'd played blackjack while they absentmindedly consumed their sandwiches. It hadn't been a good evening for Wally. By six-twenty he was down about thirteen dollars and it didn't seem like his luck was going to change. And to make matters worse, Brezowski was teasing him by flashing his toothless smile after every hand, silently saying "so long, sucker." Brezo had lost his front teeth in a barroom brawl in Lowell, Massachusetts, two years ago.

Brezo dealt Wally a face card and a four of spades. When Wally asked him for a hit, Brezo socked him with another face card, sending him over twenty-one.

"Shit!" yelled Wally, slamming the cards down and swinging his massive legs from beneath the picnic table. He pushed himself to his feet and lumbered over to the cigarette machine.

"You out, big boy?" jeered Brezo, resuming play with Angelo.

Wally didn't answer. He put his coins in the cigarette machine, punched his selection, and waited. Nothing happened. At least nothing inside the machine. Inside Wally's brain it was like snapping a piano wire stretched to its tensile limit. With a powerful kick he jarred the machine, moving it back on its supports to thump the wall. Cocking his hand back to follow up with a right cross to the coin return, he saw a light flash outside the dark window.

To Brezo and Angelo's disappointment—they had been hoping to watch the destruction of the cigarette machine—Wally's cocked arm sank and he pressed his face against the window. "What the fuck, we going to have a thunderstorm now?" asked Wally. Then he saw the flash again, but this time caught a glimpse of its source. For an instant he saw a figure, arms to his face, legs slightly spread.

"It's a goddamned camera," said Wally, astonished. "Somebody is taking pictures of the lagoon."

Wally reached for the phone and dialed Nat Archer's office. He told the super what he'd seen.

"Must be that Martel nut," said Nat Archer. "Who are you with, Wally?"

"Just Brezo and Angelo."

"Why don't you three go out there and see who it is. If it's Martel, then teach him a lesson. Mr. Dawson told me that if he showed up again to make sure it was his last visit. Remember the guy is out there illegally. He's trespassing."

"You got it," said Wally, hanging up the receiver. Turning to his buddies and cracking his knuckles, he said, "We're going to have some fun. Get your coats."

After photographing the dam, Charles worked his way over to the metal holding tanks. With the flashlight he tried to make sense out of the profusion of pipes and valves. One pipe led directly to a fenced-off area at the edge of the parking lot and obviously served as the off-load site. Another pipe coursed away from the tanks and with a T-connector joined the roof drain conduit on its way to the river bank. Using great care to keep from slipping down the embankment, Charles managed to get to the edge, which was some twenty feet above the surface of the river. The roof drain ended abruptly, spilling its contents down the embankment. The smell of benzene was intense and below the pipe was a patch of open water. The rest of the river was solidly frozen and covered with snow. After taking several pictures of the pipe, Charles leaned out with his second jar and caught some of the fluid dripping from the end. When he thought he had enough, he closed the jar and left it next to the first one. He was almost finished; his mission was more successful than he had hoped. He just wanted to photograph the T-connection between the pipe from the storage tanks and the drain conduit and the feed pipe from the storage tanks back to where it emerged from the factory.

A slight wind had come up, and the once-lazy snowflakes were now being driven into Charles's face. Before taking the picture, he dusted the snow off the pipes, then sighed through the viewfinder. He wasn't satisfied. He wanted to get the T-connector and the storage tanks in the same photo, so he stepped over the pipes, squatted down, and sighted again. Satisfied, he depressed the shutter mechanism but nothing happened. Looking at the camera, he realized he hadn't turned the flash bar around. He did so quickly, then sighed again. Now he could see the storage tank, the pipe coming from the tank, and the juncture with the roof drain. It was perfect. He pushed the shutter release.

The flash of the camera was followed instantly by a sudden, powerful jerk as the Polaroid camera was torn from Charles's fingers. He looked up from his crouching position to see three men in hooded parkas, silhouetted against the dark sky. They had him cornered against the storage tanks. Before Charles could move, the camera was tossed end over end into the center of the black lagoon.

Charles stood up, struggling to see the faces beneath the hoods. Without words, the two smaller men lunged forward and grabbed his arms. The sudden movement caught Charles off guard and he didn't struggle. The third man, the big one, went through Charles's coat pockets, finding the small collection of photographs. With a flick of the wrist they followed the camera into the chemical pond, appearing like white wafers on the surface.

The men let Charles go and stepped back. Charles still couldn't see their faces, and it made their appearance that much more frightening. Charles panicked and tried to run between one of the smaller men and the storage tank. The man reacted instantly, jabbing a fist into Charles's face and connecting with his nose. The blow stunned Charles, bringing a slight trickle of blood down his chin.

"Nice poke, Brezo," laughed Wally.

Charles recognized the voice.

The men pushed him toward the chemical lagoon so that he stumbled over the pipes underfoot. Teasing him, they cuffed his head with open hands, slapping his ears. Charles vainly tried to parry the flutter of blows.

"Trespassing, eh?" said Brezo.

"Looking for trouble, eh?" said Angelo.

"I think he found it," said Wally.

They crowded Charles to the very edge of the cesspool of acrid chemicals. A glancing blow knocked his hat into the fluid.

"How about a quick dip?" taunted Wally.

With one arm over his face, Charles drew out his flashlight with the other hand and lashed at his nearest assailant.

Brezo eluded the roundhouse blow easily by shifting his weight.

Expecting contact and not getting it, Charles slipped in the melted snow and fell to his hands and knees in the foul mud. The flashlight shattered.

Brezo, having eluded the blow, found himself teetering on the edge of the lagoon. To keep from falling bodily into the pool, he was forced into the ooze to mid-calf before Wally grabbed his jacket, pulling him free.

"Shit!" cried Brezo as he felt the corrosive chemical singe his skin. He knew he had to get his leg into water as soon as possible. Angelo pulled Brezo's arm over his shoulder, supporting him and, as if in a three-legged race, the two men hurried back toward the entrance of Recycle, Ltd.

Charles scrambled to his feet and bolted for the two planks over the old sluice. Wally made a grab for Charles but missed him, and in the process slipped and fell to his hands and knees. Belying his bulk, he was back on his feet in an instant. Charles thundered over the planks forgetting his previous nervousness at crossing. He thought about pushing the planks into the sluice but Wally was too close behind.

Fearful of being thrown into the chemical lagoon, Charles ran as fast as possible, but the going was difficult. First he had to climb through the discarded machinery, then run across the snow-covered, littered lot until he got to the hurricane fence. Wally was hindered by the same objects but, used to working out, he made better time.

Charles started up the fence but unfortunately he'd picked

a spot between two uprights. The lack of support, particularly near the top, made the climbing more difficult.

Wally Crabb reached the fence and began shaking it violently. Charles had all he could do to hold on, much less continue climbing. Then Wally reached up and grabbed Charles's right foot. Charles tried to kick free but Wally had a good hold and he merely put his weight on it.

The force overrode Charles's grasp, and he tumbled off the fence, directly on top of Wally. Desperately Charles searched beneath the snow for some object with which he could defend himself. He came up with an old shoe. He flung it at Wally, and although it missed its mark, it gave Charles a chance to stand and flee along the fence toward the river. For Charles, the situation was like being inside a cage with a raging animal.

Running in the snow along the fence was next to impossible. The crust sometimes supported Charles's weight, other times it didn't, and there was no way to tell before taking a step. Under the snow was a wide assortment of debris ranging from fresh garbage to wayward rubber tires and metal scrap that kept trapping him. Fearful he was going to be caught any moment, Charles glanced over his shoulder. One look was enough to ascertain that the obstacle course was equally difficult for Wally and Charles reached the river bank first.

His descent to the water was a marginally controlled fall. With his hands out at his sides like outriggers on a canoe, Charles slipped and slid down the embankment, coming to a jarring halt where the ice had buckled at the river's edge. Avoiding the patch of open water, Charles scrambled out onto the ice, and tried to keep his balance. Wally came down the embankment with a bit more care and consequently lost some ground. Charles was around the portion of the fence that extended out from shore and starting back up the embankment when Wally reached the river's edge.

Almost at the top of the embankment, Charles's feet suddenly slid out from under him. Panic-stricken, his hands grasped for a hold. At the last second he caught a small bush and halted his backward movement. He tried to scramble back

up but could not get any traction. Wally had already gained
the shore and started up toward Charles, closing the short distance between them.

Wally reached up to grab Charles's leg. He was inches away
when he seemed to switch to slow motion. His legs stiffened
but it was no use. Slowly at first, then rapidly, he slid backwards.

With renewed effort, Charles tried to climb the last five feet.
By jamming his toes against the embankment he discovered
he could create crude footholds. In this way, he inched up-
wards and threw his upper body over the edge. He pulled his
feet up, then raised himself on his hands and knees. In so
doing, he felt rocks and pieces of brick under the snow. He
kicked them loose and picked up a handful. Wally had begun
a new assault on the embankment and at that moment was
only five feet away.

Cocking his arm back, Charles threw the stones. One hit
Wally on the point of the shoulder and he grunted in pain. He
grabbed the area with his opposite hand only to slip back down
the embankment. Quickly Charles kicked loose additional
stones and threw them down at Wally, who put his arms over
his head and retreated out onto the ice.

Charles fled back toward the row of deserted mill buildings,
intending to run around the end of the first building and get
to the Pinto, which was parked a hundred yards back. But as
he started in that direction, he saw several flashlights coming
around the opposite end of the hurricane fence. They swung
in his direction, momentarily blinding him, and he knew he'd
been spotted. He had no choice. He ran directly for the empty
building.

Dashing through a doorless opening Charles was quickly
engulfed by impenetrable darkness. With his arms swinging in
exploratory arcs he inched forward, encountering a wall. As
if in a maze, he stumbled along the wall until he came to a
door. Bending down and searching the floor, he found some
rubble, which he tossed through the opening. It hit yet another
wall and fell back to the floor. Without letting go of the door-

jamb, Charles reached out in the darkness. His fingertips touched the wall that he'd hit with the rubble. He let go of the doorframe and walked along this new wall.

Hearing shouts behind him, Charles felt a surge of panic. He had to find a place to hide. He was convinced that these Recycle people were crazy and that they were planning to kill him. Charles was certain they had hoped to force him into the chemical lagoon, hoping perhaps to make it appear as an accident. He was, after all, a trespasser who could conceivably slip into that cesspool in the dark. And if they were willing to dump poisons into a public river, morality was not high on their priority list.

Charles came to a corner in the wall he was following. He strained to see but he couldn't even detect his own hand moving in front of his face. Bending down, he gathered a few pebbles and tossed them around the corner to see how far away the next wall was. He waited for the sound of the stone to hit a wall, then a floor. There was neither. After a long delay, Charles heard the distant splash of water. He shrank back. Somewhere immediately in front of him was a void, perhaps an old elevator shaft.

Guessing that he was in a hallway, Charles threw some pebbles perpendicular to the wall he'd been following. The stones hit immediately, and stretching out in the darkness, Charles felt the opposite wall.

With his foot Charles began to kick loose plaster ahead of him to be sure that he'd pass the shaft. It worked, and he slowly moved ahead, gaining a certain amount of confidence. He had no way of judging the distance he'd traveled, but he felt it was significant. Then his hand touched another doorjamb. Feeling ahead, his other hand grasped a wooden door, open about a foot. The knob was missing. Charles pushed and the door reluctantly opened, restricted by debris on the floor. With great care Charles inched into the room, feeling ahead with his right foot, and smelling a foul, musty odor. He encountered a bale of material, then realized it was an old, rotting rug.

Behind him he heard someone yell into the cavernous interior. "We want to talk to you, Charles Martel." The sound echoed in the blackness. Then he heard heavy footsteps and voices talking among themselves. With a surge of new fear, he let go of the door and started across the room, his hands sweeping around in front of him, hoping to find some hiding place. Almost immediately he tripped over another rug, then hit up against a low, metal object. He felt along the top of it, deciding it was a cabinet of sorts that had been tipped over. Stepping around it, he ducked down among a pile of smelly rags. He burrowed beneath the rags as best he could, feeling some movement of little feet. He hoped it was mice he'd disturbed and not something larger.

Except for the luminous dial on his watch, Charles could see nothing. He waited, his breath sounding harsh in the stillness and his heart beating audibly in his ears. He was caught. There was no place else to run. They could do to him what they wanted; no one would find his body, especially if it were thrown down the old elevator shaft. Charles had never felt such limitless terror.

A light flickered in the hallway, sending tiny reflections into Charles's room. The flashlights were moving down the hallway, coming in his direction. For a moment they disappeared and utter blackness descended. He heard a distant splash as if a large object had been thrown down the elevator shaft, followed by laughter.

The flashlight beams returned to the hallway, swaying and searching as Charles's pursuers drew nearer. Now he could hear every footstep. With a sudden, grating noise, the old wooden door was shoved open, and a sharp ray of light played around the room.

Charles pulled his head down like a turtle, hoping that his pursuer would be satisfied with a cursory glance. But such was not the case. Charles heard the man kick the roll of old rug and saw the light going over every inch of the floor. With a stab of panic he knew he was about to be discovered.

Leaping from beneath his scant cover, Charles bolted for

the door. The pursuer whirled his light, silhouetting Charles in the doorway. "Here he is!" the man yelled.

Intending to try to retrace his steps out of the maze, Charles started down the corridor. Instead he crashed into another pursuer coming down the hall who grabbed him, dropping his flashlight in the process. Charles struck blindly, desperately trying to free himself. Then, even before he felt the pain, his legs buckled beneath him. The man had hit Charles on the back of his knees with a club.

Charles collapsed to the floor as his attacker reached for his flashlight. The other man emerged from the room Charles had been hiding in and his light played over the scene. For the first time, Charles got a look at the man who'd hit him. To his astonishment he found himself looking at Frank Neilson, Shaftesbury's Chief of Police. The blue serge uniform with all its bits and pieces of decoration, including holster and hand gun, never looked so good.

"Okay, Martel, game's over, on your feet!" said Neilson, slipping his billy club into its leather holster. He was a stocky man with slicked-back blond hair and a gut that swooped out from his chest, then curved back just above his trouser tops. His neck was the size of Charles's thigh.

"Am I glad to see you," said Charles, with heartfelt sincerity despite the fact he'd been struck.

"I'll bet you are," said Frank, grabbing Charles by the collar and hauling him to his feet.

Charles staggered for a moment, his leg muscles complaining.

"Cuffs?" asked the deputy. His name was Bernie Crawford. In contrast to his boss, the deputy was tall an lanky, like a basketball forward.

"Hell, no!" said Frank. "Let's just get out of this shithole."

Bernie went first, followed by Charles, then Frank, as the trio made their way back through the deserted factory. Passing the elevator shaft, Charles shuddered to think how close he'd come to tumbling into the pit. As he walked, he thought about

Bernie's question of "cuffs." Obviously Recycle had called the police and had made a complaint.

No one spoke as they marched single file out of the old mill, across the empty lot, and to the Dodge Aspen squad car. Charles was put into the backseat, behind the thick mesh guard. Frank started the car and began to pull away from the curb.

"Hey, my car's back that way," said Charles, moving forward to speak through the mesh.

"We know where your car is," said Frank.

Sitting back, Charles tried to calm down. His heart was still thumping in his chest and his legs ached horribly. He glanced out the window wondering if they were taking him to the station. But they didn't make a U-turn. Instead they headed south and turned in at the gate for the Recycle parking lot.

Charles sat forward again. "Listen. I need your help. I need to get some hard evidence to prove that Recycle is dumping poisons into the Pawtomack. That's what I was doing here when they jumped me and destroyed my camera."

"You listen, Mack," said Frank. "We got a call you were trespassing here. And on top of that you assaulted one of the workers, pushing him into some acid. Last night you shoved around the foreman, Nat Archer."

Charles sat back, realizing that he was just going to have to wait out whatever protocol Frank had decided on. Presumably Frank wanted some positive identification. With a certain amount of exasperation clouding his relief, Charles resigned himself to having to go down to the police station.

They stopped a distance from the front entrance. Frank blew the horn three times and waited. Presently the aluminum storm door opened, and Charles watched Nat Archer come out, followed by a shorter fellow whose left leg was swathed from the knee down in bandages.

Frank struggled out from behind the wheel and came around the car to open the door for Charles. "Out," was all he said.

Charles complied. There was about an inch and a half of new snow and Charles slid a little before regaining his balance.

The bruises where he'd been hit by Frank's billy club hurt more when he was standing.

Nat Archer and his companion trudged up to Frank and Charles.

"This the man?" asked Frank, bending a stick of gum and pushing it deep into his mouth.

Archer glared at Charles and said, "It's him, all right."

"Well, you want to press charges?" asked Frank, chewing his gum with loud snapping noises.

Archer trudged off toward the factory.

Frank, still snapping his gum, walked around the squad car and got in.

Charles, confused, turned to look at Brezo. The man stood in front of Charles smiling a toothless grin. Charles noticed a scar that ran down the side of his face across his cheek, making his smile slightly asymmetric.

In a flash of unexpected violence, Brezo unleashed a powerful blow to Charles's midsection. Charles saw the blow coming and managed to deflect it slightly with his elbow. Still it caught Charles in the abdomen, doubling him up, and he crumbled to the cold earth, struggling for a breath. Brezo stood over him expecting more action, but he only kicked a bit of snow at Charles and walked off, limping slightly on his bandaged leg.

Charles pushed himself up onto his hands and knees. For a moment he was disoriented with pain. He heard a car door open and felt a tug on his arm, forcing him to his feet. Holding his side, Charles allowed himself to be led back to the squad car. Once inside, he let his head fall back on the seat.

He felt the car skid but didn't care. He kept his eyes closed. It hurt too much just to breathe. After a short time, the car stopped and the door opened. Charles opened his eyes and saw Frank Neilson looking into the back seat. "Let's go, buster. You should feel lucky you got off so easy." He reached in and pulled Charles toward him.

Charles got out, feeling a little dizzy. Frank closed the rear door, then got back into the driver's seat. He rolled down the

window. "I think you'd better stay away from Recycle. It's
got around town pretty quick that you're trying to cause trouble. Let me tell you something. If you keep at it, you'll find
it. In fact, you'll find more trouble'n you're bargaining for.
The town survives on Recycle, and we law enforcement officers won't be able to guarantee your safety if you try to change
that. Or your family's either. Think about it."

Frank rolled his window up and spun his wheels, leaving
Charles standing at the curb, his legs splattered with slush.
The Pinto was twenty feet ahead, partially buried under a
shroud of snow. Even through the pain, Charles felt a cold
rage stirring inside himself. For Charles, adversity had always
been a powerful stimulus for action.

Cathryn and Gina were cleaning up the kitchen when they
heard a car turn into the drive. Cathryn ran to the window and
pulled the red checkered curtain aside. She hoped to God it
was Charles; she hadn't heard from him since he'd fled from
the hospital, and no one had answered his extension at the lab.
She knew she had to tell Charles about the proceedings at the
courthouse. She couldn't let him learn about it when he got
the court citation in the morning.

Watching the lights come up the driveway, Cathryn found
herself whispering, "Let it be you, Charles, please." The car
swept around the final curve and passed the window. It was
the Pinto! Cathryn sighed in relief. She turned back into the
room and took the dish towel from Gina's surprised hands.

"Mother, it's Charles. Would you mind going into the other
room? I want to talk to him for a moment, alone."

Gina tried to protest but Cathryn put her fingers to her
mother's lips, gently silencing her. "It's important."

"You'll be okay?"

"Of course," said Cathryn, urging Gina toward the door. She
heard the car door slam.

Cathryn went over to the door. When Charles started up the
steps, she swung it open.

Before she could clearly see his face, she smelled him. It

was a mildewy odor like wet towels stored in a closet in summer. As he came into the light she saw his bruised and swollen
nose. There was a bit of dried blood crusted on his upper lip,
and his whole face was curiously blackened. His sheepskin
jacket was hopelessly soiled and his pants were torn over the
right knee. But most disturbing of all was his expression of
tension and barely controlled anger.

"Charles?" Something terrible was happening. She'd been
worrying about him all afternoon and his appearance suggested her concern was justified.

"Just don't say anything for a moment," demanded Charles,
avoiding Cathryn's touch. After removing his coat, he headed
for the phone and nervously flipped through the telephone pad.

Cathryn pulled a clean dish towel from the linen drawer,
and wetting the end, tried to clean off his face to see where
the blood had come from.

"Christ, Cathryn! Can you wait one second?" snapped
Charles, pushing her away.

Cathryn stepped back. The man in front of her was a
stranger. She watched him dial the phone, punching the buttons with a vengeance.

"Dawson," yelled Charles into the phone. "I don't care if
you've got the police and the whole fucking town in your
pocket. You're not going to get away with it!" Charles punc-
tuated his statement by crashing the receiver onto its bracket.
He didn't expect an answer, and wanted to beat Dawson in
hanging up.

Having made the call, his tension eased a little. He rubbed
his temples for a moment in a slow, circular motion. "I had
no idea this quaint little town of ours was so corrupt," he said
in a near-to-normal voice.

Cathryn began to relax. "What happened to you? You're
hurt!"

Charles looked at her. He shook his head and to her surprise,
laughed. "Mostly my sense of dignity. It's hard abandoning
all of one's macho fantasies in one evening. No, I'm not hurt.
Not badly anyway. Especially since at one point I thought it

was all over. But for now, I need something to drink. Fruit juice. Anything."

"I have a dinner for you in the oven, keeping warm."

"Christ. I couldn't eat," said Charles, slowly sinking into one of the kitchen chairs. "But I'm thirstier than hell." His hands trembled as he put them on the table. His stomach hurt where he'd been punched.

After pouring a glass of apple cider, Cathryn carried it to the table. She caught sight of Gina standing in the doorway with an innocent expression. In angry pantomime, Cathryn gestured for her mother to go back to the living room. She sat down at the table. At least for the moment she had abandoned her idea of telling Charles about the guardianship situation.

"There's blood on your face," she said solicitously.

Charles wiped under his nose with the back of his hand and stared at the flakes of dried blood. "Bastards!" he said.

There was a pause while Charles drank his cider.

"Are you going to tell me where you've been and what happened?" asked Cathryn finally.

"I'd rather hear about Michelle first," said Charles, putting the glass on the table.

"Are you sure?" asked Cathryn. She reached over and put her hand on top of his.

"What do you mean, am I sure?" snapped Charles. "Of course I'm sure."

"I didn't mean that the way it sounded," said Cathryn. "I know you're concerned. I'm just worried about you. You took Michelle's heart complication so hard."

"What's happened now?" demanded Charles, raising his voice, afraid that Cathryn was leading up to terrible news.

"Please calm down," said Cathryn gently.

"Then tell me what's happened to Michelle."

"It's just her fever," said Cathryn. "It's gone up and the doctors are concerned."

"Oh God!" said Charles.

"Everything else seems OK. Her heart rate has stayed normal." Cathryn was afraid to say anything about Michelle's

hair, which had started falling out. But Dr. Keitzman said it
was an expected and entirely reversible side effect.

"Any sign of remission?" asked Charles.

"I don't think so. They didn't say anything."

"How high is her fever?"

"Pretty high. It was one-oh-four when I left."

"Why did you leave? Why didn't you stay?"

"I suggested it but the doctors encouraged me to go. They
said that parents with a sick child must be careful about ne-
glecting the rest of their family. They told me there was nothing I could do. Should I have stayed? I really didn't know. I
wished you were there."

"Oh God!" said Charles again. "Someone should be with
her. High fever is not a good sign. The medications are knocking out her normal defenses and seemingly not touching her
leukemic cells. A high fever at this point means infection."

Abruptly Charles stood up. "I'm going back to the hospital,"
he said with resolve. "Right now!"

"But why, Charles? What can you do now?" Cathryn felt a
surge of panic, and she leaped to her feet.

"I want to be with her. Besides, I've made up my mind.
The medications are going to be stopped. Or at least reduced
to an orthodox dose. They're experimenting and if it were
going to work, we would have seen the circulatory leukemic
cells go down. Instead they've gone up."

"But the medicines have cured others." Cathryn knew she
had to talk Charles out of going to the hospital. If he did,
there'd be a crisis . . . a confrontation.

"I know chemotherapy has helped others," said Charles.
"Unfortunately Michelle's case is different. The normal protocol has already failed. I'm not going to let my daughter be
experimented on. Keitzman had his chance. She's not going
to dissolve in front of my eyes like Elizabeth."

Charles started for the door.

Carolyn clutched at his sleeve. "Charles, please. You can't
go now. You're a mess."

Looking down at himself, Charles realized Cathryn was

right. But did he really care? He hesitated, then ran upstairs where he changed his clothes and washed his hands and face. When he ran back down, Cathryn realized that he had made up his mind. He was going to the hospital that night and had every intention of stopping Michelle's medicines, her only chance at life. Once again, the doctors had correctly forecasted his reaction. Cathryn realized she had to tell him about the guardianship right away. She could not afford to wait.

Charles pulled on his befouled jacket, checking for his car keys in his pocket.

Cathryn leaned her back up against the counter, her hands gripping the Formica edge. "Charles," she began in a quiet tone. "You cannot stop Michelle's medicine."

Charles found his keys. "Of course I can," he said confidently.

"Arrangements have been made so that you cannot," said Cathryn.

With his hand on the back door, Charles paused. The word "arrangements" had an ominous connotation. "What are you trying to say?"

"I want you to come back, take your coat off, and sit down," said Cathryn, as if she were talking to a recalcitrant teenager.

Charles walked directly up to her. "I think you'd better tell me about these arrangements."

Although Cathryn never would have imagined it possible, she felt a touch of fear as she gazed up into Charles's narrowed eyes. "After you left the hospital so hastily this afternoon, I had a conference with Dr. Keitzman and Dr. Wiley. They felt that you were under a severe strain and might not be in the best position to make the right decisions about Michelle's care." Cathryn deliberately tried to echo the legal talk she'd heard at the meeting. What terrified her most was Charles's reaction to her complicity. She wanted to emphasize that she had been a reluctant participant. She looked up into his face. His blue eyes were cold. "The hospital lawyer said that Michelle needed a temporary guardian and the doctors agreed. They told me they could do it without my cooperation but that it would be easier if I helped. I thought I was doing the right thing although it was a hard decision. I felt one of us should still be involved."

"So what happened?" said Charles, his face becoming a dull red.

"There was an emergency hearing before a judge," said Cathryn. She was telling it poorly and at a bad time. She was making a mess of everything. Doggedly she continued, "The judge agreed that Michelle should get the recognized treatment for her condition as outlined by Dr. Keitzman. I was appointed temporary guardian. There will be a hearing on this petition in three days and a full hearing in three weeks. The court also appointed a guardian and listen, Charles, believe me, I've done all this for Michelle. I'm not doing anything against you or to come between you and Michelle."

Cathryn searched Charles's face for a flicker of understanding. She saw only rage.

"Charles!" cried Cathryn. "Please believe me. The doctor convinced me you've been under great strain. You haven't been yourself. Look at you! Dr. Keitzman is world-famous for treating childhood leukemias. I did it only for Michelle. It's only temporary. Please." Cathryn broke into tears.

Gina appeared instantly at the doorway. "Is everything all right?" she called out timidly.

Charles spoke very slowly, his eyes on Cathryn's face. "I hope to God this isn't true. I hope you're making this up."

"It's true," managed Cathryn. "It's true. You left. I did the best I could. You'll be served with a citation in the morning."

Charles exploded with a violence he'd never known he'd possessed. The only handy object was a short stack of dishes. Snatching them off the counter he lifted them over his head and crashed them to the floor in a fearful splintering of china. "I can't stand this. Everybody is against me. Everybody!"

Cathryn cringed by the sink, afraid to move. Gina was riveted to the doorway, wanting to flee but fearful for her daughter's safety.

"Michelle is my daughter, my flesh and blood," raged

Charles. "No one is going to take her away from me."

"She's my adopted daughter," sobbed Cathryn. "I feel just as strongly as you." Overcoming her fear, she grabbed the lapels of Charles's coat, shaking him as best she could. "Please calm down. Please," she cried desperately.

The last thing Charles wanted was to be held down. By reflex his arm shot up and with unnecessary force, knocked Cathryn's arms into the air. Following through with the blow, the side of his hand inadvertently caught her face, knocking her backwards against the kitchen table.

A chair fell over and Gina screamed, running into the room and positioning her corpulent bulk between Charles and her dazed daughter. She began reciting a prayer as she crossed herself.

Charles reached out and rudely shoved the woman aside. He grabbed Cathryn by both shoulders and shook her like a rag doll. "I want you to call and cancel those legal proceedings. Do you understand?"

Chuck heard the commotion and ran down the stairs. He took one look at the scene in front of him and sprang into the room, grabbing his father from behind, and pinning his arms to his side. Charles tried to twist loose but he couldn't. Instead he released Cathryn, and lunged back with the point of his elbow, digging it into the pit of Chuck's abdomen. The boy's breath came out in a forceful huff. Charles spun, then shoved Chuck backwards so that he tripped, fell, and hit his head on the floor.

Cathryn screamed. The crisis was expanding in a chain reaction. She threw herself on top of Chuck to protect him from his father and it was at this point Charles realized that he was attacking his own son.

He took a step forward but Cathryn screamed again, shielding the crumpled boy. Gina stepped between Charles and the others murmuring something about the devil.

Charles looked up to see the confused face of Jean Paul in the doorway. The boy backed away when he saw Charles staring at him. Looking back at the others, Charles felt an overwhelming sense of alienation. Impulsively he turned and stormed out of the house.

Gina closed the back door behind him, while Cathryn helped Chuck into one of the kitchen chairs. They heard the Pinto rumble down the driveway.

"I hate him! I hate him!" cried Chuck, holding his stomach with both hands.

"No, no," soothed Cathryn. "This is all a nightmare. We'll all wake up and it will be over."

"Your eye!" exclaimed Gina, coming up to Cathryn and tilting her head back.

"It's nothing," said Cathryn.

"Nothing? It's becoming black and blue. I think you'd better get some ice on it."

Cathryn got up and looked at herself in a small mirror hanging in the hallway. There was a minute cut on her right eyebrow and she was indeed getting a black eye. By the time she got back into the kitchen, Gina had the ice tray out.

Jean Paul reappeared at the doorway.

"If he ever hits you again, I'll kill him," said Chuck.

"Charles Jr.," snapped Cathryn. "I don't want to hear that kind of talk. Charles is not himself; he's under a lot of strain. Besides, he didn't mean to hit me. He was trying to get free from my grasp."

"I think he's let in the devil," said Gina.

"That's enough, all of you," said Cathryn.

"I think he's crazy," persisted Chuck.

Cathryn took a breath in preparation for reprimanding Chuck but she hesitated because the boy's comment made her wonder if Charles was having a nervous breakdown. The doctors suggested it as a possibility and they had been right about everything else. Cathryn wondered where she was going to find the reserve to hold the family together.

Her first concern was safety. Cathryn had never seen Charles lose control before. Thinking it best to get some professional advice, she called Dr. Keitzman's exchange.

Keitzman called back five minutes later.

She told him the entire series of events, including the fact that Charles had decided to stop Michelle's medications and added that Charles had left in his car, presumably en route to the hospital.

"Sounds like we petitioned for custody at the right time," said Dr. Keitzman.

Cathryn was in no mood for self-congratulation. "That may be, but I'm concerned about Charles. I don't know what to expect."

"That's precisely the problem," said Dr. Keitzman. "He may be dangerous."

"I can't believe that," said Cathryn.

"That's something that cannot be ascertained unless he's seen professionally. But, believe me, it's a possibility. Maybe you should leave the house for a day or two. You've got a family to consider."

"I suppose we could go to my mother's," said Cathryn. It was true she had others to think about besides herself.

"I think it would be best. Just until Charles calms down."

"What if Charles goes to the hospital tonight?"

"No need for you to worry about that. I'll alert the hospital, and I'll let the floor know you have guardianship. Don't worry, everything is going to be all right."

Cathryn hung up, wishing she felt as optimistic as Dr. Keitzman. She still had the feeling that things were going to get worse.

A half hour later, with a good deal of misgiving, Cathryn, Gina, and the two boys trudged out into the snow with overnight bags and piled in the station wagon. They dropped Jean Paul at a school friend's house where he'd been invited to stay, and began the drive into Boston. No one spoke.

ELEVEN

It was after nine when Charles reached Pediatric Hospital. In contrast to the daytime chaos, the street outside was quiet, and he found a parking spot in front of the medical center bookstore. He entered the hospital through the main entrance and rode up to Anderson 6 on an empty elevator.

He was accosted by someone when he passed the nurses' station, but he didn't even look in the direction of the voice. He got to Michelle's room and slipped through the partially open door.

It was darker than in the hall with light coming from a small night-light near the floor. Giving his eyes a chance to adjust, Charles stood for a moment taking in the scene. The cardiac monitor was visible on the other side of the bed. The auditory signal had been turned down but the visual signal traced a repetitive fluorescent blip across the tiny screen. There were two intravenous lines, one running into each of Michelle's arms. The one on the left had a piggyback connector, and Charles knew it was being used as the infusion route for the chemotherapy.

Charles silently advanced into the room, his eyes glued to

the sleeping face of his daughter. As he got closer he realized, to his surprise, that Michelle's eyes were not closed. They were watching his every move.

"Michelle?" whispered Charles.

"Daddy?" whispered Michelle in response. She'd thought it was another hospital technician sneaking up on her in the night to take more blood.

Charles tenderly lifted his daughter in his arms. She felt perceptibly lighter. She tried to return the embrace but her limbs were without strength. He pressed her cheek to his and slowly rocked her. He could feel her skin was flushed with fever.

Looking into her face, he noticed that her lips were ulcerated.

He felt such powerful emotion that it was beyond tears. Life was not fair. It was a cruel experience in which hope and happiness were transient illusions that served only to make the inevitable tragedy more poignant.

As he held his daughter Charles thought about his response to Recycle, Ltd. and felt foolish. Of course he could understand his urge for revenge, but under the circumstances, there were more important ways to spend his time. Obviously the people at Recycle did not care about a twelve-year-old girl, and they could conveniently blind themselves to any sense of responsibility. And what about the so-called cancer establishment? Did they care? Charles doubted it, seeing as he had the inner dynamics at his own institute. The irony was that the people controlling the megalithic cancer establishment were ultimately at equal risk to succumbing to the disease as the public at large.

"Daddy, why is your nose so swollen?" asked Michelle, looking into Charles's face.

Charles smiled. Ill as she was, Michelle was still concerned about him! Incredible!

He made up a quick story of slipping in the snow and comically falling on his face. Michelle laughed, but her face quickly became serious. "Daddy, am I going to get well?"

Without meaning to, Charles hesitated. The question had caught him off guard. "Of course," he said with a laugh, trying to make up for the pause. "In fact, I don't think you'll be needing any more of this medicine." Charles stood up, indicating the IV used for the chemotherapy. "Why don't I just take it out?"

Michelle's face clouded with worry. She detested any adjustments to the IV.

"It won't hurt," said Charles.

Deftly he removed the plastic catheter from Michelle's arm, keeping pressure on the spot. "You'll need the other IV for a little longer in case your ticker speeds up again." Charles tapped Michelle's chest.

The room light snapped on, throwing its raw fluorescent glare around the room.

A nurse came in followed by two uniformed security guards.

"Mr. Martel, I'm sorry but you are going to have to leave." She noticed the dangling IV line and shook her head angrily.

Charles did not respond. He sat on the edge of Michelle's bed and again took her into his arms.

The nurse gestured for the security men to help. They came forward and gently urged Charles to leave.

"We could have you arrested if you don't cooperate," said the nurse, "but I don't want to do that."

Charles allowed the guards to pull his arms from around Michelle.

Michelle looked at the guards and then her father. "Why would they arrest you?"

"I don't know," said Charles with a smile. "I guess it's not visiting hours."

Charles stood up, bent over and kissed Michelle, and said, "Try to be good. I'll be back soon."

The nurse turned out the overhead light. Charles waved from the doorway and Michelle waved back.

"You shouldn't have taken out that IV," said the nurse as they walked back to the nurses' station.

Charles didn't respond.

"If you wish to visit your daughter," continued the nurse, "it will have to be during regular hours, and you'll have to be accompanied."

"I'd like to see her chart," said Charles courteously, ignoring her other comments.

The nurse continued walking; obviously she didn't like the idea.

"It's my right," said Charles simply. "Besides, I am a physician."

The nurse reluctantly agreed and Charles went into the deserted chart room. Michelle's chart was innocently hanging in its designated spot. He pulled it out and placed it before him. There'd been a blood count that afternoon. His heart sank! Although he expected it, it still was a blow to see that her leukemic cell count had not decreased. In fact, it had gone up a little. There was no doubt that the chemotherapy was not helping her at all.

Pulling the phone over to him, Charles put in a call to Dr. Keitzman. While he waited for the call back, he glanced through the rest of the chart. The plot of Michelle's fever was the most alarming. It had been hovering around one hundred until that afternoon when it had shot up to one hundred four. Charles read the carefully typed cardiology report. The conclusion was that the ventricular tachycardia could have been caused by either the rapid infusion of the second dose of Daunorubicin or a leukemic infiltration of the heart, or perhaps, a combination of the two. At that point, the phone rang. It was Dr. Keitzman.

Both Dr. Keitzman and Charles made an effort at being cordial.

"As a physician," said Dr. Keitzman, "I'm sure you are aware that we doctors frequently find ourselves in the dilemma of adhering to the established and best principles of medicine or giving way to the wishes of the patient or the family. Personally, I believe in the former approach and as soon as one begins to make exception, whatever the justification, it's like opening Pandora's box. So we're having to rely on the courts more and more."

"But clearly," said Charles, controlling himself, "chemotherapy is not helping in Michelle's case."

"Not yet," admitted Dr. Keitzman. "But it's still early. There's still a chance. Besides, it's all we have."

"I think you're treating yourself," snapped Charles.

Dr. Keitzman didn't answer. He knew there was a grain of truth in what Charles said. The idea of doing nothing was anathema to Dr. Keitzman, especially with a child.

"One other thing," said Charles. "Do you think benzene could have caused Michelle's leukemia?"

"It's possible," said Dr. Keitzman. "It's the right kind of leukemia. Was she exposed?"

"Over a long period," said Charles. "A factory has been dumping it into a river that feeds the pond on our property. Would you be willing to say that Michelle's leukemia was caused by benzene?"

"I couldn't do that," said Dr. Keitzman. "I'm sorry, but it would be purely circumstantial. Besides, benzene has only been unequivocally implicated in causing leukemia in laboratory animals."

"Which you and I know means it causes it in humans."

"True, but that's not the kind of evidence acceptable by a court of law. There is an element of doubt, no matter how small."

"So you won't help?" asked Charles.

"I'm sorry but I can't," said Dr. Keitzman. "But there is something I can do, and I feel it's my responsibility. I'd like to encourage you to seek psychiatric consultation. You've had a terrible shock."

Charles thought about telling the man off, but he didn't. Instead he hung up on him. When he stood up he thought about sneaking back to Michelle's room but he couldn't. The charge nurse was watching him like a hawk and one of the uniformed security men was still there, leafing through a *People* magazine. Charles went to the elevator and pushed the button. As he waited, he began to outline what courses of action were open to him. He was on his own and would be even more on his own after the meeting tomorrow with Dr. Ibanez.

Ellen Sheldon arrived at the Weinburger later than usual. Even so she took her time because the walk to the door was treacherous. The Boston weather had been true to form the previous night, starting out with rain that turned to snow, then back to rain again. Then the whole mess had frozen solid. By the time Ellen reached the front entrance it was about eight-thirty.

The reason she was so late was twofold. First she didn't even know if she'd see Charles that day so there was no need to set up the lab. Second, she'd been out very late the night before. She'd violated one of her cardinal rules: never accept a date on the spur of the moment. But after she'd told Dr. Morrison that Charles was not following up on the Canceran work, he'd convinced her to take the rest of the day off. He'd also taken her home number in order to give her the results of the meeting with Charles and the Weinburgers. Although Ellen had not expected him to call, he had, and had told her of Charles's probationary status and that Charles had twenty-four hours to decide whether he was going to play ball or not. Then he'd asked to take her to dinner. Deciding it was a business date, Ellen had accepted, and she was glad she had. Dr. Peter Morrison was not a Paul Newman look-alike, but he was a fascinating man and obviously powerful in the research community.

Ellen tried to unlock the lab door and was surprised to find it had been opened. Charles was already hard at work.

"Thought maybe you weren't coming in today," joked Charles good-naturedly.

Ellen took off her coat and struggled with a mild wave of guilt. "I didn't think you'd be here."

"Oh?" said Charles. "Well, I've been working a good part of the night."

Ellen walked over to his desk. Charles had a new lab book

in front of him and several pages were already filled with his
precise handwriting. He looked terrible. His hair was matted
down, emphasizing the thinning area on the crown of his head.
His eyes looked tired and he was in need of a shave.

"What are you doing?" asked Ellen, trying to evaluate his
mood.

"I've been busy," said Charles, holding up a vial. "And I've
got some good news. Our method of isolating a protein antigen
from an animal cancer works just as smoothly on human cancer. The hybridoma I made with Michelle's leukemic cells has
been working overtime."

Ellen nodded. She was beginning to feel sorry for Charles
Martel.

"Also," continued Charles, "I checked all the mice we injected with the mammary cancer antigen. Two of them show
a mild but definite and encouraging antibody response. What
do you think of that? What I'd like you to do today is inject
them with another challenge dose of the antigen, and I'd like
you to start a new batch of mice using Michelle's leukemic
antigen."

"But Charles," said Ellen sympathetically, "we're not supposed to be doing this."

Charles carefully set down the vial he had in his hands as
if it contained nitroglycerin. He turned and faced Ellen. "I'm
still in charge here." His voice was even and controlled, maybe
too controlled.

Ellen nodded. In truth, she had come to be a little afraid of
Charles. Without another word, she repaired to her area and
began preparing to inject the mice. Out of the corner of her
eye she watched Charles retreat to his desk, pick up a folder
of papers, and begin reading. She looked up at the clock.
Sometime after nine she'd excuse herself from the lab and
contact Peter.

Earlier that morning Charles had been served with the citation concerning the *ex parte* guardianship hearing. He'd accepted the papers from a sheriff's department courier without
a word, and hadn't looked at them until that moment. He had

little patience with legal gibberish, and he only glanced at the forms, noticing that his presence was required at a hearing scheduled in three days. He returned the papers to their envelope and tossed it aside. He'd have to have legal counsel.

After checking his watch, Charles picked up the phone. His first call was to John Randolph, town manager of Shaftesbury, New Hampshire. Charles had met the man since he was also the owner-operator of the local hardware-appliance store.

"I've got a complaint," said Charles after the usual greetings, "about the Shaftesbury police force."

"I hope you're not talking about last night over at the factory," said John.

"As a matter of fact, I am," said Charles.

"Well, we already know all about that incident," said John. "Frank Neilson had the three selectmen meet him over breakfast at P.J.'s diner. Heard all about it. Sounded to me like you were lucky Frank came along."

"I thought so at first," said Charles. "But not after they took me back to Recycle so that some half-wit could punch me out."

"I didn't hear about that part," admitted John. "But I did hear you were trespassing, and then pushed someone into some acid. Why in God's name are you causing trouble at the factory? Aren't you a doctor? Seems like strange behavior for a physician."

Sudden anger clouded Charles's mind. He launched into an impassioned explanation of Recycle's dumping benzene and other toxic chemicals into the river. He told the town manager that for the sake of the community he was trying to get the factory closed down.

"I don't think the community would look kindly at closing down the factory," said John when Charles finally paused. "There was a lot of unemployment here before that factory opened. The prosperity of our town is directly related to Recycle."

"I suppose your gauge of prosperity is the number of washing machines sold," said Charles.

"That's part of it," agreed John.

"Jesus Christ!" shouted Charles. "Causing fatal diseases like leukemia and aplastic anemia in children is a high price to pay for prosperity, wouldn't you agree?"

"I don't know anything about that," said John evenly.

"I don't think you want to know about it."

"Are you accusing me of something?"

"You're damn right. I'm accusing you of irresponsibility. Even if there were just a chance that Recycle was dumping poisonous chemicals into the river, the factory should be closed until it is investigated. The risk isn't worth a handful of grubby jobs."

"That's easy for you to say, being an M.D. and not having to worry about money. Those jobs are important for the town and the people who work there. As for your complaint about our police, why don't you just stay out of our business? That's what the selectmen suggested this morning. We don't need you city folk with your fancy degrees from Harvard telling us how to live!"

Charles heard the familiar click as the line disconnected. So much for that approach, he thought.

Knowing anger would get him nowhere, Charles dialed the number for EPA. He asked for Mrs. Amendola of the Enforcement Division. To his surprise the line was picked up immediately and Mrs. Amendola's slightly nasal voice came over the wire. Charles identified himself and then described what he found at Recycle, Ltd.

"The tank that holds the benzene has a pipe that connects directly with the roof drain," said Charles.

"That's not very subtle," said Mrs. Amendola.

"I think it's about as blatant as you can get," said Charles. "And on top of that they have a pool of chemicals up there that regularly seeps into the river."

"Did you get some photos?" asked Mrs. Amendola.

"I tried to, but couldn't," said Charles. "I think your people might have more luck than I." Charles couldn't see any reason to get into a discussion with the EPA about the destruction of his camera. If it would have helped to get the EPA interested, he would have. As it was he was afraid it might discourage them altogether.

"I'll make some calls," said Mrs. Amendola. "But I can't promise you anything. I'd have more luck if I had the written complaint you promised to send me and a couple of photos, even if they were lousy."

Charles told her he'd get to it as soon as he could but he'd appreciate it if she'd go ahead and try to get some action based on the information he'd already given her. As he hung up he was not very confident that anything would be done.

Returning to the laboratory bench, he watched Ellen's preparation. He didn't interfere because Ellen was far more dexterous than he. Instead he busied himself with the dilution of Michelle's leukemic antigen to prepare it for injection into the mice. Since the vial was sterile, Charles used sterile technique to withdraw an exact volume of the solution. This aliquot was then added to a specific amount of sterile saline to make the concentration he desired. The vial with the remaining antigen went into the refrigerator.

With the dilution completed, Charles gave it to Ellen and told her to continue what she was doing because he was going out to find a lawyer. He told her he'd be back before lunch.

After the door closed Ellen stood there for a full five minutes watching the second hand rotate around the face of the clock. When Charles didn't return, she called the receptionist who confirmed that Charles had left the institute. Only then did she dial Dr. Morrison. As soon as he got on the line she told him that Charles was still working on his own research; in fact, expanding it, and still behaving peculiarly.

"That's it," said Dr. Morrison. "That is the last straw. No one can fault us for trying, but Charles Martel is finished at the Weinburger."

Charles's quest for legal representation was not as easy as he'd anticipated. Unreasonably equating skill and understanding with impressive quarters, he headed into downtown Boston, parking his car in the government center garage. The first impressive high-rise office building was 1 State Street. It had a fountain, wide expanses of polished marble, and lots of tinted glass. The directory listed numerous law firms. Charles picked the one closest to the top: Begelman, Canneletto, and O'Malley, hoping that the metaphorical implication of their high position would reflect itself in their performance. However, the only correlation turned out to be their estimated fee.

Apparently the firm did not expect street traffic and Charles was forced to wait on an uncomfortable Chippendale love seat which would have been as good for making love as a marble park bench. The lawyer who finally saw Charles was as junior a partner as possible. To Charles he looked about fifteen years old.

Initially the conversation went well. The young lawyer seemed genuinely surprised that a judge had granted temporary guardianship *ex parte* to a legal relative in place of a blood relative. However, the man was less sympathetic when he learned that Charles wanted to stop the treatment recommended by the specialists. He still would have been willing to help if Charles had not launched into impassioned accusations against Recycle, Ltd. and the town of Shaftesbury. When the lawyer began to question Charles's priorities, they ended up in an argument. Then the man accused Charles of barratry, which particularly inflamed Charles because he did not know what it meant.

Charles left unrepresented, and instead of trying other firms in the building, he consulted the yellow pages in a nearby drugstore. Avoiding fancy addresses, Charles looked for lawyers who were out on their own. He marked a half dozen names and began calling, asking whoever answered if they were busy or if they needed work. If there was a hesitation, Charles hung up and tried the next. On the fifth try, the lawyer answered the phone himself. Charles liked that. In response to Charles's question, the lawyer said he was starving. Charles said he'd be right over. He copied down the name and address: Wayne Thomas, 13 Brattle Street, Cambridge.

There was no fountain, no marble, no glass. In fact, 13

Brattle Street was a rear entrance, reached through a narrow, canyonlike alley. Beyond a metal door rose a flight of wooden steps. At the top were two doors. One was for a palm reader, the other for Wayne Thomas, Attorney-at-Law. Charles entered.

"Okay, man, sit right here and tell me what you got," said Wayne Thomas, pulling over a straight-backed chair. As Wayne got out a yellow pad, Charles glanced around the room. There was one picture: Abe Lincoln. Otherwise the walls were freshly painted white plaster. There was a single window through which Charles could see a tiny piece of Harvard Square. The floor was hardwood, recently sanded and varnished. The room had a cool, utilitarian appearance.

"My wife and I decorated the office," said Wayne, noticing Charles's wandering eyes. "What do you think?"

"I like it," said Charles. Wayne Thomas didn't look as if he were starving. He was a solid six-foot black in his early thirties, with a full beard. Dressed in a three-piece, blue pin-striped suit, he was a commanding presence.

Handing over the temporary guardianship citation, Charles told his story. Except for jotting down some notes, Wayne listened intently and did not interrupt like the young fellow at Begelman, Canneletto, and O'Malley. When Charles got to the end of his tale, Wayne asked a series of probing questions. Finally he said, "I don't think there's much we can do about this temporary guardianship until the hearing. With a guardianship *ad litim* they've covered their tracks, but I'll need the time to prepare the case anyway. As for Recycle, Ltd. and the town of Shaftesbury, I can start right away. However, there is the question about a retainer."

"I've got a three-thousand-dollar loan coming," said Charles.

Wayne whistled. "I'm not talking about that kind of bread. How about five hundred?"

Charles agreed to send the money as soon as he got the loan. He shook hands with Wayne and for the first time noticed the man wore a thin gold earring in his right ear.

Returning to the Weinburger, Charles felt a modicum of

satisfaction. At least he'd started the legal process and even if Wayne wasn't ultimately successful, he would at the very least cause Charles's adversaries some inconvenience. Outside of the thick glass entrance door, Charles waited impatiently. Miss Andrews, who'd obviously seen him, chose to complete a line of type before releasing the door. As Charles passed her, she picked up the telephone. That wasn't an auspicious sign.

The lab was empty. He called for Ellen and, receiving no answer, checked the animal room, but she wasn't there. When he looked up at the clock he realized why. He'd been gone longer than he'd expected. Ellen was obviously out for lunch. He went over to her work area and noticed that the dilution he'd prepared of Michelle's leukemic antigen had not been touched.

Returning to his desk, he again called Mrs. Amendola at the EPA to ask if she'd had any luck with the surveillance department. With thinly disguised impatience, she told him that his was not the only problem she was working on and that she'd call him, rather than vice versa.

Maintaining his composure, Charles tried to call the regional head of the EPA to lodge a formal complaint about the agency's organization, but the man was in Washington at a meeting about new hazardous waste regulations.

Desperately trying to maintain confidence in the concept of representative government, he called the Governor of New Hampshire and the Governor of Massachusetts. In both cases the result was identical. He could not get past secretaries who persistently referred him to the State Water Pollution Control Boards. No matter what he said, including the fact that he'd already called these people, the secretaries were adamant, and he gave up. Instead he called the Democratic senator from Massachusetts.

At first the response from Washington sounded promising, but then he was switched from low-level aide to low-level aide until he found someone conversant on environment. Despite his very specific complaint, the aide insisted on keeping the conversation general. With what sounded like a prepared speech, the man gave Charles ten full minutes of propaganda about how much the senator cared about environmental issues. While waiting for a pause, Charles saw Peter Morrison walk into the lab. He hung up while the aide was in mid-sentence.

The two men eyed each other across the polished floor of Charles's lab, their outward differences even more apparent than usual. Morrison seemed to have made particular effort with his appearance that day, whereas Charles had suffered from having slept in his clothes at the lab.

Morrison had entered with a victorious smile, but as Charles turned to face him, the administrator noticed that Charles, too, was cheerfully smiling. Morrison's own grin faltered.

Charles felt as if he finally understood Dr. Morrison. He was a has-been researcher who'd turned to administration as a way of salvaging his ego. Beneath his polished exterior, he still recognized that the researcher was the king and, in that context, resented his dependence on Charles's ability and commitment.

"You're wanted immediately in the director's office," said Dr. Morrison. "Don't bother to shave."

Charles laughed out loud, knowing the last comment was supposed to be the ultimate insult.

"You're impossible, Martel," snapped Dr. Morrison as he left.

Charles tried to compose himself before setting out for Dr. Ibanez's office. He knew exactly what was going to happen and yet dreaded the upcoming encounter. Going to the director's office had become a daily ritual. As he passed the somber oil paintings of previous directors, he nodded to some of them. When he got to Miss Evans, he just smiled and walked past, ignoring her frantic commands to stop. Without knocking, Charles sauntered into Dr. Ibanez's office.

Dr. Morrison straightened up from bending over Dr. Ibanez's shoulder. They'd been examining some papers. Dr. Ibanez eyed Charles with confusion.

"Well?" said Charles aggressively.

Dr. Ibanez glanced at Morrison, who shrugged. Dr. Ibanez

cleared his throat. It was obvious he would have preferred a moment for mental preparation.

"You look tired," said Dr. Ibanez uneasily.

"Thank you for your concern," said Charles cynically.

"Dr. Martel, I'm afraid you've given us no choice," said Dr. Ibanez, organizing his thoughts.

"Oh?" questioned Charles as if he was unaware of what was being implied.

"Yes," said Dr. Ibanez. "As I warned you yesterday and in accordance with the wishes of the board of directors, you're being dismissed from the Weinburger Institute."

Charles felt a mixture of anger and anxiety. That old nightmare of being turned out from his position had finally changed from fantasy to fact. Carefully hiding any sign of emotion, Charles nodded to indicate that he'd heard, then turned to leave.

"Just a minute, Dr. Martel," called Dr. Ibanez, standing up behind his desk.

Charles turned.

"I haven't finished yet," said Dr. Ibanez.

Charles looked at the two men, debating whether he wanted to stay or not. They no longer had any hold over him.

"For your own good, Charles," said Dr. Ibanez, "I think in the future you should recognize that you have certain legitimate obligations to the institution that supports you. You've been given almost free rein to pursue your scientific interests but, you must realize that you owe something in return."

"Perhaps," said Charles. He did not feel that Dr. Ibanez harbored the same ill will as Dr. Morrison.

"For instance," said Dr. Ibanez, "it's been brought to our attention that you have a complaint about Recycle, Ltd."

Charles's interest quickened.

"I think you should remember," continued Dr. Ibanez, "that Recycle and the Weinburger share a parent firm, Breur Chemicals. Recognizing this sibling association, I would have hoped that you would not have made any public complaints. If there is a problem, it should be aired internally and quietly rectified. That's how business works."

"Recycle has been dumping benzene into the river that goes past my house," snarled Charles. "And as a result, my daughter has terminal leukemia."

"An accusation like that is unprovable and irresponsible," said Dr. Morrison.

Charles took an impulsive step toward Morrison, momentarily blinded by sudden rage, but then he remembered where he was. Besides, it wasn't his nature to hit anyone.

"Charles," said Dr. Ibanez. "All I'm doing is trying to appeal to your sense of responsibility, and implore you to put your own work aside just long enough to do the Canceran study."

With obvious irritation that Charles might be offered a second chance, Dr. Morrison turned from the conversation and stared out over the Charles River.

"It's impossible," snapped Charles. "Given my daughter's condition, I feel an obligation to continue my own work for her sake."

Dr. Morrison turned back with a satisfied, I-told-you-so expression.

"Is that because you think you could come up with a discovery in time to help your daughter?" asked Dr. Ibanez incredulously.

"It's possible," agreed Charles.

Dr. Ibanez and Dr. Morrison exchanged glances.

Dr. Morrison looked back out the window. He rested his case.

"That sounds a little like a delusion of grandeur," said Dr. Ibanez. "Well, as I said, you leave me no choice. But as a gesture of good will, you'll be given a generous two months' severance pay, and I'll see that your medical insurance is continued for thirty days. However, you'll have to vacate your laboratory in two days. We've already contacted a replacement for you, and he's as eager to take over the Canceran study as we are to have it done."

Charles glowered at the two men. "Before I go, I'd like to say something: I think the fact that the drug firm and a cancer research institute are both controlled by the same parent company is a crime, especially since the executives of both companies sit on the board of the National Cancer Institute and award themselves grants. Canceran is a wonderful example of this financial incest. The drug is probably so toxic that it won't ever be used on people unless the tests continue to be falsified. And I intend to make the facts public so that won't be possible."

"Enough!" shouted Dr. Ibanez. He pounded his desk, sending papers swooping into the air. "When it comes to the integrity of the Weinburger or the potential of Canceran, you'd better leave well enough alone. Now get out before I retract the benefits we have extended to you."

Charles turned to go.

"I think you should try to get some psychiatric help," suggested Morrison in a professional tone.

Charles couldn't suppress his own adolescent urges, and he gave Morrison the finger before walking from the director's office, glad to be free from the institute he now abhorred.

"My God!" exclaimed Dr. Ibanez as the door closed. "What is wrong with that man?"

"I hate to say I told you so," said Dr. Morrison.

Dr. Ibanez sank as heavily as his thin frame would allow into his desk chair. "I never thought I'd say this, but I'm afraid Charles could be dangerous."

"What do you think he meant by 'making the facts public'?" Dr. Morrison sat down, arranging his slacks to preserve the sharp crease.

"I wish I knew," said Dr. Ibanez. "That makes me feel very uneasy. I think he could do irreparable damage to the Canceran project, not to mention the effect on the institute itself."

"I don't know what we can do," admitted Dr. Morrison.

"I think we can only react to whatever Charles does," said Dr. Ibanez. "Since it would be best to keep him from the press, I don't think we'd better announce that he has been fired. If anyone asks, let's say that Charles has been granted an un-specified leave of absence because of his daughter's illness."

"I don't think his daughter should be mentioned," said Dr. Morrison. "That's the kind of story the press loves. It could inadvertently give Charles a platform."

"You're right," said Dr. Ibanez. "We'll just say he's on leave of absence."

"What if Charles goes to the press himself?" asked Dr. Morrison. "They might listen to him."

"I still think that's doubtful," said Dr. Ibanez. "He detests reporters. But if he does, then we have to actively discredit him. We can question his emotional state. In fact we can say that was the reason we let him go. It's even true!"

Dr. Morrison allowed himself a thin smile. "That's a fabulous idea. I have a psychiatrist friend who, I'm sure, could put together a strong case for us. What do you say we go ahead and do it so that if the need arises, we'll be prepared?"

"Peter, sometimes I think the wrong man is sitting behind this desk. You never let human considerations interfere with the job."

Morrison smiled, not quite sure that he was being complimented.

Charles descended the stairs slowly, struggling with his anger and despair. What kind of world put the needs of business ahead of morality, particularly the business of medicine? What kind of world could look the other way when an innocent twelve-year-old girl was given terminal leukemia?

Entering the lab, Charles found Ellen perched on a high stool, flipping idly through a magazine. When she saw Charles she put down the magazine and straightened up, smoothing out her lab coat.

"I'm awfully sorry, Charles," she said with a sad face.

"About what?" asked Charles evenly.

"About your dismissal," said Ellen.

Charles stared at her. He knew the institute had an internal gossip system that was supremely efficient. Yet this was too efficient. He remembered that she'd been told of his twenty-four-hour probationary period and she'd probably just assumed. And yet . . .

He shook his head, marveling at his own paranoia.

"It was expected," he said. "It just took me a few days to admit to myself that I couldn't work on Canceran. Especially now with Michelle so ill."

"What are you going to do?" asked Ellen. Now that Charles had been tumbled from his position of power, she questioned her motivation.

"I've got a lot to do. In fact . . ." Charles stopped. For a moment he debated taking Ellen into his confidence. Then he decided not to. What he'd painfully learned over the previous twenty-four hours was that he was alone. Family, colleagues, and governmental authority were either useless, obstructive, or frankly against him. And being alone required special courage and commitment.

"In fact, what?" asked Ellen. For a moment she thought Charles might admit that he needed her. Ellen was ready if he'd only say the word.

"In fact . . ." said Charles, turning from Ellen and approaching his desk, "I would appreciate it if you'd go back up to administration, since I'd prefer not to talk with them again, and retrieve my laboratory books. Holding them hostage obviously didn't work, and I'm hoping they'd prefer to get them from under foot."

Crestfallen, Ellen slid from the stool and headed for the door, feeling stupid that she was still susceptible to Charles's whims.

"By the way," he called before Ellen got to the door. "How far did you get with the work I left with you this morning?"

"Not very far," asserted Ellen. "As soon as you walked out this morning, I knew you would be fired, so what was the point? I'll get your books, but after that I refuse to be involved any further. I'm taking the rest of the day off."

Charles watched the door close, now certain that he wasn't being paranoid. Ellen must have been collaborating with the administration. She knew too much too fast. Remembering that he'd been on the verge of taking her into his confidence, he was relieved he had remained silent.

Locking the lab door from the inside, Charles went to work. Most of the important chemicals and reagents were stored in industrial quantities, so he began transferring them to smaller containers. Each container had to be carefully labeled, then stored in an almost empty locked cabinet near the animal room. That took about an hour. Next Charles tackled his desk, looking for work tablets on which he'd outlined protocols for previous experiments. With those notes, he would be able to reconstruct his experiments even without the data in case Dr. Ibanez did not return his lab books.

While he was feverishly working, the phone rang. Quickly thinking what he'd say if it were the administration, he answered. He was relieved to find himself talking with a loan officer from the First National Bank. He told Charles that his $3,000 was ready and wanted to know if Charles wanted it deposited directly in his joint checking account. Charles told him no, he'd be over later to pick it up in person. Without letting go of the receiver, he disconnected and dialed Wayne Thomas. As he waited for the connection, he wondered what the loan officer would say if he learned that Charles had just been fired.

As he had before, Wayne Thomas himself answered. Charles told the lawyer the loan came through, and he'd bring the $500 over that afternoon.

"That's cool, man," said Wayne. "I started working on the case without the retainer. I've already filed a restraining order against Recycle, Ltd. I'll know shortly when the hearing will be."

"Sounds good," said Charles, obviously pleased. On his own initiative, at least something was started.

Charles was almost finished with his desk when he heard someone try to open the door, and being unsuccessful slip a key into the lock. Charles swung around and was facing the door when Ellen entered. She was followed by a heavy young man dressed in a tweed jacket. To Charles's satisfaction, she was carrying half of the lab books and the stranger the other half.

"Did you lock the door?" asked Ellen quizzically.

Charles nodded.

Ellen rolled her eyes for the benefit of the stranger and said: "I really appreciate your help. You can put the books any-place."

"If you would," called Charles. "Put them on that counter top." He pointed to the area above the cabinet in which he'd stored the chemicals.

"This is Dr. Michael Kittinger," said Ellen. "I was intro-duced to him up in administration. He's going to be doing the Canceran study. I guess I'll be helping him."

Dr. Kittinger stuck out a short hand with pudgy fingers, a friendly smile distorting his rubbery face. "Glad to meet you, Dr. Martel. I've heard a lot of good things about you."

"I'll bet you have," Charles mumbled.

"What a fabulous lab," said Dr. Kittinger, dropping Charles's hand and marveling at the impressive array of so-phisticated equipment. His face brightened like a five-year-old at Christmas time. "My God! A Pearson Ultracentrifuge. And, I don't believe it . . . a Dixon Scanning Electron Microscope! How could you ever leave this paradise?"

"I had help," said Charles glancing at Ellen.

Ellen avoided Charles's stare.

"Would you mind if I just looked around?" asked Dr. Kit-tinger enthusiastically.

"Yes!" said Charles. "I do mind."

"Charles?" said Ellen. "Dr. Kittinger is trying to be friendly. Dr. Morrison suggested he come down."

"I really couldn't care less," said Charles. "This is still my lab for the next two days and I want everyone out. Everyone!" Charles's voice rose.

Ellen immediately recoiled. Motioning to Dr. Kittinger, the two hurriedly departed.

Charles grabbed the door and with excessive force, sent it

swinging home. For a moment he stood with his fists tightly clenched. He knew that he'd now made his isolation complete. He admitted there had been no need to antagonize Ellen or his replacement. What worried Charles was that his irrational behavior would undoubtedly be reported to the administration, and they in turn might cut down on the two days he had left in the lab. He decided he'd have to work quickly. In fact, he'd have to make his move that very night.

Returning to his work with renewed commitment, it took him another hour to arrange the lab so that everything he needed was organized into a single cabinet.

Donning his soiled coat, he left, locking the door behind him. When he passed Miss Andrews, he made it a point to say "Hi" and inform her that he'd be right back. If the receptionist was reporting to Ibanez, he didn't want her thinking he was planning on being out for long.

It was after three, and the Boston traffic was building to its pre-rush-hour frenzy. Charles found himself surrounded by businessmen who risked their lives to get to Interstate 93 before Memorial and Storrow Drive ground to a halt.

His first stop was Charles River Park Plaza and the branch of the First National Bank. The vice president with whom Charles was passingly acquainted was not in, so Charles had to see a young woman he'd never met. He was aware that she eyed him suspiciously with his soiled jacket and day-and-a-half growth of beard.

Charles put her at ease by saying, "I'm a scientist. We always dress a little . . ." he deliberately left the sentence open-ended.

The bank officer nodded understandingly, although it took her a moment to compare Charles's present visage with the photo on his New Hampshire driver's license. Seemingly comfortable with the identification, she asked Charles if he wanted a check. He asked for the loan in cash.

"Cash?" Mildly flustered, the bank officer excused herself and disappeared into the back office to place a call to the assistant director of the branch. When she returned she was carrying thirty crisp hundred-dollar bills.

Charles retrieved his car and threaded his way into the tangled downtown shopping district behind Filene's and Jordan Marsh. Double-parking with his blinker lights on, Charles ran into a sporting goods shop where he was known. He bought a hundred of twelve-gauge number two express shot for his shotgun.

"What's this for?" asked the clerk good-naturedly.

"Ducks," said Charles in a tone he'd hoped would discourage conversation.

"I think number four or five shot would be better," offered the clerk.

"I want number two," said Charles laconically.

"You know it's not duck season," said the clerk.

"Yeah, I know," said Charles.

Charles paid for the shells with a new hundred-dollar bill.

Back in the car, he worked his way through the narrow Boston streets. He drove back the way he'd come, making his third stop at the corner of Charles and Cambridge streets. Mindless of the consequences, he pulled off the road to park on the central island beneath the MBTA. Again he left the car with the hazard lights blinking.

He ran into a large twenty-four-hour drugstore strategically situated within the shadow of the Massachusetts General Hospital. Although he had only patronized the place when he had his private practice, they still recognized him and called him by name.

"Need to restock my black bag," said Charles after asking for some of the store's prescription forms. Charles wrote out prescriptions for morphine, Demerol, Compazine, Xylocaine, syringes, plastic tubing, intravenous solutions, Benadryl, epinephrine, Prednisone, Percodan, and injectable Valium. The pharmacist took the scripts and whistled: "My God, what do you carry around, a suitcase?"

Charles gave a short laugh as if he appreciated the humor and paid with a hundred-dollar bill.

Removing a parking ticket from beneath his windshield wiper, he got into the Pinto and eased into the traffic. He recrossed the Charles River, turning west on Memorial Drive. Passing the Weinburger, he continued to Harvard Square, parked in a lot—being careful to leave his car in view of the attendant—and hurried over to 13 Brattle Street. He took the stairs at a run and knocked on Wayne Thomas's door.

The young attorney's eyes lit up when Charles handed over five crisp one-hundred-dollar bills.

"Man, you're going to get the best service money can buy," said Wayne.

He then told Charles that he'd managed to get an emergency hearing scheduled the next day for his restraining order on Recycle, Ltd.

Charles left the lawyer's office and walked a block south to a Hertz rent-a-car bureau. He rented the largest van they had available. They brought the vehicle around and Charles climbed in. He drove slowly through Harvard Square, back to the parking lot where he'd left the Pinto. After transferring the shotgun shells and the carton of medical supplies, Charles got back in the van and drove to the Weinburger. He checked his watch: 4:30 P.M. He wondered how long he'd have to wait. He knew it would be dark soon.

TWELVE

Cathryn stood up stiffly and stretched. Silently she moved over to where she could see herself in the mirror through the open door of Michelle's hospital bathroom. Even the failing afternoon light couldn't hide how awful she looked. The black eye she'd received from Charles's accidental blow had gravitated from the upper to the lower lid.

Getting a comb from her purse as well as some blush and a little lipstick, Cathryn stepped into the bathroom and slowly closed the door. She thought that a little effort might make her feel better. Flipping on the fluorescent light, she looked into the mirror once again. What she saw startled her. Under the raw artificial light she looked frightfully pale, which only emphasized her black eye. But worse than her lack of color was her drawn, anxious look. At the corner of her mouth there were lines she'd never seen before.

After running the comb through her hair a few times, Cathryn switched off the light. For a moment she stood in the darkness. She couldn't bear to look at herself a moment longer. It was too unsettling, and rather than making her feel better, the makeup idea made her feel worse.

Fleeing to her mother's apartment in Boston's North End had only eliminated the fear of Charles's violence; it had done nothing to relieve her agonizing uncertainty that perhaps she'd made the wrong decision about the guardianship. Cathryn was terrified that her action would preclude his love for her after the nightmarish affair was over.

As silently as possible, Cathryn reopened the bathroom door and glanced over at the bed. Michelle had finally drifted off into a restless sleep, and even from where Cathryn was standing, she could see the child's face twitch and tremble. Michelle had had a terrible day from the moment Cathryn had arrived that morning. She'd become weaker and weaker by the hour to the point that raising her arms and head were an effort. The small ulcers on her lips had coalesced, creating a large raw surface that pained her whenever she moved them. Her hair was coming out in thick clumps, leaving pale bald spots. But the worst part was her high fever and the fact that her lucid periods were rapidly diminishing.

Cathryn went back to her seat by Michelle's bed. "Why hasn't Charles called?" she asked herself forlornly. Several times she had decided to call him at the institute, but each time, after picking up the phone, she changed her mind.

Gina had not been much help at all. Rather than being supportive and understanding, she'd taken the crisis as an opportunity to lecture Cathryn repeatedly on the evil of marrying someone thirteen years her senior with three children. She told Cathryn that she should have expected this kind of problem because even though Cathryn had graciously adopted the children, Charles obviously thought of them as his alone.

Michelle's eyes suddenly opened and her face twisted in pain.

"What's wrong?" asked Cathryn, anxiously leaning forward on her seat.

Michelle didn't answer. Her head flopped to the other side and her slender body writhed in pain.

Without a moment's hesitation, Cathryn was out the door, calling for a nurse. The woman took one look at Michelle's squirming body and put in a call to Dr. Keitzman.

Cathryn stood by the bed, wringing her hands, wishing there was something she could do. Standing there over the suffering child was a torture. Without any clear idea why she was doing it, Cathryn rushed into the bathroom and wet the end of a towel. Returning to Michelle's bedside, she began to blot the child's forehead with the cool cloth. Whether it did anything for Michelle, Cathryn had no idea, but at least it gave her the satisfaction of doing something.

Dr. Keitzman must have been in the area because he arrived within minutes. Skillfully he examined the child. From the regular beep on the cardiac monitor, he knew that her heart rate had not changed. Her breathing was nonencumbered; her chest was clear. Putting the bell of the stethoscope on Michelle's abdomen, Dr. Keitzman listened. He heard a fanfare of squeaks, squawks, and tinkles. Removing the stethoscope, he put his hand on the child's abdomen, gently palpating. When he straightened up he whispered something to the nurse who then quickly disappeared.

"Functional intestinal cramping," explained Dr. Keitzman to Cathryn, with relief. "Must be a lot of gas. I've ordered a shot that will give her instantaneous relief."

Heavily breathing through her mouth, Cathryn nodded. She sagged back into the seat.

Dr. Keitzman could see the woman's tormented appearance and her harried expression. He put a hand on her shoulder. "Cathryn, come outside with me for a moment."

Looking at Michelle, who'd miraculously fallen back to sleep after Dr. Keitzman's examination, Cathryn silently followed the oncologist out of the room. He led her back to the now familiar chart room.

"Cathryn, I'm concerned about you. You're under a lot of stress, too."

Cathryn nodded. She was afraid to talk, thinking her emotions might all surface and overflow.

"Has Charles called?"

Cathryn shook her head. She straightened up and took a deep breath.

"I'm sorry that this has happened the way it has, but you've done the right thing."

Cathryn wondered but kept still.

"Unfortunately it's not over. I don't have to tell you because it's painfully obvious that Michelle is doing very poorly. So far the medicines that we've given her have not touched her leukemic cells, and there is no hint of a remission. She has the most aggressive case of myeloblastic leukemia I've ever seen, but we will not give up. In fact, we'll be adding another drug today that I and a few other oncologists have been cleared to use on an experimental basis. It's had promising results. Meanwhile I want to ask you if Michelle's two brothers can come in tomorrow for typing to see if either one matches Michelle's. I think we're going to be forced to irradiate Michelle and give her a marrow transplant."

"I think so," managed Cathryn. "I'll try."

"Good," said Dr. Keitzman, examining Cathryn's face. She felt his stare and looked away.

"That is quite a shiner you've got," said Dr. Keitzman sympathetically.

"Charles didn't mean it. It was an accident," said Cathryn quickly.

"Charles called me last night," said Dr. Keitzman.

"He did? From where?"

"Right here in the hospital."

"What did he say?"

"He wanted to know if I would say that benzene caused Michelle's leukemia, which I told him I couldn't do, although it's a possibility. Unfortunately there is no way it could be proven. Anyway, at the end of the conversation I suggested that he should see a psychiatrist."

"What was his response?"

"He didn't seem excited about the idea. I wish there were some way to talk him into it. With all the stress he's been under I'm concerned about him. I don't mean to frighten you, but we've seen similar cases in which the individual has become violent. If there's any way you can get him to see a psychiatrist, I think you ought to try it."

Cathryn left the chart room, eager to get back to see Michelle, but when she passed the lounge opposite the nurses' station, her eye caught the pay phone. Overcoming all of her petty reasons for not calling Charles, she put in a call to the institute. The Weinburger operator plugged in Charles's lab and Cathryn let it ring ten times. When the operator came back on the line she told Cathryn that she knew Ellen, Charles's assistant, was in the library, and she asked if Cathryn would like to speak with her. Cathryn agreed and heard the connection put through.

"He's not in the lab?" asked Ellen.

"There's no answer," said Cathryn.

"He might be just ignoring the phone," explained Ellen. "He's been acting very strangely. In fact, I'm afraid to even go in there. I suppose you know he's been dismissed from the Weinburger."

"I had no idea," exclaimed Cathryn with obvious shock. "What happened?"

"It's a long story," said Ellen, "and I think Charles should tell you about it, not me."

"He's been under a lot of stress," said Cathryn.

"I know," said Ellen.

"If you see him, would you ask him to call me? I'm at the hospital."

Ellen agreed but added that she had her doubts that she'd be seeing him.

Cathryn slowly hung up the receiver. She thought for a moment, then called Gina, asking if Charles had phoned. Gina said there hadn't been any calls. Cathryn next tried to call home but, as she expected, there was no answer. Where was Charles? What was going on?

Cathryn walked back to Michelle's room, marveling how quickly her previously secure world had collapsed around her. Why had Charles been fired? During the short time Cathryn had worked there, she'd learned that Charles was one of their most respected scientists. What possibly could have happened? Cathryn had only one explanation. Maybe Dr. Keitzman was right. Maybe Charles was having a nervous breakdown and was now wandering aimlessly and alone, cut off from his family and work. Oh God!

Slipping into Michelle's room as quietly as possible, Cathryn struggled to see the child's face in the faltering light. She hoped Michelle would be asleep. As her eyes adjusted, she realized Michelle was watching her. She seemed too weak to lift her head. Cathryn went over to her and grasped her warm hand.

"Where's my daddy?" asked Michelle, moving her ulcerated lips as little as possible.

Cathryn hesitated, trying to think of how best to answer. "Charles is not feeling too well because he's so worried about you."

"He told me last night he would come today," pleaded Michelle.

"He will if he can," said Cathryn. "He will if he can."

A single tear appeared on Michelle's face. "I think it would be better if I were dead."

Cathryn was shocked into momentary immobility. Then she bent down and hugged the child, giving way to her own tears. "No! No! Michelle. Never think that for a moment."

The Hertz people had graciously included an ice scraper with the packet of rental documents, and Charles used it on the inside of the front windshield of the van. His breath condensed and then froze on the windshield, blocking his view of the Weinburger entrance. By five-thirty it was pitch dark save for the ribbon of lights on Memorial Drive. By six-fifteen everyone had left the institute except for Dr. Ibanez. It wasn't until six-thirty that the director appeared, bundled up in an ankle-length fur coat. Bent against the icy wind, he hunched over and made his way to his Mercedes.

To be absolutely sure, Charles waited until twenty of seven

before starting the van. Switching on the lights, he drove
around the back side of the building and down the service
ramp, backing up against the receiving dock. Getting out of
the van, he climbed the stairs next to the platform and rang
the bell. While he waited for a response, he felt the first waves
of doubt about what he was doing. He knew that the next few
minutes would be crucial. For the first time in his life Charles
was counting on inefficiency.

A small speaker above the bell crackled to life. On top of
the TV camera mounted above the receiving door, a minute
red light linked on. "Yes?" asked a voice.

"Dr. Martel here!" said Charles, waving into the camera.
"I've got to pick up some equipment."

A few minutes later the metal receiving door squeaked, then
began a slow rise, exposing an unadorned, cement receiving
area. A long row of newly arrived cardboard boxes were
stacked neatly to the left. In the rear of the area, an inner door
opened, and Chester Willis, one of the two evening guards,
stepped out. He was a seventy-two-year-old black who'd re-
tired from a city job and taken the job at the Weinburger,
saying that he could watch TV at home, but at the Weinburger
he got paid for it. Charles knew the real reason the man
worked was to help a grandchild through medical school.

Charles had made it a habit over the years to work late into
the evenings, at least before Chuck had become a day student
at Northeastern, and as a consequence, Charles had become
friends with the night security officers.

"You workin' nights again?" asked Chester.

"Forced to," said Charles. "We're collaborating with a
group at M.I.T. and I've got to move over some of my equipment. I don't trust anybody else to do it."

"Don't blame you," said Chester.

Charles breathed a sigh of relief. Security did not know he'd
been fired.

Taking the larger of two dollies from receiving, Charles
returned to his lab. He was pleased to find it untouched since
his departure, particularly the locked cabinet with his books

and chemicals. Working feverishly, Charles dismantled most of his equipment and began loading it onto the dolly. It took him eight trips, with some help from Chester and Giovanni, to transport what he wanted from the lab down to receiving, storing it in the middle of the room.

The last thing he brought down from the lab was the vial of Michelle's antigen which he'd stored in the refrigerator. He packed it carefully in ice within an insulated box. He had no idea of its chemical stability and did not want to take any chances.

It was after nine when everything was ready. Chester raised the outside door, then helped Charles pack the equipment and chemicals into the van.

Before he left, Charles had one more task. Returning to his lab he located a prep razor used for animal surgery. With the razor and a bar of hand soap he went to the lavatory and removed his day-and-a-half stubble. He also combed his hair, straightened his tie, and tucked his shirt properly into his pants. After he'd finished he examined himself in the full-length mirror. Surprisingly, he looked quite normal. On the way back to the receiving area, he stepped into the main coat-room and picked up a long white laboratory coat.

When he got back outside, he buzzed once more and thanked the two security men over the intercom for their help. Climbing into the cab, he admitted that he felt a twinge of guilt at having taken advantage of his two old friends.

The drive over to Pediatric Hospital was accomplished with ease. There was virtually no traffic and the frigid weather had driven most people indoors. When he arrived at the hospital he faced a dilemma. Considering the value of the equipment jammed in the van, he was reluctant to leave the vehicle on the street. Yet pulling it into the parking garage would make a quick exit an impossibility. After debating for a moment, he decided on the garage. If he were robbed, the whole plan would disintegrate. All he had to do was make sure a quick exit was not a necessity.

Charles parked within view of the attendant's booth and

double-checked all the doors to be absolutely certain they were locked. Having purposefully left his sheepskin jacket in the van, he put on the long white coat. It afforded little protection from the cold so he ran across to the hospital, entering through the busy emergency room.

Pausing at the check-in desk, Charles interrupted a harried clerk to ask what floor radiology was on. The clerk told him it was on Anderson 2. Charles thanked him and pushed through the double doors into the hospital proper. He passed a security guard and nodded. The guard smiled back.

Radiology was practically deserted. There seemed to be only one technician on duty and she was busy with a backlog of sprained wrists and chest films from the packed emergency room. Charles went directly to the secretarial area and obtained an X-ray request form and letterhead from the department of radiology. Sitting down at one of the desks, he filled in the form: Michelle Martel, aged 12; diagnosis, leukemia; study requested: abdominal flat plate. From the stationery he selected one of the names of the radiologists and used it to sign the request form.

Back in the main corridor, Charles unlocked the wheel stops on one of the many gurneys parked along the wall and pulled it out into the hall. From a nearby linen closet he obtained two fresh sheets, a pillow, and a pillow case. Working quickly, he made up the gurney, then pushed it past the room manned by the single technician. He waited for the patient elevator, and when it came, he pushed the gurney in and pressed 6.

Watching the floor indicator jump from number to number, he experienced his second wave of doubt. So far everything had gone according to plan, but he admitted that what he'd done to that point was the easy part. The hard part was going to begin when he arrived on Anderson 6.

The elevator stopped and the door folded open. Taking a deep breath, he pushed the gurney out into the quiet hall; visiting hours were long over and, as in most pediatric hospitals, the patients had been put to bed. The first obstacle was the nurses' station. At that moment there was only one nurse, whose cap could just be seen over the counter top. Charles moved ahead, aware for the first time of the minor cacophony of squeaks emitted by the gurney's wheels. He tried altering the speed in hopes it would reduce the noise but without success. Out of the corner of his eye he watched the nurse. She didn't move. Charles passed the station and the intensity of the light diminished as he entered the long hall.

"Excuse me," called the nurse, her voice shattering the stillness like breaking glass.

Charles felt a jolt of adrenaline shoot into his system, making his fingertips tingle. He turned and the nurse had stood up, leaning on the counter.

"Can I help you?" asked the nurse.

Charles fumbled for the form. "Just coming to pick up a patient for an X-ray," he said, forcing himself to stay calm.

"No X-rays have been ordered," said the nurse curiously. Charles noticed she'd looked down at the desk and he could hear pages of a book being flipped over.

"An emergency film," said Charles, beginning to panic.

"But there's nothing in the order book and nothing was said at report."

"Here's the request," said Charles, abandoning the gurney and approaching the nurse. "It was phoned in by Dr. Keitzman to Dr. Larainen."

She took the form and read it quickly. She shook her head, obviously confused. "Someone should have phoned us."

"I agree," said Charles. "It happens all the time, though."

"Well, I'll say something. I'll ask the day people what happened."

"Good idea," said Charles, turning back to the gurney. His hands were moist. He wasn't trained for this kind of work.

With a deliberate and rapid pace, Charles moved down the corridor, hoping the nurse did not feel obligated to make any confirming calls to either radiology or Dr. Keitzman.

He reached Michelle's room and, stepping around the front of the gurney, started to push open the door. He caught a glimpse of a seated figure, head resting on the bed. It was Cathryn.

Charles averted his face, backed out of the room, and moved the door to its original position. As quickly as he could he pulled the gurney the length of the corridor, away from the nurses' station, half expecting Cathryn to appear. He wasn't sure if she'd seen him or not.

He had not anticipated her being with Michelle at that hour. He tried to think. He had to get Cathryn out of the room. On the spur of the moment he could think of only one method, but it would mean working very quickly.

After waiting a few minutes to be sure Cathryn was not coming out on her own, Charles swiftly retraced his steps back to the treatment room, which was just before the nurses' station. He found surgical masks and hoods by a scrub sink. He donned one of each and pocketed an extra hood.

Eyeing the nurses' station, he crossed the corridor to the dark lounge area. In the far corner was a public telephone. He called the switchboard and asked for Anderson 6. In a few moments he could hear the phone ringing in the nurses' station.

A woman answered the phone, and Charles asked for Mrs. Martel, saying that it was an emergency. The nurse told him to hold the line.

Quickly he put down the receiver and moved to the doorway of the lounge. Looking back at the nurses' station, he could see the charge nurse come into the corridor with an LPN. She pointed up the hall. Charles immediately left the lounge and scurried back down the hall, passing Michelle's room. In the shadow at the end of the hall, Charles waited. He could see the LPN walk directly toward him, then turn into Michelle's room. Within ten seconds she reappeared and Cathryn, rubbing her eyes, stumbled after her into the hall. As soon as the two women turned toward the nurses' station, Charles ran the gurney down to Michelle's room and pushed it through the half-open door.

Flipping on the wall switch, Charles pushed the gurney over

to the bed. Only then did he look down at his daughter. After twenty-four hours he could see she was perceptibly worse. Gently he shook her shoulder. She didn't respond. He shook her again but the child did not move. What would he do if she were in a coma?

"Michelle?" called Charles.

Slowly Michelle's eyes opened.

"It's me! Please wake up," Charles shook her again. Time was limited.

Finally Michelle woke. With great effort she lifted her arms and put them around her father's neck. "I knew you'd come," she said.

"Listen," said Charles anxiously, putting his face close to hers. "I want to ask you something. I know you are very sick and they are trying to take care of you here at the hospital. But you are not getting well here. Your sickness is stronger than their strongest medicines. I want to take you away with me. Your doctors would not like it so I have to take you right now if you want to go. You have to tell me."

The question surprised Michelle. It was the last thing she'd expected to hear. She examined her father's face. "Cathryn said you were not feeling well," said Michelle.

"I feel fine," said Charles. "Especially when I'm with you. But we haven't much time. Will you come with me?"

Michelle looked into her father's eyes. There was nothing she wanted more. "Take me with you, Daddy, please!"

Charles hugged her, then set to work. He turned off the cardiac monitor and detached the leads from her. He pulled out her IV and yanked down the covers. With a hand under her shoulders and another beneath her knees, Charles lifted his daughter into his arms. He was surprised at how little she weighed. As gently as he could, he lowered Michelle into the gurney and covered her. From the closet he retrieved her clothes and hid them beneath the sheet. Then, just prior to pushing the gurney out into the hall, he put a surgical hood over Michelle's head, tucking in what was left of her hair.

As he walked down toward the nurses' station he was terrified Cathryn would appear. It was a long shot, but under the circumstances he could not think of any safer alternatives. He had to force himself to walk at a normal pace rather than run to the elevator.

Cathryn had been sound asleep when the LPN touched her shoulder. All she had heard was that she was wanted on the telephone and that it was an emergency. Her first thought had been that something had happened to Charles.

When she got to the nurses' station the LPN had already disappeared. Not knowing what phone to use, Cathryn asked the charge nurse about her call. The woman looked up from her paperwork and, remembering the call, told Cathryn she could pick up the phone in the chart room.

Cathryn said hello three times, each time louder than the last. But no one answered. She had waited and repeated several hellos, but with no response. Depressing the disconnect button rapidly had no effect until she held it down for an instant. When she released it, she was talking to the hospital operator.

The operator didn't know anything about a call to Anderson 6 for Mrs. Martel. Cathryn hung up and walked to the doorway leading to the nurses' station. The nurse was at the desk, bent over a chart. Cathryn was about to call out when she saw a vague figure in white, complete with surgical mask and hood, push a patient across the dimly lit area in front of the elevators. Cathryn, as sensitized as she was, felt a wave of sympathy for the poor child being taken to surgery at such a late hour. She knew that it had to be an emergency.

Fearful of intruding on the nurses' important tasks, Cathryn tentatively called out to her. The nurse swung around in her chair, her face expectant.

"There wasn't anyone on the line," explained Cathryn.

"That's strange," said the nurse. "The caller said it was an emergency."

"Was it a man or a woman?" asked Cathryn.

"A man," said the nurse.

Cathryn wondered if it were Charles. Maybe he had gone

over to Gina's. "Could I make a local call from this phone?" asked Cathryn.

"We don't usually allow that," said the nurse, "but if you make it quick . . . Dial nine first."

Cathryn hurried back to the phone and quickly dialed her mother's. When Gina answered, Cathryn was instantly relieved. Her mother's voice was normal.

"What have you had to eat?" asked Gina.

"I'm not hungry," said Cathryn.

"You must eat!" commanded Gina, as if the consumption of food solved all problems.

"Has Charles called?" asked Cathryn, ignoring her mother.

"Not a word. Some father!" Gina made a disapproving clucking sound.

"How about Chuck?"

"He's here. You want to talk with him?"

Cathryn debated about discussing the need for a marrow transplant with Chuck, but remembering his previous reaction, decided to wait to do it in person. "No. I'll be home soon. I'll make sure Michelle is sleeping soundly, then I'll come home."

"I'll have some spaghetti waiting," said Gina.

Cathryn hung up, intuitively convinced that the mysterious caller had to have been Charles. What kind of an emergency could it have been? And why didn't he stay on the line? Passing the nurse, Cathryn thanked her for allowing her to use the phone.

She walked quickly, passing the partially opened doors of the other rooms, smelling pungent medical aromas, hearing the occasional cry of a child.

Reaching Michelle's room, Cathryn noticed that she had left the door completely open. As she stepped into the room, she hoped that the light from the corridor had not bothered Michelle. Quietly she pulled the door almost closed behind her and walked carefully over to her chair in the near dark. She was about to sit down when she realized that the bed was empty. Afraid to step on Michelle in case she'd tumbled onto the floor, Cathryn quickly bent down and felt around the bed. The narrow shaft of hall light glistened on the polished vinyl and Cathryn immediately could see that Michelle was not there. In a panic, she hurried to the bathroom and turned on the light. Michelle was not there, either. Returning to the room, Cathryn switched on the overhead light. Michelle was not in the room!

Cathryn ran out of the room and down the long hall, arriving back at the nurses' station out of breath. "Nurse! My daughter's not in her room! She's gone!"

The charge nurse looked up from her writing, then down at her clipboard. "That's Martel?"

"Yes! Yes! And she was there sleeping soundly when I came down here to answer the phone."

"Our report from the day shift said she was very weak?" questioned the nurse.

"That's the point," said Cathryn. "She might hurt herself."

As if she thought Cathryn was lying, the nurse insisted on returning to Michelle's room. She glanced around the room and checked the bathroom. "You're right, she's not here."

Cathryn restrained herself from making any disparaging comments. The nurse put in a call to security telling them that a twelve-year-old girl had vanished from Anderson 6. She also flipped on a series of small signal lights that called back the team of RNs and LPNs who'd been out working on the floor. She told them of Michelle's apparent disappearance and sent them back out to search all the rooms.

"Martel," said the charge nurse after the others had left. "That rings a bell. What was the name of the child taken down to radiology for that emergency flat plate?"

Cathryn looked bewildered. For a moment she thought the woman was asking her the question.

"That's probably it," said the nurse, picking up the phone and dialing radiology. She had to let it ring almost twenty times before a harried technician picked it up.

"You're doing an emergency flat plate on a patient from Anderson 6," said the charge nurse. "What is the name of the child?"

"I haven't done any emergency flat plates," said the technician. "Must have been George. He's up in the OR doing a portable chest. He'll be back in a minute and I'll have him call." The technician hung up before the charge nurse could respond.

Charles wheeled Michelle into the emergency room and, without any hesitation to suggest he didn't belong there, pushed the gurney into the examination area. He selected an empty cubicle and, pulling aside the curtain, brought Michelle in next to the table. After closing the curtain, he got out Michelle's clothes.

The excitement of the caper had buoyed Michelle's spirits and, despite her weakness, she tried to help her father as he dressed her. Charles found that he was very clumsy, and the more he hurried, the clumsier he was. Michelle had to do all the buttons and tie her shoes.

After she was dressed, Charles left her for a few moments to find some cling bandage. Luckily he didn't have to look far. Returning to the cubicle, he sat Michelle up and eyed her.

"We have to make it look like you were in an accident," he said. "I know what we'll do!"

He tore open the bandage and began winding it around Michelle's head as if she'd suffered a laceration. When he was finished he stepped back. "Perfect!" As a final touch, Charles put a regular bandage over the bridge of her nose, making her laugh. Charles told her she looked like a motorcyclist who'd fallen on her head.

Pretending that she weighed two hundred pounds, he picked up his daughter and staggered out through the curtain. Once in the corridor he quickly became serious, heading toward the entrance. To his satisfaction the emergency room had become even busier than when he'd first entered. Tearful children with all manner of cuts and bruises were waiting, while mothers with coughing infants queued up to check in. Amidst the confusion Charles was unnoticed. Only one nurse turned as Charles and Michelle passed by. When Charles caught her eye he smiled and mouthed the words, "Thank you." She waved back self-consciously as if she thought she should recognize them but didn't.

Approaching the exit, Charles saw a uniformed security man jump up from the nearby chair. Charles's heart fluttered, but the man didn't challenge them; instead he scurried to the door and said: "Hope she's feeling better. Have a good night."

With a welcome sense of freedom, Charles carried Michelle out of the hospital. Quickening his steps, he hurried to the parking garage, settled Michelle in the van, paid his parking fee, and drove off.

THIRTEEN

Cathryn tried to be both patient and understanding, but as time passed she became increasingly nervous. She castigated herself for leaving Michelle to answer the telephone. She should have had the call transferred directly to Michelle's room.

As she paced the lounge, she involuntarily thought about Michelle's comment: "I think it would be better if I were dead." She'd initially put the statement out of her mind, but now that Michelle had not reappeared, it kept coming back to haunt her. Cathryn had no idea if Michelle could do herself harm but, having heard all sorts of grisly stories, she could not dismiss her fear.

Checking her watch, Cathryn walked out of the lounge and approached the nurses' station. How could a hospital lose a sick twelve-year-old child who was so weak she could barely walk?

"Any news?" asked Cathryn, directing her question to the evening charge nurse. There were now a half dozen nurses sitting around the station chatting casually.

"Not yet," said the nurse, interrupting a discussion with a

colleague. "Security has checked all the stairwells. I'm still waiting for a call from radiology. I'm sure Martel was the name of the child radiology came and picked up."

"It's been almost a half hour," said Cathryn. "I'm terrified. Could you call radiology again?"

Not bothering to hide her irritation, the nurse called again and told Cathryn that the radiology technician had not come back from the OR but that he'd call when he did.

Cathryn turned away from the nurses' station, acutely aware how the medical people intimidated her. She was furious at the hospital, yet was unable to show her anger no matter how justified she thought it was. Instead she thanked the nurse and wandered back down to Michelle's empty room. Absentmindedly she looked into the bathroom again, avoiding her reflection in the mirror. Next to the bathroom was the closet, and Cathryn looked inside. She had the door almost closed when she reopened it and stared, dumbfounded.

Running back to the nurses' station, she tried to get the charge nurse's attention. The nurses from the evening shift who were going off duty and the night nurses who were coming on duty were grouped around the center of the nurses' station having their inviolable report. It was a time when emergencies were proscribed, medical or otherwise. Cathryn had to yell to get attention.

"I just discovered my daughter's clothes are missing," said Cathryn anxiously.

There was silence.

The charge nurse cleared her throat. "We'll be finished here in a few moments, Mrs. Martel."

Cathryn turned away angrily. Obviously her emergency wasn't as important as the ward routine, but if Michelle's clothes were gone, she had probably left the hospital.

The phone call must have been from Charles, and its purpose was to get Cathryn out of Michelle's room. All at once the image of the man pushing the child to surgery flashed before Cathryn's eyes. He was the correct height, the right build. It had to have been Charles! Cathryn rushed back to the nurses' station. Now she was sure that Michelle had been abducted.

"Now let me get it straight," said the stocky Boston police officer. Cathryn had noticed his name tag said William Kerney. "You were sleeping in here when a nurse tapped you on the shoulder."

"Yes! Yes!" shouted Cathryn, exasperated at the slow pace of the investigation. She'd hoped that calling the police would speed up the whole affair. "I've told you ten times exactly what happened. Can't you go out and try to find the child?"

"We have to finish our report," explained William. He held a weather-beaten clipboard in the crook of his left arm. In his right hand he struggled with a pencil, licking the end every so often.

The group was standing in Michelle's vacant room. It included Cathryn, two Boston police officers, the evening charge nurse, and the assistant administrator. The administrator was a tall, handsome man, dressed in an elegant gray business suit. He had a curious habit of smiling after each sentence, reducing his eyes to narrow slits. His face was gloriously tan as if he'd just returned from a vacation in the Caribbean.

"How long were you out of the room?" asked William.

"I told you," snapped Cathryn. "Five minutes . . . ten minutes. I don't know exactly."

"Uh huh," murmured William, printing the answer.

Michael Grady, the other Boston police officer, was reading the temporary guardianship papers. When he finished, he handed them to the administrator. "It's a child-snatching case. No doubt about it."

"Uh huh," murmured William, moving up to the top of the form to print "Child Snatching." He didn't know the code number for the offense and made a mental note to look it up when he got back to the station.

In desperation, Cathryn turned to the administrator. "Can't you do something? I'm sorry I can't remember your name."

"Paul Mansford," said the administrator before flashing a

smile. "No need to apologize. We are doing something. The police are here."

"But I'm afraid something is going to happen to the child with all this delay," said Cathryn.

"And you saw a man pushing a child to surgery?" asked William.

"Yes!" shouted Cathryn.

"But no child went to surgery," said the nurse.

William turned to the nurse. "What about the man with the X-ray form? Can you describe him?"

The nurse looked up toward the ceiling. "Medium height, medium build, brown hair . . ."

"That's not too specific," said William.

"What about his blue eyes?" asked Cathryn.

"I didn't notice his eyes," said the nurse.

"What was he wearing?" asked William.

"Oh God!" exclaimed Cathryn in frustration. "Please do something."

"A long white coat," said the nurse.

"Okay," said William. "Someone calls, gets Mrs. Martel out of the child's room, presents a bogus X-ray request, then wheels the child off as if he's going to surgery. Right?"

Everyone nodded except Cathryn who had put a hand to her forehead to try to control herself.

"Then, how long before security was notified?" asked William.

"Just a couple of minutes," said the nurse.

"That's why we think they are still in the hospital," said the administrator.

"But her clothes are gone," said Cathryn. "They've left the hospital. That's why you have to do something before it's too late. Please!"

Everyone looked at Cathryn as if she were a child. She returned their stares then threw up her hands in exasperation. "Jesus Christ."

William turned to the administrator. "Is there someplace in the hospital someone could take a child?" he asked.

"There are lots of temporary hiding places," agreed the administrator. "But there's no place they won't be found."

"All right," said William. "Suppose it was the father who took the child. Why?"

"Because he didn't agree with the treatment," said Cathryn. "That's why the temporary guardianship was granted: so that the treatment would be maintained. Unfortunately my husband has been under a lot of stress, not just the child's illness, but his job."

William whistled. "If he didn't like the treatment here," he said, "what was he interested in? Laetrile, something like that?"

"He didn't say," said Cathryn, "but I know he wasn't interested in Laetrile."

"We've had a few of those Laetrile cases," said William, ignoring Cathryn's last statement. Turning to his partner, Michael Grady, he said: "Remember that kid that went to Mexico?"

"Sure do," said Michael.

Turning back to the group, William said: "We've had some experience with parents seeking unorthodox treatment for their kids. I think we'd better alert the airport. They might be on their way out of the country."

Dr. Keitzman arrived in a whirlwind of nervous motion. Cathryn was tremendously relieved to see him. He immediately dominated the small gathering and demanded to be told everything. Paul Mansford and the charge nurse teamed up to give him a rapid report.

"This is terrible!" said Dr. Keitzman, nervously adjusting his rimless glasses. "It sounds to me like Dr. Charles Martel has definitely had some sort of breakdown."

"How long will the little girl live without treatment?" asked William.

"Hard to say. Days, weeks, a month at most. We have several more drugs to try on the child, but it has to be sooner rather than later. There is still a chance for remission."

"Well, we'll get right on it," said William. "I'll finish the report and turn it over to the detectives immediately."

As the two patrolmen walked out of the hospital a half hour later, Michael Grady turned to his partner and said, "What a story! Makes you feel terrible. Kid with leukemia and all that."

"It sure does. Makes you feel thankful your own kids are at least healthy."

"Do you think the detectives will get right on it?"

"Now? You kidding? These custody cases are a pain in the ass. Thankfully they usually solve themselves in twenty-four hours. Anyway, the detectives won't even look at it until tomorrow."

They climbed into their patrol car, checked in by radio, then pulled away from the curb.

Cathryn opened her eyes and looked around in confusion. She recognized the yellow curtains, the white bureau with its doily and collection of bric-a-brac, the pink vanity that had doubled as her high school desk, her yearbooks on the shelf, and the plastic crucifix she'd gotten when she'd been confirmed. She knew she was in her old room that her mother had compulsively maintained since she had left for college. What confused Cathryn was why she was there.

She shook her head to rid herself of the numbing remnants of the sleeping pills Dr. Keitzman had insisted she take. Leaning over she snatched up her watch and tried to make sense out of the numbers. She couldn't believe it. It was a quarter to twelve. Cathryn blinked her eyes and looked again. No, it was nine o'clock. Even that was later than she'd wanted to sleep.

Slipping on an old plaid flannel robe, Cathryn opened the door and hurried down to the kitchen, smelling the aroma of fresh biscuits and bacon. When she entered, her mother looked up, pleased to have her daughter home no matter what the reason.

"Has Charles called?" asked Cathryn.

"No, but I've fixed you a nice breakfast."

"Has anybody called? The hospital? The police?"

"No one has called. So relax. I made your favorite, baking-powder biscuits."

"I can't eat," said Cathryn, her mind a whirl. But she wasn't too preoccupied to see her mother's face immediately fall. "Well, maybe some biscuits."

Gina perked up and got out a cup and saucer for Cathryn.

"I'd better get Chuck up," said Cathryn, starting back to the hall.

"He's up, breakfasted, and gone," said Gina triumphantly. "He likes biscuits as much as you. Said he had a nine o'clock class."

Cathryn turned and sat down at the table while her mother poured the coffee. She felt useless. She'd tried so hard to be a wife and mother and now she had the feeling that she'd bungled it. Getting her adopted son up for school was hardly the criterion for being a good mother, yet the fact that she'd not done it seemed representative of her whole incompetent performance.

Battling her emotions, she lifted the coffee cup to her mouth, mindless of its temperature. As she took a sip, the hot fluid scalded her lips and she pulled the cup away, sloshing some of the fluid on her hand. Burned, she released her grasp on the mug and let it go. The cup fell to the table, shattering itself and the saucer. At the same moment, Cathryn broke into tears.

Gina quickly had the mess cleaned up, and repeatedly reassured her daughter that she shouldn't cry because Gina didn't care about any old cup that she'd bought as a souvenir in Venice on her only trip to that beautiful city that she loved more than any place in the world.

Cathryn got control of herself. She knew that the Venetian cup was one of her mother's treasures and she felt badly about breaking it, but Gina's overreaction helped calm down her emotions.

"I think I'll drive up to Shaftesbury," said Cathryn at length. "I'll get some more clothes for Chuck and check on Jean Paul."

"Chuck's got what he needs," said Gina. "The money it costs to drive up there, you could buy him a new outfit in Filene's basement."

"True," admitted Cathryn. "I guess I want to be around the phone if Charles calls."

"If he calls and gets no answer, he'll call here," said Gina. "After all, he's not stupid. Where do you think he's gone with Michelle?"

"I don't know," said Cathryn. "Last night the police talked about Mexico. Apparently a lot of people looking for unusual cancer cures go to Mexico. But Charles wouldn't go there. I know that much."

"I hate to say I told you so," said Gina, "but I warned you about marrying an older man with three children. It's always trouble. Always!"

Cathryn held back the anger that only her mother was capable of causing. Then the phone rang.

Gina answered it while Cathryn held her breath.

"It's for you," said Gina. "A detective named Patrick O'Sullivan."

Expecting the worst, Cathryn picked up the phone. Patrick O'Sullivan quickly reassured her, saying that they had no new information about Charles or Michelle. He said that there had been an interesting development in the case and asked if Cathryn would meet him at the Weinburger Research Institute. She agreed immediately.

Fifteen minutes later she was ready to leave. She told Gina that after stopping at the Weinburger she was going to drive back to New Hampshire. Gina tried to protest but Cathryn was insistent, saying that she had to have some time alone. She told her mother that she'd be back in time for dinner with Chuck.

The ride across Boston and down Memorial Drive was uneventful. Pulling the old Dodge into the Weinburger parking lot made her remember that summer two years before when she'd met Charles for the first time. Could it really have been only two years ago?

There were two police cars pulled up close to the entrance and when Cathryn walked by them she could hear the familiar crackle of their radios. Seeing police cars wasn't an auspicious sign, but Cathryn refused to allow herself to speculate. The front door of the institute slid open for her, and she made her way down to Charles's lab.

The door was ajar and Cathryn walked in. The first thing she noticed was that the lab had already been dismantled. She'd been in it on several occasions in the past, so she'd had an idea of what to expect. Now all the science-fiction-like machines were gone. The counter tops were bare like a store that had gone bankrupt.

There were six people in the room. Ellen, whom Cathryn recognized, was talking to two uniformed policemen who were engaged in filling out the police report. Seeing the policemen painstakingly printing brought back a memory of the previous night. Dr. Ibanez and Dr. Morrison were standing near Charles's desk talking with a freckle-faced man in a blue polyester sports coat. The man saw Cathryn enter and immediately approached her.

"Mrs. Martel?" questioned the man.

Cathryn nodded and took the man's outstretched hand. It was soft and slightly moist.

"I'm Detective Patrick O'Sullivan. I've been assigned to your case. Thanks for coming."

Over Patrick's shoulder Cathryn could see Ellen point to an empty space on the counter before she started talking again. Cathryn couldn't quite make out what she was saying but she could tell it was something about equipment. Glancing over at the doctors she could see they were engaged in heated discussion. She couldn't hear what they were saying, but she saw Dr. Morrison strike his open palm in apparent anger.

"What's going on?" asked Cathryn, looking up into the detective's soft green eyes.

"It seems that your husband, after having been dismissed from his position here at the institute, stole most of his equipment."

Cathryn's eyes widened in disbelief. "I don't believe that."

"The evidence is pretty irrefutable. The two evening security men apparently helped Charles strip the lab and load the stuff."

"But why?" asked Cathryn.

"I was hoping you'd be able to tell me," said the detective.

Cathryn glanced around the room, trying to comprehend the extent of Charles's folly.

"I haven't the slightest idea," said Cathryn. "It seems absurd."

The detective lifted his eyebrows and wrinkled his forehead as he followed Cathryn's eyes around the lab. "It's absurd all right. It's also grand larceny, Mrs. Martel."

Cathryn looked back at the detective.

The detective glanced down and shuffled his feet. "This puts a different light on your husband's disappearance. Childsnatching by a parent is one thing, and to tell you the honest truth, we don't get too excited about it. But theft is something else. We're going to have to put out the details and a warrant for Dr. Martel's arrest on the NCIC teletype."

Cathryn shuddered. Every time she thought she understood the details of the nightmare it got worse. Charles was now a fugitive. "I don't know what to say."

"Our condolences, Mrs. Martel," said Dr. Ibanez, coming up behind her.

She turned and saw the director's sympathetic expression.

"It's a tragedy," agreed Dr. Morrison with the same expression. "And to think Charles was once such a promising researcher."

There was an uncomfortable pause. Morrison's comment angered Cathryn, but she was at a loss for words.

"Exactly why was Dr. Martel fired?" asked Patrick O'Sullivan, breaking the silence.

Cathryn turned to the detective. He had asked the question she would have liked to pose if she'd had the courage.

"Basically, it was because Dr. Martel had been acting a bit bizarrely. We began to question his mental stability." Dr. Ibanez paused. "He also was not what you would call a team player. In fact, he was a loner and lately he'd become uncooperative."

"What kind of research was he doing?" asked the detective.

"It's hard to describe to a layman," said Morrison. "Basically Charles was working on the immunological approach to cancer. Unfortunately this approach is somewhat dated. Ten years ago it held great promise but initial hopes were not borne out by subsequent developments. Charles couldn't or wouldn't make the adaptation. And, as you know, the advancement of science does not wait for anyone." Morrison smiled as he finished his statement.

"Why do you think Dr. Martel took all this equipment?" asked O'Sullivan, making a sweeping gesture around the room.

Dr. Ibanez shrugged. "I haven't the faintest idea."

"I think it was spite," said Dr. Morrison. "It's like the kid who takes home his ball when the others don't want to play by his rules."

"Could Dr. Martel have taken the equipment to continue his research?" said O'Sullivan.

"No," said Dr. Morrison. "Impossible! The key to this kind of research is the highly bred animal systems we use. These animals are absolutely essential to the research, and Charles did not take any of his mice. And as a fugitive, I think he'd find it difficult to get them."

"I suppose you could give me a list of suppliers," said the detective.

"Absolutely," answered Dr. Morrison.

In the background the phone rang. Cathryn had no idea why she jumped but she did. Ellen answered it and called out for Detective O'Sullivan.

"This must be a very difficult time for you," said Dr. Ibanez to Cathryn.

"You have no idea," agreed Cathryn.

"If we can help in any way," said Dr. Morrison.

Cathryn tried to smile.

Patrick O'Sullivan came back. "Well, we've found his car. He left it in a parking lot in Harvard Square."

As Cathryn drove along Interstate 301 she felt increasingly unhappy. The reaction surprised her because one of the reasons she'd wanted to go home, besides being close to the phone in case Charles called, was to lift her spirits. She appreciated her mother's efforts to help, but she also resented Gina's disapproving comments about Charles and her self-righteous attitude. Having been abandoned herself, Gina had a low regard for men in general, particularly nonreligious men like Charles. She'd never been wholeheartedly behind Cathryn's marriage, and she let Cathryn know how she felt.

So Cathryn had looked forward to getting back to her own home although she realized it would no longer be the happy refuge she knew. Coming upon their property, Cathryn took her foot off the accelerator and braked. The first thing she saw was the mailbox. It had been knocked over and crushed. She started up the drive, moving between the rows of trees which in the summer formed a long gallery of shade. Through the now-naked branches Cathryn could see the house, stark white against the dark shadow of evergreens behind the barn.

Pulling the station wagon to a point opposite the back porch, Cathryn turned off the ignition. As she looked at the house she thought how cruel life could be. It seemed that one episode could initiate a chain reaction like a series of dominoes standing on end, each inevitably knocking over the next. As Cathryn got out of the car, she noticed the door to the playhouse was swinging in the wind, repeatedly thumping against the outside shingles. Looking more closely, she could see that most of the small panes of glass in the mullioned windows had been broken. Retrieving her keys, she walked through the snow to the back door, turned her key, and stepped into the kitchen.

Cathryn screamed. There was a sudden movement, and a figure came from behind the door and lunged at her.

In the next instant, she was pushed up against the kitchen

wall. The door crashed shut with a concussion that made the old frame house shudder.

Cathryn's scream faltered and trailed off in her throat. It was Charles! Speechless, she watched while he frantically ran from window to window, looking outside. In his right hand he held his old twelve-gauge shotgun. Cathryn noticed the windows had been crudely boarded up and Charles had to peer out between the cracks.

Before she could recover her equilibrium, Charles grabbed her arm and forced her rapidly out of the kitchen, stumbling down the short hall into the living room. Then he let go of her and again ran from window to window, looking out.

Cathryn was paralyzed by surprise and fear. When he finally turned back to her, she saw he was exhausted.

"Are you alone?" he demanded.

"Yes," said Cathryn, afraid to say anything else.

"Thank God," said Charles. His tense face visibly relaxed.

"What are you doing here?" asked Cathryn.

"This is my home," said Charles, taking a deep breath and letting it out through pursed lips.

"I don't understand," said Cathryn. "I thought you'd taken Michelle and run away. They'll find you here!"

For the first time Cathryn took her eyes off Charles. She noticed the living room had been totally changed. The gleaming, high-tech instruments from the Weinburger were grouped around the wall. In the middle of the room, in a makeshift hospital bed, Michelle slept.

"Michelle," cried Cathryn, running over and grasping the child's hand. Charles came up behind her.

Michelle's eyes opened and for an instant there was a flicker of recognition, then the lids closed. Cathryn turned to Charles.

"Charles, what in heaven's name are you doing?"

"I'll tell you in a moment," said Charles, adjusting Michelle's intravenous flow. He took Cathryn's arm and urged her to follow him back to the kitchen.

"Coffee?" he asked.

Cathryn shook her head, keeping her eyes riveted on

Charles as he poured himself a cup. Then he sat down opposite Cathryn.

"First I want to say something," began Charles, looking directly at Cathryn. "I've had a chance to think and I now understand the position you were in at the hospital. I'm sorry my own indecision about Michelle's treatment was inadvertently taken out on you. And I, more than a layman, know how doctors can bully patients and their families to get their own way. Anyway, I understand what happened in the guardianship situation. I understand there was no one at fault and there was no malevolence on anyone's part, least of all yours. I'm sorry that I reacted as I did, but I couldn't help it. I hope you'll forgive me. I know that you were trying to do what was best for Michelle."

Cathryn didn't move. She wanted to rush to Charles and throw her arms around him because all at once he sounded so normal, but she couldn't move. So much had happened and there were still unanswered questions.

Charles picked up his coffee cup. His hand shook so much he had to use his left hand to steady it.

"Deciding what was best for Michelle was a very difficult problem," continued Charles. "Like you, I hoped that orthodox medicine could give her more time. But it got to the point where I knew that they were failing and I had to do something."

Cathryn could sense Charles's sincerity. What she couldn't decide was his rationality. Had he cracked under the strain as everyone suggested? Cathryn realized that she wasn't equipped to decide.

"All the doctors agreed that the medicines were her only chance to get a remission," said Cathryn, feeling defensive about her actions. "Dr. Keitzman assured me that it was her only chance."

"And I'm sure he believed what he said."

"It's not true?"

"Of course she has to get a remission," agreed Charles. "But their chemotherapy, even in the experimentally high doses, was not touching her leukemic cells. At the same time they were destroying normal cells, particularly her own immune system."

Cathryn wasn't sure she fully understood what Charles was saying but at least it sounded consistent. It didn't sound like the product of a deranged mind.

"And I feel," continued Charles, "that if she has a chance, she has to have an intact immune system."

"You mean you have another treatment?" asked Cathryn.

Charles sighed. "I think so. I hope so!"

"But all the other doctors agreed that chemotherapy was the only way."

"Of course," said Charles. "Just like a surgeon believes in surgery. People are biased by what they know. It's human. But cancer research has been my life for the last nine years, and I think there's a chance I can do something." Charles paused.

Obviously he believed what he was saying, but was it based on reality or on delusion? Cathryn wanted desperately to believe also, but under the circumstances, it was difficult. "Do you mean there's a chance you can cure her?"

"I don't want to get your hopes up too high," said Charles, "but I think there is a chance. Maybe small, but a chance. And, more important, my treatment won't hurt her."

"Have you been able to cure any of your laboratory animals that had cancer?" asked Cathryn.

"No I haven't," admitted Charles, but then he added quickly, "I know that makes it sound unrealistic, but I think I didn't have luck with the animals because I was working so slowly and carefully. The purpose there was pure research. But I was just about to try a new technique to use healthy mice as an intermediary to cure the diseased mice."

"But you don't have any animals here," said Cathryn, remembering Detective O'Sullivan's questions.

"Not true," said Charles. "I have one large experimental animal. Me!"

Cathryn swallowed. For the first moment in the conversation

a red flag went up, questioning Charles's state of mind.

"That idea surprises you," he said. "Well, it shouldn't. In the past most great medical researchers used themselves as experimental subjects. Anyway, let me try to explain to you what I am doing. First of all my research has advanced to the point where I can take a cancerous cell from an organism and isolate a protein, or what is called an antigen, on its surface, which makes that cell different from all the other cells. That, in itself, is a major advance. My problem then was getting the organism's immune system to react to the protein and therefore rid itself of the abnormal cancerous cells. This, I believe, is what happens in normal organisms. I think cancer is a fairly frequent occurrence but that the body's immune system takes care of it. When the immune system fails, that's when a particular cancer takes root and grows. Do you understand so far?"

Cathryn nodded.

"When I tried to get the cancerous animals to respond to the isolated protein, I couldn't. I think there is some kind of blocking mechanism and that's where I was when Michelle got sick. But then I got the idea to inject the isolated surface antigen into well animals to make them immune to it. I didn't have time to carry out the tests but I'm certain it would be easy because the well animal will recognize the antigen as being very foreign to itself whereas in the sick animal the antigen is only slightly different from its normal proteins."

Cathryn's comprehension faltered, though she tried to smile.

Charles impulsively reached across the table and grasped Cathryn's shoulders. "Cathryn, try to understand. I want you to believe in what I'm doing. I need you to help me."

Cathryn felt some inner bond loosen and fall. Charles was her husband and the fact that he needed her and admitted it was a tremendous incentive.

"Do you remember that horses were used to make diphtheria antiserum?" asked Charles.

"I think so," said Cathryn.

"What I'm explaining to you is something like that. What

I've done is to isolate the surface antigen of Michelle's leukemic cells that makes them different from her normal cells,
and I've been injecting the antigen into myself."

"So you become allergic to Michelle's leukemic cells?"
asked Cathryn, struggling to comprehend.

"Exactly," said Charles with excitement.

"Then you'll inject your antibodies into Michelle?" asked
Cathryn.

"No," said Charles. "Her immune system wouldn't accept
my antibodies. But luckily modern immunology has found a
way to transfer what they call cellular immunity or sensitivity
from one organism to another. Once my T-lymphocytes are
sensitized to Michelle's leukemic antigen, I will isolate from
my white cells what is called a transfer factor and inject that
into Michelle. Hopefully that will stimulate her own immune
system to sensitize against her leukemic cells. In that way
she'll be able to eliminate her existing leukemic cells and any
new ones that evolve."

"So she'd be cured?" said Cathryn.

"So she'd be cured," repeated Charles.

Cathryn was not sure she understood everything Charles had
said, but his plan certainly seemed sound. It didn't seem possible that he could have figured it out if he were in the midst
of a nervous breakdown. She realized that from his point of
view, everything he'd done had been rational.

"How long will all this take?" asked Cathryn.

"I don't know for sure it will even work," said Charles.
"But from the way my body is reacting to the antigen, I'll
know in a couple of days. That's why I've boarded up the
house. I'm prepared to fight any attempts to have Michelle
taken back to the hospital."

Cathryn glanced around the kitchen, noting again the
boarded windows. Turning back to Charles, she said: "I guess
you know the Boston police are looking for you. They think
you've fled to Mexico to get Laetrile."

Charles laughed. "That's absurd. And they can't be looking
for me too hard because our local police know very well that

I'm here. Did you notice the mailbox and the playhouse?"

"I saw that the mailbox was crushed and the windows were broken in the playhouse."

"That's all thanks to our local authorities. Last night a group came up from Recycle, Ltd. bent on vandalism. I called the police and thought they'd never showed up until I noticed one of the squad cars parked down the road. Obviously they condoned the whole thing."

"Why?" asked Cathryn, aghast.

"I retained a young aggressive lawyer and apparently he's successfully giving Recycle some trouble. I think they believe they can frighten me into calling him off."

"My God!" exclaimed Cathryn, beginning to appreciate the extent of Charles's isolation.

"Where are the boys?" asked Charles.

"Chuck's at Mother's. Jean Paul is in Shaftesbury, staying with a friend."

"Good," said Charles. "Things might get rough around here."

Husband and wife, both at the limits of their emotional reserves, stared at each other across the kitchen table. A surge of love swept over them. They stood up and fell into each other's arms, holding on desperately as if they were afraid something would force them apart. They both knew nothing was resolved, but the reaffirmation of their love gave them new strength.

"Please trust me, and love me," said Charles.

"I love you," said Cathryn, feeling tears on her cheek. "That's never been a problem. The issue has only been Michelle."

"Then trust that I have only her best interests at heart," said Charles. "You know how much I love her."

Cathryn pulled away to look up into Charles's face. "Everyone thinks you've had a nervous breakdown. I didn't know what to think, particularly with your carrying on about Recycle when the real issue was Michelle's treatment."

"Recycle just gave me something to do. The most frustrating part of Michelle's illness was that I couldn't do anything, which is what happened with Elizabeth. Back then all I could do was watch her die, and it seemed as if it was going to be the same situation with Michelle. I needed something to focus on, and Recycle galvanized my need for action. But my anger about what they're doing is real enough, as well as my commitment to get them to stop. But obviously my main interest is Michelle, otherwise I wouldn't be here now."

Cathryn felt as if she'd been freed from an enormous weight. She was now certain that Charles had never lost contact with reality.

"What about Michelle's condition?" asked Cathryn.

"Not good," admitted Charles. "She's a terribly sick child. It's amazing how aggressive her disease is. I've given her morphine because she's had awful stomach cramps." Charles embraced Cathryn again and averted his face.

"She had some while I was with her, too," said Cathryn. She could feel Charles tremble as he fought back his tears. Cathryn held him as tightly as she could.

They stood together for another five minutes. There were no words but the communication was total. Finally Charles pulled away. When he turned back she saw that his eyes were red, his expression serious.

"I'm glad we had the opportunity to talk," said Charles. "But I don't think you should stay here. Without doubt there will be trouble. It's not that I don't want you to be with me; in fact, selfishly I'd like you to stay. But I know it would be better if you got Jean Paul and went back to your mother's." Charles nodded his head as if he were convincing himself.

"I want you to be selfish," said Cathryn. She experienced a new sense of confidence that she could be a wife. "My place is here. Jean Paul and Chuck will be all right."

"But Cathryn . . ."

"No buts," said Cathryn. "I'm staying and I'm helping."

Charles examined his wife's face. She looked positively defiant.

"And if you think," she continued with a vehemence that

he had never seen, "that you can get rid of me now that you've convinced me what you're doing is right, you *are* crazy! You'll have to throw me out bodily."

"All right, all right," said Charles with a smile. "I won't throw you out. But we could be in for a rough time."

"It's as much my responsibility as yours," said Cathryn with conviction. "This is a family affair and I'm part of this family. We both recognized that when we decided to get married. I'm not here just to share the happiness."

Charles experienced a mixture of emotions, but the primary one was pride. He had been guilty of not giving Cathryn the credit she deserved. She was right; Charles had tried whenever it was possible to shield her from the negative aspects of their life, and that was wrong. He should have been more open, more trusting. Cathryn was his wife, not his child.

"If you want to stay, please do," he said.

"I want to stay," said Cathryn simply.

Charles kissed her gently on the lips. Then he stepped back to look at her with an admiring eye.

"You really can help," he said, checking his watch. "It's almost time to give myself another dose of Michelle's antigen. I'll explain what you can do to help after I get it prepared. Okay?"

Cathryn nodded and let Charles squeeze her hand before he walked back to the living room.

Holding on to the back of one of the kitchen chairs, Cathryn felt a little dizzy. Everything that had happened in the last several days was unexpected. There had never been a moment that she'd thought Charles would have taken Michelle to their home. She wondered if there were some way to cancel the guardianship proceedings and eliminate one of the reasons Charles was being sought by the police.

Picking up the phone, she dialed her mother. While she waited for the connection, she realized that if she told her mother that Charles was there it would precipitate an argument, so she decided to say nothing.

Gina answered on the second ring. Cathryn kept the conversation light, not mentioning her visit to the Weinburger or the fact that Charles was suspected of grand larceny. When there was a pause, she cleared her throat and said: "Provided you don't mind seeing that Chuck gets some dinner and gets off to school in the morning, I think I'll spend the night here. I want to be available in case Charles calls."

"Honey, don't feel that you have to sit around and wait for that man. I tell you, he'll call here if there's no answer at your house. Besides, I've been planning on having a wonderful dinner tonight. Try and guess what I'm making."

Cathryn let out her breath in a quiet sigh. It never failed to amaze her that her mother always believed that a good meal could fix everything.

"Mother, I don't want to guess what you are having for dinner. I want to stay here tonight in my own home."

Cathryn could tell she'd hurt her mother's feelings, but under the circumstances she didn't feel she had much choice. As quickly as she could without seeming to be rude, Cathryn hung up.

Thinking of food, Cathryn checked the refrigerator. Except for being low on milk and eggs, they were reasonably well stocked, especially with the old-fashioned root cellar in the basement. Closing the refrigerator, Cathryn looked around her boarded-up kitchen, marveling at being a prisoner in her own house.

She wondered about Charles's treatment for Michelle. She acknowledged that she didn't understand its details, but it sounded good. At the same time, she recognized that if she were with Dr. Keitzman, she'd probably believe what *he* said. Medicine was too complicated for her to feel confident enough to question the experts. As a lay person she was put in an impossible situation when the doctors disagreed.

When she went into the living room, Charles was holding a syringe with its needle up, tapping it with his index finger to get rid of air bubbles. Quietly she took a seat and watched. Michelle was still sleeping, her thin hair splayed out on the white pillow. Through the boards on the windows, Cathryn could see it was snowing again. In the basement, she could hear the oil burner kick on.

"Now I'm going to inject this into my arm vein," said Charles, looking for a tourniquet. "I don't suppose you'd be willing to do it for me."

Cathryn felt her mouth go dry. "I can try," she said reluctantly. In truth she wanted no part of the syringe. Even looking at it made her feel faint.

"Would you?" asked Charles. "Unless you're an addict, it's harder than hell to stick yourself in a vein. Also I want to tell you how to give me epinephrine if I need it. With the first intravenous dose of Michelle's antigen, I developed some anaphylaxis, meaning an allergic reaction which makes breathing difficult."

"Oh, God," said Cathryn to herself. Then to Charles she said: "Isn't there another way to take the antigen, like eating it?"

Charles shook his head. "I tried that but stomach acid breaks it down. I even tried sniffing a powdered form like cocaine, but the mucous membrane in my nose swelled unbelievably. Since I'm in a hurry I decided I'd have to mainline it. The problem is that my body's first response has been to develop a simple allergy, what they call immediate hypersensitivity. I've tried to cut down on that effect by altering the protein slightly. I want delayed hypersensitivity, not immediate."

Cathryn nodded as if she understood, but she'd comprehended nothing except the cold feel of the syringe. She held it with her fingertips as if she expected it to injure her. Charles brought a chair over and placed it in front of hers. On a counter top within reach he put two smaller syringes.

"These other syringes are the epinephrine. If I suddenly go red as a beet and can't breathe, just jam one of these into any muscle and inject. If there's no response in thirty seconds, use the next one."

Cathryn felt a strange terror. But Charles seemed blithely unconcerned. He unbuttoned his sleeve and rolled it up above his elbow. Using his teeth to hold one end of the tourniquet,

Charles applied the rubber tubing to his own upper arm. Quickly his veins engorged and stood out.

"Take off the plastic cover," instructed Charles, "then just put the needle into the vein."

With visibly trembling hands, Cathryn got the cover off the needle. Its sharp point glistened in the light. Charles tore open an alcohol pad with his right hand, holding the packet in his teeth. Vigorously he swabbed the area.

"Okay, do your stuff," said Charles looking away.

Cathryn took a breath. Now she knew why she'd never considered medicine as a career. Trying to hold the syringe steady she put the needle on Charles's skin and gently pushed. The skin merely indented.

"You have to give it a shove," said Charles, still looking away.

Cathryn gave the syringe a little push. It indented Charles's skin a little more.

Charles looked down at his arm. Reaching around with his free hand he gave the needle a sudden forceful lunge and it broke through the skin, impaling the vein.

"Perfect," he said. "Now draw back on the plunger without disturbing the tip."

Cathryn did as Charles asked and some bright red blood swished into the syringe.

"Bull's-eye," said Charles, as he took off his tourniquet. "Now slowly inject."

Cathryn pushed the plunger. It moved easily. When it was slightly more than halfway, her finger slipped. The needle dove into Charles more deeply as the plunger completed its movement. A small egg rapidly appeared on his arm.

"That's okay," said Charles. "Not bad for your first time. Now pull it out."

Cathryn pulled the needle out and Charles slapped a piece of gauze over the site.

"I'm sorry," said Cathryn, terrified that she'd hurt him.

"No problem. Maybe putting some of the antigen subcutaneously will help. Who knows?" Suddenly his face began to get red. He shivered. "Damn," he managed. Cathryn could hear his voice had changed. It was much higher. "Epinephrine," he said with some difficulty.

She grabbed for one of the smaller syringes. In her haste to remove the plastic cover she bent the needle. She grabbed for the other one. Charles, who was now blotching with hives, pointed to his left upper arm. Holding her breath, Cathryn jammed the needle into the muscle. This time she used ample force. She pressed the plunger and pulled it out. Quickly she discarded the used syringe, and picked up the first one, trying to straighten the bent needle. She was about to give it to Charles when he held up his hand.

"It's okay," he managed, his voice still abnormal. "I can already feel the reaction subsiding. Whew! Good thing you were here."

Cathryn put down the syringe. If she thought she was trembling before, now she was shaking. For Cathryn, using a needle on Charles had been the supreme test.

FOURTEEN

By nine-thirty they were settling in for the night. Earlier Cathryn had prepared some food while Charles worked in the makeshift lab. He'd taken a sample of his blood, separated the cells, and isolated some T-lymphocytes with the aid of sheep erythrocytes. Then he'd incubated the T-lymphocytes with some of his microphages and Michelle's leukemic cells. While they had dinner he told Cathryn that there still was no sign of a delayed, cell-mediated hypersensitivity. He told her that in twenty-four hours, he'd have to give himself another challenge dose of Michelle's antigen.

Michelle had awakened from her morphine-induced sleep and was overjoyed to see Cathryn. She'd not remembered seeing her stepmother arrive. Feeling somewhat better, she had even eaten some solid food.

"She seems better," whispered Cathryn as they carried the dishes back to the kitchen.

"It's more apparent than real," said Charles. "Her system is just recovering from the other medicines."

Charles had built a fire and brought their king-sized mattress down to the living room. He had wanted to be close to Michelle in case she needed him.

Once Cathryn lay down, she felt a tremendous fatigue. Believing that Michelle was as comfortable and content as possible, Cathryn allowed herself to relax for the first time in two days. As the wind blew snow against the front windows, she held on to Charles and let sleep overwhelm her.

Hearing the crash and tinkle of glass, Cathryn sat up by pure reflex, unsure what the noise had been. Charles, who had been awake, reacted more deliberately, rolling off the mattress onto the floor and standing up. As he did so he hefted his shotgun and released the safety catch.

"What was that?" demanded Cathryn, her heart pounding.

"Visitors," said Charles. "Probably our friends from Recycle."

Something thudded up against the front of the house, then fell with a thump on the porch floor.

"Rocks," said Charles, moving over to the light switch and plunging the room into darkness. Michelle murmured and Cathryn made her way over to the child's side to comfort her.

"Just as I thought," said Charles, peering between the window boards.

Cathryn came up behind him and looked over his shoulder. Standing in their driveway about a hundred feet from the house was a group of men carrying makeshift torches. Down on the road were a couple of cars haphazardly parked.

"They're drunk," said Charles.

"What are we going to do?" whispered Cathryn.

"Nothing," said Charles. "Unless they try to get inside or come too close with those torches."

"Could you shoot someone?" asked Cathryn.

"I don't know," said Charles, "I really don't know."

"I'm going to call the police," said Cathryn.

"Don't bother," said Charles. "I'm sure they know about this."

"I'm still going to try," returned Cathryn.

She left him by the window and made her way back to the kitchen where she dialed the operator and asked to be connected to the Shaftesbury police. The phone rang eight times before a tired voice answered. He identified himself as Bernie Crawford.

Cathryn reported that their house was being attacked by a group of drunks and that they needed immediate assistance.

"Just a minute," said Bernie.

Cathryn could hear a drawer open and Bernie fumbled around for something.

"Just a minute. I gotta find a pencil," said Bernie, leaving the line again before Cathryn could talk. Outside she heard a yell, and Charles came scurrying into the kitchen, going up to the window on the north side facing the pond.

"Okay," said Bernie coming back on the line. "What's the address?"

Cathryn quickly gave the address.

"Zip code?" asked Bernie.

"Zip code?" questioned Cathryn. "We need help right now."

"Lady, paperwork is paperwork. I gotta fill out a form before I dispatch a car."

Cathryn gave a zip code.

"How many guys in the group?"

"I'm not sure. Half a dozen."

Cathryn could hear the man writing.

"Are they kids?" asked Bernie.

"Cathryn!" yelled Charles. "I need you to watch out the front. They're torching the playhouse but it may be just a diversion. Somebody has got to watch the front door."

"Listen," shouted Cathryn into the phone. "I can't talk. Just send a car." She slammed down the phone and ran back into the living room. From the small window next to the fireplace she could see the flickering glow from the playhouse. She turned her attention to the front lawn. The group with the torches was gone but she could see someone lifting something out of the trunk of one of the cars. In the darkness, it looked like a pail. "Oh, God, don't let it be gasoline," said Cathryn.

From the back of the house Cathryn could hear glass breaking. "Are you all right?" she called.

"I'm all right. The bastards are breaking the windows to your car."

Cathryn heard Charles unlock the rear door. Then she heard the boom of his shotgun. The sound reverberated through the house. Then the door slammed shut.

"What happened?" yelled Cathryn.

Charles came back into the living room. "I shot into the air. I suppose it's the only thing they respect. They ran around this way."

Cathryn looked back out. The group had reassembled around the man coming from the car. In the light of the torches, Cathryn could see that he was carrying a gallon can. He knelt down, apparently opening it.

"Looks like paint," said Cathryn.

"That's what it is," said Charles.

While they watched the group began to chant "Communist" over and over. The man with the paint can approached the house seemingly building up the courage of the rest of the group. As they got closer, Cathryn could see that the men were carrying an assortment of clubs. The chanting got progressively louder. Charles recognized Wally Crabb and the man who had punched him.

The group stopped about fifty feet from the house. The man with the paint kept walking as the others egged him on. Charles pulled away from the window, making her stand behind him. He had a clear view of the door, and he slipped his finger around the trigger.

They heard the footsteps stop and then the sound of a paint-brush against the shingles. After five minutes there was a final sound of paint splashing up against the front door, followed by the clatter of the can hitting the front porch.

Rushing back to the window, Charles could see that the men were yelling and whooping with laughter. Slowly they walked back down the drive pushing and shoving each other into the snow. At the base of the driveway and after several vociferous arguments, the men climbed into the two cars. With horns blaring they drove off into the night, heading north on Interstate 301 toward Shaftesbury.

As abruptly as it had been broken, the wintry silence returned. Charles let out a long breath. He put down the shotgun and took Cathryn's hands in his. "Now that you've seen how unpleasant it is, perhaps it would be better for you to go back to your mother's until this is over."

"No way," said Cathryn, shaking her head. Then she broke away to tend to Michelle.

Fifteen minutes later the Shaftesbury police cruiser skidded up the driveway and came to a sudden stop behind the station wagon. Frank Neilson hurried from the front seat as if he were responding to an emergency.

"You can just get right back inside your car, you son-of-a-bitch," said Charles, who had come out on the front porch.

Frank, standing defiantly with his hands on his hips and his feet spread apart, just shrugged. "Well, if you don't need me."

"Just get the fuck off my land," snarled Charles.

"Strange people this side of town," said Frank loudly to his deputy as he got back into the car.

Morning crept over the frozen countryside, inhibited by a pewter-colored blanket of high clouds. Charles and Cathryn had taken turns standing watch, but the vandals had not returned. As dawn arrived Charles felt confident enough to return to the bed in front of the fireplace and slip in next to Cathryn.

Michelle had improved considerably and, although she was still extremely weak, she could sit up, courageously managing to smile when Charles pretended to be a waiter bringing in her breakfast.

While he drew some of his blood and again tested his T-lymphocytes for signs of delayed hypersensitivity to Michelle's leukemic cells, Cathryn tried to make their topsy-turvy house more livable. Between Charles's equipment and reagents, Michelle's bed, and the king-sized mattress, the living room was like a maze. There was little Cathryn could do there, but the kitchen soon responded to her efforts.

"No sign of any appropriate reaction with my lymphocytes," said Charles, coming in for some more coffee. "You're going to have to give me another dose of Michelle's antigen later today."

"Sure," said Cathryn, trying to buoy both her own and Charles's confidence. She wasn't sure she could do it again. The thought alone gave her gooseflesh.

"I must think of some way to make us more secure here," said Charles. "I don't know what I would have done if those men last night had been drunk enough to storm the back door."

"Vandals are one thing," said Cathryn. "What if the police come, wanting to arrest you?"

Charles turned back to Cathryn.

"Until I finish with what I'm doing, I have to keep everybody out of the house."

"I think it's just a matter of time before the police come," said Cathryn. "And I'm afraid it will be a lot more difficult to keep them out. Just by resisting, you'll be breaking the law, and they might feel obligated to use force."

"I don't think so," said Charles. "There's too much for them to lose and very little to gain."

"The stimulus could be Michelle, thinking they need to recommence her treatment."

Charles nodded slowly. "You might be right, but even if you are, there's nothing else to be done."

"I think there is," said Cathryn. "Maybe I can stop the police from looking for you. I met the detective who's handling the case. Perhaps I should go see him and tell him that I don't want to press charges. If there are no charges, then they would stop looking for you."

Charles took a large gulp of coffee. What Cathryn said made sense. He knew that if the police came in force, they could get him out of the house. That was one of the reasons he'd boarded up the windows so carefully; afraid of tear gas or the like. But he thought they probably would have other means which he hadn't wanted to consider. Cathryn was right; the police would be real trouble.

"All right," said Charles, "but you'll have to use the rental van in the garage. I don't think the station wagon has any windshield."

Putting on their coats, they walked hand in hand through the inch of new snow to the locked barn. They both saw the charred remains of the playhouse at the pond's edge and both avoided mentioning it. The still-smoldering ashes were too sharp a reminder of the terror of the previous night.

As Cathryn backed the van out of the garage, she felt a reluctance to leave. With Michelle ostensibly feeling better and despite the vandals, Cathryn had enjoyed her newly found closeness with Charles. With some difficulty, since driving a large van was a new experience, Cathryn got the vehicle turned around. She waved good-bye to Charles and drove slowly down their slippery driveway.

Reaching the foot of the hill, she turned to look back at the house. In the steely light, it looked abandoned among the leafless trees. Across the front of the house, the word "Communist" was painted in careless, large block letters. The rest of the red paint had been splashed on the front door, and the way it had splattered and ran off the porch made it look like blood.

Driving directly to the Boston Police Headquarters on Berkeley Street, Cathryn rehearsed what she was going to say to Patrick O'Sullivan. Deciding that brevity was the best approach, she was confident that she'd be in and out in a matter of minutes.

She had a great deal of trouble finding a parking spot and ended up leaving the van in an illegal yellow zone. Taking the elevator to the sixth floor, she found O'Sullivan's office without difficulty. The detective got up as she entered and came around his desk. He was dressed in exactly the same outfit as he'd had on twenty-four hours earlier when she'd met him. Even the shirt was the same because she remembered a coffee stain just to the right of his dark blue polyester tie. It was hard for Cathryn to imagine that this seemingly gentle man could muster the violence he obviously needed on occasion for his job.

"Would you like to sit down?" asked Patrick. "Can I take your coat?"

"That's okay, thank you," said Cathryn. "I'll only take a moment of your time."

The detective's office looked like the set for a TV melodrama. There were the obligatory stern photos of some of the police hierarchy on the chipped and peeling walls. There was also a cork bulletin board filled with an assortment of wanted posters and photographs. The detective's desk was awash with papers, envelopes, soup cans full of pencils, an old typewriter, and a picture of a chubby redheaded woman with five redheaded little girls.

O'Sullivan tipped back in his chair, his fingers linked over his stomach. His expression was entirely blank. Cathryn realized she had no idea what the man was thinking.

"Well," she said uneasily, her confidence waning. "The reason I came is to tell you that I'm not interested in pressing charges against my husband."

Detective O'Sullivan's face did not alter in the slightest detail.

Cathryn looked away for a moment. Already the meeting was not going according to plan. She continued: "In other words, I don't want guardianship of the child."

The detective remained unresponsive, augmenting Cathryn's anxiety.

"It's not that I don't care," added Cathryn quickly. "It's just that my husband is the biological parent, and he is an M.D., so I think he's in the best position to determine the kind of treatment the child should receive."

"Where is your husband?" asked O'Sullivan.

Cathryn blinked. The detective's question made it sound as if he hadn't been listening to her at all. Then she realized she shouldn't have paused. "I don't know," said Cathryn, feeling she sounded less than convincing.

Abruptly O'Sullivan tipped forward in his chair, bringing

his arms down on the top of his desk. "Mrs. Martel, I think I'd better inform you of something. Even though you initiated the legal proceedings, you cannot unilaterally stop them before the hearing. The judge who granted you emergency temporary guardianship also appointed a guardian *ad litim* by the name of Robert Taber. How does Mr. Taber feel about pressing charges against your husband in order to get Michelle Martel back into the hospital?"

"I don't know," said Cathryn meekly, confused at this complication.

"I had been led to believe," continued Detective O'Sullivan, "that the child's life was at stake unless she got very specific treatment as soon as possible."

Cathryn didn't say anything.

"It's apparent to me that you have been talking with your husband."

"I've spoken with him," admitted Cathryn, "and the child is doing all right."

"What about the medical treatment?"

"My husband is a physician," said Cathryn, as if stating Charles's qualifications answered the detective's question.

"That may be, Mrs. Martel, but the court will only agree to accepted treatment."

Cathryn marshaled her courage and stood up. "I think I should go."

"Perhaps you should tell us where your husband is, Mrs. Martel."

"I'd rather not say," said Cathryn, abandoning any pretense of ignorance.

"You do remember we have a warrant for his arrest. The authorities at the Weinburger Institute are very eager to press charges."

"They'll get every piece of their equipment back," said Cathryn.

"You should not allow yourself to become an accessory to the crime," said Patrick O'Sullivan.

"Thank you for your time," said Cathryn as she turned for the door.

"We already know where Charles is," called Detective O'Sullivan.

Cathryn stopped and turned back to the detective.

"Why don't you come back and sit down."

For a moment Cathryn didn't move. At first she was going to leave, but then she realized she'd better find out what they knew and more importantly, what they planned to do. Reluctantly, she returned to her seat.

"I should explain something else to you," said O'Sullivan. "We didn't put out the warrant for your husband's arrest on the NCIC teletype until this morning. My feeling was that this was not a usual case, and despite what the people at the Weinburger said, I didn't think your husband stole the equipment. I thought he'd taken it, but not stolen it. What I hoped was that somehow the case would solve itself. I mean, like your husband would call somebody and say 'I'm sorry, here's all the equipment and here's the kid; I got carried away . . .' and so forth. If that happened I think we could have avoided any indictments. But then we got pressure from the Weinburger and also the hospital. So your husband's warrant went out over the wires this morning and we heard back immediately. The Shaftesbury police phoned to say that they knew Charles Martel was in his house and that they'd be happy to go out and apprehend him. So I said . . ."

"Oh God, no!" exclaimed Cathryn, her face blanching. Detective O'Sullivan paused in mid-sentence, watching Cathryn. "Are you all right, Mrs. Martel?"

Cathryn closed her eyes and placed her hands over her face. After a minute she took her hands down and looked at O'Sullivan. "What a nightmare, and it continues."

"What are you talking about?" asked the detective.

Cathryn described Charles's crusade against Recycle, Ltd. and the attitude of the local police, also the police's reaction to the attack on their house.

"They did seem a bit eager," admitted O'Sullivan, remembering his conversation with Frank Neilson.

"Can you call them back and tell them to wait?" asked Cathryn.

"It's been too long for that," said O'Sullivan.

"Could you just call and make contact so that the local police don't feel they are operating by themselves," pleaded Cathryn.

O'Sullivan picked up his phone and asked the switchboard operator to put him through to Shaftesbury.

Cathryn asked if he would be willing to go to New Hampshire and oversee things.

"I don't have any authority up there," said the detective. Then as the call went through he directed his attention to the receiver.

"We got him surrounded," said Bernie loud enough so that when O'Sullivan held the phone away from his ear, Cathryn could hear. "But that Martel is crazy. He's boarded up his house like a fort. He's got a shotgun which he knows how to use and he's got his kid as a hostage."

"Sounds like a difficult situation," said O'Sullivan. "I suppose you've called in the state police for assistance?"

"Hell, no!" said Bernie. "We'll take care of him. We've deputized a handful of volunteers. We'll give you a call as soon as we bring him in so you can make arrangements to ship him down to Boston."

Patrick thanked Bernie, who in turn told the detective not to mention it and that the Shaftesbury police force was always ready and willing to help.

O'Sullivan looked over at Cathryn. The conversation with Bernie had substantiated her claims. The Shaftesbury deputy seemed a far cry from a professional policeman. And the idea of deputizing volunteers sounded like something out of a Clint Eastwood western.

"There's going to be trouble," said Cathryn, shaking her head. "There is going to be a confrontation. And because of

Michelle, Charles is very determined. I'm afraid he'll fight back."

"Christ!" said O'Sullivan, standing up and getting his coat from a rack near the door. "God, how I hate custody cases. Come on, I'll go up there with you, but remember, I have no authority in New Hampshire."

Cathryn drove as fast as she thought she could get away with in the van while Patrick O'Sullivan followed in a plain blue Chevy Nova. As they neared Shaftesbury, Cathryn could feel her pulse quicken. Rounding the last turn before the house she was almost in a panic. As she came up to their property, she saw a large crowd of people. Cars were parked on either side of Interstate 301 for fifty yards in both directions. At the base of their driveway two police cruisers blocked the entrance.

Parking the van as close as she could, Cathryn got out and waited for O'Sullivan, who pulled up behind her. The crowd gave the scene a carnival aspect despite freezing temperatures. Across the road some enterprising individual had set up a makeshift charcoal grill. On it sizzled Italian sausages which were selling briskly in a pocket of pita bread for $2.50. Next to the grill was an ash can of Budweiser beer and ice. Behind the concession a group of kids were building opposing snow forts in preparation for a snowball fight.

O'Sullivan came up beside Cathryn and said, "Jesus, this looks like a high school outing."

"All except for the guns," said Cathryn.

Grouped behind the two police cruisers was a throng of men dressed in all manner of clothing, from army fatigues to ski parkas, and each armed with a hunting rifle. Some carried their guns in one hand, Budweiser in the other. In the center of the group was Frank Neilson, with his foot on the bumper of one of the police cars, pressing a small walkie-talkie to his ear and apparently coordinating unseen, armed men as they completed surrounding the house.

O'Sullivan left Cathryn and walked up to Frank Neilson, introducing himself. From where Cathryn was standing, she could tell that the Shaftesbury police chief viewed the detective as an intruder. As if it were an effort, Neilson withdrew his foot from the car bumper and assumed his full height, towering a foot over O'Sullivan. The two men did not look as if they shared the same profession. Neilson was wearing his usual blue police uniform, complete with massive leather-holstered service revolver. On his head he had a Russian-style fake fur hat with all the flaps tied on top. O'Sullivan, on the other hand, had on a weather-beaten, wool-lined khaki coat. He wore no hat and his hair was disheveled.

"How's it going?" asked O'Sullivan casually.

"Fine," said Neilson. "Everything under control." He wiped his snub nose with the back of his hand.

The walkie-talkie crackled and Neilson excused himself. He spoke into the machine saying that the tomcat group should approach to one hundred yards and hold. Then he turned back to O'Sullivan. "Gotta make sure the suspect doesn't sneak out the back door."

O'Sullivan turned away from Neilson and eyed the armed men. "Do you think it's advisable to have this much firepower on hand?"

"I suppose you want to tell me how to handle this situation?" asked Neilson sarcastically. "Listen, detective, this is New Hampshire, not Boston. You've got no authority here. And to tell you the honest truth, I don't appreciate you big city boys feeling you gotta come out here and give advice. I'm in charge here. I know how to handle a hostage situation. First secure the area, then negotiate. So if you'll excuse me, I got work to do."

Neilson turned his back on O'Sullivan and redirected his attention to the walkie-talkie.

"Pardon me?" said a tall, gaunt man tapping O'Sullivan on the shoulder. "Name's Harry Barker, *Boston Globe*. You're Detective O'Sullivan from the Boston police, right?"

"You guys don't waste any time, do you?" said O'Sullivan.

"The Shaftesbury *Sentinel* was good enough to give us a

jingle. This could be a great story. Lots of human interest. Can you give me some background?"

O'Sullivan pointed out Frank Neilson. "There is the man in charge. Let him give you the story."

As O'Sullivan watched, Neilson picked up a bull horn and was preparing to use it when Harry Barker accosted him. There was a brief exchange of words, then the reporter stepped aside. Pressing the button on the bull horn, Frank Neilson's husky voice thundered out over the winter landscape. The deputized men stopped laughing and shouting and even the children were silent.

"Okay, Martel, your place is surrounded. I want you to come out with your hands up."

The crowd stayed perfectly still and the only movement was a few snowflakes drifting down among the branches of the trees. Not a sound emanated from the white Victorian house. Neilson tried the same message again with the same result. The only noise was the wind in the pines behind the barn.

"I'm going closer," said Neilson to no one in particular.

"I'm not so sure that's a good idea," said O'Sullivan, loud enough for everyone in the immediate vicinity to hear.

After glaring at the detective, Neilson took the bull horn in his right hand and with great ceremony started around the police car. As he passed O'Sullivan he was laughing. "The day that Frank Neilson can't handle a piss pot of a doctor will be the day he turns in his badge."

While the crowd murmured excitedly, Neilson lumbered up the driveway to a point about fifty feet beyond the two police cruisers. It was snowing a little harder now and the top of his hat was dusted with flakes.

"Martel," boomed the police chief through the bull horn, "I'm warning you, if you don't come out, we'll come in."

Silence descended the instant the last word issued from the cone of the horn. Neilson turned back to the group and made an exasperated gesture, like he was dealing with a garden pest. Then he began walking closer to the house.

Not one of the spectators moved or spoke. There was an

excited anticipation as they all hoped something would happen. Neilson was now about a hundred feet from the front of the house.

Suddenly the red-paint-spattered front door burst open and Charles Martel emerged holding his shotgun. There were two almost simultaneous explosions.

Neilson dove headfirst into the snowbank lining the drive, while the spectators either fled or took cover behind cars or trees. As Charles slammed the front door, bird shot rained harmlessly down over the area.

There were a few murmurs from the crowd, then a cheer as Frank scrambled to his feet. Then he ran as fast as his legs would carry his overweight body. As he neared the cars, he tried to stop but lost his footing and slid the last ten feet on his buttocks, slamming into the rear wheel of the police cruiser. A handful of deputies scurried around the car and pulled him up.

"Goddamn motherfucker!" Neilson shouted. "That's it! That little bastard is going to get what he deserves."

Someone asked if he'd been hit with any bird shot, but the chief shook his head. Meticulously he shook off the snow, and adjusted his uniform and holster. "I was much too fast for him."

A local TV news van pulled up and a camera crew alighted, quickly finding their way over to the police chief. The commentator was a bright young woman, dressed in a mink hat and a long, down-filled coat. After a brief word with Neilson, the camera lights went on, flooding the immediate area. The young woman made a rapid introduction, then turned to the police chief and stuck the microphone about an inch from his pug nose.

Frank Neilson's personality underwent a 180-degree change. Acting shy and embarrassed, he said, "I'm just doing my job the best way I know how."

With the arrival of the TV camera, the politically minded town manager, John Randolph, materialized out of the crowd. He squeezed his way into the sphere of lights and put an arm around Neilson. "And we think he's doing a splendid job. Let's hear it for our police chief." John Randolph took his arm off the police chief and began clapping. The crowd followed suit.

The reporter pulled the microphone back and asked if Frank could give the audience an idea of what was happening.

"Well," began Frank, leaning into the mike, "we got a crazy scientist holed up here." He pointed awkwardly over his shoulder at the house. "He's got a sick kid he's keeping from the doctors. The man's heavily armed and dangerous, and there's a warrant for his arrest for child-snatching and grand larceny. But there's no need to panic because everything is under control."

O'Sullivan wormed his way back out of the crowd, searching for Cathryn. He found her near her car, her hands pressed against her mouth. The spectacle terrified her.

"The outcome of all this is going to be tragic unless you intervene," said Cathryn.

"I can't intervene," explained O'Sullivan. "I told you that before I came up here. But I think everything will be all right as long as the press and the media are here. They'll keep the chief from doing anything crazy."

"I want to get up to the house and be with Charles," said Cathryn. "I'm afraid he might believe I brought the police."

"Are you crazy?" asked O'Sullivan. "There must be forty men with guns surrounding this place. It's dangerous. Besides, they're not going to let you go up there. It just means one more hostage. Try to be a little patient. I'll talk to Frank Neilson again and try to convince him to call in the state police."

The detective started back toward the police cruisers, wishing he'd stayed in Boston where he belonged. As he neared the makeshift command post, he again heard the police chief's voice magnified by the bull horn. It was snowing harder now and one of the deputies was asking whether the chief could be heard up at the house. One way or the other, Charles did not answer.

O'Sullivan went up to Neilson and suggested that it might

be easier to use the portable phone and call Charles. The chief
pondered the suggestion and although he didn't respond, he
climbed into his cruiser, got Charles's number, and dialed.
Charles answered immediately.

"Okay, Martel. What are your conditions for letting the kid
go?"

Charles's reply was short: "You can go to hell, Neilson."
The line went dead.

"Wonderful suggestion," said Neilson to O'Sullivan as he
put the phone back into the car. Then to no one in particular
he said, "How the fuck can you negotiate when there's no
demands? Huh? Somebody answer me that!"

"Chief," called a voice. "How about letting me and my buddies storm the place."

The suggestion horrified O'Sullivan. He tried to think of a
way to get the chief to call in the state police.

In front of Neilson stood three men dressed in white,
hooded militarylike parkas and white pants.

"Yeah," said one of the smaller men, who was missing his
front teeth. "We've checked out the place. It would be easy
from the back. We'd run from the side of the barn, blow out
the back door. It'd all be over."

Neilson remembered the men. They were from Recycle,
Ltd. "I haven't decided what I'm going to do," he said.

"What about tear gas?" suggested O'Sullivan. "That would
bring the good doctor out."

Neilson glared at the detective. "Look, if I want your opinion, I'll ask for it. Trouble is that out here we don't have all
sorts of sophisticated stuff and to get it I'd have to call in the
state boys. I want to handle this affair locally."

A yell pierced the afternoon, followed by a burst of shouting. O'Sullivan and Neilson turned in unison, seeing Cathryn
run diagonally across the area in front of the cars.

"What the hell?" exclaimed Neilson.

"It's Martel's wife," said O'Sullivan.

"Jesus Christ!" exclaimed Neilson. Then to the nearest

group of deputies he yelled, "Get her. Don't let her get up to the house!"

The faster Cathryn tried to run, the more trouble she had as her feet broke through the crusted snow. Upon reaching the driveway, the snowdrift left from the plowing acted like a barrier, and Cathryn was reduced to scrambling over it on all fours. Sliding down the opposite side, she got to her feet.

With a whoop of excitement, a half dozen of the idle deputies responded and struggled around the squad cars. It was a competition to see who got to the prize first. But the new-fallen snow made the going treacherous and the deputies inadvertently inhibited each other. Eventually two of them made it around the cars and began running up the drive as fast as they could. A murmur of excitement escaped from the crowd. O'Sullivan, on the other hand, found himself clenching his fists and urging Cathryn to greater efforts even though he knew her presence in the house would only complicate the situation.

Cathryn found herself gasping for breath. She could hear the heavy breathing of her pursuers and knew they were gaining on her. Desperately, she tried to think of some evasive maneuver but a growing pain in her side made thinking difficult.

Ahead she saw the red-spattered door swing open. Then there was a flash of orange light and an almost simultaneous explosion. Cathryn stopped, gasping for breath, waiting to feel something. Looking back, she could see that her pursuers had dropped into the snow for cover. She tried to run but couldn't. Reaching the front steps she had to pull herself up with her arms. Charles, holding the shotgun in his right hand, reached out to her and she felt him yank her forward and into the house.

Cathryn collapsed on the floor, her chest heaving. She could hear Michelle calling but she didn't move. Charles was running from window to window. After a minute, Cathryn pulled herself to her feet and walked over to Michelle.

"I missed you, Mommy," said Michelle, putting her arms around her.

Cathryn knew she'd done the right thing.

Charles came back into the living room and checked out the front again. Satisfied, he came over to Cathryn and Michelle, and putting gun down, enveloped them in his arms. "Now I have both my women," he said with a twinkle.

Cathryn immediately launched into an explanation of what happened, saying over and over that she had had nothing to do with the arrival of the police.

"I never thought for a second you did," said Charles. "I'm glad to have you back. It's hard watching in two directions at once."

"I don't trust the local police," said Cathryn. "I think that Neilson is a psychopath."

"I couldn't agree more," said Charles.

"I wonder if it wouldn't be better if we gave up now. I'm afraid of Neilson and his deputies."

Charles shook his head, silently mouthing, "No."

". . . but listen to me . . . I think they're out there because they want violence."

"I'm sure they do," admitted Charles.

"If you give up, give the equipment back to the Weinburger, and explain to Dr. Keitzman what you are trying to do for Michelle, maybe you could continue your experiment at the hospital."

"No way," said Charles, smiling at Cathryn's naiveté. "The combined power of organized research and medicine would bar me from doing anything like this. They'd say that I wasn't mentally stable. If I lose control over Michelle now, I'll never get to touch her again. And that wouldn't be so good, would it?" Charles tousled Michelle's hair while Michelle nodded her head in agreement. "Besides," continued Charles, "I think my body is starting to show some delayed hypersensitivity."

"Really?" said Cathryn. It was hard for her to generate enthusiasm, having just witnessed the frenzied crowd outside. Charles's apparent calm amazed her.

"The last time I tested my T-lymphocytes there was some mild reaction to Michelle's leukemic cells. It's happening, but it's slow. Even so, I think I should take another challenge dose of the antigen when things quiet down."

Outside Cathryn could hear the bull horn but it was muffled by the falling snow. She wished she could stop time. For the moment she felt secure, even as she sensed the evil outside.

Because of the snow, night came early. Charles chose dinner-time to have Cathryn help him take another injection of Mich-elle's antigen. He used a different technique, encouraging Cathryn to slip a catheter into one of his veins. It took Cathryn several tries but to her surprise she did it. With an intravenous line open, Charles gave her explicit instructions how to handle the expected anaphylactic reaction. He took epinephrine al-most immediately after the antigen and the rather severe re-action was easily controlled.

Cathryn made dinner while Charles devised methods to se-cure the house. He boarded up the second-story windows and increased the barricades behind the doors. What worried him most was tear gas, and he put out the fire and stuffed the chimney to prevent someone from dropping in a canister.

As evening turned into night, Cathryn and Charles could see the crowd begin to disperse, disappointed and angry that there hadn't been any violence. A few persistent gawkers re-mained, but they, too, drifted off by nine-thirty as the ther-mometer dipped to a chilling five degrees above zero. Cathryn and Charles took turns either watching the windows or reading to Michelle. Her apparent improvement had leveled off and she was again weaker. She also had a mild bout of stomach cramps, but they abated spontaneously. By ten she fell asleep.

Except for the occasional sound of the oil burner kicking on, the house was silent, and Charles, who was taking the first watch, began to have difficulty staying awake. The wired feel-ing he'd gotten from the dose of epinephrine had long since worn off to be replaced by a powerful exhaustion. He poured himself a cup of lukewarm coffee and carried it back into the living room. He had to move by feel because he'd turned out all the indoor lights. Sitting down next to one of the front windows, he looked between the planks and tried to visualize the police cars, but it wasn't possible. He let his head rest for a moment and in that moment fell into a deep, encompassing sleep.

FIFTEEN

At exactly 2 A.M. Bernie Crawford gingerly put his arm over the front seat of the police cruiser and prepared to wake the snoring chief as he had been asked. The problem was that Frank hated being pulled from sleep. The last time Bernie had tried to wake the chief on a stakeout, the chief had punched him ferociously on the side of the head. When he'd finally become fully conscious, he'd apologized, but that didn't erase the pain. Pulling his arm back, Bernie decided on a different ploy. He got out of the car, noticing that the new snow had accumulated to three inches. Then he opened the rear door, reached in, and gave the chief a shove.

Neilson's head popped up and he tried to grab Bernie, who quickly backed up. In spite of his bulk, the chief bounded out of the car, obviously intent on catching his deputy, who was prepared to flee down Interstate 301. But as soon as Neilson hit the five-degree air, he stopped, looking disoriented.

"You all right, chief?" called Bernie from fifty feet away.

"Of course I'm all right," grumbled Frank. "What the hell time is it?"

Back in the front seat of the cruiser, Neilson coughed for

almost three minutes, making it impossible to light up his cigarette. After he'd finally taken several puffs, he took out his walkie-talkie and contacted Wally Crabb. Neilson wasn't entirely happy with his plan, but as the deputies said, he didn't have a better idea. Midway through the evening, everyone had run out of patience and Neilson had felt obligated to do something or lose respect. It was at that time he had agreed to Wally Crabb's idea.

Wally had been a marine and had spent a good deal of time in Vietnam. He told Frank Neilson that as long as you went in fast, the people inside a house never had a chance to resist. Simple as that. Then he pointed out that after it was over, Neilson could personally take the suspect to Boston and the kid to the hospital. He'd be a hero.

"What about the guy's shotgun?" Frank had asked.

"You think he's going to be sitting there with the thing in his hot little hand? Naw. After we blow the back door away, we'll just sail in there and grab him. They'll be so surprised they won't move a muscle. Believe me, you'd think I'd do it if I didn't know it would work? I might be stupid, but I'm not crazy."

So Neilson had relented. He liked the idea of being a hero. They decided on 2 A.M. as the time and chose Wally Crabb, Giorgio Brezowski, and Angelo DeJesus to hit the door. Neilson didn't know the guys, but Wally Crabb said they'd been in Nam with him and were "real" experienced. Besides, they'd volunteered.

The walkie-talkie crackled in Frank's hand, and Wally's voice filled the cab. "We read you. We're all set. As soon as we open the front door, come on up."

"You sure this will work?" asked Neilson.

"Relax, will you? Jesus Christ!"

"All right, we're standing by."

Neilson switched off the walkie-talkie and tossed it in the back seat. There was nothing more he could do until he saw the front door open.

Wally slipped the tiny walkie-talkie into his parka and

zipped it up. His large frame shivered with anticipatory excitement. Violence for Wally was as good as sex, maybe even better because it was less complicated.

"You guys ready?" he asked the two forms huddled behind him. They nodded. The group had approached the Martel house from the south, moving through the pine trees until they came upon the barn. Dressed in white, courtesy of the management of Recycle, Ltd., they were almost invisible in the light but persistent snow.

Reaching the barn, they'd made their way around the eastern end until Wally, who was in the lead, had been able to look around the corner at the house. Except for a light on the back porch, the house was dark. From that point it was about a hundred feet to the back door.

"Okay, check the equipment," said Wally. "Where's the shotgun?"

Angelo passed the gun to Brezo who passed it to Wally; the gun was a two-barrel, twelve-gauge Remington, loaded with triple zero magnum shells capable of blasting a hole through a car door. Wally flipped off the safety. Each man also had been issued a police thirty-eight.

"Everybody remember their job?" asked Wally. The plan was for Wally to lead, blast open the rear door, then pull the door open for Brezo and Angelo to rush inside. Wally thought it was a good plan, the kind that had kept him alive through five years of Vietnam. He'd made it a habit only to volunteer for the safe part of any assault.

Angelo and Brezo nodded, tense with excitement. They'd made a bet with each other. The one who got Martel first would be a hundred bucks richer.

"Okay," said Wally. "I'm off. I'll signal for Angelo."

After checking the dark house once more, Wally scrambled around the edge of the barn, running low to the ground. He crossed the hundred feet quickly and noiselessly, pulling himself into the shadows below the lip of the back porch. The house remained quiet so he waved to Angelo. Angelo and Brezo joined him holding their flashlights and pistols.

Wally glanced at the two men. "Remember he has to be shot from the front, not the back."

With a burst of energy, Wally thundered up the back steps and aimed the shotgun at the lock of the back door. A blast sundered the peaceful night, blowing away a section of the back door. Wally grabbed the edge and yanked it open. At the same moment Brezo ran up the steps and past Wally, heading into the kitchen. Angelo was right behind him.

But when Wally opened the door it triggered Charles's trap. A cord pulled a pin from a simple mechanism which supported several hundred-pound bags of Idaho potatoes which had been in the root cellar. The potatoes were hung by a stout rope from a hook directly above the door, and when the pin was pulled the potatoes began a rapid, swinging plunge.

Brezo had just snapped on his flashlight when he saw the swinging sacks. He raised his hands to protect his face at the moment Angelo collided into the back of him. The potatoes hit Brezo square on. The impact made him accidentally pull the trigger of his pistol as he was knocked straight back off the porch into the snow. The bullet pierced Angelo's calf before burying itself in the floor of the porch. He, too, was knocked off the porch, but sideways, taking with him part of the balustrade with the gingerbread trim. Wally, not sure of what was happening, vaulted back over the railing and scrambled off toward the barn. Angelo was not aware he'd been shot until he tried to get up and his left foot refused to function. Brezo, having recovered enough to get to his feet, went to Angelo's aid.

Charles and Cathryn had bolted upright at the blast. When Charles recovered enough to orient himself, he reached frantically for the shotgun. When he found it, he ran into the kitchen. Cathryn rushed over to Michelle, but the child had not awakened.

Arriving in the kitchen, Charles could just make out the two sacks of potatoes still swinging in and out of the open back door. It was difficult to see beyond the sphere of light from the overhead back porch fixture, but he thought he made out two white figures heading for the barn. Switching off the light, Charles could see the men better. One seemed to be supporting the other as they frantically moved behind the barn.

Pulling the splintered door closed, Charles used some rope to secure it. Then he stuffed the hole made by the shotgun blast with a cushion from one of the kitchen chairs. With a good deal of effort he restrung the potatoes. He knew that it had been a close call. In the distance he could hear the sound of an ambulance approaching, and he wondered if the man who'd been hit with the potatoes was seriously hurt.

Returning to the living room, he explained to Cathryn what had happened. Then he reached over and felt Michelle's forehead. The fever was back with a vengeance. Gently at first, then more forcibly, he tried to wake her. She finally opened her eyes and smiled, but fell immediately back to sleep.

"That's not a good sign," said Charles.

"What is it?" questioned Cathryn.

"Her leukemic cells might be invading her central nervous system," said Charles. "If that happens she's going to need radiotherapy."

"Does that mean getting her to the hospital?" asked Cathryn.

"Yes."

The rest of the night passed uneventfully, and Cathryn and Charles managed to keep to their three-hour watch schedule. When dawn broke, Cathryn looked out on six inches of new snow. At the end of the driveway only one police car remained.

Without waking Charles, Cathryn went into the kitchen and began making a big country breakfast. She wanted to forget what was happening around them, and the best way was to keep busy. She started fresh coffee, mixed biscuits, took bacon from the freezer, and scrambled eggs. When everything was ready, she loaded it on a tray and carried it into the living room. After awakening Charles, she unveiled the feast. Michelle woke up and seemed brighter than she had been during the night. But she wasn't hungry, and when Cathryn took her temperature, it was 102.

When they carried the dishes back to the kitchen, Charles told Cathryn that he was concerned about infection and that if Michelle's fever didn't respond to aspirin, he would feel obliged to start some antibiotics.

When they were done in the kitchen, Charles drew some blood from himself, laboriously separated out a population of T-lymphocytes, and mixed them with his own macrophages and Michelle's leukemic cells. Then he patiently watched under the phase contrast microscope. There was a reaction, definitely more than the previous day, but still not adequate. Even so, Charles whooped with a sense of success, swinging Cathryn around in a circle. When he calmed down, he told Cathryn that he expected that his delayed sensitivity might be adequate by the following day.

"Does that mean we don't have to inject you today?" asked Cathryn hopefully.

"I wish," said Charles. "Unfortunately, I don't think we should argue with success. I think we'd better inject today, too."

Frank Neilson pulled up at the bottom of the Martels' driveway, skidding as he did so, and bumped the front of the cruiser that had sat there overnight. Some of the snow slipped off with a thump, and Bernie Crawford emerged, heavy with sleep.

The chief got out of his car with Wally Crabb. "You haven't been sleeping, have you?"

"No," said Bernie. "Been watching all night. No sign of life."

Neilson looked up at the house. It appeared particularly peaceful with its fresh blanket of snow.

"How's the guy that got shot?" asked Bernie.

"He's okay. They got him over at the county hospital. But I tell you, Martel is in a lot more trouble now that he's shot a deputy."

"But he didn't shoot him."

"Makes no different. He wouldn't have got shot if it hadn't

been for Martel. Rigging up a booby trap is a goddamn crime in itself."

"Reminds me of those gooks in Nam," snarled Wally Crabb. "I think we ought to blow the house right off its fucking foundation."

"Hold on," said Neilson. "We got a sick kid and a woman to think about. I brought some sniper rifles. We'll have to try to isolate Martel."

By midday, little had happened. Spectators from town drifted to the scene and, although as yet there weren't quite as many as the day before, it was a considerable crowd. The chief had issued the rifles and positioned the men in various spots around the house. Then he'd tried contacting Charles with the bull horn, asking him to come out on the front porch to talk about what he wanted. But Charles never responded. Whenever Frank Neilson called on the phone, Charles would hang up. Frank Neilson knew that if he didn't bring the affair to a successful conclusion soon, the state police would intervene and control would slip from his hands. That was something he wanted to avoid at all costs. He wanted to have the credit of resolving this affair because it was the biggest and most talked-about case since one of the mill owners' children had been kidnapped in 1862.

Angrily tossing the bull horn into the back seat of his cruiser, Neilson crossed the road for an Italian sausage in pita bread. As he was about to bite into the sandwich, he saw a long black limousine come around the bend and stop. Five men got out. Two were dressed in fancy city clothes, one with white hair and a long fur coat, the other with almost no hair and a shiny leather coat cinched at the waist. The other two men were dressed in blue suits that appeared a size too small. Neilson recognized the second two: they were bodyguards.

Frank took a bite from his sandwich as the men approached him.

"Neilson, my name is Dr. Carlos Ibanez. I'm honored to meet you."

Frank Neilson shook the doctor's hand.

"This is Dr. Morrison," said Ibanez, urging his colleague forward.

Neilson shook hands with Morrison, then took another bite of his sausage sandwich.

"Understand you got a problem here," said Ibanez, looking up at the Martel house.

Frank shrugged. It was never good to admit to problems.

Turning back to the chief, Ibanez said, "We're the owners of all the expensive equipment your suspect has up there in his house. And we're very concerned about it."

Frank nodded.

"We rode out here to offer our help," said Ibanez magnanimously.

Frank looked from face to face. This was getting crazier by the minute.

"In fact, we brought two professional security men from Breur Chemicals with us. A Mr. Eliot Hoyt and Anthony Ferrullo."

Frank found himself shaking hands with the two security men.

"Of course we know you have everything under control," said Dr. Morrison. "But we thought you might find these men helpful and they have brought some equipment you might find interesting."

Mr. Hoyt and Mr. Ferrullo smiled.

"But it's up to you, of course," said Dr. Morrison.

"Absolutely," said Dr. Ibanez.

"I think I have enough manpower at the moment," said Frank Neilson through a full mouth.

"Well, keep us in mind," said Dr. Ibanez.

Neilson excused himself and strolled back to his makeshift command post, confused after meeting Ibanez and his friends. After he told Bernie to contact the men with the rifles and tell them there was to be no shooting until further notice, he got into his car. Maybe help from the chemical company wasn't a bad idea. All they were interested in was the equipment, not the glory.

Ibanez and Morrison watched Neilson walk away from them, talk briefly with another policeman, then get into his squad·car. Morrison adjusted his delicate horn-rimmed glasses. "Frightening that someone like that is in a position of authority."

"It's a travesty, all right," agreed Dr. Ibanez. "Let's get back into the car."

They started off toward the limousine. "I don't like this situation one bit," said Dr. Ibanez. "All this press coverage may whip up sympathy for Charles: the quintessential American guarding his home against outside forces. If this goes on much longer, the media is going to plaster this on every TV screen in the country."

"I couldn't agree more," said Dr. Morrison. "The irony is that Charles Martel, the man who hates the press, couldn't have created for himself a better platform if he tried. The way things are going he could cause irreparable damage to the whole cancer establishment."

"And to Canceran and the Weinburger in particular," added Dr. Ibanez. "We've got to get that imbecile police chief to use our men."

"We've planted the idea in his head," said Morrison. "I don't think there's much else we can do at this point. It has to look like his decision."

Neilson was jarred from a little postprandial catnap by someone tapping on the frosted window of the cruiser. He was about to leap from the car when he regained his senses. He rolled down the window and found himself looking into a sneering face behind thick, milk-bottle glasses. The guy had curly hair that stuck out from his head in a snow-covered bush; the chief guessed it was another big-city spectator.

"Are you Chief Neilson?" asked the man.

"Who wants to know?"

"I do. My name is Dr. Stephen Keitzman and this is Dr. Jordan Wiley behind me."

The chief looked over Dr. Keitzman's shoulder at the second man, wondering what was going on.

"Can we talk to you for a few minutes?" said Dr. Keitzman, shielding his face from the snow.

Neilson got out of the car, making it clear that it was an extraordinary effort.

"We're the physicians of the little girl in the house," explained Dr. Wiley. "We felt it was our duty to come up here in case there was anything we could do to help."

"Will Martel listen to you guys?" asked the chief.

Dr. Keitzman and Dr. Wiley exchanged glances. "I doubt it," admitted Dr. Keitzman. "I don't think he'll talk with anyone. He's too hostile. We think he's had a psychotic break."

"A what?" asked Neilson.

"A nervous breakdown," added Dr. Wiley.

"Figures," said the chief.

"Anyway," said Dr. Keitzman, swinging his arms against the cold, "we're mostly concerned about the little girl. I don't know if you realize how sick she is, but the fact of the matter is that every hour she's without treatment, the closer she is to death."

"That bad, huh?" said Neilson, looking up at the Martel house.

"Absolutely," said Dr. Keitzman. "If you procrastinate too long, I'm afraid you'll be rescuing a dead child."

"We're also concerned that Dr. Martel might be experimenting on the child," said Dr. Wiley.

"No shit!" exclaimed Neilson. "That fucking bastard. Thanks for letting me know. I think I'll tell this to my deputies." Neilson called Bernie over, spoke to him a minute, then reached in for the walkie-talkie.

By midafternoon the crowd was even larger than the previous day. Word had drifted back to Shaftesbury that something was going to happen soon and even the schools were let out early. Joshua Wittenburg, the school superintendent, had decided that the lessons in civil law to be learned from the episode should not be passed up; besides, he felt that it was the biggest scandal in Shaftesbury since Widow Watson's cat had been found frozen solid in Tom Brachman's freezer.

Jean Paul drifted aimlessly on the periphery of the crowd. He'd never been subjected to derision before, and the experience was extremely disquieting. He'd always felt his father was a little weird but not crazy, and now that people were accusing him of being insane, he was upset. Besides, he couldn't understand why his family hadn't contacted him. The people with whom he was staying tried to comfort him but it was obvious they, too, questioned his father's behavior.

Jean Paul wanted to go up to the house but he was afraid to approach the police, and it was easy to see the property was surrounded.

Ducking a snowball thrown by one of his former friends, Jean Paul walked back through the crowd, crossing the road. After a few minutes he thought he saw a familiar form. It was Chuck, dressed in a torn and tattered army parka with a fur-tipped hood.

"Chuck!" called Jean Paul eagerly.

Chuck took one look in Jean Paul's direction, then turned and fled into a stand of trees. Jean Paul followed, calling out several more times.

"Chrissake!" hissed Chuck, when Jean Paul caught up to him in a small clearing. "Why don't you yell a little louder so everybody hears you?"

"What do you mean?" asked Jean Paul, confused.

"I'm trying to keep a low profile to find out what the hell is going on," said Chuck. "And you come along yelling my name. Jesus!"

Jean Paul had never considered the idea of concealing himself.

"I know what's going on," said Jean Paul. "The town is after Dad because he's trying to shut down the factory. Everybody says he's crazy."

"It's more than the town," said Chuck. "It was on the news last night in Boston. Dad kidnapped Michelle from the hospital."

"Really?" exclaimed Jean Paul.

"Really. Is that all you can say? I think it's a goddamn miracle, and all you can say is really. Dad's given the finger to the whole friggin' establishment. I love it!"

Jean Paul examined his brother's face. A situation he found disturbing Chuck seemed to find exhilarating.

"You know, if we worked together, we might be able to help," said Chuck.

"Really?" said Jean Paul. It was a rare occurrence when Chuck offered to cooperate with anyone.

"Jesus. Say something a little more intelligent."

"How could we help?" asked Jean Paul.

It took about five minutes for the boys to decide what they would do, then they crossed the road and approached the police cars. Chuck had appointed himself spokesman, and he went up to Frank Neilson.

The chief was overjoyed to find the boys. He did not know how to proceed when the kids had presented themselves. Although he dismissed their request to go up to the house to reason with their father, he convinced them to use the bull horn, and spent a good thirty minutes coaching them on what they should say. He hoped that Charles would talk to his sons and communicate his conditions for resolving the situation. Frank was pleased that the boys were so cooperative.

When everything was ready, Frank took the bull horn, greeted the spectators, then pointed it at the house. His voice boomed up the driveway calling for Charles to open the door and speak to his sons.

Neilson lowered the bull horn and waited. There was no sound or movement from the house. The chief repeated his message, then waited again, with the same result. Cursing under his breath, he handed the instrument to Chuck and told the boy to try.

Chuck took the bull horn with trembling hands. Pushing the button, he started speaking. "Dad, it's me, Chuck, and Jean Paul. Can you hear me?"

After the third time, the paint-splattered door opened about six inches. "I hear you, Chuck," Charles called.

At that moment, Chuck clambered over the front bumpers of two squad cars, discarding the bull horn. Jean Paul followed at his heels. Everyone, including the deputies, was intent on watching the house when the boys made their move, and for a moment they didn't respond. It gave the boys a chance to clear the cars and start up the driveway.

"Get them, goddamn it! Get them!" shouted Neilson.

A murmur went up from the crowd. Several deputies led by Bernie Crawford sprinted around the ends of the two squad cars.

Although younger, Jean Paul was the athlete, and he quickly overtook his older brother, who was having difficulty making headway on the slippery driveway. About forty feet beyond the squad cars, Chuck's feet went out from under him and he hit the ground hard. Gasping for breath he struggled up, but as he did so Bernie grabbed a handful of his tattered army parka. Chuck tried to wrench himself free but instead managed to yank Bernie off balance. The policeman fell over backwards, pulling the boy on top of him. Chuck's bony buttocks knocked the wind out of Bernie with an audible wheeze.

Still entangled, the two slid a few feet back down the driveway, rolling into the next two deputies on their way up. The men fell in a comical fashion reminiscent of a silent-movie chase sequence. Taking advantage of the confusion, Chuck pulled himself free, scrambled out of reach, and ran after Jean Paul.

Although Bernie was temporarily winded, the other two deputies quickly resumed pursuit. They might have caught Chuck again had it not been for Charles. He stuck the shotgun through the door and fired a single round. Any thought of heroics on the deputies' part vanished, and they instantly took refuge behind the trunk of one of the oaks lining the driveway.

As the boys reached the front porch, Charles opened the door, and they dashed inside. Charles slammed the door behind them, secured it, then checked the windows to make sure no one else was coming. Satisfied, he turned to his sons.

The two boys were standing self-consciously near the door, gasping for breath, and amazed at the transformation of their living room into a science-fiction laboratory. Chuck, an old-movie buff, noticing the boarded-up windows, said it looked like the set of a Frankenstein movie. They both began to smile, but became serious when they saw Charles's dour expression.

"The one thing I thought I didn't have to worry about was you two," said Charles sternly. "Goddamn it! What on earth are you doing here?"

"We thought you needed help," said Chuck lamely. "Everyone else is against you."

"I couldn't stand to hear what people were saying about you," said Jean Paul.

"This is our family," said Chuck. "We should be here, especially if we can help Michelle."

"How is she, Dad?" asked Jean Paul.

Charles didn't answer. His anger at the boys abruptly dissolved. Chuck's comment was not only surprising, it was correct. They were a family, and the boys should not be summarily excluded. Besides, as far as Charles knew, it was the first unselfish thing Chuck had ever done.

"You little bastards!" Charles suddenly grinned.

Caught off guard by their father's abrupt change of mood, the boys hesitated for a moment, then rushed to give him a hug.

Charles realized he couldn't remember the last time he'd held his sons. Cathryn, who'd been watching since the boys first appeared, came up and kissed them both.

Then they all went over to Michelle, and Charles gently woke her. She gave them a broad grin and Chuck bent over and put his arms around her.

SIXTEEN

Neilson had never been in a limousine before, and he wasn't sure he was going to like it. But once he'd ducked through the door and settled back in the plush seat, he felt right at home: it had a bar. He refused a mixed drink on account of being on duty but accepted straight brandy for its medicinal powers against the cold.

After the Martel boys had managed to get up to the house, Neilson had had to admit the situation was deteriorating. Rather than rescuing hostages, he was adding them. Instead of a crazy guy and a sick kid, he was now confronted by a whole family barricaded in their home. Something had to be done right away. Someone suggested calling in the state police but that was just what Neilson wanted to avoid. Yet it would be inevitable if he wasn't successful in resolving the incident within the next twelve hours. It was this time pressure that had made him decide to talk to the doctors.

"Knowing how sick the little girl is, I felt I couldn't turn down your offer to help," he said.

"That's why we're here," said Dr. Ibanez. "Mr. Hoyt and Mr. Ferrullo are ready and willing to take orders from you."

The two security men, positioned on either side of the bar, nodded in agreement.

"That's great," said Frank Neilson. The trouble was that he didn't know what kind of orders to give. His mind raced in circles until he remembered something Dr. Ibanez had said. "You mentioned special equipment?"

"I certainly did," said Dr. Ibanez. "Mr. Hoyt, perhaps you'd like to show us."

Mr. Hoyt was a handsome man, lean but obviously muscular. Frank recognized the bulge of a shoulder holster under his suit.

"My pleasure," said Hoyt, leaning toward Frank. "What do you think this is, Mr. Neilson?" He handed Frank a weighty object that was shaped like a tin can with a handle protruding from one end.

Frank turned it in his hands and shrugged. "Don't know. Tear gas? Something like that?"

Mr. Hoyt shook his head. "Nope. It's a grenade."

"A grenade?" exclaimed Frank, holding the object away from him.

"It's called a concussion grenade. It's what antiterrorist units use to rescue hostages. It's thrown into a room or airplane and when it detonates, instead of hurting anything—except perhaps for breaking a few eardrums—it just befuddles everyone for ten, twenty, sometimes thirty seconds. I think you could use it to advantage in this situation."

"Yeah, I'm sure we could," said Frank. "But we got to get it into the house. And the guy's boarded up all the windows."

"Not all the windows," said Mr. Hoyt. "We've noticed that the two attic windows which are easily accessible from the roof are free. Let me show you what I'd suggest." Hoyt produced floor plans of the Martels' house and, noticing the chief's surprise, said: "It's amazing what you can get with a little research. Look how the attic stairs come down to the main hall on the second floor. From that stairway it would be easy for someone like Tony Ferrullo, who's an expert at this sort of thing, to toss a concussion grenade into the living room where the suspect is obviously staying. At that point, it would be easy to rush both the front and back doors and rescue the hostages."

"When could we try it?" asked Frank Neilson.

"You're the boss," said Mr. Hoyt.

"Tonight?" asked Frank Neilson.

"Tonight it is," said Mr. Hoyt.

Neilson left the limousine in a state of suppressed excitement. Dr. Morrison reached out and pulled the door closed.

Hoyt laughed: "It's like taking candy from a child."

"Will you be able to make it look like self-defense?" asked Dr. Ibanez.

Ferrullo straightened up. "I can make it look any way you want."

At 10 P.M. exactly, Charles reached over and switched off the dialyzer. Then, as carefully as if he were handling the most precious commodity on earth, he reached into the machine and withdrew the dialyzate in a small vial. His fingers trembled as he transferred the crystal clear solution to the sterilizer. He had no idea of the structure of the small molecule contained in the vial except that it was dialyzable, which had been the final step in its isolation, and that it was not affected by the enzymes that broke down DNA, RNA, and peptide linkages in proteins. But the fact that the structure of the molecule was unknown was less important at this stage than knowledge of its effect. This was the mysterious transfer factor which would hopefully transfer his delayed hypersensitivity to Michelle.

That afternoon, Charles had again tested his T-lymphocyte response with Michelle's leukemic cells. The reaction had been dramatic, with the T-lymphocytes instantly lysing and destroying the leukemic cells. As Charles had watched under the phase contrast microscope, he couldn't believe the rapidity of the response. Apparently the T-lymphocytes, sensitized to a surface antigen on the leukemic cell, were able to pierce the leukemic cells' membranes. Charles had shouted with joy the moment he saw the reaction.

Having found his delayed hypersensitivity response adequate, he had canceled the next dose of antigen he'd planned to give himself. This had pleased Cathryn, who had been finding the procedure increasingly distasteful. Instead he had announced that he wanted to draw off two pints of his blood. Cathryn had turned green, but Chuck had been able to overcome his distaste for blood and, along with Jean Paul, was able to help Charles with the task.

Before dinner, Charles had slowly separated out the white blood cells in one of the sophisticated machines he had taken from the Weinburger. In the early evening he had begun the arduous task of extracting from the white blood cells the small molecule that he was now sterilizing.

At that point, he knew he was flying blind. What he'd accomplished would have taken years under proper research conditions where each step would have been examined critically and reproduced hundreds of times. Yet what he'd accomplished so far had been essentially done before with different antigens like the one for the tuberculosis bacillus. But now Charles had a solution of an unknown molecule of an unknown concentration and of an unknown potency. There was no time to determine the best way to administer it. All he had was a theory: that in Michelle's system was a blocking factor, which had to that point kept her immune system from responding to her leukemic cells' antigen. Charles believed and hoped that the transfer factor would bypass that blocking or suppressor system and allow Michelle to become sensitized to her leukemic cells. But how much of the factor should he give her? And how? He was going to have to improvise and pray.

Michelle was not happy with the idea but she let Charles start another IV. Cathryn sat holding her hand and trying to distract her. The two boys were upstairs watching for any suspicious movement outside.

Without telling Cathryn or Michelle, Charles prepared for any eventuality when he gave his daughter the first dose of the transfer factor. Although he had diluted the solution with sterile water, he was still concerned about its side effects. After giving her a minute dose, he monitored her pulse and blood pressure. He was relieved when he could detect no response whatever.

At midnight the family came together in the living room. Charles had given Michelle approximately one-sixteenth of the transfer factor. The only apparent change in her status was a slight rise in her fever, and she had fallen asleep spontaneously.

They decided to take two-hour watches. Although they were all exhausted, Chuck insisted on taking the first watch and went upstairs. Charles and Cathryn fell asleep almost instantly. Jean Paul lay awake for a while, hearing his brother wander from room to room upstairs.

The next thing Jean Paul knew was that Chuck was gently nudging him. It seemed like he'd just fallen asleep but Chuck said it was 2 A.M. and time for him to get up. "It's been quiet, except a van came about an hour ago and stopped by the police cars. But I haven't seen anybody."

Jean Paul nodded, then went into the downstairs bathroom to wash his face. Coming back into the dark living room, he debated whether to stay on the ground floor or go upstairs. Since it was difficult to move around in the living room, he went up to his own room. The bed looked inviting but he resisted the temptation. Instead he looked out between the planks covering the window. He couldn't see much, or even enough to tell if it was snowing or just blowing. In any case there was lots of snow in the air.

Slowly he went from room to room as he'd heard Chuck do, gazing out at the dark. It was utterly silent except for an occasional gust of wind which would rattle the storm windows. Sitting in his parents' bedroom which looked down the driveway, Jean Paul tried to make out a van but he was unable to. Then he heard a sound, like metal against stone. Looking in the direction of the noise, he found himself facing the fireplace. It shared the same chimney as the living room fireplace. He heard the sound again.

With no further hesitation, he ran back down to the living room.

"Dad," whispered Jean Paul, "wake up."

Charles blinked, then sat up.

"Four o'clock?" asked Charles.

"No," whispered Jean Paul. "I heard a noise up in your bedroom. Sounded like it came from the fireplace."

Charles sprang up, waking Cathryn and Chuck.

"Jean Paul thinks he heard a noise," whispered Chuck.

"I know I heard a noise," returned Jean Paul, indignant.

"Okay! Okay!" said Charles. "Listen, we need at least one more day. If they're trying to break in, we've got to stop them."

Charles gave the gun to Cathryn and sent her to the back door. He positioned the boys by the front door with Jean Paul's baseball bat. Taking the poker for himself, Charles climbed the stairs and went into the master bedroom. Standing by the fireplace he congratulated himself on having the foresight to pack the chimneys. But he heard nothing except the wind under the eaves.

After several minutes Charles walked out of the master bedroom, crossed the hall, and entered Michelle's room. From here he could see the barn, where the previous night's assault had originated, but all he saw now were the pines, rustling in the wind.

Anthony Ferrullo placed an aluminum ladder against the chimney and climbed onto the roof. Catlike, he moved along the ridge to one of the attic windows. Then, using a rope as a precaution against slipping, he worked his way down the slope of the roof to the base of one of the dormers, where he cut out a small circle of glass. Slowly he opened the window, smelling the musty odor of the attic. Turning on his flashlight, he looked inside. There were the usual trunks and cartons, and he was pleased to see a floor rather than widely spaced beams. He dropped into the room without making the slightest noise.

Ferrullo waited, listening for sounds of movement in the

house. He was in no hurry. He was certain Hoyt was already in position below the front porch, ready to storm the front door. Neilson had insisted that two of his deputies participate. They were to storm the back door after the explosion, but if things went the way Ferrullo intended, the job would be over before they entered.

Satisfied all was quiet, Anthony moved forward slowly, testing each place he put his foot before he shifted his weight onto it. He was directly over Charles's head.

Charles stared at the barn for some five minutes, until he was convinced there was no activity there. Wondering what Jean Paul could have heard, he turned back toward the hall. Suddenly the ceiling joists above him squeaked. Freezing, Charles listened intently, hoping he'd imagined the sound. Then it was repeated.

A shiver of fear passed through his exhausted body. Someone was in the attic!

Gripping the poker and feeling the perspiration on his hands, Charles began to follow the sounds above him. Soon he'd advanced to the wall of Michelle's room, behind which were the attic stairs. Looking out into the hall, he could just make out the attic door in the darkness. It was closed but not locked. The skeleton key protruded temptingly from the mechanism. Hearing the first step on the stairs, his heart began to pound. He'd never experienced such terror. Frantically he debated whether to lock the door or just wait for the intruder to appear.

Whoever was coming down the stairs was agonizingly slow. Charles gripped the poker with all the force he could muster. Abruptly the furtive steps halted and there was nothing but silence. He waited, his panic growing.

Downstairs, Charles heard Michelle stir in her sleep. He winced, hoping no one would call up to him, or worse yet, come up the stairs. He heard Jean Paul whisper something to Chuck.

The noises coming from the living room seemed to activate the movement on the attic stairs. Charles heard the sound of another step, then to his horror the knob began to turn very slowly. He grasped the poker with both hands and lifted it above his head.

Anthony Ferrullo slowly opened the door about eight inches. He could see across the short hall to the balustrade connecting to the banister of the main stairs. From there it was a straight drop to the living room. After checking the position of his holster, he unclipped the concussion grenade from his belt and pulled the pin from the timing fuse.

Charles could not stand the waiting another second, especially since he was sure he wouldn't be able to actually strike the intruder. Impulsively he lifted his foot and kicked the attic door closed. He felt a slight resistance but not enough to keep it from slamming shut. He leaped forward, intending to turn the key in the lock.

He never got to the door. There was a tremendous explosion. The attic door burst open, sending Charles flying back into Michelle's room with his ears ringing. Scrambling on all fours, he saw Ferrullo topple from the attic stairs to the hall floor.

Cathryn and the boys jumped at the explosion, which was followed by a rush of footsteps on the front and back porches. In the next instant a sledgehammer crashed through the glass panel and its wooden cover next to the front door just inches from Chuck's head. A groping hand reached through the opening for the doorknob. Chuck reacted by grabbing the hand and pulling. Jean Paul dropped the bat and leaped to his brother's aid. Their combined strength pulled the unwilling arm to its limit, forcing it up against the shards of glass left in the panel. The unseen man yelled in pain. A pistol sounded and splinters flew from the door, convincing the boys to let go.

In the kitchen Cathryn tightened her hold on the shotgun as two men wrestled with the already broken back door. They succeeded in releasing the securing rope and pulled the door open. The potatoes swung out, but this time the men were able to duck. Wally Crabb grabbed the sack on its return swing, while Brezo headed through the door. With the gun pointed downward, Cathryn pulled the trigger. A load of bird shot roared into the linoleum, ricocheting up and spraying the doorway and Brezo. Brezo reversed direction and followed Wally off the porch as Cathryn pumped another shell into the chamber and blasted the empty doorway.

As abruptly as the violence started it was over. Jean Paul ran into the kitchen to find Cathryn immobilized by the experience. He closed the back door and resecured it, then took the gun from her shaking hands. Chuck went upstairs to see if Charles was all right and was surprised to see his father bending over, examining a scorched and dazed stranger.

With Chuck's help, Charles got the man downstairs and bound him to a chair in the living room. Cathryn and Jean Paul came in from the kitchen and the family tried to pull themselves together after the nerve-shattering excitement. There was no hope for sleep for anyone except Michelle. After a few minutes the boys volunteered to resume watch and disappeared upstairs. Cathryn went into the kitchen to make fresh coffee.

Charles returned to his machines, his heart still pounding. He gave Michelle another dose of the transfer factor through her IV, which she again tolerated with no apparent ill effects. In fact, she didn't even wake up. Convinced the molecule was nontoxic, Charles took the rest of the solution and added it to Michelle's half-empty intravenous bottle, fixing it to run in over the next five hours.

With that done, Charles went over to his unexpected prisoner, who had regained his senses. Despite his burns, he was a handsome man with intelligent eyes. He looked nothing at all like the local thug Charles expected. What worried him was the fact that the man seemed to be a professional. When Charles had examined him, he'd removed a shoulder holster containing a Smith & Wesson stainless steel .38 special. That wasn't a casual firearm.

"Who are you?" asked Charles.

Anthony Ferrullo sat as if carved from stone.

"What are you doing here?"

Silence.

Self-consciously, Charles reached into the man's jacket pockets, finding a wallet. He pulled it out. Mr. Ferrullo did not move. Charles opened the wallet, shocked at the number of hundred-dollar bills inside. There were the usual credit cards, as well as a driver's license. Charles slipped the driver's license out and held it up to the light. Anthony L. Ferrullo, Leonia, New Jersey. New Jersey? He turned back to the wallet and found a business card. Anthony L. Ferrullo; Breur Chemicals; Security. Breur Chemicals!

Charles felt a shiver of fear pass over him. Up until that moment he had felt that whatever risk he was taking in standing up against organized medical and industrial interests could be resolved in a court of law. Mr. Anthony Ferrullo's presence suggested the risk was considerably more deadly. And most disturbing, Charles realized that the risk extended to his whole family. In Mr. Ferrullo's case, "security" was obviously a euphemism for coercion and violence. For a moment the security man was less an individual than a symbol of evil, and Charles had to keep himself from striking out at him in blind anger. Instead he began turning on lights, all of them. He wanted no darkness, no more secrecy.

Calling the boys down from upstairs, the family gathered in the kitchen.

"Tomorrow it's over," said Charles. "We're going to walk out of here and give up."

Cathryn was glad, but the boys looked at each other in consternation. "Why?" asked Chuck.

"I've done what I wanted to do for Michelle, and the fact of the matter is that she might need some radiotherapy at the hospital."

"Is she going to get better?" said Cathryn.

"I have no idea," admitted Charles. "Theoretically there's no reason why not, but there's a hundred questions I haven't answered. It's a technique outside of all accepted medical practices. At this point all we can do is hope."

Charles walked over to the phone and called all the media

people he could think of, including the Boston TV stations. He told anyone who'd listen that he and his family would emerge at noon.

Then he called the Shaftesbury police, told a deputy who he was, and asked to speak to Frank Neilson. Five minutes later the chief was on the phone. Charles told him that he'd called the media and informed them that he and his family were coming out at noon. Then he hung up. Charles hoped that the presence of so many newspaper and TV reporters would eliminate any possible violence.

At exactly 12 o'clock, Charles removed the planks securing the front door and released the lock. It was a glorious day with a clear blue sky and a pale winter sun. At the bottom of the drive, in front of a crowd of people, were an ambulance, the two police cars, and a handful of TV news vans.

Charles looked back at his family and felt a rush of pride and love. They'd stood behind him more than he could have hoped. Walking back to the makeshift bed, he scooped Michelle into his arms. Her eyelids fluttered but remained closed.

"All right, Mr. Ferrullo, after you," said Charles.

The security man stepped out onto the porch, his scorched face gleaming in the sun. Next came the two boys, followed by Cathryn. Charles brought up the rear with Michelle. In a tight group they started down the driveway.

To his surprise Charles saw Dr. Ibanez, Dr. Morrison, Dr. Keitzman, and Dr. Wiley all standing together near the ambulance. As they got closer and the crowd realized there would not be any violence, a number of the men began to boo, particularly those from Recycle, Ltd. Only one person clapped, and that was Patrick O'Sullivan, who was immensely pleased the affair was coming to a peaceful close.

Standing in the shadow of the trees, Wally Crabb was silent. He slid his right index finger under the trigger of his favorite hunting rifle and pressed his cheek against the cold stock. As he tried to sight, the front of the rifle shook from all the bourbon he'd consumed that morning. Leaning up against a nearby branch helped considerably, but Brezo's urging to hurry made him nervous.

The sharp crack of a firearm shattered the winter stillness. The crowd strained forward as they saw Charles Martel stumble. He didn't fall but rather sank to his knees, and as gently as if handling a newborn infant, he laid his daughter in the snow before he fell facedown beside her. Cathryn turned and screamed, then threw herself to her knees, trying to see how badly her husband was hurt.

Patrick O'Sullivan was the first to react. By professional reflex, his right hand sought the handle of his service revolver. He didn't draw the gun but rather held on to it as he bullied his way between several onlookers and charged up the driveway. Hovering over Cathryn and Charles like a hawk guarding its nest, his eyes scanned the crowd, looking for suspicious movement.

SEVENTEEN

Never having been a hospital patient before, Charles found the experience agonizing. He'd read some editorials in the past about the problems associated with the technological invasion of medicine, but he never imagined the state of insecurity and powerlessness he would feel. It had been three days since he'd been shot and then operated on, and as he looked up at the tangle of tubes and bottles, monitors and recorders, he felt like one of his own experimental animals. Thankfully, the day before he had been transferred out of the frenzied terror of the intensive care unit, and deposited like a piece of meat in a private room in the fancy section of the hospital.

Trying to adjust his position, Charles felt a frightening stab of pain that tightened around his chest like a band of fire. For a moment he held his breath, wondering if he had opened his incision, and waited for the pain to return. To his relief it didn't, but he lay perfectly still, afraid to move. From his left side, between his ribs, protruded a rubber tube that ran down to a bottle on the floor next to the bed. His left arm was strung up in traction by a complicated net of wires and pulleys. He was immobilized and totally at the mercy of the staff for even the most basic of functions.

A soft knock caught his attention. Before he could respond, the door silently opened. Charles was afraid it was the technician who came every four hours to forcibly inflate his lungs, a procedure Charles was sure had not been equaled in pain since the Inquisition. Instead it was Dr. Keitzman.

"Could you stand a short visit?" he asked.

Charles nodded. Although he didn't feel like talking, he was eager to hear about Michelle. Cathryn had not been able to tell him anything except that she wasn't worse.

Dr. Keitzman came into the room self-consciously, pulling a metal and vinyl chair over next to Charles's bed. His face contorted with the tic that usually connoted tension and he adjusted his glasses.

"How do you feel, Charles?" he asked.

"Couldn't be better," said Charles, unable to keep the sarcasm from surfacing. Talking, even breathing, were risky affairs and at any moment he expected the pain to return.

"Well, I have some good news. It might be a little premature, but I think you should know."

Charles didn't say anything. He watched the oncologist's face, afraid to let his hopes rise.

"First," said Dr. Keitzman. "Michelle responded to the radiotherapy extremely well. A single treatment seems to have taken care of the infiltration of her central nervous system. She's alert and oriented."

Charles nodded, hoping that was not all Dr. Keitzman had come to say.

There was a silence.

Then the door to the room burst open and in walked the respiratory technician, pushing the hated IPPB machine. "Time for your treatment, Dr. Martel," said the technician brightly, as if he were bringing some wonderfully pleasurable service. Seeing Dr. Keitzman, the technician skidded to a respectful halt. "Excuse me, Doctor."

"That's quite all right," said Dr. Keitzman, seemingly pleased at the interruption. "I've got to be going anyway." Then looking down at Charles, he said: "The other thing I wanted to say was that Michelle's leukemic cells have all but disappeared. I think she's in remission."

Charles felt a warm glow suffuse his body. "God! That's great," he said with enthusiasm. Then he got a sharp twinge that reminded him where he was.

"It certainly is," agreed Dr. Keitzman. "We're all very pleased. Tell me, Charles. What did you do to Michelle while she was in your house?"

Charles had trouble containing his joy. His hopes soared. Maybe Michelle was cured. Maybe everything worked as he had guessed. Looking up at Keitzman, Charles thought for a moment. Realizing that he didn't want to go into a detailed explanation at that point, he said: "I just tried to stimulate her immune system."

"You mean by using an adjuvant like BCG?" asked Dr. Keitzman.

"Something like that," agreed Charles. He was in no shape to get into a scientific discussion.

"Well," said Dr. Keitzman, heading for the door. "We'll have to talk about it. Obviously whatever you did helped the chemotherapy she'd been given before you took her from the hospital. I don't understand the time sequence, but we'll talk about it when you feel stronger."

"Yes," agreed Charles. "When I'm stronger."

"Anyway, I'm sure you know the custody proceedings have been canceled." Dr. Keitzman adjusted his glasses, nodded to the technician, and left.

Charles's elation over Dr. Keitzman's news dulled the painful respiratory treatment, even better than the morphine. As the technician stood by, the positive pressure machine forcibly inflated Charles's lungs, something a patient would not do himself because of the severity of the pain. The procedure lasted for twenty minutes and when the technician finally left, Charles was exhausted. In spite of the lingering pain, he fell into a fitful sleep.

Unsure of how much time had passed, Charles was roused by a sound from the other side of the room. He turned his head toward the door and was shocked to discover he wasn't alone. There, next to the bed, not more than four feet away, sat Dr. Carlos Ibanez. With his bony hands folded in his lap and his silver hair disheveled, he looked old and frail.

"I hope I'm not disturbing you," said Dr. Ibanez softly.

Charles felt a surge of anger, but remembering Keitzman's news, it passed. Instead he looked with indifference.

"I'm glad you're doing so well," said Dr. Ibanez. "The surgeons told me you were very lucky."

Luck! What a relative term, thought Charles with irritation. "You think getting shot in the chest is lucky?" he asked.

"That's not what I meant," said Dr. Ibanez with a smile. "Hitting your left arm apparently slowed the bullet so that when it entered your chest, it missed your heart. That was lucky."

Charles felt a little stab of pain. Although he didn't feel particularly fortunate, he wasn't in the mood for an argument. He shook his head slightly to acknowledge Dr. Ibanez's comment. In truth, he wondered why the old man had come.

"Charles!" said Dr. Ibanez with renewed emphasis. "I'm here to negotiate."

Negotiate? thought Charles, his eyes puzzled. What the hell is he talking about?

"I've given a lot of thought to everything," said Dr. Ibanez, "and I'm willing to admit that I made some mistakes. I'd like to make up for them if you're willing to cooperate."

Charles rolled his head and looked up at the bottles over his head, watching the intravenous fluid drip from the micropore filter. He controlled himself from telling Ibanez to go to hell.

The director waited for Charles to respond, but seeing that he would not, the old man cleared his throat. "Let me be very frank, Charles. I know that you could cause us a great deal of trouble now that you've become a celebrity of sorts. But that wouldn't be good for anyone. I have convinced the board of directors not to press any charges against you and to give you your job back . . ."

"The hell with your job," said Charles sharply. He winced with pain.

"All right," said Ibanez consolingly. "I can understand if you don't want to return to the Weinburger. But there are other institutions where we can help you get the kind of job you want, a position where you'll be able to do your research unhindered."

Charles thought about Michelle, wondering about what he'd done to her. Had he really hit on something? He didn't know but he had to find out. To do that he needed laboratory facilities.

He turned and examined Dr. Ibanez's face. In contrast to Morrison, Charles had never disliked Dr. Ibanez. "I have to warn you that if I negotiate, I'm going to have a lot of demands." In actuality Charles had not given one thought to what he was going to do after he recovered. But lying there, looking at the director, his mind rapidly reviewed the alternatives.

"I'm prepared to meet your demands, provided they are reasonable," said Dr. Ibanez.

"And what do you want from me?" asked Charles.

"Only that you won't embarrass the Weinburger. We've had enough scandal."

For a second, Charles was not sure what Dr. Ibanez meant. If nothing else, the events of the previous week had impressed him with his own impotence and vulnerability. Isolated first in his house, then in intensive care, he had not realized the extent to which he had become a media figure. As a prominent scientist who had risked his life to save his daughter, the press would be happy to hear any criticism he might have of the Weinburger, particularly after the bad notices the institute had already received.

Dimly Charles began to assess his negotiating strength. "All right," he said slowly, "I want a research position where I'll be my own boss."

"That can be arranged. I've already been in contact with a friend in Berkeley."

"And the Canceran evaluation," said Charles. "All the existing tests have to be scrapped. The drug has to be studied as if you'd just received it."

"We already were aware of that," said Dr. Ibanez. "We've started an entirely new toxicity study."

Charles stared, his face reflecting astonishment at what Ibanez was saying. "And then there's the matter of Recycle, Ltd. Dumping of chemicals into the river must stop."

Dr. Ibanez nodded. "Your lawyer's activities got the EPA involved in that affair and I understand the problem will be solved shortly."

"And," said Charles, wondering how far he could go, "I want Breur Chemicals to make a compensatory payment to the Schonhauser family. They can keep their name out of the affair."

"I think I can arrange that, particularly if it remains anonymous."

There was a pause.

"Anything else?" asked Dr. Ibanez.

Charles was amazed that he'd gotten so far. He tried to think of something else but couldn't. "I guess that's it."

Dr. Ibanez stood up and placed the chair back against the wall. "I'm sorry that we are going to lose you, Charles. I really am."

Charles watched Ibanez as he closed the door silently behind him.

Charles decided if he ever drove cross-country again, it would be without kids and with air conditioning. And if he had to choose between those two conditions, it would be without children. The three had been at each other's throats ever since they left New Hampshire, though that morning they had been relatively quiet as if the vast expanse of the Utah desert awed them into silence. Charles glanced in the rearview mirror. Jean Paul was directly behind him, gazing out his side of the car. Michelle was next to him, bored and fidgety. Way in the back of the refurbished station wagon, Chuck had made a nest for himself. He had been reading for most of the trip—a chemistry text, of all things. Charles shook his head, acknowledging that he was never going to understand the boy, who now said he wanted to take a summer session at the university. Even if it were a passing fancy, Charles was inordinately pleased when his older son announced that he wanted to be a doctor.

As they crossed the Bonneville Salt Flats west of Salt Lake City, Charles hazarded a glance at Cathryn sitting next to him. She'd taken up needlepoint at the beginning of the trip and seemed absorbed in the repetitive motion. But sensing Charles's stare, she looked up and their eyes met. Despite the annoyance of the kids, they both shared a building joy as the harrowing experience of Michelle's illness and that last violent morning faded into the past.

Cathryn reached over and placed a hand on Charles's leg. He'd lost a lot of weight, but she thought he appeared handsomer than he had in years. And the tension that normally tightened the skin around his eyes was gone. To Cathryn's relief, Charles was at last relaxed, hypnotized by the rushing road and the numbing blur of scenery.

"The more I think about what's happened, the less I understand it," said Cathryn.

Charles shifted in his seat to find a position that accommodated the fact that his left arm was in a cast. Although he had yet to come to terms with most of the emotions engendered by the affair, there was one thing he had acknowledged. Cathryn had become his best friend. If nothing else, that made the experience worthwhile.

"So you've been thinking?" said Charles, letting Cathryn pick up the conversation wherever she wished.

Cathryn continued pushing her bright-colored yarn through the canvas mesh. "After all the frenzy of packing and actually leaving, I've never really sorted out exactly what happened."

"What is it you don't understand?" asked Charles.

"Dad!" called Jean Paul from the back seat. "Do they play hockey in Berkeley? I mean is there ice and all that?"

Craning his neck so he could see Jean Paul's face, Charles

said, "I'm afraid there's no ice. It's more like continuous spring in Berkeley."

"How stupid can you be?" groaned Chuck, tapping Jean Paul on the top of the head.

"Shut up," said Jean Paul, twisting in his seat to swipe at Chuck's boot. "I wasn't talking to you."

"All right, pipe down," yelled Charles harshly. Then in a calmer voice he said, "Maybe you can learn to surf, Jean Paul."

"Really," said Jean Paul, his face brightening.

"They only surf in Southern California," said Chuck, "where all the weirdos are."

"Look who's talking," retorted Jean Paul.

"Enough!" yelled Charles, shaking his head for Cathryn's benefit.

"It's all right," said Cathryn. "It reassures me to hear the kids bicker. It convinces me that everything is normal."

"Normal?" scoffed Charles.

"Anyway," said Cathryn, looking back at Charles. "One of the things I don't understand is why the Weinburger made such an about-face. They all couldn't have been more helpful."

"I didn't understand it, either," said Charles, "until I remembered how clever Dr. Ibanez really is. He was afraid the media would get hold of the story. With all those reporters milling around, he was terrified I'd be tempted to tell them my feelings about their brand of cancer research."

"God! If the public ever knew what really goes on," said Cathryn.

"I suppose if I were a real negotiator, I should have asked for a new car," laughed Charles.

Michelle, who had been vaguely listening to her parents, reached down in her canvas tote bag and pulled out her wig. It was as close a brown to Cathryn's hair as she had been able to get. Charles and Cathryn had implored her to get black, to match her own hair, but Michelle had remained adamant. She had wanted to look like Cathryn, but now she wasn't so sure. The idea of going to a new school was terrifying enough without having to deal with her weird hair. She'd finally realized she couldn't be brunette for a few months and then become black-haired. "I don't want to start school until my hair grows back."

Charles looked over his shoulder and saw Michelle idly fingering her brown wig and guessed what she was thinking. He started to criticize her for stupidly insisting on the wrong color but checked himself and said mildly: "Why don't we just get you another wig? Maybe black this time?"

"What's the matter with this one?" teased Jean Paul, snatching it away, and jamming it haphazardly on his own head.

"Daddy," cried Michelle. "Tell Jean Paul to give me back my wig."

"You should have been a girl, Jean Paul," said Chuck. "You look a thousand times better with a wig."

"Jean Paul!" yelled Cathryn, reaching back to restrain Michelle. "Give your sister back her wig."

"Okay, baldy," laughed Jean Paul, tossing the wig in Michelle's direction and shielding himself from the last of his sister's ineffectual punches.

Charles and Cathryn exchanged glances, too pleased to see Michelle better to scold her. They still remembered those dreadful days when they were waiting to see if Charles's experiment would work, if Michelle would get better. And then when she did, they had to accept the fact that they would never know whether she had responded to the immunological injections or to the chemotherapy she had received before Charles took her out of the hospital.

"Even if they were sure your injections had effected the cure, they wouldn't give you credit for her recovery," said Cathryn.

Charles shrugged. "No one can prove anything, including myself. Anyway, in a year or less I should have the answer. The institute in Berkeley is content to let me pursue my own approach to studying cancer. With a little luck I should be able to show that what happened to Michelle was the first example of harnessing the body to cure itself of an established leukemia. If that . . ."

"Dad!" called Jean Paul from the back of the car. "Could you stop at the next gas station?"

Charles drummed his fingers on the steering wheel, but Cathryn reached over and squeezed Charles's arm. He took his foot off the accelerator. "There won't be a town for another fifty miles. I'll just stop. We could all use a stretch."

Charles pulled onto the dusty shoulder of the road. "Okay, everybody out for R-and-R and whatever."

"It's hotter than an oven," said Jean Paul with dismay, searching for some sort of cover.

Charles led Cathryn up a small rise, affording a view to the west, an arid, stark stretch of desert leading up to jagged mountains. Behind them in the car, Chuck and Michelle were arguing. Yes, thought Charles. Everything is normal.

"I never knew the desert was so beautiful," said Cathryn, mesmerized by the landscape.

Charles took a deep breath. "Smell the air. It makes Shaftesbury seem like another planet."

Charles pulled Cathryn into his right arm. "You know what scares me the most?" he said.

"What?"

"I'm beginning to feel content again."

"Don't worry about that," laughed Cathryn. "Wait until we get to Berkeley with no house and little money and three hungry kids."

Charles smiled. "You're right. There is still plenty of opportunity for catastrophe."

EPILOGUE

When the snows melted in the lofty White Mountains in New Hampshire, hundreds of swollen streams flooded the Pawtomack River. Within a two-day period, its level rose several feet and its lazy seaward course became a torrent. Passing the town of Shaftesbury, the clear water raged against the old granite quays of the deserted mill building, spraying mist and miniature rainbows into the crystal air.

As the weather grew warmer green shoots thrust up through the ground along the river, growing in areas previously too toxic for them to survive. Even in the shadow of Recycle, Ltd., tadpoles appeared for the first time in years to chase the skittish water spiders, and rainbow trout migrated south through the formerly poisoned waters.

As the nights became shorter and hot summer approached, a single drop of benzene appeared at the juncture of an off-load pipe in one of the new chemical holding tanks. No one supervising the installations had fully understood the insidious propensities of benzene, and from the moment the first molecules had flowed into the new system, they began dissolving the rubber gaskets used to seal the line.

It had taken about two months for the toxic fluid to eat through the rubber and drip onto the granite blocks beneath the chemical storage tanks, but after the first, the drops came in an increasing tempo. The poisonous molecules followed the path of least resistance, working their way down into the mortarless masonry, then seeping laterally until they entered the river. The only evidence of their presence was a slightly aromatic, almost sweet smell.

The first to die were the frogs, then the fish. When the river fell, as the summer sun grew stronger, the concentration of the poison soared.

Seizure
by Robin Cook

Biotechnology has become the buzzword in the
campaign of Senator Ashley Butler, a self-appointed
guardian of "traditional American values."
The conservative politician has come down
staunchly against stem cell research. But when he
develops Parkinson's disease, the senator must
make an unwilling pact with the very doctor whose
groundbreaking—yet untested—technology
he is trying to destroy.

"LEAVE IT TO DOCTOR-TURNED-NOVELIST
ROBIN COOK TO SCARE US ALL TO DEATH."
—LOS ANGELES TIMES

"ROBIN COOK KNOWS HOW TO MAKE THE PAGES FLY."
—KIRKUS REVIEWS

0-425-19794-8

Available wherever books are sold or at
www.penguin.com